By the same author:

In Six Hours ... *the world changed*

An apocalyptic thriller

In six hours the Middle East – and the world – will change forever

The Whore and her Mother:

9/11, Babylon and the Return of the King

Oh What Rapture!

Is a 'secret rapture' going to spare believers from tribulation to come?

Ireland – now the good news!

The best of *'Bread'* – personal testimonies and church/fellowship profiles from around Ireland

Edited by **Raymond & Gerry McCullough**

A wee taste a' craic

all the Irish craic from the *Celtic Roots Radio* shows 2-25

Cover design: Raymond McCullough
Cover photo: India trucks © **Pjhpix** – Dreamstime.com

In One Hour
... Babylon will fall

Raymond McCullough

Comments on *The Whore and her Mother*:

"... AMAZED when I read this book ... in awe of your extensive knowledge on so many levels: Christian, Jewish, and Muslim culture; the Jewish diaspora ... Greek & Hebrew; and your panoramic view of history through a biblical world view ... thought-provoking and trouble-some ... many will be offended, but you consistently build your case instead of being sensationalistic."

James Revoir, author of *Priceless Stones*

"... thoughtful, insightful ... and you have a knack for putting complicated topics in an easily accessible way."

Jim Darcy, author of *The Firelord's Crown*

".. has the makings of a best seller in its field ... you open up real ideas some of which are somewhat scary to say the least ... difficult to leave down because you have created the 'Must turn the page' feeling threaded right through every line"

Colin T Mercer, author & poet, UK

"Love this kind of stuff ... grounded in research and common sense"

Francis Albert McGrath, author, Dublin, Ireland

"... most thought provoking ... meticulously researched and written with style and passion"

Sheila Belshaw, UK, author of *Pinpoint*

"It's very thought-provoking and solidly presented."

Katherine Holmes, author of *The Swan Bonnet*

"I did not feel you were preaching at all, more laying your cards on the table ... An evocative read, which left me 'thoughtful'"

Molly Hopkins, author of *It Happened in Paris*

"I was so impressed with the level of detail you give and your breadth of knowledge ... well-researched and thorough"

Kevin Alex Baker, author of *Head Games*

In One Hour
... Babylon will fall

The Middle East has been re-shaped and an epic exodus has begun, meanwhile, across the Atlantic, judgement is coming and former comrades need to help their families to escape the coming destruction

Raymond McCullough

Published by

Precious Oil
PUBLICATIONS
www.preciousoil.com/publications

ISBN 13: 978-09955404 1 5

ISBN 10:   09955404 1 1

First published 2019

10a Listooder Road, Crossgar,

Downpatrick, Northern Ireland BT30 9JE

Contents

Introduction   1

PART ONE – The Ingathering   3

1 – The 2nd Exodus   5

2 – The desert road   13

3 – Basra beginnings   24

4 – Haifa and Akko   32

5 – An Afternoon in Lebanon   40

6 – Shabbat in Galilee   50

7 – Boston visit   54

8 – To Steal a Bridge   58

9 – Leaving Kabul   71

10 – Basra: day two   81

11 – Basra: day three   101

12 – Trouble in Raleigh   113

13 – Flight across Iran   125

14 – Email from Kabul   137

15 – Bridge Building   141

16 – Day Six: Shabbat in Basra   149

17 – The Adventure Begins   155

18 – Second week, a second bridge   161

19 – Journey across Iran   163

20 – Tragedy Averted   171

21 – Caught Up, or Caught Out   185

22 – Home Run   191

23 – Riverside Reunion   199

24 – Good News in Triplicate   207

25 – Smooth running   221

26 – Reunited in Jerusalem   225

27 – Preparations and conversations 243

28 – Weddings and interactions 257

PART TWO – Babylon rising 275

29 – Time to flee Babylon? 277

30 – Um Qasr 287

31 – The Ark revealed 289

32 – To your own land 293

33 – The dedication of the Temple 299

34 – Ireland: halfway house 307

35 – The conspiracy of ten 311

36 – The lights go out in Times Square 315

37 – Death of America 319

38 – Nightmare journey 323

39 – Saved by 'Alice!' 334

40 – Brothers reunited 340

Epilogue 342

The End 342

Glossary 343

Bibliography 346

About the author: 348

In Six Hours 350

... the world changed 350

Neighbours from Hell: 351

Thanks to my wife, Gerry, for editing and general encouragement.

Introduction

The wise man looks ahead. The fool attempts to fool him-self and won't face facts. (**Proverbs 14:8** *Living Bible*)

In that day there will be a highway from Egypt to Assyria.
(**Isaiah 19:23**)

This thriller series is fiction – i.e. the characters active in it are straight out of my own imagination. However, the events they are involved in are based directly upon the predictions of the Hebrew prophets – and, of course, my interpretation of them.

A hundred years ago the State of Israel was only a faint hope in the hearts of a few pioneering Jews, scoffed at even by their fellow Israelites. Today, Israel is the most advanced and powerful nation in the Middle East, yet still continually under threat from the surrounding nations.

The Middle East, and much of the world, are today dominated by Islamic fundamentalism. Will that continue? Today, America is the world's only superpower. Could a time come when that is no longer the case?

My previous non-fiction book, *The Whore and Her Mother: 9/11, Babylon and the Return of the King*, investigated some of the unfulfilled Hebrew prophecies concerning the last days – particularly those concerning the modern day city and nation of Mega-Babylon and God's plan for the Middle East and other nations of the world.

That book was based on the logical argument that, if we can see one of the most significant of these prophecies being fulfilled today, then we surely ought to pay attention to *all* of those unfulfilled prophecies and perhaps start to live our lives accordingly. Since that book was

1

published (2011), week by week there have been even more fulfillments of those biblical prophecies.

This Six Hours thriller series is an attempt to bring to life some of the events foretold by the Hebrew prophets and covered in *The Whore and Her Mother*. The first book in this fiction series, *In Six Hours ... the world changed*, ended with the miraculous deliverance of the nation of Israel from certain destruction in the form of an all-out nuclear and conventional attack from all those nations surrounding her. In just six hours the world changed fundamentally!

Now, the face of the Middle East has been transformed forever. Iran and her Arab allies have been scattered like dust and chaff – Iran and Saudi Arabia bombing each other into oblivion with nuclear missiles.

And Israel, miraculously, has triumphed once again over those who sought her annihilation. Radical Islam has been shown to be impotent in the face of the tiny Jewish State – even Mecca has been destroyed. And the oil and gas resources of the entire Middle East are now under Israeli control. The tables have been turned. Israel is no longer beholden to Russia, or anyone else, for oil supplies.

The scattered Ten Tribes – and the remnant of the tribe of Judah – are now eager to return to their greatly expanded land, Eretz Israel. And – perhaps only for a very limited period – the way is now actually open for their return, the promised Israelite 'ingathering'.

Russia, China and, in particular, the USA – once Israel's greatest ally – look upon this triumph with great dismay and seek to hinder those scattered Israelites who would return to this newly enlarged country. Life in America especially, for Jews and for others, is getting more and more difficult.

This ingathering involves a voluntary population transfer of perhaps more than one hundred million people – travelling many thousands of miles through remote and dangerous war-devastated areas! Shaul Levine – recently promoted to Major in the IDF, after his eventful role in the only just ended *'Six Hour War'* – is now given a role in the task of facilitating this transfer. It is time to call upon his friends – fellow Americans, Devlin and Thomas, and the Afghani, Ali Yusufzai – to aid him in this mammoth task.

But their families back in the USA are increasingly under threat. Will the comrades succeed in aiding their loved ones escape in time – before destruction overwhelms the nation?

PART ONE – The Ingathering

Four weeks after the Six Hour War

1 – The 2ⁿᵈ Exodus

BBC News - Sudan-Egypt border

'I'm standing near the southern Egyptian border with Sudan. As far as the eye can see they keep coming – cars, pickup trucks, buses, tractors ... The vehicles are piled high with household belongings, children clinging precariously to the tops of many. A biblical exodus appears to be well under way.

'In the wake of the recent war in the Middle East, and the overwhelming victory of Israel in that war, millions upon millions of the Nigerian Igbo people are heading 'home' – as they see it – to their promised land. Israel has just recently given them permission to come, as they have also to the Pashtuns, Kashmiris and Menashe from Afghanistan, Pakistan and India.

'The Jewish prophet, Jeremiah, referred to a highway stretching all the way from Egypt to ancient Assyria – roughly the area of modern-day Afghanistan – and that that highway will pass through Israel. It seems that this prediction may now be coming to pass.

'One convoy begins in Nigeria, west Africa, travelling east into Cameroon, Central African Republic and South Sudan, then north into Sudan and Egypt. Another convoy, of the Lemba tribe, in Zimbabwe and South Africa, is travelling north through Zambia, Tanzania, Kenya and Ethiopia, to join up with the western convoy from Sudan into Egypt. It seems likely that many of the Tutsi tribe, from Rwanda and Burundi, are also ready to join this exodus.

'Just a few weeks ago, Karen, it would have been impossible for these people to travel through Sudan or Egypt to Israel, but those countries joined forces with Iran and other Middle East nations in the recent failed attempt to wipe out Israel – and now they are a defeated and subdued enemy, currently dependent upon Israel.

'*Amazingly, the great Nile River seems conveniently to have dried up to a fraction of its normal size, enabling this huge convoy to bypass the congested bridges on new crossings engineered by the Israeli Army.*

'*These people travelling across Africa seem to be exuberantly happy. They sing hymns and cheer as they travel. If a vehicle breaks down – as many of them do – there is always plenty of help to get them going again.*

'*Israeli military vehicles are patrolling along the column of refugees, while helicopters pass over the vehicles periodically. The Israelis are not taking any chances on this massive exodus being attacked en route – especially with members of the extreme Islamist group, Boko Haram, still in the area. Transit camps are being set up all along the route, with Israeli field kitchens and medical teams ready to deal with heat exhaustion, child-birth, or any other emergency.*

'*Israel has put a call out worldwide for volunteer engineers and mechanics to help repair vehicles and roads. Earlier today we watched as huge Caterpillar bulldozers were air-lifted to help build those extra Nile crossings. The same thing, I believe, is happening all along the convoy routes.*

'*This is an absolutely incredible scene! Some experts reckon that there are perhaps thirty million people on the move here from western Africa alone – with more from the south, plus some Tutsi from Rwanda and Burundi, joining them. Karen, this must be the largest people movement the modern world has ever seen.*

'*This is David Hawthorne, BBC news, on the Sudan-Egypt border.*'

* * *

'*That was David Hawthorne reporting from Africa. I'm Karen Wignall and, in case you missed our headlines, the story of the day is of the continuing massive people movement of the huge Igbo tribe, from Nigeria, and other African tribes who regard themselves as of Israelite origin, heading for the newly expanded State of Israel.*

'*On their way these travellers will actually be covering more or less the same ground as the many millions who recently fled from the Middle East in the other direction during the recent 'Six Hour War'.*

'Another similar mass movement is taking place in Asia, also travelling towards Israel. We're going to go now to our correspondent in southern Iraq, Susan Reilly ...'

* * *

Basra, near the Iran-Iraq border

'Thank you, Karen. I'm standing by the main road east of Basra, near the border between what used to be Iran and Iraq. Both those countries have been totally devastated by the recent war and are now almost completely empty of their original inhabitants. Their populations fled originally in fear of Israeli retaliation for Iran and Syria's failed nuclear attack, just a few weeks ago – and then later because of the missile and land attack from Saudi Arabia. Apart from Israeli soldiers and relief organisations, Basra is deserted.

'That attack on Israel was accompanied by massive rocket and mortar attacks across the borders from Gaza, Lebanon, Jordan, Saudi Arabia and Egypt. Unbelievably, instead of Israel being wiped out, as everyone fully expected, their attackers fled in advance of the unexpected Israeli counter-attack.

'In that short time the Middle East has changed forever. All of Iran's military facilities and most of their cities, too, are now a smoking ruin. It seems that Iran – together with Saudi Arabia and Egypt – badly miscalculated the affect of their attempt to wipe out Israel and the result is the total destruction of a former major power in the Middle East.

'This convoy of immigrants stretches as far as I can see. There must be many millions of Pashtuns, from eastern Afghanistan, and the Swat and North West Frontier Provinces of Pakistan. Karen, many of these people were linked to the Taliban that US and UK coalition forces have been fighting against for many years.

'Former members of the Taliban – an extreme Islamist force before the war – are apparently now willing to join with the State of Israel! The forces of militant Islam have indeed been dealt a great blow and many have lost their faith in the Islamic religion.

'What is happening here is something quite unbelievable. I wouldn't believe it myself if I wasn't witnessing it with my own eyes. Even at the end of the Second World War when the Indian subcontinent was

partitioned into modern India and Pakistan, there were nowhere near as many people involved.

'These people are not Jews, but they regard themselves as belonging to the 'people of Israel' – just as the Jews do. And this convoy doesn't just come from Afghanistan and Pakistan – I am told that there are potentially six million Kashmiri's also on the move from northern India and another four million of the Menashe tribe from eastern India. All of these tribes apparently regard themselves as 'Israelite', also.

'In the past, Israel had permitted several thousand of the Menashe – regarded as part of the biblical tribe of Manasseh – to emigrate, or 'make aliyah' to Israel, though many more thousands had applied to emigrate. Until Israel recently dramatically changed their immigration policy, it would have taken a couple of hundred years at the previous rate to allow in those who had applied. Now, even those who are professedly Christian – the majority of the Menashe – want to make 'aliyah', and Israel have said, 'Yes, they can come!'

'There are Israeli military vehicles in evidence everywhere here, with helicopters flying overhead periodically and a pair of Israeli jets every now and then, also. The convoy is accompanied by well armed Israeli patrols, aided by transport planes who set them down all along the route of this migration. You can see that the mighty Euphrates River – normally full at this time of year – is now almost completely dried up, enabling Israeli engineers to create several new vehicle crossings here quite easily.

'Israel are keeping a watchful eye on this transfer of humanity, but they are going to have their work cut out for them when they reach their destination – rehousing of so many millions of new immigrants will be an almost superhuman task.

'This is Susan Reilly, BBC news, on the former Iran-Iraq border.'

* * *

'Well, recent events in the Middle East have caused a great deal of response around the globe. Russia and China have both condemned Israel for their sharp response to an all-out attack from all the surrounding Arab countries, along with Iran.

'The United States, who in recent years have distanced themselves more and more from their former ally, Israel, have also spoken *out strongly against the Israeli occupation of the former territories of Syria, Lebanon, Jordan and parts of Saudi Arabia, Iraq and Egypt.*

'We go now to our Jerusalem correspondent, Michael Farr, who is currently in south Lebanon. Michael, how are the Israelis coping with such a massive influx of refugees?'

* * *

South Lebanon

'Well, first of all, Karen, these are not really what we would normally refer to as refugees. They are not fleeing from any threat such as famine, or war. This is a massive ideological people movement of totally biblical proportions. These people have simply decided that, after two thousand seven hundred years of separation, now is the right time to return to their original homeland.

'And by the way, it was pointed out to me just recently that where I'm standing now – just outside the town of Sour, or Tyre, in former south Lebanon – was originally part of the British Mandate territory of Palestine in 1920, originally destined by the League of Nations to become part of the Jewish State. That was until Britain and France began a bit of wheeler-dealing, which resulted in Britain gaining control of the oilfields in what we now call the Kurdish area of Iraq, while the French added this area south of the Litani River to their newly created country, named after Mount Lebanon.'

'Michael, how are the Israelis coping with the situation?'

'Well, it is unbelievable that a nation that two weeks ago we believed was about to disappear from the map is now taking on an influx of people that will increase its population by around ten times! This has never been done before – unless you count the original biblical Exodus of two and a half million people from Egypt all those centuries ago!

'Don't forget, I'm standing here in what used to be Lebanon – where the vast majority of the population has fled from what they obviously believed would become a holocaust in retaliation for their attempt to wipe out Israel.

'As much as possible the new immigrants are being organised on the basis of their town or village of origin, with empty towns and

villages here being matched with those now being emptied in Asia and Africa.

'*Back in those towns and villages, Israeli officials are carefully co-ordinating the exodus so that the new immigrants know in advance where they are going. Other Israeli officials, along with the military, are organising the clearing of streets and repairing and securing empty homes for their new tenants – here in Lebanon, and in Syria, Jordan, the Sinai and north-eastern Saudi Arabia.*

'*An interesting development, overshadowed by this absolutely huge people movement, is that many of the Palestinian refugees, who for decades have lived in Lebanon refugee camps, by and large have NOT fled along with their Lebanese countrymen. The same is true of many of the Palestinians in the west bank and Gaza Strip. They at least appear to have learned a lesson from their previous flights, which have only resulted in their own misery. Their former leaders in Hamas and the Palestinian Authority, of course, have either fled or been destroyed by Israeli forces, after their attempt to destroy Israel. and, of course, their former supporters in Saudi Arabia, Egypt, etc. are no longer in any position to help them.*

'*It has been voiced in recent years that many, perhaps even the majority, of those we refer to as 'Palestinians' actually have Jewish roots – just like those who are now coming from Afghanistan and other countries. DNA and historical evidence has tended to confirm this. So, in the changed regional situation, the Israelis have extended an open welcome to those Palestinians who sincerely want to remain as part of the new Israel. They are welcome to stay and become full Israeli citizens. No-one yet knows just how that might work out in practice, but some potential new leaders among them have cautiously welcomed the Israeli government's offer.*

'*Certainly, there can be no conceivable going back to the pre-war days of conflict, with outside backing in terms of missiles and monetary support – those backers have gone! And so a separate Palestinian State is no longer a realistic option! The Israeli government have officially dissolved the Palestinian authority – although in practice it had mostly dissolved itself! Their own terrorist leaders have either fled or been annihilated and the Arab world's exploitation of the Palestinians for their own ends has seemingly come to an end – especially with Iran, Syria, Qatar and Hezbollah now out of the picture.*

'*It remains to be seen, Karen, just how big a task Israel has taken on in allowing so many millions to return. The population of the* new Israel could become seventy, eighty – even a hundred million – probably greater than that of former Iran! This truly is a biblical exodus. And it will completely transform the make-up of the new Israel.

'No-one knows yet how this will affect the political climate in Israel – most of these immigrants are not even Jewish in terms of religion. The majority are either Christian or some variety of Muslim – the Pashtuns have their own Pashtunwali code – so at least they might feel at home in former Muslim, or Christian, towns and villages here in Lebanon, or Syria.

'How the Israelis will house and find employment for all these people is anybody's guess. Not to mention that they will presumably need to learn Hebrew to integrate fully into Israeli society. How will the present day Israelis cope with such an influx of immigrants? Could Israel even be reduced to a third world country by accepting so many poverty-stricken people?

'The current Israeli government is really an interim government. When things settle down a bit there will have to be new elections representing the changed political reality. There will probably be new political parties – a Pashtun party, perhaps? an Igbo party? No-one can really imagine how these new realities will affect the post-war Israel – but affect it they certainly will!

'Zionism has certainly been given a whole new lease of life. Israel no longer needs to apologise or bend to any outside powers. The UN have been remarkably silent in the wake of the attempt to completely destroy Israel by several of their former members.

'But the new Israel will no longer be an exclusively Jewish state. It remains to be seen how that will be received by the present population of Israel. The new immigrants will possibly outnumber the indigenous population by a factor of ten to one.

'On the other hand, Israel almost ceased to exist forever – and the collective thankfulness for what is being received as miraculous divine intervention on their behalf, has led the Israeli leadership to take this unprecedented step. One cannot conceive of another nation making such a bold move.

'From Israel's point of view it also solves the question of occupation of these former Arab lands, by immediately peopling them with outside immigrants. Those new immigrants will be a security buffer in the future. Even the Kurds are happy – as Israel have agreed to support them in setting up their own government in the parts of Syria *north east of the Euphrates River. That, combined with their present autonomous area of former northern Iraq, and the surviving Iranian Kurds, would give them their longed for new state of Kurdistan. Turkey, of course, will not be at all happy with that development!*

'This is Michael Farr, BBC News, Tyre, in former south Lebanon.'

* * *

'Thank you, Michael.

'Well, the recent developments in the Middle East and Africa have taken the world by storm. The unexpected survival of Israel after an all-out nuclear and conventional attack from all the surrounding nations has left the world community reeling. Stock markets still really don't know how to gauge the current economic climate.

'Oil prices have risen due to the expected reduction in supply – though Israel have assured the world that any damage to oil production equipment in the Persian Gulf will soon be repaired and back in operation as soon as possible.

'Israel have announced that their own Leviathan oil and gas field in the eastern Mediterranean will soon be producing commercial quantities of oil. Leviathan gas is already supplying a large part of Europe and the Middle East with energy. The government have also confirmed that the newly discovered oilfield in the Golan Heights will also be producing oil in the very near future.

'Israel are working with the fledgeling Kurdish State to provide oil supplies direct to the Mediterranean by creating a new pipeline through former Syria, connecting the existing oil terminal at Baniyas to the existing pipe-line from Kirkuk. Obviously, it is in Israeli economic interest to get this pipeline up and running in record time and the Israeli company in charge of the project are currently recruiting expert engineers to facilitate this.

'In other news ...'

2 – The desert road
Iraq - one week after the Six Hour War

Shaul (Sol, or Solly) Levine lay back lazily in the front passenger seat of the almost new *CombatGuard* armoured personnel carrier as it led a convoy of vehicles across the desert from Jordan into former Iraq. Behind came the rest of his company in an assortment of APCs, *Hummvees*, jeeps, buses, tanks on transporters, and trucks – many of these captured from the Syrian, Jordanian, Saudi and Egyptian forces they had recently defeated.

They were accompanied by the tank troops who had helped them achieve such success in Saudi Arabia in the recent war. The convoy also included supply trucks loaded with food, water, vehicle parts and other essential supplies for an expected whole nation on the move.

The road ahead of them had been mainly empty so far – apart from some reserve military vehicles, travelling to supply outlying Israeli posts in Iraq, or returning from doing so. For the last hour, though, they had begun to meet increasing traffic coming in the opposite direction. This became the most amazingly motley display of humanity Sol had ever witnessed.

Increasingly, the opposite side of the road became filled with a convoy of trucks, farm tractors with overloaded trailers, buses, commandeered military vehicles, cars, three-wheeler tuk-tuks, even a few men on horseback. Many vehicles were garishly painted with Magen Davids and slogans in mis-spelt English and a few even in Hebrew – *'Isreal, or bust!' 'Shalom, Israel!'*, *'Pashtuns cuming home'*, **'ישראל**.

Most of the vehicles sounded their horns loudly and their occupants cheered when they recognised the approaching convoy as Israelis, many flying a home-made Israeli Star of David flag out of the window. Cries of *'Shalom, aleichem',* 'Eretz Israel' and 'We coming home!' could be heard. The soldiers in Shaul's company responded in kind. These interludes helped brighten the long journey through the Iraqi desert.

In between, Shaul mused over the recent three weeks of war, followed by the political upheaval while they had been on leave. After losing their original commander to injury, Shaul's company had achieved some success in capturing Jordanian and Saudi territory – the cities of Aqaba and Tabuk, plus the ancient biblical 'land of Midian' – during the recent *'Six Hour War'.*

The action though had actually continued for much longer after that first morning, when the war had already begun to turn in Israel's favour. Those who had conspired together to 'wipe Israel off the map' had subsequently responded in complete terror when it became clear that Israel were still very much a force to be reckoned with.

Expecting the Israelis to respond – as they would have themselves – by slaughtering their Arab enemies, the forces of Islam, together with their families, took no chances on the possibility of Israel being merciful, but fled, just as the prophets had predicted – *'like dust and chaff in the wind, like tumbleweed in a gale'.*

Again and again – in Jordan, Lebanon, Syria, northern Saudi Arabia and in the Egyptian Sinai – the self-confessed enemies of Israel had left all and fled to east, west, north and south. Many times all that the Israeli forces had to do was try to keep up with their fleeing enemies – over and over again entering enemy towns and villages to find them empty and undefended.

Israeli tanks were now at the Turkish border – Turkey having opted out of the conflict this time and the Turks having conveniently reinforced their former Syrian border with a massive concrete wall back in 2018. The funds for this expensive construction – more than 80 million Euros – had been mostly supplied by the countries of the EU. Now, all that Israel needed to do was to add an access/patrol road and some lookout towers on their own side of the border – already under construction!

They now controlled all of Lebanon and Syria west of the Euphrates River and their forces were well into southern Iraq – almost to the Iranian border – though they were being forced to avoid some city areas where nuclear missiles had struck. Israel's natural allies, the Kurds, had taken control of the remaining north eastern corner of Syria, along with northern Iraq – their enemies having fled to the east and north.

Iran and the remainder of southern Iraq – from where the majority of nuclear missiles had been launched against Israel – were now mostly a smouldering wasteland. Their inhabitants were presently scattered to the four winds – again in fulfilment of the words of the prophets. Israel's borders – once places of tension and threat – now consisted either of unpopulated desert areas, friendly Kurdish forces or the well-fortified – and currently peaceful – Turkish border. These were easily controlled with a minimum of forces – just as well, considering the gargantuan task Israel now faced in bringing such a staggering number of immigrants 'home' to their newly-expanded state.

The original post World War I *San Remo Agreement* (in 1920) for a Jewish State in the former Turkish-controlled area of Southern Syria – then re-named 'Palestine' by the British – had first been reduced in area by Britain and France, who removed the northern section of Palestine, south of the Litani River – giving part to the newly-formed state of Lebanon and part to Syria. This was in exchange for Britain gaining control of the oil rich area of modern day Kurdistan, in northern Iraq.

The planned Jewish State had then been further reduced by Britain, who gave away 78% of the remaining mandate area to create Trans-Jordan – which then became Jordan. Israel lost the water resource of the Litani River and half the control of the Jordan River. Almost one hundred years later the original San Remo plan had now been more than fulfilled – poetic justice , thought Shaul – and most Israelis would have agreed with him!

He reflected that Israel now controlled not only the area originally promised them at San Remo, but in addition also the remainder of Lebanon, almost all of Syria, the Sinai Peninsula in Egypt and the ancient land of Midian (north eastern Saudi Arabia) – a direct fulfilment of the prophecies in Genesis (15:18), Exodus (23:31), Deuteronomy (11:22-25) and Isaiah (27:12). Further to this, Egypt, Sudan, Saudi Arabia, Iran and most of Iraq, were now effectively under Israeli dominance.

Immediately following the conclusion of the war, and their brief three-day leave, Shaul and his company – including their tank contingent –

had been given command of a newly acquired base in Basra, close to the former Iran/Iraq border. At the end of the war the company had travelled through the desert from Tabuk – formerly a city of 500,000 in Saudi Arabia, but an almost deserted city now under Israeli military and civilian control – to the outskirts of Amman, Jordan.

New Israel Plan officials were currently surveying the accommodation available in Tabuk and the forerunners of a convoy of Igbo from Nigeria were already en route across Africa towards Egypt and the Red Sea. The Duba Port ferry terminal liberated by Shaul's forces was now controlled by the Israeli Navy. Ships would now be made available to take the Igbo and others across the Red Sea to Midian to settle in Tabuk and the surrounding area. Some of the Pashtun convoys would be heading there also, eventually.

Shaul's company had left their temporary base in Tabuk – the *Fahad Bin Sultan University*, which they had captured – which was now being repaired and made ready as an absorption centre for the coming new immigrants. A few days ago the company had moved north along Saudi Highway 15 and Jordanian Highway 5 to Ma'an, Jordan – also under Israeli control – then north on Highway 15 to the south eastern outskirts of Amman, the former Jordanian capital. Their vehicles and equipment had been left there under guard as they took a well-earned three-day leave back home in 'Israel proper', as it was now being called.

When they returned from their brief leave they were joined by a convoy of trucks from Israel carrying much-needed food, vehicle parts and medical supplies, as well as low-loaders carrying bulldozers and road-making equipment, and more trucks carrying stone, asphalt and other materials.

The convoy also included two coaches containing quite a number of volunteers – doctors, nurses, mechanics and others with various skills, who wanted to be of service in the unbelievably massive task of bringing home the Ten Tribes.

Since the government decision to welcome the new immigrants home – many of whom, to be truthful, were already en route to Israel – and the Prime Minister's heartfelt speech to the nation explaining that decision and the need for a new pioneering spirit, the Israeli media had been putting out numerous calls for such volunteers.

The Prime Minister had summed up the miraculous deliverance of Israel during the recent war and the devastating affect of that victory on the former Islamist enemies of the nation – who had been dealt a massive blow, which only time would tell the full extent of.

The government of Israel had received requests from Pashtun leaders in Afghanistan, Pakistan and India, Kashmiris also, Igbo from Nigeria, Lemba from South Africa and Zimbabwe. But many of those people had pre-empted any Israeli government decision and simply packed essential supplies and extra fuel and begun the unbelievable trek towards Israel.

Unless they wanted to risk a huge humanitarian disaster in their name, the Israeli government really had only one choice – to accept the fait accompli thrust upon them and to throw all the resources of the nation into making this second Exodus a success.

Whether it would in fact be successful was not a foregone conclusion – no country in the world had ever dealt with such an enormous population transfer. Even the Israeli government at present were unable to determine the total number of people en route towards the new Israel – guesses were anything from fifty million to perhaps in excess of one hundred million people!

In addition, the world – especially the region surrounding the Middle East – was still reeling from the after-effects of the recent *Six Hour War* and the flight of so many millions of Arabs, Iranians and others from the war zone. Many of those countries who might have been disposed to provide aid to Israel in these circumstances were already overwhelmed in coping with refugees moving in the opposite direction.

Amman – like Tabuk, Ma'an and many other cities in the former countries neighbouring Israel – was also largely deserted by its former inhabitants and an Israeli interim city council was in the throes of being set up to prepare for re-population by the incoming tribes.

Shaul's greatly enlarged convoy had headed east from Amman early that morning, through the Jordanian/Iraqi desert, towards Iraq's Highway 1, Ramadi and Falluja, then skirting to the south of Baghdad and heading south. Not so long ago the coalition forces of US, UK, Australia, etc. had been in control here – mostly the Brits in Basra.

Then the coalition had pulled out, leaving Iraq and its Shi'ite government to fall more and more under Iranian domination – until ISIS came into the picture in early 2014, taking over the north and west of Iraq. Now not only former Iraq, but former Iran also, were under Israeli control – and the Iranians were scattered to the four corners of the earth, as prophesied hundreds of year before by the Hebrew prophet, *Yeshayahu* (Isaiah).

Iran, as far as Shaul knew, was mostly a smoking wasteland after their attempt to wipe out Israel by nuclear and conventional attack had misfired so badly. Many of those missiles which managed to reach Israeli airspace had been successfully intercepted by Israel's defensive shield, mostly blown up high above the Jordanian desert by Israeli missiles.

But the vast majority of the missiles aimed towards Israel had been electronically intercepted by the Israelis – in an advanced version of their previously highly acclaimed *StuxNet* software – and re-directed against Iranian, Syrian and other hostile targets. Israel had also retaliated with several hundred conventional missiles of their own, aimed primarily at military targets in the surrounding nations.

The result, Shaul mused, had been unbelievable pandemonium among Israel's Arab neighbours, as well as non-Arab Iran. Their populations had reacted to what seemed a doomsday scenario – panicked flight the only thought left in their minds.

As a result, Israel now controlled the Sinai desert and part of Egypt proper, a large part of northern Saudi Arabia – the ancient land of Midian, through which Moses had led the children of Israel on their way to the promised land – all of Jordan, Lebanon and Syria, plus southern Iraq and Iran. The ancient prophecy to Abraham had been fulfilled – that God would grant him everywhere that the soles of his feet (and his descendants) had trod.

He remembered reading that when the Israelites crossed the Red Sea into Midian all those centuries ago they had amused themselves by carving petroglyphs – the outline of thousands of pairs of feet etched onto the rocks – wherever they wandered. Now, he thought, those rocks were, for the first time, under Israel's control.

Shaul's mind moved on to the thought that he was going to be extremely busy for the next few months, running the equivalent of a small town with an ever-changing population. Quite a change from his last mission – charging through the heat of the Midian desert in the wake of the fleeing Saudis.

They had just passed through Fallujah when, ahead, he noticed some confusion and a break in the flow of traffic. As they drew nearer he could make out the cause – an oncoming ancient Nissan truck had broken down and the traffic behind had turned into a chaotic melee. Some were manoeuvring slowly past, while others were impatiently blowing horns and shouting abuse at the vehicles in front.

'Right, Bar-Ilan,' Shaul radioed to his second lieutenant, 'This is the sort of thing we're gonna have to get used to dealing with. Take one APC and a mechanic and find a suitable spot ahead to tow that truck off the road. We'll need to move our own vehicles off the road, too. Get the mechanic ready to start on repairs as soon as we've got the road cleared. I'll get Tamari to organise the tow.'

'Yes, sir,' she replied, immediately grabbing a pair of binoculars from her own vehicle. 'I can see what looks like a disused gas station about a kilometre ahead, we can probably pull in there.'

'*Tov ma'od,* Bar-Ilan (Very good). Let me know when you've checked it out. Out.'

Her APC pulled up on the right hand side of the road and Bar-Ilan hopped out and went back along the column to select the men she needed. Sol radioed for the rest of the column to wait where they were, except for one truck full of troops, which he asked to accompany him.

'Sergeant Tamari, he radioed, 'I need one APC to tow the broken down truck. Bar-Ilan is looking for somewhere off-road ahead to repair it and to park our own vehicles off the road. We'll need to clear the road and get it turned around, then tow it to that location.

'Yes, sir,' replied Tamari – now promoted to *Rav Samal* (First Sergeant) after the recent war.

Shaul directed his driver towards the confused collection of humanity ahead, instructing him to pull in well ahead of the disabled vehicle to allow room for Tamari and his men to attach a tow to the truck and get it turned around. 'Stay with the APC,' he commanded the remaining men with him.

Shaul jumped out and walked to the truck which had pulled in behind their APC. 'Traffic duty! I want all you guys out behind the broken down truck. We want as few accidents as possible with these people, so keep them in line.'

He walked over and spoke to the driver of the disabled Nissan truck, 'Do you speak any English? What's the problem?'

'Yes, English a leetle. Radiator boil up. Engine just stop,' the driver said in broken English.

'OK, we're going to tow you off the road to where we can fix your vehicle, fix your truck – you understand?'

'Yes, fix truck. Good, very good!' he said.

A dozen men had dropped into the roadway from the rear of the Israeli truck and now followed Shaul past the disabled vehicle. As those drivers behind saw the Israeli soldiers they raised another cheer and shouts of 'Israel, Israel!' Shaul walked back along the slowly approaching column of vehicles, shouting up to each one, 'Anyone here speak good English?'

Most had very little, but eventually he heard a clipped almost British accent reply, 'Yessir, I speak very good English. Can I help you, sir?' The man was about thirty, slim and fit-looking, with an impressive moustache. 'Where did you learn your English,' Shaul asked him.

'Please, sir, with the British forces, sir. I was an interpreter for the British troops in Helmand province,' the moustached man replied. 'How can I be of service to you, sir?'

'I don't want to hold you up for too long,' Shaul replied, 'But I need you to translate for me for a short while. Can you pull your car off the road here? Two of my men will stay with your family while you assist me.'

'OK, sir. I will do what you ask. My name is Daoud, Daoud Shinwari. I am very happy to be of service to the State of Israel, sir,' Daoud stated.

They moved Shinwari's dusty Toyota car to a suitable spot at the side of the road, and Daoud explained the situation briefly to his family before following Shaul back to the head of the queue of vehicles now squeezing slowly past the disabled Nissan truck.

As they walked, Shaul explained what he wanted from Daoud and Daoud spoke in turn to each of the drivers, explaining what was happening. When they returned to the broken down truck again, he got Daoud to translate for him so the truck driver knew exactly what was happening. Then Shaul sent two of his men back down the convoy with Daoud, to explain things to the drivers further back, while he radioed Bar-Ilan ahead.

'I was just about to call you, sir,' said Bar-Ilan. 'There is plenty of room here for our convoy and the disabled truck.'

'*Beseder*, Bar-Ilan. Tamari will be with you soon. I'll get the convoy moving behind him in a minute.'

'*Beseder*, sir.'

Tamari and his team had already reversed one of their own *Namer* tracked APCs in front of the Nissan and attached a steel towing bar. While Shaul's men halted the convoy, the articulated vehicle was swung slowly around in the width of the highway behind the *Namer* APC and the two vehicles began to move slowly east along the crowded roadway, finally pulling into the area Rebekkah Bar-Ilan had selected as a suitable repair location, two of her men guiding them in.

Shaul directed his own driver to the east-bound side of the highway again and waved forward the convoy once the offending obstruction had freed the highway and a chorus of yells and sounding horns from the once again freely moving vehicles greeted Shaul. He found his own men and thanked the interpreter, Daoud, for his help.

'Once you have reached wherever you are staying in Israel, if you want a job in Basra, helping with the convoys, just contact me. I'll arrange for you to be transported back to our base. We need all the interpreters we can get, right now,' said Shaul, handing him a piece of paper with his contact details in Basra. 'If you know any others with excellent English like yourself, we could use them, too.'

'Indeed, God has sent you to meet me,' cried a joyful Daoud, 'We have not even reached Israel yet and already I have an offer of a job.' He went back to his car to share the happy news with his wife and children. Shaul's men held a place for Daoud to pull out into the Israel-bound convoy and as he passed Shaul again he beamed out of the open window, 'May God bless you, Major Levine. I will be seeing you again very soon, *Insh'allah!*'

'Welcome to Israel, David Shinwari, and your family, too. *Shalom!*' Shaul called back, as they disappeared westwards.

Shaul directed his APC east down the highway, the rest of the convoy following behind, and pulled into the deserted former gas station, parking alongside the disabled truck, whose occupants were now sitting in the shade of the vehicle, sharing some food. At the front of the truck the IDF mechanic poked his head out from the engine compartment to explain that it was only a broken fan belt, which he had already replaced. They were only waiting now for the engine to cool sufficiently to top up the radiator and the truck and its occupants could soon be on their way again.

Bar-Ilan and Tamari, meanwhile, had already organised their own vehicles off the highway and the traffic had begun to flow freely in both directions, fellow IDF soldiers waving to them and calling *'Shalom'* as they passed. Shaul returned to his own APC.

A short while later they waited as Tamari held up the Israel-bound traffic briefly again, to allow the repaired Nissan truck to rejoin the convoy west, before returning to join Shaul and the others. Two of Tamari's men then held up the eastbound traffic to allow Shaul's company to return to the highway and then they were able to resume their interrupted journey to Basra.

The dust covered convoy finally pulled off Iraq's Highway 1 onto Highway 31, which passed Basra International Airport – now badly damaged by the recent war, although IDF troops were guarding it and it was hoped to have the runway functioning quite soon to facilitate Shaul's mission.

The highway suddenly ended at a new junction and they turned right onto Highway 6, then left into another divided highway which led to the Shatt al-Arab Waterway and the *Shatt Al-Arab Hotel* beside it, which seemed to have escaped any major war damage. This was to be their base of operations for the foreseeable future.

The hotel commanded a view of the main bridge to the north, across the Shatt al-Arab Waterway, via Sinbad Island. The main bridge was incomplete – one half having been damaged in the 1991 Iraq War – so traffic had to leave the main road, do a long loop around the island, underneath the damaged bridge, then across one of two temporary pontoon bridges – one lane each way – and onto a divided highway leading to the former Iran border and Iran's Highway 96 to Khorramshahr, Abadan and Bandar Mahshahr.

A weary Sol climbed down from his APC and walked stiffly across to a water tap he had spotted against the rear wall of the building. Stooping to allow the water to flow over his head he washed the dust from his face and then drank deeply from the tap.

Chapter 2 – The desert road, Jordan/Iraq

Turning to his second lieutenant and first sergeant he said, 'Let's get these guys fed and bedded down for the night. We'll meet first thing in the morning to plan our strategy.'

'Yes, sir,' said Bar-Ilan and Tamari together. They walked back to where the tank transporters and most of the trucks and buses were being parked, showing the men and all the volunteers towards the back entrance to the hotel.

'*Rav Seren* Levine?' a young Israeli Corporal walked out stiffly from the hotel, eager to please. '*Rav turai* Lev. I'm here to show you your accommodation, sir.'

'Yes, I'm *Rav Seren* Levine,' said Shaul, 'and you can show us the dining room, *Rav turai*. That will do for now. My men are hungry and road-weary. Once they're fed and watered you can show me the rest of the facilities.'

'No problem, sir,' the young soldier replied, 'This way, then.' He led them through the rear entrance to the hotel.

3 – Basra beginnings

Next morning Shaul gathered his officers around the breakfast table. Present were Lieutenant Alon Peled, the commander of Shaul's tanks; Second Lieutenant Rebekkah Bar-Ilan, First Sergeant Musa Tamari, newly promoted Sergeant Ari Gold, Peled's second in command; Corporal Avi Katz and – also newly promoted – Corporal Samir Junbalat, plus the new addition to their number, Corporal Doron Lev – who had already organised a squad to prepare breakfast for them.

'OK, comrades,' Shaul began. 'I won't pretend we don't have a huge task ahead of us. It will probably take us weeks to get a full grasp of it. We may no longer be in a combat situation, but we could face life and death situations every day from now on – so we need to be ahead of the game. We have limited resources and, though we can call upon Southern Command and the government for any help we need, we need to get a plan together ASAP.

'Yesterday was a good example of the sort of thing we're gonna have happening regularly – breakdowns. These vehicles in the convoys are not the latest models – many of them are too old and decrepit for such a journey. Some will just need a quick repair – a new tyre, a replacement hose, or fan-belt or battery.

'Where there are accidents with serious damage we will have to write off some vehicles – then we have the problem of what to do with the occupants. So, that's the first thing – vehicles, maintenance, repairs. I'm asking *Rav Samal* Tamari to handle that side of things from now on, with *Rav Turai* Katz at his side. Anyone who comes across a vehicle or road problem report it to Tamari or Katz, right?

The convoys are travelling unaccompanied at the moment – apart from the Israeli Air Force flying some patrols along the nearer part of the route, reporting any problems they spot. I don't think that is the best way, so we need to decide how to police this thing. We'll need patrols going out each day, several times a day, then accompanying the convoy back to their next staging post.

'*Seren* Peled, I'm going to use you in that capacity. You'll need to decide where tanks are best deployed – probably as semi-permanent check-points – otherwise you can use APCs, trucks, whatever is needed, *beseder*? *Samal* Gold will obviously be your right-hand man in that role.

Next problem is the purely human one. These are people who have uprooted themselves from their whole way of life, to travel 3,500 kilometres or more to a new land they have never seen before, whose language they do not speak. There will be illnesses, babies born, accidents, disputes ... and the whole business of getting these people to Israel safely and settled into homes, jobs, schools, etc. A humanitarian nightmare, but one we have to have an answer to.

Bar-Ilan, I'm putting you in charge of all personnel and medical issues. You will liaise with our doctors and nurses and with the Ministry of the Interior back home. Corporal Junbalat will work with you, plus Corporal Lev here, and I will be available to help iron things out with Command, or Jerusalem, OK? We'll be liaising with the *New Israel Plan* people in placing the immigrants.'

'OK, that's the rough breakdown. Now we need to consider the nitty gritty – foresee as many problems as we can before they land in our faces. I want everyone to feel free to chip in on this, but first we'll hear from those taking the responsibility. So, Tamari – vehicles?'

'Well, you saw what happened yesterday, sir, one truck overheats and the convoy descends into chaos. That's going to happen several times every day. We'll need regular stops where vehicles can be taken off the road and rested, or, if necessary, repaired. We need teams of mechanics and spares to back them up. If vehicles have to be written off we'll need buses or trucks to transport those people the rest of the way. And we'll need drivers for those, of course.' Tamari paused.

'Katz, anything to add?' asked Shaul.

'Sir, we have a two lane highway – parts of it here in Iraq are even divided highway, as we saw last night. This is pretty much one way traffic, so we could keep the other lane for our own exclusive use – both ways. We'll need to be able to get to emergency situations quickly. When the convoys get to the divided highway, obviously they can use both lanes and speed things up a little.

'We've also got alternative routes – not just one single road for most of the way – so we'll have to patrol all the roads. Unless we close some roads and keep them for our own use?'

'Excellent, Katz. Some great ideas, there. Any thoughts on those ideas, anyone?'

'I like the idea of keeping some roads exclusively for our own use, sir,' Bar-Ilan responded. 'Say we have a real medical emergency, we need to get people to our hospital as speedily as possible – a separate road might facilitate that?'

'OK, said Shaul, 'We'll need maps and decisions on what roads are for the convoys, what roads are excluded. We also need to get a good picture of what's on the ground, pick out places for stops and repairs, etc.

'Another thing is fuel. A lot of these vehicles are simply gonna run out of fuel. In fact, I don't know where they managed to get the fuel to get this far. We'll need strategic fuel dumps set up along the main routes and regular checks on vehicles to make sure they're topped up – perhaps there are some existing gas stations which we can make operational again? I don't imagine we're gonna be expecting them to pay for it, either!

'Peled, you'll need to add fuel checks to your responsibilities – at least for now.' Peled was making notes as he spoke.

'OK, Peled, any thoughts on your responsibilities?'

'Yes, sir,' he responded, setting down his notebook, but glancing at it briefly. 'We'll need properly set up regular check-points. We can use some of our tanks for that purpose, but to avoid excessive wear and tear on the tanks I suggest we use *Hummvees*, or trucks, to get to and from from those checkpoints.

'On the security front, I take it the Air Force will likely be the first to spot any infiltration – I'm thinking bandits, thieves, anyone seeking to prey on the convoys. We'll need to respond with rapid action if they report anything to us.

'Just another quick thought, sir, but what about contraband. Do we turn a blind eye, or what?'

'I take it you're thinking of a certain Afghan export that my colleagues and I had often had to deal with in Kabul? I think we'll have to cope with it, but maybe in a fairly subtle way so that we don't make a big public exhibition of the culprits. I don't think we can blame people for trying to bring what they see as a valuable commodity with them. At the same time we don't allow narcotics free access to Israel. So, we don't turn a blind eye, as such, but give some careful thought to how we might deal with it.

'Good, we're making some progress. I imagine we'll need more brain-storming sessions as we progress.

'Bar-Ilan, the medical/human side of things? Any thoughts?'

'Well, we'll need some of our APCs dedicated as ambulances – re-painted with the Magen David Adom. Maybe have sirens fitted? The check-points could be staffed by some medical personnel, who could deal with any medical problems brewing before they get out of hand – offering a check-up for anyone who needs it. Sift out the less severe cases and refer the more serious ones early, before it becomes a real emergency?

'Our biggest problem, as I see it, will be communication. That man Daoud we met on the desert highway – there must be many more like him. Otherwise we're relying on pot luck as to whether anyone can speak English or not. None of them are going to have any Hebrew, though there might be the odd French speaker, I suppose.'

'Yes, that is a major problem, Bar-Ilan. One thing we can do is what I did yesterday, only in a more official way. If we come across a suitable translator we give them an official document – that will be recognised by *New Israel Plan*, or whoever – so that they can show they have a job offer back here and get themselves transported back here as soon as possible.

'We may possibly come across some potential translators who are unattached,' she added, 'single men, free to start right away – in which case I say we grab them straight off. Put them on the payroll and sort it out later with *NIP*, etc.

'OK, we've got a lot of great suggestions already. Anyone care to add anything at this point?'

'Just the idea of doing a survey, sir,' said Tamari. 'Maybe each of us here need to run over the route, or routes, at some point in the near future. Then we'll all know better what we're dealing with and can come up with suitable suggestions.'

'I agree, Tamari. We'll make sure that happens over the next day or two, *beseder*?'

Bar-Ilan spoke up, 'We could probably do with some road signs – just saying *'Israel'* should be enough – to direct traffic onto the routes we want them to take. I can organise that at the same time as painting the ambulance APCs.'

'*Beseder,* Bar-Ilan, that's great. Go ahead.'

Peled also responded, 'I don't know if anyone noticed last night, but there is quite a smell about this place already. It's only going to get worse, too. There must be hundreds of bodies lying unburied in the rubble out there. We don't want an epidemic on our hands among the new immigrants. There's our own health and safety to consider, also.'

'Excellent, Peled. We're gonna have to set aside one of the bull-dozers to make a mass grave and a team to collect and bury the bodies – not a pleasant task. I think we'll need to rotate men on that one. Bar-Ilan, I hate to add to your responsibilities, but it does seem to fall on your plate. Perhaps you could delegate that to Lev, here. Tamari can let you have one of the bulldozers and a driver.

'You'll need a couple of trucks and a squad of men – use some of the trucks we took from the Saudis. That way, if they break down, we won't have far to go to retrieve them. We'll need a suitable burial site, too – somewhere outside the city in the desert, preferably.

'Tamari, I suggest you get your men organised. Pick out any with mechanical expertise, or aptitude. Take most of the transporter drivers and their toolkits – a couple of drivers should be enough to unload whatever tanks Peled needs at the moment. We'll keep the transporters with us for the moment. I think we may need their vehicles, but we certainly need their mechanical expertise.

'Decide with Peled and Bar-Ilan which vehicles are going to be used for what purpose. Then take some men and APCs, or *Hummvees*, and head east out of here towards Abadan and Bandar Mahshahr. The road splits after that, but make a note of where the main traffic is coming from. Take a couple of the road engineers with you. Check out everything that strikes you – places for check-points, repair stops – anything that occurs to you, OK?'

'Peled, you can start organising your men into shifts and patrols – day and night at the moment. Do the first patrol yourself – again as far as Bandar Mahshahr – that's about eighty to one hundred kilo-metres. We'll have to widen our area eventually, but that will keep us busy for now – one step at a time. Can you organise a few men to guard this hotel HQ, also?'

Junbalat, you can take charge of our own accommodation and food. We may also need to get some of these immigrants fed and accommodated overnight, before sending them on the next stage of their journey – much better if they're well rested and fed first. Take an APC and crew and do a recce of what's available and make a note of it, OK? See you back here in a couple of hours?

'Now, Bar-Ilan, you'll need to check out that road, too, in the near future, but I think we need to get organised at this end first. Let's you and I go talk to the medical people now and then we'll also do a recce to see which hospital we're going to use.'

Shaul and Rebekkah grabbed a couple of APCs and Shaul waited while Rebekkah selected four *Namer* APCs to become ambulances and organised a detail to paint suitable markings on them. Peled preferred the nimbler *CombatGuard* APCs or jeeps for patrol work, but the *Namer* had more room for carrying stretchers, etc.

She also commandeered two of the captured Saudi trucks and organised Doron Lev with two squads of men to begin patrolling for bodies – initially in the area adjacent to their HQ. They could widen their search once this area was clear. When they had a full load they were to report by radio to find out the location of the new burial site.

'Come with us and get some masks and gloves from the medical guys, OK?' she told him.

When she had finished she and Lev joined Shaul and they headed for the area of the hotel in which the medical staff were currently residing. The doctors and nurses had been busy sorting through their supplies and discussing their coming roles in the present situation. They looked up with interest when Shaul and Rebekkah arrived.

Rebecca quickly selected one of the junior nurses, introducing Lev and explaining that he needed masks and gloves. He then accompanied the nurse to get his supplies. She turned back to the senior medical team and nodded to Shaul.

'*Boker tov*, my friends. I'm *Rav Seren* Shaul Levine and this is *Segen Mishne* Rebekkah Bar-Ilan. She'll be taking charge of anything related to medical and personnel issues. So she'll be the person you go to with any queries or problems – and of course we're open to any positive suggestions. We're in very new, uncharted territory here. We're going to have to learn our responsibilities as we go along.

'Bar-Ilan has already designated four of our larger *Namer* APCs to be used as ambulances. They are being painted with the Magen David Adom on the sides as we speak and made ready for use as

Chapter 3 – Basra beginnings

ambulances. When they're finished, and we know where the hospital is going to be, we'll send them over to you, complete with drivers.'

'So, unless you have any urgent questions I suggest we take your main personnel on a tour to find suitable facilities right now?'

A tall man in his forties introduced himself. I'm Dr. Cohen – Emmanuel Cohen. I will be in charge of this new medical facility. This is Staff Nurse Stein, who will be in charge of the nursing. These are my chief colleagues, Dr. Bergman and Dr. Lewinsky. Nurse Stein was a solid-looking grey-haired woman of around forty, Dr. Bergman was another tall slim man in his thirties and Dr. Lewinsky was a petite, intelligent looking woman of around thirty. They all shook hands with Shaul and Rebekkah, who escorted them out to the waiting APCs.

Rebekkahh took the two younger doctors with her to the left side of the *CombatGuard* APC, while Shaul escorted Dr. Cohen and the Staff Nurse to the right hand side. Shaul got into the front passenger seat and turned around to speak to the medical personnel. The clam-shell doors were shut and they drove off into what was left of the city of Basra.

'It seems that Basra remained free of any nuclear attack, so there is no danger of radiation here. Most of the destruction you see around you was the result of Saudi conventional missiles and artillery. We'll check out the nearest hospital first. If it is too badly damaged we'll go further afield, until we find something that is suitable.'

They drove south along Dinar Street, parallel to the Shatt Al-Arab Waterway, for more than two kilometres, until they came to a large intersection with a roundabout offset on their right. They swung right, heading towards Highway 6, and drove almost two kilometres until they reached *Al Faihaa General Hospital.*

'There is another, probably larger, general hospital several kilometres further south,' said Shaul, 'but I reckon that if this one is in any way usable it's better to be closer to our HQ and the bridge nearby.'

From the outside the building looked to be intact, so they exited the APC and ventured into the hospital building – a fairly recently built modern concrete structure, surrounded by a high concrete wall. There were signs of last minute confusion and panic. The hospital was in a state of disarray, but didn't appear to be badly damaged. Dr. Cohen and his colleagues reckoned they could put it to good use.

'*Beseder*', Shaul told them, 'we'll start our operation here, but we'll check out the other hospital first, so we know what is available if we need it later.'

The doctors and nurse agreed. They returned to their vehicles and drove one kilometre west to Highway Six, then south again on Highway Six for nearly six kilometres, before turning north east again towards the city centre. All the way they were meeting a steady flow of immigrant traffic, which had crossed the Shatt Al-Arab via the city centre Corniche Bridge.

After another five hundred metres they turned left into the *Basra General Hospital*. There appeared to be some damage to the old building, but they parked and the medical staff accompanied Shaul and Rebekkah on a tour of the facilities. Dr. Cohen seemed interested in the hospital, which had a new building, mostly undamaged. They discussed the merits of using this hospital, which had some more modern equipment and was also right on the route many of the immigrants were already travelling.

Shaul summed up the discussion, 'As we get ourselves established I think we'll definitely want to make use of this facility, so we'll put a guard on it and perhaps borrow some of the equipment there, as needed? I'll leave that to you medical experts. In the meantime, I think we need to get the other hospital up and running as soon as we possibly can. It is only one kilometre from Highway Six, also – so pretty accessible.

'Bar-Ilan here will take you back and get some men organised to help you. In the meantime you can continue to billet in the hotel, but if the hospital has any suitable facilities, it might be more convenient to move some of you closer to your base of operation.

'I'm going to take the other APC and inspect the bridges, now,' he said to Bar-Ilan. 'I'll leave these people in your capable hands.'

'*Beseder*, sir,' she responded. 'Just a thought, sir – should we rename the hospital? I mean, *Al Faihaa* is a bit of a tongue-twister, isn't it? How about something in Hebrew, *'Ben Gurion'*, or even the present Prime Minister's name, if you prefer?'

'I think *Ben Gurion* sounds fine. What do the rest of you think?'

The doctors and nurse agreed. 'Avoids any potential political conflict, too,' said Dr. Bergman.

'*Beseder*,' said Rebekkah, hopping into the front seat and directing the APC driver back to their hotel base to begin moving personnel and equipment. By the end of the day a rudimentary hospital would be established.'

4 – Haifa and Akko
One week earlier – immediately after the Six Hour War

At the end of the war Shaul and his men had arrived back from Amman, Jordan, in an Israeli Air Force *Hercules C-130* transport plane, landing at *Ramat David* airfield in Galilee. A bus took them from there to the nearby city of Haifa, dropping them at the Central Bus Station.

Shaul said goodbye to the rest of his troops and then collected Rebekkah Bar-Ilan from outside, where she was already waiting for him. She had changed out of her IDF uniform into tight jeans and a pale blue tank top, which not only showed off her slim figure, but emphasised her blue eyes and pale blonde hair. Her light beige jacket hung from her thumb over her shoulder.

Shaul was impressed and whistled to show his appreciation, adding, 'You sure look a lot different out of uniform – great improvement, in my humble opinion.'

'Oh yeah,' Rebekkah replied with a grin, raising her eyebrows suggestively.

They walked the short distance to a car-hire office nearby and Shaul organised a Toyota Jeep to take them around the Galilee. When they came out to collect the vehicle Shaul handed the keys to Rebekkah.

'OK, we're on leave now, Rebekkah. No more 'sir', OK?'

'Sure, Sol – and you can call me Bekkah. That's how I'm known on the kibbutz.'

'OK, Bekkah, let's go find some food first, eh? I know a good Italian place near Paris Square. Want to try that?'

'That sounds good, Sol. I could eat a horse by now.'

'Don't think the Italians here *do* horse – something about it not being kosher – but I'm sure they can produce something suitable. I had a very enjoyable meal here a few months ago.'

Rebekkah drove the jeep to Paris Square and found a parking spot, after a little searching. Then they walked the few yards to the Italian restaurant.

Over their pasta Shaul asked Rebekkah about her family, 'Are they all kibbutzniks, Bekkah?'

'Well, my mum and dad are still very much an integral part of the kibbutz. I have two older brothers – both of them served in combat brigades, as did my dad, so I suppose that's where I got my motivation to stay in the Army from. My brothers are both in business, now. Yoel, the oldest, runs a medium size electronics company in Petach Tikva. Daniel is the head of research for a computer firm in Haifa.'

'So they're both into high-tech – what Israel is now famous for?'

'Yeah, we're the original start-up nation. Probably our biggest asset – technology and innovation,' said Rebekkah. 'What about your family, Sol?'

'My dad owned an insurance company in New York, which my brother Reuben now controls. Reuben is a lawyer – and he acts like the typical lawyer. Money is all important to him, and position and prestige. None of those things mean a whole lot to me – I mean, I'm thankful that I wasn't brought up in poverty, of course, but other than the basic necessities I don't really think a lot about material things.

'I prefer to be doing something constructive – though not everyone sees the Army as constructive, I understand. But where would we be as a western capitalist society if we didn't have an army to protect and make our way of life secure? Where would Israel be today if they didn't have a strong military?'

'Israel wouldn't exist,' said Rebekkah, 'It's as simple as that.'

'Yes,' said Shaul, 'I agreed with former Prime Minister Netanyahu when he said, "The truth is that if the Arabs were to put down their arms there would be no more war. If Israel were to put down its arms there would be no more Israel." Well, now they've been forced to put down their weapons and Israel has no enemies within or around her.'

'Yeah, it's hard to realise that we don't have to fight with the whole world any more about a *two state solution*,' said Rebekkah,

'Everything has changed so much in such a short time. Wasn't it some British politician who said, "A week is a long time in politics"?'

'Yeah, it might have been Harold Wilson, back in the sixties – but he sure got it right as far as the Middle East is concerned,' Shaul answered. 'Israel are in a completely new situation, now. I mean, we can pretty much disregard world opinion at the moment. We don't have to try to please anyone. Not one nation came to our aid when they all believed we were about to be eliminated – just like they did nothing during the holocaust!

'So, now we owe *them* nothing' agreed Rebekkah, 'Not a single thing. Israel can hold her head up around the world again. We no longer need to apologise for daring to defend ourselves. Our enemies have proved to the rest of the world that they meant exactly what they said when they talked about "wiping Israel off the map".

'*Ken*,' Shaul agreed. 'No one at the time believed Hitler would really attempt to wipe out the Jews of Europe and no one – until now – wanted to believe that Iran and the Arab states would really try to wipe out Israel. Now that they've tried to do it – and failed – they *can* believe it! And they can't blame Israel for acting decisively to prevent her own annihilation.'

'Yes,' said Rebekkah, 'we're spread thin all over the Middle East at the moment, but yet we have no enemy in sight. That's really weird when you've lived all of your life surrounded by enemies. I mean, a lot of Israelis used to go abroad – to America, Europe, or whatever – just to get away from the tension, that sense of being under pressure all the time. I think when it really sinks in it will make a profound difference to how we view ourselves as Israelis in future.'

'I think Israel are now on their way to becoming one of the strongest nations,' said Shaul. 'I mean, Britain, for instance, have always been considered a world power, with a population of sixty million. If all of the Ten Tribes come home to eretz Israel we could have a population of over one hundred million.

'With all of our technology resources and our ability to make the desert bloom and to harvest solar power, rejuvenate the Dead Sea, etc. we should be able to turn this into one of the most advanced countries in the world. I mean, it will take a good few years to achieve it, but then Israel really would be a light to the nations – as HaShem intended.'

'HaShem? You really believe in God, then, Sol?' Rebekkah asked.

'I don't see how anyone could doubt His existence after what has just happened. I mean, even the most secular reporters are referring to the 'miracle' of Israel's survival. I'm referring to YHWH – the God of the bible, of Avraham, Yitzhak and Yaakov – not the Allah of the Muslims. That god has been totally discredited by recent events – even the Muslims are beginning to admit that. What about you? Don't you believe in God, Bekkah?'

'I don't know. It was never a big thing in my life. I mean, being brought up on a kibbutz, God didn't figure highly in anything. We were taught to rely pretty much on our own resources. That's why we're called *sabras*, you know – a prickly cactus on the outside, but soft and sweet on the inside. Most people outside Israel only see the tough outside, though. But God – God has been left up to our own choice. We certainly weren't taught to expect anything from Him.'

'Well, I wasn't brought up religious, or anything,' said Shaul. 'I don't know for sure, but I sometimes wonder if my dad thought God was just there to make his business profitable. You know, like his relationship with God was just another business deal? My brother probably thinks the same way. But when you've been in combat you don't tend to think that way any more. You see how fragile life really is. And you begin to realise there might be something more out there.'

'I suppose that's true,' Rebekkah admitted.

'It was after a pretty rough day in Kabul, when we'd been attacked in an area of the city that had normally been quite peaceful. We ended up in a fire-fight and we lost one ANA soldier dead, and two more – one American – injured. It was later that day that we had one of those 'bible' conversations with my friend, Brandon.

'I mean, it started off by us just taking a rise out of him for reading his bible all the time. But, you know, he never did that to appear religious, or anything like that. Sometimes he was hardly even aware that we were talking to him. Anyway, the way he answered got us intrigued – because he related it to right were we were. And now, after the war he told us about has come to pass, I'm seriously wondering about whether the rest of what he told us is also going to be fulfilled?'

'What was the rest of it then, Sol?'

'Well, first of all the ingathering of all the ten tribes – that seems to be about to happen, if it isn't happening already. I mean we're about to go back to Basra, Iraq, of all places. I mean, who would ever have thought Israeli soldiers would be operating in Iraq and Iran? So that part looks to be coming true. But it's the other part that really scares me.'

'And what's that?' Rebekkah encouraged him.

'Well, apparently the bible talks a lot about Babylon – or mega-Babylon, or the *'daughter of Babylon'*. These are prophesies in the *Tanakh* that have not yet been fulfilled. I mean, ancient Babylon got taken over by the Medes and Persians, and the Jews – or 50,000 or so of them, anyway – were allowed to return to Israel. But it was never destroyed *'in one hour'* the way those prophecies described. Ancient Babylon just kinda faded out after a few hundred years – until some German archaeologist re-discovered it about a hundred years ago.

'No, it's like these unfulfilled prophesies are referring to Babylon as a code – especially when it says the *'daughter of Babylon'* – one verse actually says that her mother will be ashamed of her. OK, how many nations can refer to a mother nation? Most of them are the remains of the British Empire – Australia, New Zealand, South Africa – and, of course, the United States.'

'So what you're saying – or Brandon was saying, anyway – is that when the bible says 'Babylon' it actually refers to a modern nation in the world today? And that these things the prophets foretold have still to happen – to this modern nation?'

'Yes, that's exactly it,' said Shaul. 'And all the prophetic clues point to it being my own country of birth – the United States!'

'So, they foretell that the United States will be destroyed – in one hour, did you say?'

'Yes, that's about it. It *is* scary, isn't it?'

'It is, especially if you happen to have friends and family back there – like your brother and his family, and your friends from the Army.'

'That's what I mean. Brandon believes these things, obviously. And I think Dev was beginning to take some of it to heart – especially from what I've heard from him recently.'

'Oh – what has been happening with him, then?'

'Well, he was over in Ireland recently – his family in Boston are originally from there – at his cousin's wedding. And apparently he's fallen in love with one of his cousin's friends – the same girl apparently who picked him up at the airport. Well, it turns out that his cousin, and her new husband, belong to some church in Ireland that Dev refers to as the 'born agains'. I think he means it's like what Brandon's into, sort of Pentecostal? I'm not too well up on Christian denominations.

'Anyway, This girl – her name is pronounced Neev, spelt some funny Irish way – has been to some of their meetings, too – and she and Dev hit it off and they have some discussion about the stuff we've just been talking about. So, they go along to this pastor guy, from his cousin's church – have a talk with him and the upshot is they pray together and both of them have some kind of powerful spiritual experience.

'So now Dev is getting really into this prophecy stuff as well – particularly the bits about America being the Babylon referred to in the *Tanakh*. Actually, there is apparently some prophecy in the Christian New Testament about it as well, but it all seems to link together.'

'Well, America sure haven't been much of an ally to Israel, in recent years,' said Rebekkah. 'And they're still complaining about us winning the war and gaining control over so much of the Middle East – as if it was Israel's fault that we were attacked by our neighbours and nearly wiped out!'

'Well, that was Brandon's whole point – the reason for God's judgement of America was her attitude towards Israel. That the USA was responsible for all this bloodshed and loss of life in Israel. You've got to admit, if the US hadn't allowed Iran to develop nuclear weapons in the first place, we probably wouldn't have been attacked – and all those tens of thousands of Israelis wouldn't be dead now.'

'Very true,' said Rebekkah, 'What a wonder hindsight is. That policy has been the cause of many millions of deaths, not just Israelis. Look at Gaza, Damascus, Beirut, Iran, Iraq, Saudi Arabia, Egypt, Sudan – millions of people dead.'

'Yeah, well there's a prophecy in Isaiah – or *Yeshayahu*, I should say – I found this one myself. It talks about God loving Israel so much that he will give other nations in exchange for her – Egypt is specifically mentioned. If it applies to Egypt, it could well apply to America as well?'

'Hmm,' mused Rebekkah, 'it's kind of interesting – all this prophecy stuff – I can see that.'

'Anyway,' Shaul concluded, 'We have a car outside and only three days to make use of it. Where are you taking me to, then?'

'Oh,' Rebekkah replied, 'I thought we might have a look at Akko and Nahariyyah – you haven't been up there yet, have you, Sol?'

'No,' he answered, 'but I'd love to see the old Crusader walls.'

'Well, there's also an old Crusader fort inland a bit from Nahar-iyyah, in the Yehiam Forest. We could see that as well – it's kind of on the way to my kibbutz, Kfar Giladi. And then there are the grottoes at the Lebanese border, at Rosh Hanikrah. Lot's to see.'

'We'd better get moving, in that case,' Shaul said, producing a credit card to pay the bill.

They made their way to the car, but before getting in Shaul took Rebekkah's hand and pulled her towards him. 'I've been wanting to do this all through the meal,' he said, then kissed her long and thoroughly. She responded in kind and they clung to one another for several minutes, before finally releasing one another and quietly getting into the jeep.

Rebekkah started the vehicle, drove through the city centre traffic and quickly accessed Highway 4, which passes through the centre of Haifa, keeping in the left hand lane which brought them onto the fairly new Highway 22 heading first south east, then east, then swinging northwards. The freeway was now passing the *Krayot* – the 'villages', large suburbs of Haifa – to the north.

'We need to decide where we're staying tonight – I'd suggest we find a hotel in Akko. All right with you?' she said softly. The formerly tense atmosphere between them had dissipated with the intimate contact and they both felt much more relaxed, more at ease with one another.

A bridge had been crossed in their relationship and they both felt quite happy about it. There was no need to rush to develop things any further right at this point, but they both expected that in due course, that would happen and were each eagerly anticipating it.

In just a few minutes they were entering Akko and turning off west towards Palm Beach. Shaul, browsing local hotels on his phone, told Rebekkah to keep going. They passed the *Palm Beach Hotel* and turned inland, then left past the Nautical College and back to the sea front again. Just over one hundred metres along the street they came to the *Akko Hotel* – built right into the old Crusader city walls.

'This looks nice,' Shaul said.

'It looks very expensive,' answered Rebekkah, parking the jeep in a convenient space just past the hotel entrance.

When she switched off the ignition, Shaul reached over and pulled her towards him, kissing her soundly. 'Perhaps we could save money by sharing a room?' he suggested.

'Are you planning on seducing me, *Rav Seren?*' she asked.

'Mmmm, definitely,' Shaul replied.

'Okay, then we'd better find out if they actually have a room, don't you think?' she asked.

They discovered that the hotel indeed had a room available – one with a good view of Haifa Bay to the south – and Shaul insisted on paying for it.

'Would you care for a walk by the sea, first,' he asked Rebekkah.

'That would be nice, yes,' she replied.

He explained to the young man on reception that they were going to take a walk across the road to the beach for a short while.

'That's OK, sir,' he said. 'We'll make sure your luggage is taken up to your room in the meantime.' He then handed Shaul a couple of key-cards for their room.

Shaul took Rebekkah by the hand and led her out of the hotel and beyond the city walls to the edge of the Mediterranean Sea. The night was warm and a gentle breeze rustled the palm trees near the beach, while soft waves caressed the sand below.

'It looks very romantic,' Rebekkah said, 'with all the lights of Haifa in the distance and the sound of the waves.'

'Yes,' said Shaul, 'and you can see all the ships waiting outside the bay as well.'

He took her in his arms and kissed her once again.

'No last minute regrets, *Segen mishne?*' he asked.

In reply she pulled him towards her and kissed him fiercely again, '*Lo,*' she answered abruptly – no!

After a short while they returned to the hotel and retired to their room together.

5 – An Afternoon in Lebanon

Shaul and Rebekkah woke early the next morning.

'How about breakfast in the old city of Akko?' Shaul suggested, as he came back from the shower.

'Mmmm,' Rebekkah murmured sleepily, 'Sounds good. Think I might need a shower first to come alive, though.'

'Be my guest,' replied Shaul.

Ten minutes later they had checked out and parked their belongings in the jeep and began walking through narrow streets and covered alleys, into the heart of the Old City of Akko. Built by the Crusaders, with massive fortifications on the north and west, the city was a complete contrast to Haifa, where they'd eaten their meal last night.

Every few metres was a reminder of the past – a wall, an arch, an isolated stone column – now leading into a quiet plaza shaded by trees, now into a dark stone arched passageway, now into the broad expanse of an ancient khan, surround by an arched portico, and with a tall clock tower rising above the city.

They emerged from the khan into a narrow street bordering the sea wall. Every few metres there were gaps where they could see out across the bay inland through a metal railing. They caught glimpses of the marina to the south and walked towards it. They passed an old mosque, with stone minarets and came out into the port area, filled with small open fishing boats, with the tall masts of the yacht marina beyond.

As they walked south past the port they could see across Haifa Bay to Mount Carmel and Haifa City beyond. On the edge of the sea wall was a large sculpture of a whale with a person-sized hole through its middle.

'Want to be Jonah?' Rebekkah asked, pointing to the whale.

Shaul dutifully climbed into the whale and Rebekkah took his picture. They reversed positions and Shaul took hers also.

'OK, I think I've worked up an appetite, now,' Rebekkah remarked.

'What about that restaurant beside the waves?' suggested Shaul.

'Sounds good,' replied Rebekkah, as they walked back towards a restaurant which bordered the sea between the harbour and an old ruined section of wall, which still resisted the sea's impact. They found a table at the very back, where they could look out between the ruined wall sections across Haifa Bay to Mount Carmel. Large waves were coming in from the Mediterranean Sea just outside the bay and breaking on the rocks and sea wall below them.

'It reminds me of the Old City in Jerusalem,' remarked Shaul, as they tucked into an Israeli breakfast, 'and Jaffa, too. 'The same kind of stone – cream and golden in the light – dark tunnels and arches over the street.'

'Yes, it's very similar,' Rebekkah agreed.

Sol was studying a pamphlet about the city he had picked up at the hotel. 'It says Acre is one of the oldest continually inhabited cities in the world – dates back to around 1500 BCE! The Crusaders – under Richard I – captured it from the Saracens in 1191 CE. Despite being lion-hearted, he still managed to execute 2,700 Saracens! When the Mamluks invaded exactly a hundred years later they in turn killed every remaining Crusader – the end of the kingdom.'

'Yeah, bloodthirsty lot, weren't they – all of them?' commented Rebekkah wryly.

'This place was ancient long before America was ever discovered!' Shaul continued.

'It also says the British used the fortress as a high-security prison to hold members of the Jewish underground. Men from the Irgun staged a dramatic rescue in May 1947 – only a few of the prisoners escaped, but it was a major blow to the British and a big morale boost for the Jewish forces.

'Apparently there's a whole subterranean Crusader city,' Shaul added. 'The entrance to it is opposite the mosque. Shall we invest-igate?'

'Beseder,' Rebekkah replied. 'Let's check it out.'

41

Chapter 5 – An Afternoon in Lebanon

Shaul and Rebekkah spent another couple of hours wandering around ancient Akko, then returned to their hired jeep and drove north on Highway 4 to Nahariyya, where they found a restaurant along the pleasant tree-lined main street of Sderot Haga'aton. The street was divided either side of the river, which flowed down the middle towards the beach to the west.

After a relaxed lunch in Nahariyya, Rebekkah drove north again past the Kibbutz of Rosh HaNikra, perched high on the south side of the ridge that had previously separated Israel from Lebanon. They turned west towards the Mediterranean Sea and, just before it turned north again, the road widened and Rebekkah was able to park the jeep facing the sea.

'This used to be as far as you could travel north along the Mediterranean,' Rebekkah explained. There used to be an Army checkpoint here and no-one was allowed beyond that point.'

Carrying towels and swimming costumes they had bought in Nahariyya, they walked westward along a wooden walkway on the left side of the road, which led to the cable car station. After a short wait a yellow cable car arrived and they descended quite steeply to sea level. Half-way down they passed a red car on its way up. As they descended they had a clear view of the white chalk cliffs forming the promontory.

At the bottom the cable car stopped in a concrete enclosure on the seaward side of a concrete road, which ran between two tunnels and over a small bridge on the southern side.

'These railway tunnels were made by the British forces from New Zealand and South Africa during the Second World War,' Rebekkah explained. 'The northern tunnel used to take you into Lebanon, but it was walled off when Israel became independent in 1948. I wonder if they've opened it up again yet?'

They walked northwards past a viewing area beside the sea and on into the tunnel, where the remains of railway lines were still visible in the floor. After less than a hundred metres the tunnel was closed off by a concrete wall. However, the door in the wall was open – with no sign of anyone guarding it – and Shaul and Rebekkah were able to walk through it into what had recently been Lebanese territory. Eventually, they came out of the tunnel into the sunshine again on the Lebanese side of the former border.

'And here we are in Lebanon,' Rebekkah announced, sounding like a tour guide. 'Y'know, it's really weird being here. I've lived all my life beside the Lebanese border – with Katyusha rockets being fired at us every now and then – and now it doesn't exist any more! We can just walk right into Lebanon – and, I suppose, Syria too?'

'Yes,' agreed Shaul, 'the reality of the new Israel. I wonder if the government will consider rebuilding the railway line? I don't think there *is* a railway system in Lebanon any more – not since the civil war in the seventies and eighties – but there are railways in former Syria and I'm sure Israel will want to connect them to the existing Israeli railway system. It would make it much easier to get around the new Israel.

'There's probably no better time to do it – y'know, with so many houses and businesses being empty. The government could easily set aside the land needed for the railway line, before allocating houses to new immigrants. I suppose that will all come under the *New Israel Plan*, now. They're gonna be the ones responsible for the re-building of infrastructure and settling the new *olim.*'

'*Ken,*' said Rebekkah, 'I wonder how soon it will be before we can get a train from Tel Aviv to say Aleppo, or Latakia? Don't think there'll be many tourists wanting to visit Beirut, or Damascus, though!'

'Actually,' said Shaul, 'Israel might just go ahead and build the line the Jordanians were planning to build – from the Jordan River, near Beth Shean, to Idlib – y'know, connecting on from the new Haifa to Beth Shean railway line. Then they could link that in to an upgraded Amman-Damascus line and connect into the whole Syrian system that way. There's a new Jordanian line connecting Amman to Aqaba, as well, so Israel could link into it from the new Eilat Station and then we'd have a complete circuit.'

'Well, there's certainly plenty of potential for development there,' agreed Rebekkah. 'And we're definitely gonna need imaginative projects to provide employment for all these new *olim.* Shall we go and see the grottoes, now?'

They walked back through the railway tunnel into Israel proper and after a short distance turned left into the tunnel leading to the spectacular sea grottoes that Rosh Hanikrah was named after. They spent some time wandering from grotto to grotto, admiring the spectacular colours formed on the walls by light reflected from the sea below – everything from white and golden orange, through pale yellow and green, to deep blue and indigo at sea level and below the water.

Once back out into the daylight again, Rebekkah handed her phone to a passing visitor and asked him to take a picture of Shaul and herself in front of the wall showing the cable car and the distance to Jerusalem (205 km) and Beirut (120 km).

After a short swim in the adjacent Mediterranean they ascended via the cable car again and gazed out at the coast to the south. Shaul asked Rebekkah, 'Shall we see if we can drive into Lebanon, as well as walk?'

'Yeah, sure, why not? That was the first time I've ever set foot in Lebanon.'

Rebekkah drove up the slope to what had been the Frontier Post only a week ago. The gate was now fixed wide open and a soldier waved to them from beside it. 'Can we drive on into the Lebanon?' Rebekkah asked him.

'Of course you can,' he replied. 'It's not Lebanon any more – it's all part of Israel, now. *Shalom aleichem!* Where are you from?'

'I'm from HaGalil – Kfar Giladi,' replied Rebekkah, 'and Shaul is a lone soldier, originally from the US.'

Immediately they were into conversation about the Army and where they had been posted during the recent war. Eventually, another couple of cars pulled up behind them and the young soldier wished them an enjoyable trip, saying, *'L'hitraot.' (see you)*.

L'hitraot,' they both replied.

Rebekkah accelerated away and they rounded the bend with steep white cliffs on their right. As they turned northwards they began to see the coast of Lebanon ahead and she drove on slowly for three or four kilometres until they reached the village of Naqoura – the same word as *Hanikra*, in Arabic – also named after the grottoes. The village was almost deserted – apart from other Israeli sightseers viewing it for the first time, like themselves.

In the middle of the village a sign in English pointed to the former UNIFIL *Camp Green Hill* base. 'Shall we take a look?' asked Rebekkah.

'Sure,' Shaul replied.

The road forked and Rebekkah took the southerly direction, which climbed the side of the hill parallel to the sea, then turned left and ascended a steep hill to the very top of the camp. Several roads led off on the left to buildings belonging to the camp. At the very top of the hill they came to the heliport, where only a couple of weeks ago UN helicopters had still been transporting UNIFIL troops to their posts along the border.

The only troops visible now were a few Israeli soldiers, who were using the camp as a base. They waved to them cheerfully. There was a kind of holiday atmosphere around that Shaul remarked on.

'Yeah,' said Rebekkah, as she parked facing out to sea. 'It's all a bit unreal, I think. It's hard to believe we're in the Lebanon and there are no enemies in sight. Even when we were here in the eighties there would have been South Lebanese Army and PLO shooting at one another. You couldn't have just wandered around like a tourist – which, I guess, is just what we are at the moment.

'Well,' Shaul pondered, 'I think it might have been Ezekiel who prophesied that one day the people of Israel would no longer have malicious neighbours who are painful briers and sharp thorns.'

'Well he certainly got that right, then! Want to see more?' she added. 'If you don't mind missing the Crusader fortress at Yehiam I think we could actually drive to Kfar Giladi through Lebanon, if the roads are passable.'

'Sure. Why not,' Shaul answered. 'We might not get this chance for a long time. Do you think you can find the way?'

'I hope so,' she answered. 'As long as we go roughly east and only a little bit to the north we shouldn't wander *too* far off.'

She started the jeep again and they headed across the hill and back down by the other road, along the side of a wooded gully.

At the northern edge of Naqoura Rebekkah turned right onto another road that climbed south towards the former border.

'This part of the border is all forest,' Rebekkah remarked.

'Yes,' said Shaul, 'It's quite unusual to see such a wild forest.'

The road grew steeper and there were several hairpin bends. In places the surface was damaged – probably by Israeli shellfire during the war – and Rebekkah had to manoeuvre slowly around the obstacles.

'I'm quite glad now that we hired a jeep,' she said.

'Me too,' Shaul agreed.

The road came to a tee junction, where Rebekkah turned left. They could see the former border fence ahead of them and to the south.

'This looks like the road UNIIFIL and the Lebanese Armed Forces used to patrol the border,' said Rebekkah. 'I think we can stay fairly close to the border fence for the first fifteen kilometres, or so. Then we have to go more to the north. That's where we are more likely to get lost.'

'So, it's going to be a bit of a mystery tour, eh?' said Shaul, laughing.

'Yeah,' Rebekkah agreed, 'but let's hope we can solve the mystery.'

The border fence had mostly disappeared from view, having taken a sharp turn to the south. They caught brief glimpses of it south of them, in the bottom of a valley, as they travelled eastwards along a ridge. It disappeared completely as the road turned sharply northwards to the village of Aalma Ech Chaab.

Rebekkah turned right in the centre of the deserted village, heading south eastwards again, through cultivated fields. The road led between steep hills and east into a wide flat valley, where there were several more empty villages. They caught sight of the border fence again as the road ran along an east-west ridge, with terraced sides to the north. They could see the buildings of an Israeli kibbutz just beyond the border.

'All those border settlements were built with defence in mind,' said Rebekkah. 'I suppose they'll take the fence down, now – no more need for it.'

'Yeah, the only border that might need a fence now is the northern one with Turkey,' Shaul agreed, 'and I think the Turks have already built one!'

The road forked ahead and there were no signs to say which road went where. Rebekkah took the one on the right, and again at the next fork – because the surface looked slightly better kept – and they soon found themselves in another Arab village.

'The trouble with Arab villages is that they tend to have been designed by donkeys,' Rebekkah remarked with a sigh.

'You mean by people who weren't very clever?' asked Shaul, slightly puzzled.

'No, I'm not being derogatory, I mean *literally* designed by donkeys. When the Canaanites, or whoever, first created all these terraces they built retaining walls and then filled the baskets on each side of the donkey with soil and allowed the donkey to find its own way up the hill to where the terraces where. Of course the donkey didn't go straight up – it wandered back and forwards along the side of the hill. Those donkey tracks often became the roads we have today and they meander all over the place as a result.

'Ahh, a sign for Bint Jbail,' she exclaimed. 'At last, somewhere I'm familiar with. Markaba is what we really want – it's the Lebanese village opposite Kfar Giladi – but Bint Jbail is a large village on the way there.'

The road took them through another deserted village, where they turned left – now heading north east – and then through a village on the side of a tall ridge, from which they could see across to the east, to a collection of buildings that, presumably, made up Bint Jbail.

They came to a junction and Rebekkah turned right, driving south now towards the centre of Bint Jbeil. This village seemed much larger than any they had passed through on the way across southern Lebanon. There were many shops, a gas station, some banks, even some industrial buildings. The main street turned eastwards, leading to a large square surrounded by tall buildings. Rebekkah took the road leading eastwards out of the square and was gratified to see a sign in English which mentioned Markaba.

'We seem to be on the right road, after all,' she said.

'Well done,' said Shaul. 'I'm beginning to feel quite hungry and I wouldn't mind a cool drink – something better than this warm water.'

'Well, one thing about a kibbutz on a Friday night, we may not be religious, but we do believe in a good Shabbat meal.'

The road turned from east, to north east and then north, and as it did so the hills grew more barren and mountainous. They caught glimpses of 'the good fence' and sometimes, far below, of Israel's green and fertile Huleh Valley spread out beyond it.'

'The early pioneers drained the Huleh Lake into the Jordan and turned the whole valley into one of the most productive in Israel,' Rebekkah explained. 'They brought in lots of eucalyptus trees from Australia to dry up the swampy ground, but they deliberately left some areas in their natural form to preserve the wildlife.'

They passed the turnoff to Markaba and shortly after the road turned east and continued north along the fence itself. On the Israeli side another road ran parallel.

'Look,' said Rebekkah, 'they've cut the fence already. That means we don't have to drive on to Metulla to cross back into Israel, we can take a shortcut now.'

She turned the jeep through the wide hole cut in the border fence and, manoeuvring over some rough ground, turned right onto a road on the former Israeli side running south, which skirted the border kibbutz of Misgav Am and meandered down the valley towards Kibbutz Kfar Giladi. Rebekkah pointed out the Kfar Giladi quarry immediately below them, with the kibbutz beyond.

All the way down they had a spectacular view of the Huleh Valley and the last of the sun was lighting up the huge majestic snow-covered bulk of Mount Hermon beyond to the north east. They passed the quarry entrance on the left and then the kibbutz entrance appeared just beyond and Rebekkah swung the jeep left through the open gateway. Turning to Shaul she announced, 'Welcome to my home – Kfar Giladi.'

They drove through quiet tree shaded avenues until Rebekkah pulled up near a small red-roofed bungalow. 'This is my parents' home. Come on in and I'll introduce you.'

Shaul followed Rebekkah into her parents' house. He found his hand gripped firmly by her father, Yuval, while her mother, Ronit, hugged Rebekkah enthusiastically. When she finally let go of Rebekkah, she hugged Shaul briefly as well.

'Shabbat shalom!' said Yuval. 'Welcome to our home, Shaul. You are *Seren* (Captain) Levine, now, *ken*?'

'Shabbat shalom!' Shaul responded. 'Actually, I'll be going back to Basrah as *Rav Seren*, (Major)'. 'I started the war as *Segen* (Lieutenant), but my commander – *Seren* Gefen – was wounded in Aqaba and I took his place. They promoted me then to *Seren*.'

Thus began a discussion of the recent war and comparison with several previous wars, which was soon interrupted by Ronit, who said, 'You men can discuss the Army and wars all you want – *after* we've eaten.'

The four of them walked across to the canteen building and – true to Rebekkah's prediction the shabbat food was excellent. The war discussion continued both during the meal and afterwards, when they walked around the south of the kibbutz to the pub, which was nearly empty.

Rebekkah explained that the pub would normally be a busy place – well populated with international volunteers, but that they had left as soon as they possibly could when the war began and none of them had yet returned. Later, they all headed back to the Bar-Ilan home for coffee and more conversation – Yuval and Ronit soon excusing themselves to go to bed. Eventually, Shaul and Rebekkah also retired to her old room for the night.

In One Hour – Babylon will fall – *Raymond McCullough*

6 – Shabbat in Galilee

Next morning – after another Israeli breakfast in the kibbutz dining room – Rebekkah, wearing a revealing light blue tank top and tight shorts, showed Shaul around the kibbutz – the original kibbutz houses in black Galilee stone, the chickens, dairy cows, fish ponds, nurseries and the apple and avocado orchards. Here and there, on dead tree stumps, bright yellow *Katyusha* rockets had been placed.

'Those are the ones that *failed* to explode,' said Rebekkah. 'We had plenty that did – mostly in the fields and orchards, thankfully. Hezbollah were trying to hit Kiryat Shmona to the south, of course, but many of them fell short.'

'Must have been a bit scary, not knowing when one of these might hit?' Shaul said.

'You just got used to it,' Rebekkah said. 'We carried on as normal – business as usual. We wouldn't let them change our way of life. The worst hit was during the 2006 war with Hezbollah, when twelve reserve soldiers were killed by a *Katyusha* rocket.'

Rebekkah suggested taking Shaul for a trip on the cable car up to Manara kibbutz, the cliff train and then the mountain slide back down for 1.2 kilometres. 'We used to love going there as kids,' she told him.

They drove south through the town of Kiryat Shmona and stopped just beyond it at the cable car station. 'Yesterday we went on the steepest cable car in the world,' Rebekkah informed Shaul. 'Today we're going on the longest one in Israel – nearly two kilometres.'

The view over the Huleh valley to Mount Hermon and the Golan Heights was stunning, as they climbed up over the steep cliff. They rose to the top and then took the Cliff Train – trailer carriages towed by a kibbutz tractor – up to the former border fence and along the patrol road to the former UN checkpoint, then back to the kibbutz, through the forest and to the fruit orchards. There was plenty of commentary at different points as they rode around.

'That was interesting,' said Shaul, as they returned to the cable car.

'Ahh, but the best is yet to come,' said Rebekkah.

They left the cable car halfway down and Rebekkah led Shaul to the mountain slide – a roller-coaster-style run down the mountain slopes in karts that held one or two persons.

'You can use the brake if you really want to,' she laughed, as she strapped herself into the front seat of one of the karts.'

Shaul strapped himself in behind her and the kart was towed up the track to the top of the run, then began a long, fast descent of the slopes – careening madly around the many bends. The ride was fast, scenic and exhilarating and Shaul thoroughly enjoyed it.

'That was great!' he told her when they left the slide. 'I really enjoyed that – in fact, the whole day, so far. *Toda.*'

He pulled Rebekkah towards him and kissed her fervently. 'You're a lot of fun to be with,' he told her.

'You're not so bad, yourself,' she retorted, laughing. 'Fancy a swim, now?'

'Yeah, why not – it's hot enough!' Shaul answered. 'Where do we go?'

'Come on and I'll show you, she replied, heading down the trail towards the lower cable car station, where their jeep was parked. Rebekkah drove again, heading towards the middle of the Huleh Valley, to the Jordan River. They parked just off a small road and walked to the river. The Jordan at this point was more of a fast-flowing stream than a river, with a deep channel on the far side and shallow water on the outside of the bend.

They quickly changed into swimming gear and walked into the shallow water, which suddenly got deeper, colder and much swifter, making it impossible to swim. They would simply hold onto a tree root, float for a few seconds and then let go and allow the strong current to carry them around the bend for a hundred metres, or so – then wade out and walk back to the starting point. The water was quite chilly where the current flowed.

'Very refreshing,' said Shaul. 'I've been to the Jordan where it flows out of the Sea of Galilee – wide and slow – this is like a different river.'

'Yeah,' replied Rebekkah, 'it's much livelier up here.'

'And much colder,' added Shaul.

'That's because its source is from melting ice from Mount Hermon and the mountains of Lebanon,' Rebekkah answered. 'The Dan stream just suddenly appears out of the bottom of a hill as a fully flowing stream. The Banyas stream comes from the same source and the Hasbani, or Snir, stream flows in from Lebanon – in fact it used to form part of the border between Israel and Lebanon.

'There is an Alawite village, called Ghajar – about five kilometres from Kfar Giladi ...' Rebekkah pointed to the north east, 'which was taken by Israel when we captured the Golan in 1967. Half of it was in Israel and half in Lebanon. The villagers preferred to be called Syrian, but were happy to have Israeli passports and to work in Israel. When Israel withdrew from Lebanon in 2000 the villagers all wanted to remain part of Israel, but the UN said the northern half of the village belonged to Lebanon and insisted Israel had to withdraw.

'So we built a fence right around the village – to keep out Hezbollah and the LAF, who patrolled north of the fence – and the IDF patrolled the northern part of the village, but had no permanent troops there. Eventually, we agreed to pull our troops out of the northern part and the UNIFIL forces were allowed to patrol the northern part instead.'

'Sounds like a crazy situation, indeed,' said Shaul.

'Yeah, well, they should be happy enough, now,' Rebekkah concluded. 'All the other Alawites from the Lebanese side have fled – though the people of Ghajar have had no real contact with the other villages in all that time, anyway. The Lebanese Alawites always regarded them as traitors.'

'I suppose we'd better get back to say goodbye to your parents and return to Haifa, now,' said Shaul.

'Yeah,' Rebekkah sighed, 'Back to work again, eh?'

They were already dry in the sun so they dressed and Rebekkah headed the jeep back to the kibbutz. They said goodbye to Yuval and Ronit – who assured Shaul he was very welcome to come and visit them anytime, and drove down Highway 90 to the junction with Highway 85, which took them across the Galilee to Akko, then south to Haifa. Because it was still Shabbat the roads were quiet and the journey took them only an hour and thirty minutes.

Rebekkah filled the jeep's gas tank at an Arab-owned filling station, then parked it close to the hire company and they embraced fervently in the vehicle before parting. Shaul remarked, 'Don't know when we'll be able to have time together again, but it's been a lovely weekend. I've really enjoyed it. Your parents were great, too.'

'Me too,' Rebekkah whispered. They kissed one last lingering time. 'I'll see you at the bus, then,' she said, leaving Shaul to return the keys of the jeep to the car hire company.

They walked to the bus station – arriving separately – and found the IDF bus waiting with the rest of their company to take them back to the Ramat David airbase and an IDF transport plane back to Amman, in the former Kingdom of Jordan.

7 – Boston visit

Dev and Niamh had met when he travelled to Ireland for his cousin's wedding and they had been in touch regularly since his return from there. They often met up on *Skype* to chat and refresh their memory of each other. Now Niamh had agreed to come to Boston for two weeks. Devlin met her at Logan International Airport.

When Niamh saw him she rushed into his arms and they embraced tightly, then kissed one another hungrily in the middle of the Arrivals area.

'It's so good to see you face to face again,' Dev told her.

'Yes,' she replied. 'I've been so keyed up on the journey over – wondering if we'd both still feel the same way after all this time. I feel much better already.'

'Well, *I've* certainly not changed my mind about *you*,' Dev assured her.

'I can see that, now,' Niamh said. 'But I couldn't convince myself it was real until you held me again, there now.' She put both her arms around his neck and kissed him again. Dev responded enthusiastically.

'Well?' he said, 'Happier now?'

'Definitely,' she answered. 'Would you like to take my case?'

'Sure,' he replied, grabbing the handle of her wheeled case, then feasting his eyes on her once again. 'There's a lot to be said for Skype,' he told her, 'but it sure don't beat the real thing.'

'I should hope not, Mr Devlin,' she replied, looking up at him mischievously.

He led the way out of the airport and across the car park and they climbed into his dark blue Chevy Suburban, after placing her case and hand luggage on the back seat.

'So I'm now in Boston. You'll have to introduce me to your city,' she told him.

'T'will be moi pleasure, ma'am' he assured her in a mock Irish accent, starting the vehicle and pulling carefully into the traffic.

'What have you been up to back in Ireland,' he asked her.

'Oh, still trying to sell a few properties,' she answered. 'There's been a slight improvement in the housing market, but it's certainly not taking off for the foreseeable future.'

'Actually, I've had a bit of an idea about that,' said Micky.

'Oh, yes,' Niamh raised her eyebrows at him.

'You know the way we were talking about prophecy and about Babylon and all that?'

'Yes,' said Niamh.

'Well, part of that was a warning for people – Jews and others – to flee America, right? So there must be a certain number of people who believe that and are already thinking about leaving the USA? Quite a number of those would also have an Irish background and might well be interested in moving to Ireland – do you think?'

'Yeah,' pondered Niamh, 'maybe. We'd have to know if there really was an interest and also how to contact such people. Any ideas how to do that?'

'Well, I was thinking you could set up a new website – promoting the whole idea of moving to Ireland and showing some of the properties that are currently available.'

'Yeah, that might work. It would take a lot of thought put into it. And we'd need to make sure we got into contact with the right people. but it's an idea. You thinking of doing this yourself?' she asked.

'I thought it might be something we could work on together. I've got some pay gathered up from the Army and if we needed more capital my Dad might be willing to help. It's worth thinking about, anyway.'

'Yes, it could be a great idea – if it was handled right,' Niamh agreed.

'What sort of price could these properties be bought for, do you reckon?' Dev asked.

'You mean buy up a property and then re-sell it?' she asked.

'I was thinking more of buying up a whole street, part of a development, or whatever – with maybe an option to buy the rest later. If nobody's buying surely they could be bought at a rock bottom price?'

'Oh yeah, we've got developers going bankrupt, or just managing to hang on by the skin of their teeth. They might jump at the chance to off-load. The government have ordered the worst forty estates to be demolished at the developers expense. But they were mostly in rural areas where there was never going to be a demand for them, anyway.'

'Why were they built, then,' Devlin asked.

'The short answer is greed. They were built to make a profit. Everybody thought the economic boom was going to go on and on and that you just couldn't fail to make money. It was a collective craziness – and the developers and investors weren't the only ones to blame – the government and local authorities really did nothing to keep a check on those developments.

'Some of them are small developments close to Dublin, which would be more likely to sell in future. The problem is there were hardly any Building Control inspections during the boom years. Some of the houses are sub-standard, or they have faulty sewers, or have no infrastructure nearby – public transport, schools and shops.'

'OK, so you'd need to check out what you were buying very carefully, first – before making a decision,' Dev mused.

'Aye, ye would that,' Niamh agreed. 'Having said that, it should be possible to make some money if you went about it in the right way.'

'Well, I would think you would be the ideal person to decide what is a good investment, Niamh. You have the local experience.'

'Yeah, I suppose so,' she said.

'Anyway, we'll discuss it later,' said Micky. 'This is my parents' place.'

They stopped in a car park to the side of a large, dark green painted, Irish pub, with *'Devlin's'* written in Celtic-style lettering on a huge sign across the front.

'Looks impressive,' said Niamh.

'Yeah, we get a good regular crowd,' Dev explained. It's a restaurant as well, y'know. The weekends are the busiest.'

IIn One Hour – Babylon will fall – *Raymond McCullough*

8 – To Steal a Bridge
One week after the Six Hour War

Shaul directed his driver to go south on Highway Six until the first major junction – 'You'll see the University buildings straight ahead as you approach it. Turn left then and straight on to the River. As the driver obeyed, Shaul radioed Peled and then Tamari, informing them of the location of the newly designated Ben Gurion Hospital – in case they had come across any urgent medical needs in the meantime.

Peled reported, 'We've unloaded four of the tanks so far, sir. I've left Gold supervising another four, but I'm keeping two on transporters in case we want to transport them some distance away. Tamari can have the drivers once they're finished unloading.

'I've set up a check-point at this side and one across the Sinbad Island bridge, which only goes halfway across now – as far as the island. Apparently the other half was destroyed in the 1991 Gulf War, so there are two single-lane pontoon bridges carrying the traffic to and from the other side.

'I've also set up a check-point at the turn-off leading to the main bridge further south. It seems to have the heaviest traffic at the moment, sir. I'm on my way into former Iran now against the flow of traffic. I'm making notes of everything I notice along the way, relevant to our operation.'

'*Tov*, Peled, I need a checkpoint set up at both hospitals. We're using the *Al Faihaa* – the northerly one – at present, but we will need equipment from the *Basra Hospital* and we eventually hope to get it operational, too – so we need to protect the building and its equipment.'

'*Beseder*, sir, I'll contact Gold to get that organised – a couple of *Namer* APCs and some troops should do it.'

'I'll leave it with you, Peled. *L'hitraot*.'

Tamari reported that he was on the highway east between Abadan and Bandar Mahshah. 'The roads are generally good, sir, but there has been missile or mortar damage in several places. When I get back I'm gonna organise a couple of repair teams, with a bulldozer, to patch up those sections.

'There are bottlenecks going through the towns – the main Highway 96 goes right through the middle of Khorramshar and through a good part of Abadan, also. The road I'm on at the moment is in good condition, just coming to a divided section, actually. We're stopping every kilometre or so and giving out what information we can, in the hope that it will get passed along and ease people's minds a little. *Beseder?*'

'*Ken, tov ma'od* (Yes, very good), Tamari. Out.'

Shaul's APC was travelling along the right hand side of a waterway by this time, passing Lion of Babylon Square – actually a roundabout – and rounding the corner onto Corniche Street, was just approaching the city centre bridge. The original bridge had gone – only the supports in the middle and a section of bridge cantilevered out from either end remained – but about one hundred metres south a pontoon bridge had been constructed, with a single lane of traffic slowly crossing it.

He asked the driver to pull over and took two of the young soldiers in the rear with him for a look. The immigrant vehicles were travelling quite slowly over a bridge that looked less than secure.

Shaul and the two soldiers returned to the APC and Shaul directed the driver to retrace his route, 'Back north, round the corner, through Lion of Babylon Square, then turn right at the next large roundabout, over the waterway. That's Dinar Street – just follow it until we pass our hotel. We'll come to the other bridge, then.'

They travelled north for several minutes, crossing two more waterways, passing through several roundabouts, some with statues in the centre. Eventually, the street began to travel close to the Shatt Al-Arab waterway. When another large waterway appeared on their left the road crossed a bridge over it, suddenly doing a sharp loop to the left and along the opposite side of this waterway, heading south for a couple of hundred metres, then doubling north west again, as it passed by their hotel HQ.

About a kilometre along, the straight road swung north east and approached the Sinbad Island bridge. Two tanks were positioned at the bend in the road. Shaul told his driver to turn left across the oncoming convoy traffic. The soldiers from the tanks halted the convoy and waved Shaul's vehicle through. Just one hundred metres from the bend was a small bridge over the water channel.

Hmm, Shaul thought, *we could send the convoy across this, but maybe we'd be better keeping it for our own use and building a proper road and bridge to connect to Highway 6.*

He instructed the driver to turn around and they headed east to cross through the convoy again. Before they did so Shaul beckoned one of the soldiers on duty over. 'Keep the convoy heading south for the moment. We're gonna build a new road across to Highway 6, but we'll need to keep that little bridge for our own use for now, *beseder.*

'Beseder, sir.'

The soldier again halted the convoy and Shaul's APC continued on to the Sinbad Bridge. As Peled had reported, the second span of the original bridge was destroyed and instead two single-lane pontoon bridges were operating – one in each direction. Again Shaul instructed the APC driver to pull in, just south of the broken bridge.

As he and another pair of his troopers walked under the damaged bridge they could see the mass of traffic gingerly crossing the west-bound pontoon bridge. It looked much more flimsy in construction than its southern counterpart, which was currently empty of traffic. Across the river Shaul could see Peled's two tanks watching the convoy crossing. He made a decision and they returned to the APC. 'Drive across the bridge,' he told the driver, 'We're gonna direct traffic for a little while.'

As they began crossing the empty southern bridge Shaul radioed Sergeant Gold, 'We need your tank crew on the northern bridge – the Sinbad Island one – to direct the traffic onto the southern pontoon. I'm nearly with them now.'

'Beseder, sir, I'll contact them straight away and let them know you're coming.'

'Toda raba,' replied Shaul.

As they approached the tanks a few minutes later the forward hatch of one opened, 'Need our help, sir? I'm Kravitz. Gold just radioed us.'

'Ken, Kravitz. We want to move the traffic onto the southern bridge – it's much more robust and the traffic should be able to move

faster. So, I'd like your tanks to close off the northern approach and a couple of your men to supervise the traffic, re-directing it onto the southern bridge instead.

'One minute, sir.'

The rear clam-shell doors of the tank opened and two soldiers soon appeared, then both tanks began to move toward the stream of traffic.

'Come with me,' Shaul told the two men, as he began to walk towards where the highway separated, raising his arm in the signal to halt. As the traffic ahead slowed and stopped, he began to wave them onto the southern approach. Once the first driver understood what was required and complied, the vehicles behind began to follow him.

As a gap in the traffic opened up Kravitz manoeuvred his tanks to block off the northern route. The traffic was now flowing smoothly onto the previously empty southern bridge. Shaul explained to the two soldiers what he wanted from them and then walked over to the tanks to also explain to Kravitz.

We need your men to stop the traffic and allow our vehicle to cross into the right hand lane – same when we come back again. Peled and Tamari will be back this way in due course, so we need the same operation then. That's gonna be a regular as we start to patrol this section of the highway, so you may as well get used to being traffic policemen.'

'*Beseder*, sir. We'll look after it.'

'*Toda*,' Shaul replied, returning to his APC, which he directed towards the former Iranian border. The two soldiers left on duty held up the traffic for a few minutes as Shaul's vehicle approached. Once they had negotiated their way through the oncoming column they sped away down the empty half of the highway. After a couple of kilometres the road crossed a river and began to turn east, then south. As it did so it became a divided highway for several kilometres, before reducing to single again a few kilometres before what had been the Iranian border.

Halfway along the divided section they found Peled's second checkpoint – at a roundabout where the main road branched off into Basra, leading to the city centre bridge. A couple of Peled's men were directing traffic to divide here – waving some vehicles north east to the Sinbad Island bridge and some south east to the city centre one.

Chapter 8 – To Steal a Bridge

The tanks were parked in the centre of the small roundabout. They sounded their horn to the troops as they passed.

As they crossed into former Iranian territory the highway divided again until they reached the outskirts of Khorramshahr, where it reduced to single after crossing a river. A kilometre further on Shaul directed his driver to turn off to the right, towards the Shatt Al-Arab Waterway, which had originally also been the Iran/Iraq border at this point.

When they reached the waterway the road turned south east along the river for another couple of kilometres, then it turned inland at a small roundabout, followed by a larger one, and headed north east to Highway 96 again. Shaul directed the driver to turn right at the first small roundabout and to stop the vehicle close to the waterway.

He got out and walked to the water's edge. The river level was very low and Shaul remembered the prophesy in *Yirmeyahu* (Jeremiah) which talked about the Euphrates River drying up into seven streams, *'so that my people can walk across dry shod.'* Across the river he could see a large island, with another beyond it.

The river here was narrower than further north or south.

I wonder? Shaul thought to himself. *Need to get an engineer down here.*

He returned to the APC and told the driver to head back to Basra. When they reached the city he instructed him to return to the hotel and park, releasing him and the other occupants to get some lunch in the hotel, but asking them to take one of the engineers wherever he wanted to go after they'd finished lunch.

Shaul grabbed something to eat in the APC and selected another driver and a couple of crew to accompany him south of the city. He also found the group of engineers and asked one of them – Barkat – to take a look at the western approaches to Sinbad Bridge, pointing out his earlier driver and the other men, who would take them there shortly.

Another couple of the engineers, both with bridge-building experience, agreed to accompany him to the river further south. He and the engineers climbed into the APC with his new crew and headed to Highway Six – which became a single highway just as they reached the southern extremes of the city.

About forty kilometres down the highway – which would need some repairs in places, but was mostly in good condition – they turned off into a small lane on their left. This brought them to a channel of the river, on the other side of which was an island, with another larger island beyond that. They were just opposite the northern part of Khorram-shahr, where Shaul had explored earlier.

The driver asked him if he wanted to go across to the island, as the water level was quite low. 'These *CombatGuard* babies are able to negotiate five feet of water, sir.'

'You could be right, *Turai*, but we'd look awfully stupid if we got stuck in the middle of all that mud, with no one here to tow us out. So I think maybe I'll pass this time. The engineers looked relieved, and they and Shaul got out of the APC and surveyed the low islands in front of them and the former Iranian town of Khorramshahr beyond.

The engineers looked thoughtful and one – Wolfson was his name – remarked, 'There have been bridges here in the past. You can see the remains of them. I take it that we'll need to go down the other side to get a proper look at the main channel?'

'Yes,' agreed Shaul. 'I'll have my crew take you down the far side once we get back. I've got to do some other stuff. But do you think a pontoon bridge across the islands is feasible?'

'Yes,' replied Wolfson, 'it's certainly feasible. And that would be the ideal spot, where the river divides into three streams. The main channel is bound to be narrower at that point.'

'We'd need the Navy's help, wouldn't we, to get the pontoons into place?' Shaul asked, 'I'd thought for the main channel that we could use some of the Iranian ships that are at the port – straight across there.'

'Yes,' Wolfson replied, 'Several small ships of the same size would be ideal. But where will we get the bridge sections from?'

'I have an idea about that, too,' said Shaul, 'I thought mebbe we could just steal a bridge.'

'Steal a bridge,' asked the other engineer – Becker. 'How could we steal a bridge, Major?'

'Well,' said Shaul, 'I've looked at the satellite map online. Of course, you can't see much detail on a satellite map, though I could ask command for a military version of the locations. There are four existing pontoon bridges that I know of – all further north on the Tigris River. One is just north of Baghdad, one at Madain, one at Aziziyah, and one just north of Az Zubaydiyah. '

There are another two pontoon bridges just north of Basra on the Shatt Al-Arab – one is just north of Al Haritah, more than twenty kilometres further north, and the other at Ad Dayr, which is forty kilometres further. We could send convoy vehicles there, but using them would mean adding forty five, or even eighty, kilometres to the journey. If we have an emergency, we might have to use them, so I don't want to dismantle them.

Tomorrow, I'd like you to thoroughly survey this area from both sides. You can have whatever transport you need – we'll find a small boat somewhere along this river to get you to the islands. Then, the day after, I'd like to send you north with an escort to survey the four bridges on the Tigris that I mentioned – see which are the most suitable for dismantling and removal. We may need more than one to cross this waterway. The Tigris is bound to be narrower further north than the Shatt Al-Arab here.

'I don't know what's the best way to transport the sections. We have ten tank transporters here, if that's any help. Otherwise I thought maybe we could float them down the River on barges. You decide what is possible. You're the engineers. Just build me a bridge – and we need it yesterday!'

'*Beseder*,' said Wolfson thoughtfully, looking across at Becker and raising his eyebrows. 'You've certainly given us a challenge. We will try our best to meet it. We'll let you know if it's possible as soon as we reach a decision ourselves. But using barges would not be possible, anyway, if, as you've said, there are already other pontoon bridges in the way.'

'*Toda raba*, gentlemen. Just do your best. That's what we Israelis are about, eh?'

Shaul and the two engineers climbed into the APC and they headed back to the hotel HQ, discussing the bridge problem on the way. Shaul retrieved his driver from earlier in the day and asked him to take the engineers to the same place in Khorramshahr, where Shaul and the driver had been that morning.

As he sought out Tamari, whose APCs he had noted outside, he heard the sound of more vehicles arriving – either Bar-Ilan making another trip, though he didn't see any trucks arriving – or more likely Peled returning from his first patrol to Bandar Mahshahr.

Good, he thought, *we can pool our ideas, now.*

He found Tamari, grabbing some food with his drivers, almost at the same time as Peled appeared through the back door. I'll let you get something to eat, Alon, then you and Musa can join me in my office.

'Your office, sir, ' they chorused. 'Where is that?'

'Ahh, I'm just going to look for a suitable room, now. I'm sure you'll be able to find me.'

Ten minutes later the two officers tapped lightly on the open door of a large room, where they found Shaul trying out a desk and chair.

'There you are. Find a seat somewhere and come on in.'

Both men retreated to find chairs and returned with them to Shaul's new office.

'*Beseder*, gentlemen. Perhaps you can let me know what you've found out on your travels today. Tamari?'

'I've made a note of all the bad patches on the highway over that 160 kilometres. I'm gonna go shortly and organise all the drivers, trucks and workmen I reckon I'll need to get a good start made early tomorrow. I was planning on leaving before sunup, sir.

'Tomorrow, I thought we'd get to work on the nearest section – from here to Khorramshahr. I've picked out a truck compound just this side of Khorramshahr – just one hundred metres north of that roundabout with the pagoda thing in the middle. There are gates on it, so I reckon we can leave all the heavy equipment there and truck the drivers back here tomorrow night. We can lock it up and leave a small guard overnight.'

'*Beseder*, that sounds good. Do you need Peled here to organise a guard for tomorrow night, then?'

'That would help, sir.' he nodded at Peled.

'What about the vehicles, then? Breakdowns? Fuel?'

'We took one fuel tanker with us – just diesel, no gas yet – and three teams of mechanics. We found plenty of breakdowns, so they were all kept busy, sir. We played catch-up with one another all day.

65

We took the fuel tanker up to Abadan – didn't want to stretch our-selves too thin on the first day, sir.

'We found a petrol station there – as the Iranians seemed to call it – just this side of the large roundabout on the far side of Abadan. It's an ideal spot, sir. Highway 96 and Highway 39 meet there. There was occasional traffic on Highway 39, but most of it was coming from Bandar Mahshahr on Highway 96.

'The only problem with the gas station is that it's not enclosed, sir – no gates. However, we figured it would be pretty difficult for anyone to steal a whole tanker-full of diesel fuel, once its been pumped into the underground tanks.

'We had a few vehicles that ran out of fuel before they got to Abadan, but we also had a truck with a lot of Jerrycans – both gas and diesel – so we topped them up and and then bled them where necessary and got them as far as the fuel depot in Abadan.

'I think the next step, sir, is to set up something similar in Bandar Mahshahr. The only problem there is the greater distance, sir. There is a small truck depot just beside the entrance to Mahshahr Airport. It's enclosed and can be secured, so we can put our equipment there when we get that far. I think we need to set up a forward base there, sir. What do you think, Peled?'

'Yes,' replied Peled, 'Tamari and I met up when he was on his way back. We stopped to compare notes and yes, I *do* think we need to set up a forward base – either there or at Omidiyeh, which is closer to halfway between here and Shiraz. It also has an airfield.

'Mahshahr is where the roads diverge a bit,' Peled continued. 'There are two main ways they're coming at the moment – Highway 86 is the main route, but some are coming in via 96 to the south, and just a few from 43, more to the north. The main route is through the city of Shiraz, sir – 640 kilometres. That would take about eight and a half hours normally, though depending on the speed of the convoy and the state of the road it will probably take much longer.

'That's another thing I've been thinking, sir. We have trucks in the convoy, which can carry quite a load – especially the articulated ones. But we also have cars, the odd tractor, motorbikes – all of these are very inefficient in terms of fuel and more trouble to repair. What if we loaded several of them onto a tank transporter, then we'd only be using fuel in one vehicle?'

'It's an idea, Peled. How about if we implement it at the moment only for dead vehicles – those that can't be repaired quickly? We could send say one transporter per day to Mahshahr and maybe a bus as well. Then they can make a return trip, picking up stopped vehicles and carrying the passengers in the bus?'

'OK, sir. Will I leave it to Tamari to organise that, sir? I know he's got a lot on his plate.'

'Tamari, we've got a few engineers, haven't we? I sent one to look at the approaches to the Sinbad Bridge today and I took another two down Highway Six to a point opposite Khorramshahr, where I hope we might be able to build another pontoon bridge. They're down in Khorramshahr at the moment and tomorrow they're going to do a proper survey.

'We have boats across there on the Iranian side that could be used as the pontoons and we can possibly steal the bridging sections from existing pontoon bridges up north on the Tigris River.'

Peled's face broke into a grin, 'Steal a whole bridge, sir. I like it. I like it!'

He grinned at Tamari, who returned the grin.

'Well, we might have a few immigrants crossing on bridges further south, but there are other permanent bridges they can use, anyway, so *we* can make better use of them down here. As you both know from crossing over today, we're really hampered by the lack of even one proper bridge. Another pontoon bridge would help ease the congestion.

'Anyway, the point I was going to make, Musa, was that you can send an engineer to supervise the road repairs. That leaves you freer to concentrate on fuel and breakdowns.'

'*Beseder*, sir. Maybe if I get them started tomorrow, I'll be able to leave them to it after that?'

'*Beseder, Samal*. We're all very stretched here at the moment, and for the next few weeks, or longer. So we need to delegate as much as we can. The volunteers and even some of our own men have had a fairly easy time of it today, while we've been running ourselves ragged, trying to get a picture of what's needed.

'Tomorrow, I want everyone stretched to the limit. Peled, get patrols organised both day and night. Both of you look out for a suitable base, either in Mahshahr or Omidiyeh. Bar-Ilan has her hands full today with setting up the hospital, but she will be able to leave a lot of that in the medic's hands from now on. For instance, they can run the ambulances, using our drivers.

'However, she'll also be dealing with the burial detail, plus a lot of other personnel stuff, so I don't think she'll have much free time, either. Which reminds me, did you have any casualties today at all?'

Tamari answered first, 'I brought a couple of people back who were fairly elderly and ill from heat exhaustion, plus a mother with a sick child. I've left them over to *Ben Gurion Hospital* – as I see it's now called.' He smiled.

'Yes,' said Shaul, 'Bar-Ilan's idea – easier to refer to than *Al Faihaa*, for sure!

'I took a truck of bottled water with me – left it at the fuel stop in Abadan and it went back empty a couple of hours later. Katz radioed for another one to come. This time they brought peanuts and bananas as well to give out. I think we'll need to do that every day, sir – and at Mahshahr, too, as soon as we're able. Then we might have less people sick, sir.'

'*Beseder*, Musa, that is a good point.

'Alon?'

'Yes we picked up several patients, too – a mother with two kids suffering eye complaints – I think from all the dust, an elderly man with exhaustion, and a pregnant woman who thought she was going into labour. Thankfully, it still hadn't happened by the time we got her to the hospital.'

'Well, it's happened now!' Bar-Ilan's voice sounded from the doorway. 'We've just welcomed our first brand new Israeli citizen in *Ben Gurion. Mazel tov!*'

'*Mazel tov*, indeed, Rebekkah!' agreed Shaul. 'Find yourself a chair, then come in and join us in my new office.'

'We've been mulling over what we've learnt today and planning tomorrow a little,' he added, once she'd got herself seated.

'*Ken*, the Major thinks we should steal ourselves a bridge,' said Peled, chuckling.

'How on earth do you go about stealing a bridge,' Rebekkah queried.

'Well, Shaul's sending some engineers up north to find out – day after tomorrow, isn't it?' Peled asked Shaul.

'I hope so. They're doing a full survey tomorrow – at Khorramshahr and at this side of the River, then they're going north after that, all being well. We need more bridge capacity. At the moment we have three single lane pontoon bridges – a bridge and a half, in total!'

'A new pontoon bridge will bring that up to the equivalent of two full bridges, though we'll be using three lanes for traffic coming in and only one the other way. If you're going across, Bar-Ilan, we're using the most northerly pontoon bridge to go both east and west. Peled's men are operating a check-point at the far side, so they will stop traffic when necessary for us to cross over left to right.

'How is everything at the hospital? Is it fully operational yet?'

'Well, we've got a capable bunch running things,' she replied. 'The doctors are organising shifts for themselves. I've left the ambulances under their care, with our drivers and crew, of course. Though I've been thinking that the ambulances need to be outside Basra, really – somewhere about halfway. Otherwise they've got a long distance to go every time?'

Tamari responded, 'There *is* nothing exactly halfway – except empty road, but Abadan might be the best spot. We've got a fuel stop there and we could easily park up the ambulances in that truck yard. It's not enclosed, Rebekkah, but we'll have a guard on it from now on.'

'OK, that sounds good. I'll tell the ambulance crews, then, shortly. We've got four ambulances set aside, and eight crews, taking six hour shifts. We can just move say two of them to Abadan, at the moment?'

'That sounds OK to me, Rebekkah,' said Shaul. 'We'll adjust if necessary when we see how it's working in practice.'

Junbalat arrived at the office at this point, 'Are you guys ready for something to eat,' he asked.

'I'd say that's a *Ken'*, Peled said for all of them.

'Come and get it then. What about Gold and Katz?' he asked.

'I'll give Katz a shout,' said Tamari. 'He's here somewhere.'

'Gold is out on a patrol. He may be a while, yet,' said Peled.

'Lev should be here shortly, too,' Rebekkah said.

'OK, we'll keep something for them. We've got volunteers in the kitchen today and they're really quite good,' Junbalat encouraged them.

Chapter 8 – To Steal a Bridge

'Tamari is off early in the morning with his engineer and road crews, also taking fuel to Mahshahr and handling breakdowns, said Shaul. 'I suggest you take one truck of water with you – hand it out where needed, Musa.'

'Yes, sir,' Tamari replied, 'Katz will be covering the full distance with another truck tonight and he'll be organising another team to cover the same route tomorrow.'

'OK, let's eat!' said Shaul.

By the time they had eaten Corporal Lev had joined them and Gold had arrived back from patrol and the others went to bed straight away, exhausted.

9 – Leaving Kabul

Sergeant Ali Yusufzai had been out of Kabul for more than a week and, consequently, had not had any contact with his new friend, Khaista, for a while. His Afghan National Army (ANA) unit had been sent down to Kandahar – first of all to deal with the influx of Iranian refugees, but now also to cope with the ever-increasing tide of Pashtun Afghanis packing up their belongings and heading into what had until recently been Iran – on their way to Israel.

So much had changed in the last couple of weeks that Ali had difficulty taking it all in. The devastating nuclear war in the Middle East had had repercussions far beyond the region. First were the waves of Iranian and Iraqi refugees pouring over the Iran border into Afghanistan. Other countries bordering Iran – Pakistan, Turkey, Azerbaijan and Turkmenistan, in particular – had had to cope with this influx, also.

The United Nations had called for other countries around the world to relieve some of the pressure on Iran's neighbours by allowing a certain quota of refugees into their states, but there were refugees also from many other countries in the region. Turkey, in particular, was overwhelmed with Arab – Syrian, Lebanese, Jordanian and Iraqi – refugees.

Another difficulty was that these Iranians were Shi'ite Muslims and that both Afghanistan (80%) and Pakistan (85-90%) were predominantly Sunni. Neither country wanted to upset the delicate religious balance that an influx of Shi'ites would cause.

Now the traffic had become a two way flow. At first only a small number of Pashtuns had declared that they were reverting to their ancestral – Israelite – origins and were determined to return to their original homeland in Israel. The Israeli government had been debating their response to this, but those same groups had then decided unilaterally to begin the long trek – more than 3,500 kilometres – to the now greatly enlarged State of Israel.

At first this involved only a few hundred Pashtuns, but as others saw their neighbours moving away, or heard the reports on the news, this seemed to suddenly awaken a deep urge within them to return to their land of origin – even though they had been estranged from it for nearly 3,000 years, and even though it would mean a whole new – and Jewish – way of life.

The hundreds became thousands, overnight, and now was heading towards hundreds of thousands, eventually to become millions. Of course, it did make some accommodation available for the refugees, who were evident everywhere – and, even if the Afghan government had at first been reluctant to provide them with homes, the refugees were becoming desperate and would soon have begun invading recently emptied homes and taking them over, anyway.

This didn't solve the problem, however – the new immigrants had no jobs, no official recognition and most of them didn't even speak any of the local languages. Leaflets and posters were hurriedly being drafted in the Persian – Farsi – language and in Arabic and, for the foreseeable future, the country would have to adjust to these new inhabitants – unless they could be persuaded to move elsewhere, of course. Then some of them, at least, might become someone else's problem.

As a Pashtun himself, who had begun to study the prophecies about the ten tribes returning to their homeland, Ali had been thinking seriously about all that had been happening. He and Khaista – the Pashtun woman he had befriended just a few short months ago – had both downloaded many of the books of the *Tawrat* (the Jewish *Torah*) and had begun to discuss their meaning to them.

Ali's family name was Yusufzai – literally 'children of Joseph', one of the twelve tribes of Israel. Khaista's family name was Afridi – a variation of Ephraim – part of that same tribe, in fact the half tribe that, combined with the other half tribe of Manasseh, made up Joseph. They were both aware that their heritage was from the *Bnei Israel* – the children of Israel – and the way now appeared to be open for them also to join the other Pashtuns, plus Kashmiris and Menashe (Manasseh – from eastern India).

Ali was tempted to buy a pickup truck, or similar, load it with jerry cans of fuel and a week's supply of food and water and join the road to Basra and, ultimately, Israel. The distance to Basra, in former Iraq, was over 2,500 kilometres. He'd made an agreement a few years back with his comrades in the ISAF forces – three American soldiers – that they would re-unite in Jerusalem after the *Six Hour War* that Brandon has assured them was prophesied in the *Tawrat*.

Well, that war had come, and Israel had been victorious – just as Brandon had foretold. What was there to stop him joining the other Pashtuns and arriving in Israel to meet his friends. What had previously been just a dream was now beginning to look like it could become a reality.

Would Khaista be willing to join him? He remembered the poem she had written and read out at the poetry evening in Kabul some time ago. He had asked her for a copy of it and she had emailed it to him. It was a yearning for freedom – freedom which was not really possible in a place such as Kabul – hedged about with the restrictions of extremist Islam.

Ali knew those restrictions would probably continue – particularly if those who wanted freedom expressed that desire by leaving the country. Everything was in an upheaval right now. Now it was possible for them to leave but, in the future, that opportunity might no longer be available.

Ali made two decisions that day. One, he would try to contact his friend Shaul, in Israel, to enquire if there was a role for him to play in this ingathering. Two, he would ask Khaista if she would be willing to leave with him and to marry him in Israel. *Yes*, he thought, *the future for us is in Israel, where we can be among our own people.*

At the moment he could do neither, but what he could do was begin to make a plan. How would he go about this journey? He needed to think it all through carefully. He would need a weapon for a start – there was no telling what problems or opposition they might face on such a journey.

Another problem was money. Should he withdraw his savings from the bank in Kabul and attempt to take cash with him – a very risky proposition, no matter how carefully you stashed it in a vehicle. Could the money be transferred electronically – he knew that was theoretically possible, but had no first hand experience of doing it from Afghanistan.

What about his current position in the Army? He had served quite a few years by now and had the option to leave in the very near future. But would they allow him to leave earlier, under the present circumstances?

Ali spent the next few days agonising over these matters, when he was suddenly and surprisingly given the task of transporting to Kabul a truckload of men who had been arrested for several offences – from looting and threatening the emigrants, to drug smuggling and even murder. He was given four men to help guard the prisoners and they had been given two day's leave in Kabul before they needed to return to Kandahar.

Two of the men travelled with him in the front of the truck – one driving. The other two travelled in the rear with the prisoners. Every two hours Ali would rotate their duties – it meant a change of conversational topics, apart from anything else! Eventually, after more than ten hours of driving, they completed the almost five hundred kilometre journey and handed over their charges to ANA headquarters.

Ali dropped off the other four soldiers around the city, arranging to pick them up again early at the depot in two days time. Then he drove back to his own small apartment. He managed to get an internet connection and composed an email to his friend, and former commander, Shaul.

Hi there my friend,

I got your email and I thank God that He has kept you safe through the war that you have been fighting in Israel. I have been posted south to Kandahar recently, helping with the refugees arriving in Afghanistan and now also with those who have to chosen leave our country.

Many of my Pashtun compatriots are packing and beginning the long journey to Israel. I have been giving this some thought and I have decided that – if Khaista is willing to go with me, and I am hoping that she will – I also will leave Afghanistan and come to Israel. At least, as soon as the Army will let me go!

I will probably use some of the money I have saved to buy a pickup truck, or something similar, and load it with fuel, food and water for the journey. The route seems fairly obvious, but perhaps you can advise me on that.

Also, you can tell me if there would possibly be any kind of job available for me when I arrive. As you know I do not speak any Hebrew, – and will have to start learning it, as you have done – but my English is good. My friend, Khaista, is studying Computer Science part-time at Kabul University, in regular contact with the University of Mary-

land, in America – so she is also very fluent in English. She works for the government here in administration the rest of the time.

Another question I have is the problem of bringing money with me on such a long and hazardous journey. Is there a simple way I can transfer most of this money electronically – I have no experience of doing this from Kabul?

Now that I have made up my mind to go – make aliyah, I think you say in Israel? – I hope to begin as soon as it is possible. I will be in touch with Khaista very soon and will then know her answer. I have two days leave at the moment, so please, if you get this, contact me soon – before I have to return to Kandahar.

I hope to hear from you soon, my friend.

Your former comrade,

Khan Ali Yusufzai

After this he sent a text message to Khaista, whom he hadn't seen for well over a week:

Back in Kabul for a day, or so. Can we meet tomorrow, early?

He received a reply only a few minutes later:

Certainly, Ali. Meet me at the University canteen – 8 am?

OK, see you then, Ali replied.

Next morning Ali arrived early at the university and parked his Army truck near to the dining area. Khaista was waiting near the doorway and they held one another's hands briefly.

'I've never seen you in your uniform, before, Ali – you look very smart in it,' she said, before they headed inside to choose their food. Ali paid once again and they sat down at a table well away from the others eating.

'Are you intending to make this a regular occurrence, then, Ali?' she asked.

'What's that?' asked Ali.

'Paying for my food,' she answered.

'Well, that's something we really need to discuss,' he said.

'Oh, you have me intrigued already!' she smiled at him.

'Khaista, I've been doing a lot of thinking while I've been away in Kandahar – and I've made an important decision. Well, two decisions, really.'

Khaista went pale and began to look worried, 'What decisions are those, then, Ali?' she asked quietly.

'After watching so many of my fellow Pashtuns packing up all their possessions and leaving for Israel I've decided that I really would like to join them.'

Khaista's hand went to her mouth in trepidation. She said nothing, fearing she might break down. Was she about to lose Ali? She suddenly found that she couldn't bear that thought.

Ali continued, 'The thing is, Khaista, I've become really fond of you. I know we haven't known each other for very long, but I think I *do* know my own mind. I'd like to spend the rest of my days with you by my side. And I want to know if you'd be willing to come with me to Israel and marry me when we arrive there?'

Khaista stared at him in stupefaction.

Ali began explaining, 'I know this is probably very sudden …'

'No, Ali,' she interrupted, 'it's not too sudden. I, too, know my own mind and I want to be with *you*, Ali – wherever you go. Yes, I will go to Israel with you and, yes, I will marry you, Ali.'

Ali grabbed both of her hands and they sat for several minutes staring into one another's eyes.

Eventually, Ali said, 'You know, I am really looking forward to being in a country where I can express myself freely. I've kept thinking about that poem you wrote – the one you read out in Kabul that night? We can't really be free here, can we? I'm so glad you have agreed to go with me. I was dreading that your answer might not be what I wanted to hear. You're definitely sure, now – no second thoughts.'

'I am quite sure, Ali. No second thoughts. But when? And how will we go? I mean, I have a little money saved. But how will we do this?'

'Well, first of all I'm going to talk to my superiors in the Army, to see how soon they would be willing to discharge me. Once I know that we can make more definite plans. Oh yes, I've emailed

76

my friend, Shaul, and I mentioned you as well. I asked him if there might be a job for each of us when we get there.'

'Oh, Ali, this so exciting!' she said. 'I can hardly think straight. But we need to be clear thinking, right now. How do you plan to go there?'

'Well, I have some money saved, too. I hope to buy a fairly decent pickup truck and load it with fuel, water and enough food to last the journey. The main problem is how to take money with us? I wondered if we could transfer some electronically, but it is not something I have ever done. Do you know anything about that?'

'Yes, Ali,' Khaista replied. 'It's quite simple, really. Friends of mine at the University here have often bought items from abroad. I think transferring money is quite simple too. There are many Western Union offices all over the city – some of them are in banks. If there is not one in your own bank you can take the money out and take it to the nearest Western Union office.

'We would need to know the details of the bank in Israel, of course. Perhaps your friend, Shaul, can help set up an account?'

'Yes, of course. I'm hoping he will reply quickly, because I will probably be going back to Kandahar in a day, or so – unless the Army are happy to let me go sooner?'

'What will we do when we get there,' she asked.

'Well, I've told Shaul that we both speak good English – he knows that *I* do, anyway. And I said that you were doing a Computer Science course. Hopefully, you can finish your studies in Israel? We will have to find out about all these things.'

'Do we need passports, Ali? Do we need permission to leave Afghanistan?'

'Well, I've been on patrol with those leaving through Kandahar and, as far as I have been able to find out, our government are so overwhelmed with the number of refugees who have come from Iran, that they are making no attempt to stop those who want to leave. It makes the problem just a little bit less for them.

'That's another thing, though,' Ali added. 'They *could* change their attitude in the near future and stop Pashtuns from leaving. So, the sooner we leave Afghanistan, the better.'

'OK, I will have to wind up my affairs at the Government office and with the University, here,' she said. 'Also, I will ask them if I can transfer credit for my course here. If possible, I don't want to waste the time I have spent studying on this course.'

'Well, I will leave you to work some of these things out,' Ali arose from the table. 'I will go home and check if there is any reply from Shaul. I asked him about the best route to take, as well.'

'You could check your email from the University here,' said Khaista. 'I can show you where the computers are.'

'Are you sure no one will mind?' he asked.

'No one will know you are not just another student, even in your uniform,' she answered.

'Ok, let's go and see,' said Ali.

They walked through the University grounds to the computer suite where Khaista spent a lot of her time. She showed Ali to a computer and left him to check his email. Sure enough a reply from Shaul was in his inbox.

Ali, great to hear from you. You have decided to join us in the new Israel, then. Fantastic! I am actually based in Basra, now – in former Iraq. We too are dealing with the convoys of immigrants coming through from Afghanistan and Pakistan – policing part of the route, providing medical care, repairing roads and bridges. Life is extremely busy!

But your email comes at an ideal time. One of the things we need most here are interpreters who can speak to the people travelling. Only a few of them have any English, which means we often have difficulty in communicating with them.

I can offer both of you a job here in Basra, immediately. Khaista's skills would be extremely useful in running the office I have now set up here at the hotel, which is our base for the moment. You would both be working directly to me and paid by the government. I can ask for accommodation to be organised for you in Israel, but if you are working here, that will be taken care of in the meantime.

The main route is through Kandahar, Zabol, Zahedan, Kerman, Shiraz and Bandar Mahshahr. We are currently responsible for the section from Shiraz to Basra, but we've only been here for one day, so we are operating as far as Mahshahr at the moment. People are getting through, but we don't yet know how good, or bad, the roads

78

are. My men are organising road repairs, starting from this end and working east.

If you are buying a vehicle, try to get one with four-wheel-drive, in case you need to go off road where the surface has been damaged. There are craters and obstructions – especially in the towns and cities, where buildings have been destroyed. Again we are repairing roads, but that will take some time. You can also help us as you travel by making careful note of the sections of worst damage, any gas (petrol) stations that we could use for refuelling vehicles, etc.

As regards transferring money, I can set up an account with one of the Israeli banks in your name – or do you need two accounts? Anyway, you should be able to transfer money to that from a Western Union office in Kabul. I'll email you the details of the account as soon as I have them. Let me know if you have any difficulties.

It is so good to hear from you, comrade, and it will be great to be working together again. We really do need your help – and that of Khaista – I hope she has agreed to come?

Get back to me quickly with your details and I will get things rolling, here.

Your comrade in arms,

Solly.

Ali quickly typed a reply to Shaul's email, including his and Khaista's full names, ages, skills, etc. and texted the good news to Khaista. He then set off for the ANA base to request his release from the Afghan National Army. Their adventure was beginning!

In One Hour – Babylon will fall – *Raymond McCullough*

10 – Basra: day two

Shaul met with most of his officers the next morning over breakfast. Tamari had left much earlier with his road-mending crew, after supervising the despatch of another breakdown patrol, complete with water truck and other supplies. Gold was still sleeping, having been on patrol for a good part of the night.

'OK,' Shaul began, when they were all seated and munching heartily. 'I've just had some good news. A former comrade of mine back in Afghanistan has been in touch by email. He's in the Afghan National Army at present, but he's hoping to leave the Army soon, buy a pickup truck and travel here.

'He will, hopefully, be bringing a young lady with him who has good computer skills. Both of them have good English, so I've offered them both a job with our mission, here. Both are Pashtuns, obviously, and they speak both Pashto and Dari, which will be a very useful asset in our communication with the immigrants.'

'That sounds great, sir,' Peled spoke. 'Any idea how soon they will be coming?'

'Not yet – it depends on when the ANA will let him go. So I'll update you once I know. Ali will also be useful in gathering information on the whole immigrant route. I've asked him to make a careful note of all the damage to roads and streets as he travels here. Once he leaves Kandahar he'll be out of range of any cellphone transmission until he arrives here.'

'Yeah, Iran, Iraq and Saudi Arabia have managed to bomb each other back to the dark ages!' said Katz.

'I've also been in contact with Southern Command. I've asked them to send us more volunteer personnel, trucks with drinking water, fruit and peanuts, etc. We will be receiving a new contingent of troops for burial detail, along with dogs and their handlers to find the bodies – which will be necessary in other cities along the immigrant route as well as here in Basra.

'I also discussed the problem of the bridges over the Shatt Al-Arab, and my plan to possibly build another pontoon bridge further downstream. If we can determine the feasibility of moving the bridge sections from up north, they will let us have some Navy personnel to move the Iranian boats into position, ready for the bridge sections. So, we need to keep moving on that one – get the survey done, then send our engineers up north with an escort to check out those bridges up there. Once we know it's possible – including some way to transport them – then we can get the Navy here to start moving the boats.'

'Sounds like a plan, sir,' Bar-Ilan commented. The others nodded.

'OK, back to our ongoing program here. We've made a start on burying the corpses in the town – that's a big operation, which is why I've asked for help with it. We will gradually widen our search area west and south, so that the route of the convoys is free of bodies, at any rate. Bar-Ilan, are you happy to continue looking after that end?'

'Yes, Major,' she replied. 'I'm hoping the hospital will begin to run itself, more or less, from now on. So I should have more time to organise the ambulance service and the burials.'

'*Beseder.* Well, we need to discuss any ideas we have to improve our control of this thing. At the moment we have a runaway truck situation – a fait accompli. We need, as quickly as we possibly can, to bring this *aliyah* under our control. That's why the military have been given this job – it's a task only the military could hope to accomplish.'

'Sir?' Peled queried.

'Go ahead, Alon,' Shaul said.

'I've been thinking. What help can we get from the Air Force on this? I mean, if we had an airport operational at, say, Shiraz – which will probably mean a lot of repair work, of course – we could possibly load a *Hercules* transport with mebbe three *CombatGuard* APCs, or Hummvees, and fly them there. Then they would travel back along the route, overtaking the convoy, helping with repairs, giving out water, and giving medial aid.

'The crews would save several hours on the journey out and their time would be better used travelling *with* the convoy. The plane could also bring back any serious medical emergencies, or those whose vehicles have been abandoned. When it returned it could immediately load up another three vehicles and do another run. Would that be possible, do you think, sir?'

Chapter 10 – Basra: day two

'I don't know, Peled, but it sounds like an excellent idea. We've been told we can call on HQ for any help we need. They are as much in the dark at the moment as we are. They are relying on our reports on the ground to determine what is really needed. In fact, we could maybe pioneer that idea on our Shiraz to Basra leg and, if it is a success, we could replicate it on the other sections of the route.

'The first thing we would need,' Shaul continued, 'is a working airport here, then another at the Shiraz end – or possibly in between. There is an airport at Bandar Mahshahr and another airfield at Omidiyeh. The problem is that the airports have been major targets for Saudi missiles during the war, so a lot of repairs are going to be needed. That means we will have to get repair equipment out there in the first place.

'As far as I know our Air Force have some sort of standard air-field repair strategy. We have an IAF team out at Basra Airport at the moment. I'll check with them this morning on what progress they're making getting Basra Airport functioning again, and I'll also discuss with them how we can get the next airfield in line operational.

'We may be able to get some help from the IAF on that, as well as supplying the ferry service for our vehicles, of course. I'll make that a priority, today. That is a pretty useful idea, Peled. *Toda.'*

Peled nodded in response.

'As you can see, I've put up a map of the main convoy routes here. I'll also add the potential airfields – commercial, or military, either will serve our purpose – and I might ask my friend Yusufzai to survey them en route. It would probably be a good idea, then, to have our forward bases on, or close to these airfields.'

'Good idea, sir,' Bar-Ilan said.

'OK, Junbalat, how did your survey of accommodation go yesterday?'

'Well, sir, this seems to be the only hotel in the immediate vicinity – i.e. the north of the city. There are three hotels close to the Corniche bridge, in the centre – the *Basra International*, which is on the Corniche, just south of the bridge; the *Shams Al-Basra* is in a street behind it, less accessible; and the *Hamdan Hotel*, on the main route from the Corniche to Highway 6. There's an empty lot just north of the *Basra International*, where the vehicles could park.

'Those are the best possibilities, sir, but they're all well south of here. The other possibility is *Shatt Al-Arab College*, which is just off the same road the Ben Gurion Hospital is on. There's an empty lot beside it we could use for parking the vehicles. There's also the larger *University of Basra* – just north of the junction between Highway 6 and 31. It has student Halls of Residence and the main entrance to it is off Highway 6.'

'*Tov,* Junbalat, sounds like we should probably use the *International* for the traffic coming via the Corniche, and either one of the University sites for the Sinbad bridge traffic. Good work, Samir. In fact, if the engineers can have the new road from Sinbad Bridge to Highway 6 ready in another day or two, the main University site would seem ideal.

'Not everyone is going to want to stop overnight, anyway. A lot of the vehicles have more than one driver, taking turns. They obviously want to get the journey over and done with as quickly as possible. But there are others who really need a break and a good night's sleep by this stage – especially families with several kids. Those are the people we are thinking of.'

'Peled,' Shaul asked, 'What are your plans for today?'

'I'm taking the two remaining tanks still on their transporters to set up a checkpoint in either Mahshahr or Omidiyeh. I'll take two water trucks as well. If you like I can take a look at both the airfields, get a rough idea of the damage needing repair?'

'*Beseder,*' said Shaul, 'if there's nothing else urgent to discuss I'll be in my office for a short while, then I'm going to check on that new road and after that the airport. I should be back here before lunchtime.'

They all rose and left on their various tasks. Shaul went to his office and switched on the computer which had now been set up for him by the engineers. He even had access to the internet via a satellite connection – the internet generally being a thing of the past now in former Iraq and Iran. He discovered a new email from Ali in Kabul:

Shalom Shaul,

Khaista and I were so pleased to hear that you can provide jobs for us – and helping with the Pashtun/Kashmiri immigration, too. We will be very pleased to accept your offer.

Chapter 10 – Basra: day two

As you can tell, Khaista has agreed to come with me – she has also agreed to marry me when we get there. Perhaps that would be possible in Basra, I don't know? We will be very happy to carry out a survey of the roads along the way.

Khaista thinks we can transfer money quite easily using Western Union – there is actually an office at my own bank – so, as soon as you can set up an account we will be able to do that. One account will be sufficient.

I am now on my way to talk to my superiors about leaving the ANA. Pray for my success.

Let me know any other information you think I may need.

I will be in touch very soon.

Your friend and new Israeli citizen,

Ali.

Shaul typed a brief reply and left the office. He collected an APC and crew and headed first north west to see how the engineers were progressing with the road between Highway 31 – the road west past the airport – and the Sinbad Bridge, as they were now calling it. He pulled the APC off the road filled with immigrant vehicles, currently heading south east along Dinar Street past their hotel HQ – a convoluted route which Shaul hoped to bypass very soon with the new road.

The engineer – Efraim Barkat – showed him the road which was now levelled from the bridge to the first obstacle, a water channel running roughly north-south. Barkat explained, 'We don't have any material to create a proper bridge, so we're just using the rubble from demolished buildings nearby and filling the channel up.

'We managed to locate a yard nearby with some large concrete pipe sections, so we're laying those first, then filling between and over them with the rubble. At the moment, as you can see, we are about halfway across. On the other side there are some roads which we can link up with to connect to the main highways.

'What we're gonna need very soon is enough asphalt to surface about five hundred metres of road. We have approximately three hundred metres to surface here, plus some needed across the bridge and some for repair and straightening of the road sections between here and the highways.'

'How soon will this causeway be ready?' Shaul asked.

'We should have a road, of sorts, by the end of tomorrow – but we'll need asphalt before we can surface it properly. And ask them to supply it in trucks with 'hot boxes' – to keep the material usable overnight, or longer.'

'Beseder, Efraim,*'* said Shaul, making a note to ask for 'hot boxes'. 'Looks like a good job. When I get back to the office I'll contact Southern Command for more asphalt to be delivered ASAP. I expect Tamari will need more supplies as well. I'm going out to the airport first, to liaise with the Air Force team working there. *L'hitraot!'*

He returned to his APC and headed back past the convoy towards Highway 6, where they turned north west to the main junction with Highway 31. Shaul turned right off the highway onto the side roads that Barkat had mentioned.

After five hundred metres they came to a crossroads where the road ahead was unsurfaced and looked unusable at present. They turned left, then right, into a parallel road which had a reasonable surface. This road ended at a point only one hundred metres from the causeway being built by Barkat across the channel.

'Good,' said Shaul to his driver. 'This should be a much better route than the present one. It should cut off at least three kilometres. We can use the unsurfaced road for our own vehicles. Let's head west to the airport, now.'

'Yes, sir,' his driver replied.

They travelled south west along Highway 31 for six kilometres, then followed the airport road north west for another six kilometres, arriving at what had been Basra International Airport. As they skirted the airport buildings – mostly destroyed – they came on a scene of much activity.

Shaul told the driver to halt beside a group of men working at the edge of the runway. They were hooking up a very long narrow trailer to a waiting truck. It held a rolled up section of what appeared to be interlocking aluminium sheet, rather like a giant roller-shutter door. They directed Shaul across the runway to where their officer was controlling operations.

As Shaul stepped out of the APC the commander came over and saluted him. Shaul returned the salute and said, *'Rav Seren* Shaul Levine. We're stationed in Basra, overseeing the *aliyah* convoys.'

Chapter 10 – Basra: day two

'*Seren* Ben Ezra – Moshe. I'm in charge of this Airfield Damage Recovery unit. What can I do for you, *Rav Seren?*'

'Well, one of my staff had an idea of using *Hercules* transports to leapfrog along the *aliyah* route, delivering three APCs or Hummvees each trip – with medical personnel and supplies, breakdown crews with parts, and water and basic sustenance for those *olim* en route. So, I thought I'd check on your progress here first, before we start making any serious plans.'

'Well, Levine, we've been here only two days so far, but we're making progress. The runways were pretty badly damaged, so we're concentrating our effort on getting one runway serviceable. This is never gonna be an International Airport again, so one decent runway ought to suffice.'

'And how long will that take?' Shaul asked.

'Are you familiar with ADR?' he asked.

'ADR? Don't even know what it means,' Shaul laughed. 'You'll have to explain it to me.'

'Well ADR is a British term meaning Airfield Damage Recovery. An airfield is not like an ordinary road, where you can fill in the holes and just lay some asphalt over them. The surface here has to be capable of taking the weight of a fully loaded heavy transport plane – like the *Hercules C-130* you were referring to – landing on the surface.

'A bomb can create a crater maybe twenty metres in diameter and up to five metres deep. There are two ways we can repair the damage – one is called the *Clean Bowl* technique, the other is *Dynamic Compaction*. Clean Bowl is where we scoop out all the loose material and replace it with new very coarse aggregate to fill the crater to within half a metre of the surface. It behaves something like a big bag of marbles and doesn't need compacting. Then we fill the remainder with finer grades of aggregate, compact it and pour a very fine grout over the surface, which penetrates the 18 mm aggregate to a depth of about 200 mm.

'That method requires a lot of machinery and material readily available, which is possible on your own airfield – like back in Israel, for instance. But here we don't have material readily available, so we're using the other method, Dynamic Compaction, and BDRMs – Bomb Damage Repair Mats.

'With that method we re-use the material in and around the crater, bulldoze it into the crater until it is overfilled, forming a hump. Then we use a heavy machine called a Dynamic Compactor, which you can see operating over there to compact the material level with the surrounding surface.' He pointed to a large excavator type machine with a vertical ram like a pile driver, which was systematically pounding the surface of a recently filled crater.

'Instead of using the grouting method, we can employ Bomb Damage Repair Mats (BDRMs), which you can also see the guys working with over there.' He pointed to another already-filled crater, where the men Shaul had spoken to earlier had positioned their trailer, unloaded the aluminium mat, with the help of an excavator, and were beginning to unroll it over the filled area.

'The BDRM is bolted down to the existing surface and will take the weight of a fully loaded plane on landing. So, that's what we're up to here, Levine.'

'Very impressive,' said Shaul. 'This has been a bit of an education. So, how long until you have a useable runway, then?'

'Well, you can see just how many craters there are …'

Shaul looked across the runway where large excavators were filling in several more bomb craters.'

'Unfortunately, we don't have enough BDRMs to deal with all the craters here – you can blame the Iraqis for that lack of fore-sight. This airport must have got a real heavy pounding from Saudi missiles – the closest target to Saudia, I suppose. We'll have to bring in grout and find dumps of the right coarse aggregate – hopefully nearby – to bring in. I reckon it will be at least a week before air-craft will be able to land here.

'And the runway is only part of the job. We need to restore essential services – to be able to re-fuel, for instance. So, fuel pipes have to be repaired, or bypassed. A lot of stuff like that.'

'So,' Shaul began, 'when you've finished here your team would be available to do the same thing with another airport? I'm thinking of Shiraz, actually – although there's an airport in Bandar Mahshahr that would be useful, also another airfield at Omidiyeh.'

'OK, I tell you what. Give me a couple of days to get things more under control here and I'll leave my sergeant in command and take a trip with you to survey these three airports. If there is one with only light damage it would make sense to get that one operational as soon as possible and leave the others until that one is sorted?'

'That sounds like a good idea,' Shaul replied. 'How about transporting your machinery to another airport? I take it you drove here in convoy from Israel?'

'Yes, we did – on low-loaders – but, being the Air Force, we *could* get some machines moved by helicopter. We should be able to land helicopters at these airfields fairly easily, I would think – they're landing here to refuel from tankers at present. So, once some machinery is freed up in Basra, we could transport it to another airfield and a team can begin filling craters there. I'll have to check this all out with my superiors, of course, but I don't imagine there'll be any big problem. We're all working towards the same end, aren't we?'

'Yes,' replied Shaul, 'facilitating the biggest *aliyah* known to mankind! Actually, we have several tank transporters – they can carry a 60-tonne Merkavah tank. We may be sending them north in the near future – to bring some bridge sections back to Basra. But, otherwise, we could use them to transport your machinery.

'Actually, there's another airport close by – in Abadan. It's really too close to here to be of much use for our purposes, but you might want to check it for more of your BDRM things? That should speed things up a little, I imagine?'

'*Ken.* Good idea, Levine, I'll do that. *Toda.*'

'Well, thank you for showing me what's involved. I'd better get back to my HQ and leave you to get on with your job. I'll be in touch soon about that road trip. OK?'

'Yes, I'll look forward to it, *Rav Seren. L'hitraot!*'

'*L'hitraot,*' Shaul replied.

Shaul rejoined his APC and they headed back to headquarters at the *Shatt Al-Arab Hotel*. He went to the office and used the radio to contact Southern Command.

'Levine, here, sir. We are beginning to get a bit of a handle on this whole exercise. I've just come from supervising our road-building effort next to the Sinbad Bridge. The engineer tells me he needs enough asphalt for about five hundred metres of normal roadway. But we will need more than that to keep up with repairs on the main convoy route. Maybe the same again. And the engineer specified it will need to be in trucks with 'hot boxes', sir. Apparently, that's so it can be kept usable for several days.'

'Beseder, Levine. I'll get a convoy assembled and heading out to you very soon. I've made a note to supply it in hot boxes. Anything else you need?'

'Well, sir, my second-in-command, Peled, had a very good suggestion, I think. It depends on us having usable airfields for a *Hercules* transport plane. I've just checked with the Air Force here – the Airfield Damage Recovery Unit, they call it. *Seren* Ben Ezra showed me what is required and is going to accompany me on a trip as far as Shiraz, to check on the damage to it and the four airfields en route.

'If possible we would want to have two of them operational. Peled's idea is to take three of our APCs – complete with medics and medical supplies, mechanics and spare parts and a third vehicle carrying water and fruit and so forth. The idea is to get the APCs there quickly, pick up any serious medical cases, or stranded people, and return to Basra, unload and then take out another small convoy of three vehicles.

'That way we can have patrols travelling *with* the convoy and spending most of their time in contact with it, instead of half their time being spent just getting there. The plane would speed up our operation, sir.'

'Hmm. Sounds like an excellent idea, Levine.'

'Well, sir, we thought we could try it out on the Shiraz-Basra section. Then, if it works as we hope, we could replicate the idea on the further sections. This section has more intervening towns and probably better highways. The outer sections cross some pretty inhospitable terrain, sir. And there are only two other towns with airfields, as far as we know – Kerman and Zahedan.

'Regarding those, sir, I have a former comrade from my time in Afghanistan – a soldier at present with the Afghan National Army. He is planning on making *aliyah* very soon from Kabul, and he has agreed both to survey the route and the airfields in those two cities, sir.'

'That sounds excellent, Levine. I think your man – Peled, is it? – has come up with a very sound idea. Leave it with me for now and I'll have a chat with the IAF about it. At the moment we're using helicopters to patrol part of the route, which is very costly. Your idea would be a much better use of our resources.

'And I believe you have a hospital up and running, now, in Basra?'

'Yes, sir, *Segen mishne* Bar-Ilan is in charge of that – and also of the burial squads, sir.'

'*Tov,* Levine. So we can send our helicopters to your hospital now, with any urgent cases. Too costly on fuel to keep flying all the way back to Israel. We need to do shorter hops where possible.'

'Yes, sir, we have a good medical team here, and I'm sure they will only send on to Israel the extreme cases that are beyond their abilities, or equipment.'

'Very good, *Rav Seren.* Anything else?'

'Yes, sir,' Shaul replied. 'We have two engineers surveying at Korramshahr for the new bridge. Tomorrow I'm sending them as far north as Baghdad to see if there are bridge sections we can use down here. If they are suitable then, hopefully, we'll be able to use our tank transporters to collect them. But we'll need a mobile crane ASAP. I wondered if the Air Force could airlift a suitable crane to the required site, then move it down here afterwards for unloading and building the bridge, sir?'

'*Beseder,* I'll check out the possibilities for that, Levine. We'll be in touch soon.'

'Thank you, sir,' said Shaul, ending the communication.

He had just settled back in his chair when the radio crackled again, 'Tamari, contacting base.'

'Levine here. How is it going, *Rav Samal?*'

'We're making progress, sir. We've repaired the first section up to the old Iran border and now we're working towards Korramshahr. I'm planning to work until sunset, sir. Then we'll take the heavy equipment to the yard in Korramshahr and lock it up with a guard for the night. Some of the men can head straight back when we finish. The drivers we'll bring back in a couple of APCs. See you this evening, sir.'

'Fine, Tamari. How are your asphalt supplies holding out?'

'We'll be OK for tomorrow, sir, but we'll need more supplies, soon.'

'Just as well I've put in an order for more then. A convoy is being assembled and will be on its way soon. We need enough for the new road at Sinbad Bridge – about five hundred metres of road – so I've ordered twice that amount. We'll need more for the approach road to the new bridge, anyway. It will be supplied in 'hot boxes', if that means anything to you.'

'Yes, sir – means we can keep the asphalt usable for days. That's great. I'll get back to work, now. See you later. sir.'

'Levine out,' Shaul replied.

Shaul sat back in his chair and contemplated the map on the wall. He had marked the main route and the airports along it. It was more than 2,500 kilometres from Kabul in Afghanistan, or from Quetta in Pakistan, to Basra.

From Kandahar on there was some very inhospitable territory – especially the section from the Afghan/Pakistan border to the city of Kerman. As far as he knew there was only one airport in the whole area, just east of Zahedan – a ten hour journey from Kandahar under normal conditions. Shaul didn't envy Ali and Khaista their journey through that terrain.

According to the map – and closer inspection using *Google Maps* – the roads were quite good. A lot of it was divided highway – especially in the western sections – but there was no telling how much damage there had been from the recent war. The same applied to the towns en route – although most of them could be bypassed. Still, a bomb crater in a narrow section of mountain road could become a very dangerous hazard indeed for such a convoy.

He did a more comprehensive search and discovered to his satisfaction that there were, in fact, four more airports, or airfields, that could be useful to the *aliyah* – Zabol, a town close to the Afghan border; Bam, a small town between Kerman and Zahedan; Sirjan, between Shiraz and Kerman; and Gachsaran, between Shiraz and Omidiyeh.

Still thinking about the logistics of the *aliyah*, Shaul headed for the dining room, where he found Katz also having lunch. 'Are you about to go out on patrol, *Rav Turai*,' he asked him.

'In a few minutes, sir,' Katz replied. '*Seren* Peled is already out as far as Omidiyeh. He should be heading back this way very soon, after unloading the two tanks. He'll pick up any abandoned vehicles and passengers with the transporters on the way. I'll probably meet him about halfway.'

'I wonder could you check something for me on your way, *Rav Turai?* You know the airport just west of Abadan? Could you take a careful look around it for very long narrow trailers, with what looks like a large aluminium roller-shutter door rolled up on them. Or for stacks of those shutters, themselves? They're actually BDRMs – Bomb Damage Repair Mats – and if the Air Force can get some more of them over here to Basra Airport, they can have the runway operational all the more quickly.'

'Certainly, sir, I'll have a good look for them. They're pretty important, then, I take it.'

'Yes, corporal, it might mean we could implement Peled's idea all the sooner. All our travel on the ground would then be east-west – in the direction of the convoy, catching up with those in trouble. We'd also be able to do about twice as many patrols with the same personnel and equipment.'

'*Beseder,* sir, I'll check it out on the way. *L'hitraot!*'

'*L'hitraot!*' Shaul replied.

After a quick lunch Shaul collected his APC crew and headed across the Sinbad Bridge towards Korramshahr, in search of the two engineers, Wolfson and Becker. On his way he noticed that the traffic was now moving much more freely on this section since Tamari's crew had repaired the road. The only problem was that now there was an increasing tailback from both bridges. *A new bridge is going to be essential,* he thought.

He found the engineers by the docks in Korramshahr. They had been busy that day, surveying both sides of the river. Now they were examining boats moored alongside the wharf. Shaul asked them how they were getting on.

'We're just picking out boats suitable to use as pontoons. There are plenty to choose from but, as far as possible, we want to have them all pretty much one size and draught. That will make the bridge building all the easier.'

'How much longer will you need to finish?' Shaul asked them.

'About another half an hour. You need us?'

'Yes, I would like you to pick up Barkat from his own project and show him where you want the access road on the western side. While you guys are off up north he can make a start on paving a road to the islands. By the way, he has found a supply of large concrete pipes, some of which he's using under the causeway he's building over a water channel. I thought they might also be useful for your project – at least for the island to island connection?'

'Yes,' said Wolfson, 'that's quite a narrow channel. We could use large diameter pipes there, I think. What do you say, Becker?'

Becker agreed.

'Beseder,' said Shaul. 'You can discuss the details with Barkat, then.'

'Beseder, we'll do that,' Becker replied.

'Toda, l'hitraot,' Shaul replied, as he returned to his APC.

Another little step along the way, he thought to himself.

Back at the Sinbad Bridge Shaul halted briefly to tell Barkat that the other two engineers would be collecting him in about an hour, and explained what he had in mind. Leaving Barkat he headed back to the Hotel HQ and his office.

Bar-Ilan found him there a few minutes later. 'Southern Command were on a short while ago, sir. They have a convoy of asphalt trucks heading our way tomorrow morning. They should arrive here by the end of the day.'

'That's great, Rebekkah, Shaul replied. 'We're making progress. Though I won't be happy until we have this *aliyah really* under control.'

'I understand, sir,' she answered.

'Are things under control with your end, Rebekkah?' he asked.

'I think so, sir. Some volunteers arrived this afternoon to help with the body retrieval and burials. So, I've been able to take some guys off that duty and put them on ambulance work. When the two outlying ambulances report in I immediately send out the other two to replace them. So far, that seems to be working – although, since your radio call earlier, I've had to co-ordinate with the IAF and ferry more patients from the airport. We will need a couple more ambulances for that job now.'

'*Beseder,* Rebekkah. Go ahead with whatever you need to do. Are you free for an hour or so, at the moment?'

'I can be, sir,' she replied.

'OK, come with me for now.'

'*Beseder.*'

Shaul collected the empty APC he had been using earlier and they drove south east towards the city centre, along Dinar Street, following the convoy of vehicles.

As they crossed the bridge over a side channel and came level with five large storage tanks on the left, Shaul pulled the APC in to the right, beside a sign which said *Basra Family Park*. He switched off the engine and reached across to Rebekkah, pulling her towards him. They kissed passionately for a few minutes, then sat back a little.

'Phew,' we really haven't had a minute to ourselves this last couple of days, have we?' said Shaul.

'No, that three days in Galilee seems like another world,' she answered. I was beginning to wonder if you'd gone off me,' she smiled at him.

'No chance!' he responded. 'Maybe we should get off this road. We're kind of conspicuous, here – in full view of the convoy.'

'Luckily they don't know us from Adam and they don't speak Hebrew, either,' she replied.

They left the APC and walked hand in hand into the small park. In the middle a yellow tower from one of the rides had fallen across the path – a casualty of the recent war. They ducked under it and walked to the waterside. The sun was low in the western sky, reflecting dazzlingly off the water in the channel, as Shaul and Rebekkah sat on the bank and gazed at the sunset.

I can see this is going to be a difficult few weeks – until we get things more under control,' said Shaul.

'Just remember,' Rebekkah said, thoughtfully, 'we're doing something which has never been done before. There are no textbooks about this. No one has any experience of it. And we're bound to make some mistakes.'

'Yeah, I suppose so. It's just that, being the Jewish State – and even more so now that we're an expanded Jewish State – we want to show the world that we can do this, and do it right, y'know?'

'I understand. But I think you might need to relax and let the world slip off your shoulders for a little while, huh?'

'And how would you suggest I do that, oh wise one?'

'Let me demonstrate,' she said and pulled him towards her.

After a while they sat just gazing at the continually changing colours of the sunset. There was a great sense of stillness, even though the roar of *aliyah* traffic was just across the road.

'Do you think any of the others suspect?' Shaul asked.

'About us? I don't think so. Let's face it, we've been so absorbed in our task here that there would be absolutely nothing to give any grounds for suspicion.'

'Somehow, we'll have to find a way to spend some time together, though. I don't think I can keep on not seeing you, except as *Segen Mishne* Bar-Ilan.

'It's difficult, I must admit,' she said. 'And yet it would be a lot worse if everyone knew.'

'Oh, yes, my friend, Ali? He's bringing his girlfriend – well, fiancée, now, I guess – Khaista, with him and they're planning to get married soon after they get here.'

'Wow. I bet she's excited – both of them, in fact. I wonder what it's like to live in such a restricted country as Afghanistan and then arrive into Israeli society. It will be quite a culture shock for them, I imagine.'

'Yes. I've been thinking about the journey itself. I know all these people have made it this far,' he said, pointing towards the convoy across the road, 'but it is quite an undertaking – about two and a half thousand kilometres just to get here to Basra. Some of the road is really remote desert country – though I suppose so is a lot of Afghanistan.'

'Quite an adventure for them,' she replied. 'A road trip into a new future – new country, new language, new life together. It's all in front of them, as they say!'

Chapter 10 – Basra: day two

The sun had set and it was rapidly getting darker. They embraced and kissed once again, then held hands as they walked back to the APC.

Ten minutes later they were back at the hotel and Shaul joined Peled at a table for dinner. Rebekkah had gone upstairs to wash up and appeared a short while later.

'I have a message for you from *Rav Turai* Katz,' Peled began.

'OK,' said Shaul.

'He says those BDRMs – have I got that right?' Shaul nodded. 'Apparently, he says, there's a stockpile of them at Abadan Airport. I take it that's good news?'

'Yes,' Shaul replied, 'very good news. There aren't enough of them at Basra Airport to finish the repairs to the runway. But, hopefully, with these extra they can now get the airport operational very soon. I want to try out your air relay idea, and to do that we need two operational airfields – the one here in Basra, of course, plus another at Mahshahr, or Omidiyeh, or Gachsaran, or Shiraz – whichever is the most feasible to repair quickly.

'*Seren* Ben Ezra is the Air Force guy in charge of the repair squad. He's going to take a trip with me to Shiraz in a day or two – inspecting the four airfields. Whichever one is the least damaged, he'll move onto that job next. He can send some of his equipment by helicopter, if necessary, to start preliminary work, filling in the craters.

'They're using some heavy equipment over there. Apparently, Airfield Damage Repair is much more complicated than repairing a road, or street. The surface has to take the impact of a fully loaded transport plane on landing. They overfill the crater and they have this kind of pile driver machine – a Dynamic Compactor – which then compresses the fill down level with the surrounding surface.

'Then, if they have them, they simply unroll one of these BDRMs over the filled area and bolt it down to the surrounding surface. What you've just told me could take days off the task of getting the airport ready. Once we have a second airport to fly to we can try out your air ferry idea.'

'You really like that idea, huh?'

'Yes, and Command like it too. By the way, where did you set up your checkpoint?'

'Decided to go all the way to Omidiyeh, sir,' Peled replied. 'There was an ideal spot there just off a roundabout. I also took a look at the airfield. It didn't look too badly damaged to me. Just a few craters. Probably too small a place to warrant too much attention from the Saudis.'

'That sounds hopeful, Alon.' He looked towards the doorway, 'Aah, there you are Bar-Ilan. Come and join us. Tamari should be here in less than an hour. I think we could all do with an early night, eh?'

'Yes, sir,' Rebekkah agreed. 'I just got a radio call earlier from one of the helicopters. They were bringing several people in to our hospital. Multiple injuries.'

'What happened?' Shaul asked.

'Well, it was out in the remote country between Kerman and Zahedan – actually between Bam and Zahedan. The road was partly blocked with rock where a rocket had struck the cliff face. An over-loaded minibus was manoeuvring past and went too close to the edge. The edge crumbled and the minibus slid over onto its side, rolling over until a tree stopped it's movement. It's fortunate the tree was there, because there was a sheer drop beyond that, and they would all have been killed.

'As it turns out their injuries are not as serious as they might otherwise have been. Our ambulances took them from the airport to the hospital and they're being made comfortable now. In a few days they'll be able to travel again.'

'Hmm, there must be quite a few dangerous stretches of road like that and how can we get a repair crew out beyond Kerman. We don't even have an airfield here in Basra, yet, never mind at Kerman.' Shaul looked very serious and Rebekkah and Alon exchanged looks.

'We're already doing the very best that we can sir,' said Rebekkah. 'It's a mercy that not one of them was killed. They will all recover in a day or two. Just some broken limbs, scrapes and shock.'

'I know,' Shaul answered, 'but the same thing could happen again – even tonight – with worse results. We need to get those roads sorted. The sooner Yusufzai can travel, the sooner he can survey the roads for us – and maybe the airports, too.'

Tamari arrived at that moment and the conversation largely repeated itself for his benefit.

'Well,' he said, when they had finished bringing him up-to-date, 'at least one section is repaired, now. We can only do so much you know.'

'Yes,' Rebekkah replied, 'that's what we've been trying to tell him.

'Beseder,' said Shaul. 'Tomorrow the engineers need to travel north to investigate the possible use of those bridge sections for our bridge here at Khorramshahr. Tamari, I suggest we send Gold along with them, accompanied by a small force. They will report to me by radio and, if the sections can be dismantled and moved by road, we will then send our tank transporters up north to collect them. I've asked Command to see if the Air Force can transport a mobile crane to the location, for loading there and then unloading again here.'

'Fine, sir,' Tamari agreed.

Gold nodded. 'We'd better make an early start, then,' he said, and went off to agree a time with the engineers and his men.

'By the way,' said Rebekkah, 'I think someone suggested a while ago that we all get an early night. I, for one, am gonna do that.'

She rose and bid them all *leila tov* – good night. Shaul excused him-self a few minutes later and also went to bed.

'You notice anything about those two, Musa?' asked Peled, after Shaul had departed.

'What's to notice?' Tamari answered.

'I don't know. Seems all of a sudden they are very formal and official with each other, all the time. 'Sir, this' and 'Bar-Ilan, that.' I wonder if they're hiding something since that three day leave we had?'

'You think there's something going on between them – Bar-Ilan and the Major?'

'Mmmm, I wouldn't be surprised,' said Peled.

'I suppose we'll just have to wait and see, Alon,' said Tamari.

'Yes,' he replied. 'Anyway, let's get a few hours sleep. You off at sun-rise again?'

'Indeed,' Musa answered. *'L'hitraot.'*

'It's been a long day,' said Peled. *'Leila tov.'*

In One Hour – Babylon will fall – *Raymond McCullough*

11 – Basra: day three

Shaul again met with his officers as they shared an Israeli breakfast together – minus Tamari, who was off before dawn again, and Gold, who was already on his way north with the engineers, Wolfson and Becker. Bar-Ilan brought up the subject of the accident victims brought in by helicopter the night before. 'We really need some way of reaching those remote roads, sir,' she said.

'Yes,' replied Shaul, 'I've been thinking about that. It would take a major operation involving a helicopter and aerial refuelling to reach as far as Zabol, the nearest airport to the Afghan border. I've taken the step of listing all the airfields – military, or civilian – that we are aware of. There are nine – not including Basra, here, and Abadan, which is too close for our purposes.

'I'm going to suggest to Command that *Seren* Ben Ezra and I take a helicopter trip to visit each of these. Moshe has the expertise to assess the level of damage at each airfield. Zabol is the furthest, north east of the town, and fairly close to the Afghan border. Then there's one east of Zahedan, the next major point on the route and the nearest to the Pakistan border. There's also an airport east of Bam, near the accident from last night, and roughly halfway between Zahedan and Kerman.

'As well as Kerman and Shiraz International airports, there's also one just north of Sirjan, approximately halfway between. Between Shiraz and here we have airfields at Gachsaran, Omidiyeh, Bandar Mahshahr and, of course, Abadan. Gold has checked the airport at Abadan and reported the existence of some BDRMs there, which can be used to speed repairs at Basra Airport.'

'We'll be looking for more of those at the other airfields and coming to a decision on which airfields to make a priority and which to simply cannibalise. If we can organise a heavy transport helicopter, we could take two APCs with us and set down a patrol further east than we are able to at the moment – say at Kerman.'

'Are *we* gonna be expected to patrol those further sections, sir,' Peled inquired. 'I kind of understood that our responsibility was only from Basra to Shiraz?'

'At the moment we have no way of setting up, or supplying, a forward base, beyond what we can handle from here,' Shaul replied. 'We will have to work out what is possible and who will be responsible as we go. We've been told that we can ask for more personnel and equipment at any time, as we need it.

'At the moment the Air Force are trying to cover the route, using helicopters and aerial re-fuelling from tanker aircraft. That's a very costly method and it's only happening because our government are concerned for the safety of the *olim*.'

'Understood, sir,' Bar-Ilan said. 'So, we *could* end up patrolling as far away as the Afghan and Pakistan borders?'

'*Ken*, it's a possibility,' Shaul agreed.

'Now, the engineers are on their way north today – I hope to hear from them by this evening. Peled, I take it you'll be sending replacements to your outpost at Omidiyeh?'

'That's right, sir,' Peled replied. We're taking two *hummvees* and some trucks, with water and food. Katz here and his service crews are coming with us – one as far as Bandar Mahshahr and the other to Omidiyeh, so there'll be two repair patrols today.'

'*Tov ma'od*, Alon, Avi (very good),' Shaul said to them both. Katz nodded in response.

'I'll be in touch with Command this morning and then I'll be over at the airport to organise a trip with *Seren* Ben Ezra. Bar-Ilan, everything going well at your end?'

'Yes, sir,' she replied. 'I thought I'd send two ambulances with Peled and Katz this morning. I've organised two more for the airport run – meeting the helicopters when they return. The other two will return from Abadan when Peled's convoy passes.'

'*Beseder*,' said Shaul. 'Everything is under control so far. *Boker tov*, men.'

'*L'hitraot, Shalom*,' they replied, as they each left for the day's duties.

Shaul headed to his office to make contact with Command.

'*Shalom, boker tov,* Levine,' HQ replied. 'We have some good news for you. First of all your consignment of asphalt is already on its way to Basra – should be with you this afternoon, or evening.'

'*Toda raba,* sir,' Shaul replied.

'Next, we can do better than transporting a mobile crane. The IAF have agreed to supply you with a Sky Crane – an *Mil Mi-26,* which we've already hired in from Europe. When your transporters are ready let us know and we'll get the IAF to send it to Baghdad, or wherever you need it. It will load the bridge sections onto your transporters and then travel down to Basra to offload and place the sections.

'Now you'll need to have the boats in position before they can be placed, so we've organised a Navy engineering crew to be with you later today, complete with welding equipment and materials to make the boats ready. A couple of marine diesel road tankers will be coming with them to ensure the boats have enough fuel to be manoeuvred into position. Their engines will also need to be run once a day – for half an hour or so, I'm told, to keep the batteries up and operate the bilge pumps – otherwise you might end up with a sinking bridge, instead of a floating one!'

'*Tov ma'od,* sir,' Shaul replied. *Humour from Southern Command!* he thought.

'I'm also informed that we have a Rapid Deployment Bridge available. It will span a gap of over thirty metres. That should be enough for your inter-island bridge, shouldn't it?'

'Yes, sir, indeed. When will that be arriving?'

'As soon as the bridge sections have arrived from up north, we can despatch the bridge. I take it you will set up the western section first, while the navy get to work on the eastern side?'

'Yes, that's correct, sir,' Shaul answered.

'Then the bridge team can take their trucks across and erect the second bridge, while your engineers and the helicopter are concentrating on the wider span. Your operation is being given top priority from the government on down, so that's why the fast response. Now, anything else you need?'

'Yes, sir,' Shaul reported the story of the truck accident the night before. 'I would like to take a helicopter trip with *Seren* Ben Ezra to the nine airports along the route. He can make an assessment of which ones are worth repairing and which we should cannibalise for BDRMs, etc.

'It would mean mid-air refuelling, sir. And if we could use a transport helicopter I was hoping we could drop off a pair of APCs with repair crews and medical supplies as far as Kerman. It would be the first patrol along that section and they could assess what's needed on that road section as they go.'

'I agree with you that we need to extend your operation ASAP. I'll contact the IAF again and see if I can expedite that. When do you hope to go?'

'Well, I'm about to go and see *Seren* Ben Ezra in a few minutes, sir. If he can make himself available, then perhaps tomorrow morning?'

'Very well, Levine. Contact us when you return and we should have an answer for you,' Command replied.

'*Toda raba,* sir,' said Shaul.

Shaul collected his APC crew and they drove north to the new road, which was almost ready for surfacing. Shaul stopped the APC and spoke with Barkat, the engineer in charge of the work. 'I see you are nearly finished here,' said Shaul.

'Well, apart from surfacing, yes. Any news of some asphalt, sir?'

'Command have just told me it's on its way as we speak. Should be here late this afternoon.'

'*Beseder,*' the engineer replied. 'Then I can start moving some of my equipment down to the riverside site, to begin work on the road there.'

'*Tov ma'od,*' Shaul replied. '*Lhitraot.*'

He jumped back into the APC and headed west to the airport. The APC stopped on the runway beside *Seren* Ben Ezra.

Shaul alighted and greeted Moshe, '*Boker tov.*'

'*Shalom, boker tov,*' Ben Ezra replied. 'What can I do for you today, Levine?'

'Well, first, one of my men has located more BDRMs for you at Abadan Airport. I've also been in touch with Command about our proposed trip to check out the other airfields. I think they're prepared to send us a transport helicopter and refuelling aircraft so we can check out all nine airports along the route to the Pakistan and Afghan borders. I will know this morning.'

'Well, that's great news about the BDRMs. I'll send a crew over now to start transporting them.'

'Just use the outbound side of the highway, there and back – except for the Sinbad Bridge, where we use the opposite side – the northern bridge – both ways. My men will stop the convoy there to let you through.'

'Beseder,' Ben Ezra replied. 'Just give me a minute to organise these guys.' He called over his sergeant and repeated Shaul's instructions to him.

Shaul added, 'If you follow the route of the convoys until you enter Abadan, then keep straight on at the roundabout, where the convoy comes in from the left. You'll see the airport on your right, between the town and the river. You can also drive straight on now towards Sinbad Bridge from the Highway 6 intersection. The new road is not surfaced yet, but that won't be a problem for your vehicles.'

'Toda, sir,' the sergeant replied. He then went off to organise several trucks and trailers to collect the BDRMs.

'Great, Levine,' Ben Ezra began, 'that will speed things up greatly here. Which means I can give some time to assessing these other airports. My men here are pretty experienced now at what they're doing, so I can leave my sergeant in charge for a day. We'll have all the craters filled today, I hope, so tomorrow he can carry on with compacting them and laying the mats. And I'll be at your disposal, sir.'

'Tov, Moshe,' replied Shaul, 'It will be a very busy day – nine airports, spread over 2,000 kilometres – plus mid-air re-fuelling ...'

'Oh, I wouldn't worry about that,' Moshe replied. 'Our pilots are well used to aerial re-fuelling. It's routine. It *will* be a long day, though.'

'Well, I'll radio through to you as soon as I hear from Command. Your IAF guys should be in touch, anyway. So, I'll probably see you back here tomorrow morning. Until then, *l'hitraot.'*

'Yom tov, Shaul.'

Shaul returned to the hotel base and radioed command from his office as requested.

'Well, Levine, you and Ben Ezra will be picked up by transport helicopter at 08:00 hours tomorrow. It's one of these new *Yas'ur* (Petrel) *2025*s – the Israeli version of the *Sikorsky CH-53K*. They can carry two of your *CombatGuard* APCs, or *Hummvees*, and drop them off and pick up again wherever you tell them.

'Slight change of plan, now. We're sending you the Rapid Deployment Bridge tomorrow – seven trucks in all, with a team who know how to erect it. You can keep the transport helicopter for another day and it can transport the bridge sections and the men onto the first island, so they can go ahead with erecting it while the other bridge sections are being transported down.

'You might want to transfer some of your road-making machinery to the island while you have the chance. I take it you will be able to ferry the men back to your side by boat? When you've finished with the helicopter please send it back home. All the best with your mission tomorrow, *Rav Seren.*'

'*Toda*, sir,' Shaul replied.

Shaul then radioed Ben Ezra to inform him of the time of departure. 'Just got word from the Air Force, myself. So, I'll see you at 08:00 hours, Levine. It should be an interesting trip.'

'See you then,' Shaul ended.

He then radioed Bar-Ilan and asked her to call at the office when she was free.

Half an hour later she arrived in Shaul's office. 'Sir?' she inquired.

'Come in, Rebekkah,' said Shaul. 'I'm flying out with *Seren* Ben Ezra at 08:00 hours tomorrow. It's a transport helicopter, so we can also carry two vehicles as far as Kerman. Can you set one up with medical personnel and drivers for tomorrow? I want you to travel with them.

'I'll ask Tamari, or Katz, to set aside a repair crew also, to travel with you in another APC. *Your* task will be to assess and record the damage to the road and the route through towns and cities. Also take note of any gas stations en route – petrol stations, the Iranians called them.'

'Yes, sir,' she replied. 'And I think the Iraqis called them Benzine stations.'

Chapter 11 – Basra: day three

'Confusing, but in their absence I think we'll revert to calling them gas stations, eh? Now I'll leave Peled in charge here, tomorrow. We'll fly straight from here to Kerman, refuelling before we get there, and drop you guys off at Kerman. You can begin heading back towards Shiraz. We'll check out Kerman airfield, then fly on to Bam, and then Zahedan, refuel again before flying to Zabol, refuelling again on the way back to Sirjan, then pick you up again at Shiraz airport.

'After that we'll have three more stops – at Gachsaran, Omidiyeh and Bandar Mahshahr – then refuel a fourth time and return to Basra, where the medics can transfer any patients to the hospital. It will be a pretty full day's work for all of us.'

'It certainly sounds like a busy day, sir.!' Rebekkah commented.

'Perhaps you'd like to join me for a picnic lunch, Ms. Bar-Ilan?' said Shaul.

'Certainly, sir,' Rebekkah replied with a knowing grin.

They selected sandwiches and a couple of bottles of grape juice from the counter and left the hotel. They took Shaul's APC, leaving the crew relaxing and eating their lunch. Shaul drove west along the new road – now awaiting a delivery of asphalt which, hopefully, would arrive in a few hours – and turned south at the intersection onto Highway 6.

'We're not going to have any private time in the next few days, I reckon,' Shaul commented.

'I guess not,' Rebekkah replied. 'The price of being a soldier, eh?'

'I think once we get things more in hand and it starts to become routine, we should be able to get some leave,' Shaul added. 'Hopefully, there won't be a problem with us getting time off at the same time. Ali and Khaista should be here by that time. It would be nice to introduce them to Israel. And we should be able to tell *them* our situation without it putting any pressure on them.'

'That's an idea,' she said, 'We could be together on the understanding that we were accommodating Ali and Khaista. They'll probably want to be on their own a lot, anyway, so we wouldn't be crowding them, or they us. That might work.

'You're under a lot of pressure at the moment, Sol. It was showing last night. I know you relish the idea of being in command of such an important project – we all do – but you can't take on more than any person is capable of. Non of us are superhuman, you know.'

'I guess,' said Shaul. 'But what do you suggest I can do about it?'

'I don't know, said Rebekkah. 'Mebbe just share the load with the rest of us as much as you can.'

'*Beseder,*' Shaul replied. 'I'll try to keep that in mind.'

They drove south for roughly forty kilometres and then Shaul turned off to the left towards the river. Already they could see a Caterpillar shovel and another excavator at work widening and straightening the small road leading to the water's edge. 'We're making progress,' Shaul commented.

'Yes, but even with a new bridge the river is going to continue to be a bottle-neck,' she said.

'I have some thoughts on that. Although I'm making it a priority at the moment – and we need to – you'll notice how low the river is. What if it continued to drop so low that we could make several crossings with just some rubble and some of those concrete pipes that Barkat used for the water channel near the hotel?'

'But how do we know it will?' asked Rebekkah.

'We don't, but *Yermeyahu* prophesied that the Euphrates River would dry up into seven streams '*so that my people can cross over dryshod*'. What if that prophecy is fulfilled right now? That would sure help clear the congestion, wouldn't it?'

'It would, certainly, but I guess I don't have your confidence in old *Torah* prophecies being fulfilled,' she replied. 'The *Torah* was regarded more as a history book in our house, not something we could plan the future on.'

'But look at how much has been fulfilled in these last two weeks,' Shaul argued. 'I used to be skeptical, too, when my friend Brandon was telling us these things. But now that I've seen so much of it come to pass, I find it's not such a big step to believe what it says. I've even begun to consider his position on *Moshiach* – y'know, Yeshua? What if he really was/is the Jewish Messiah?'

'Hmm, that would *not* be a popular idea in Israel,' she answered.

'I know, and it's not something *I'm* totally convinced of, at the moment. But I think it *is* worth thinking about.'

Shaul drove along a track that paralleled the river, until they were out of sight of the machines, around the bend, then he stopped again – just south of the bottom end of the larger island.

Chapter 11 – Basra: day three

'Shall we take a walk by the river?'

'Beseder,' she replied.

They left the APC and walked, now holding hands, towards the bank of the much reduced Shatt Al-Arab River. Across from them they could see the southern part of Khorramshahr, with the convoy visible as it approached the bridges over the Karun River, flowing in from the other side. Further south they could just make out the Control Tower of Abadan Airport, where Ben Ezra's men would be busy at the moment collecting the BDRMs to compete the work at Basra Airport.

They sat on the bank of the River and Shaul pulled Rebekkah towards him, kissing her fervently. Eventually, as they parted for air, he said quietly, 'I really enjoyed that time we spent together in Galilee and Lebanon.'

'Me too, Sol,' Rebekkah murmured. 'It just seems so long ago, now.'

'Yes, it does,' Shaul agreed.

They sat for a short while, eating their lunch and watching the sluggish flow of the river and the odd waterbird swimming by. Then Shaul said, 'I suppose we'd better get back to work.'

They stood up and held each other in an embrace, kissing one another hungrily. Then they walked slowly back to the APC and returned to Basra. When they reached the Hotel, Rebekkah collected her APC and headed to the hospital and burial site. Shaul returned to his office and stared for a minute at the map of Iran on his wall. *Well, after to-morrow we'll know a little bit more about how things stand*, he mused.

He sat at his computer and began to type an email to Ali Yusufzai:

Hi Ali,

I really hope things are going well for you in Kabul. Have the Army given you permission to leave, yet. We could really do with your help this end. I'm off on a trip all day tomorrow, so you won't be able to reach me.

We will be flying by helicopter to all the airports on the route – to see which ones we might be able to make usable again. We'll also be dropping off two APCs at Kerman and picking them up again later at Shiraz. So, the part of the route we'll need you to survey is from the Afghan border to the Kerman bypass. Once you reach that you can just make all speed for Basra.

Make sure the truck has four-wheel-drive and that you carry a spare can of engine oil, enough fuel for 2,500 kms and food and water for five to seven days. About 35 kms before Kerman you can bypass it by turning left at a small place called Mahan. After another 50 kms you can turn left onto Highway 86 for Sirjan and Shiraz.

At Basra use the northern bridge (Sinbad Island) as you approach the Shatt Al-Arab River. When you cross the bridge you cross over Dinar Street and then turn left out of the flow of traffic. About one kilometre south east the road turns north again. Keep going north (do NOT turn right, or cross the small waterway). Our HQ is the Shatt Al-Arab Hotel just a few hundred metres along the waterway. You will see trucks, Hummvees and APCs parked at the rear entrance and the Israeli flag on the roof..

After our trip tomorrow I will be able to update you with more details. We will know then which airports we are going to repair first, etc.

Your bank account has been set up by the IDF command and is ready to use. The account is in Tel Aviv – though you can change that when you know where you'll be living. Command sent me the details by email, so I have already forwarded that email to you separately. They are also sending me your cheque book and a debit card for the account. You will be on salary from when you leave Kabul and your salary will be paid directly into that account. However, you won't need any actual money here in Basra. Your food and rooms will be covered by the IDF and New Israel Plan.

Your comrade,

Shaul (Solly)

As he hit *'Send'* the radio squawked beside him. It was the delivery of asphalt announcing their arrival.

'We are at the end of Highway 31 at a large intersection, where this highway stops, after crossing another one – Highway 6. Over.'

'Tov,' Shaul replied, 'carry on straight ahead onto the minor road. There's a left and then right turn to stay on the surfaced road. At the end you'll be opposite a newly-bridged water channel. That's the road we need your material for. I'll radio the engineer to expect you. He'll tell you exactly where he wants your material. Out.'

Chapter 11 – Basra: day three

Shaul then radioed the engineer, Barkat, to let him know his asphalt had arrived. *More progress,* Shaul said to himself. *We're getting there step by step.*

He headed out the long way round to Highway 6 – avoiding the busy crews laying the new surface and drove north to the University of Basra campus. The campus had some halls of residence at the north eastern end, which Shaul examined carefully. *Junbalat was right,* he thought, *these would be ideal overnight accommodation for some of our exhausted olim.*

When Shaul returned to his office – going the long way around again – he received a radio call from Gold, who was with the two engineers.

'We've been to all four bridges, now, sir. Wolfson and Becker reckon we'll need to use material from three of them to build the two bridges we need. The first bridge we looked at – in northern Baghdad – they believe will be sufficient for the Iraqi side of the crossing. They reckon we can use the pontoons there as well for that side. Then we'll need material from two more bridges to complete the Iranian side. They also reckon we can transport the sections on our tank transporters. We just need a crane and a team to start taking the first bridge apart.'

'Well,' said Shaul, 'you can tell Wolfson and Becker that the Air Force are gonna help us on that score. They have a *Sky Crane* hired in from Europe at the moment – a Russian *Mil Mi-26* – that they are willing to despatch to the first site as soon as I let them know where. Where do they want to start work, Ari?'

'They'd like to start with the first bridge we looked at – the one in Baghdad,' Gold replied.

'Beseder,' said Shaul. 'How many men will they need for the operation?'

'They think twenty should be enough, *Rav Seren,'* he replied.

'Beseder,' Shaul said, 'I'll send Tamari up with the transporters and extra men tomorrow. I'll also contact Command and get the *Sky Crane* organised. You can start work as soon as the helicopter arrives, I take it?'

111

'I think they're planning to start work straight away tomorrow morning, sir,' he replied. 'They're eager to get started. We're planning to drive back up to Baghdad as soon as I finish this call.'

'Have you got somewhere to stay for yourselves and the extra men while you're working there?' Shaul asked.

'Yes, we picked out a small hotel near the bridge when we were there the first time – that's where we're heading for in a few minutes. We should have enough food with us until Tamari arrives.'

'*Beseder,* Ari,' Shaul told him. 'I'll send more supplies with him, then. We'll be in touch tomorrow.'

'*Leila tov, Rav Seren,*' Gold replied.

The engineer, Barkat, and his men worked until darkness fell to get the new road completed. At last, weary and dust-covered, they made their way back to the Hotel HQ. Barkat reported to Shaul in his office, 'Just thought I'd let you know, sir, the new road is now operational. Your men have directed the first traffic onto it and the rest of the convoy are now following.

Saul listened and could no longer hear the roar of traffic outside that he had become accustomed to. '*Tov ma'od,* Efraim, *toda raba,*' he answered. 'Care to join me for dinner?'

'Sure, let me just get washed up first.'

Shaul headed for the dining room and after his meal bid goodnight to Barkat and his comrades and headed to bed. Rebekkah and the others followed shortly after.

12 – Trouble in Raleigh

Shaul's former comrade in Kabul, Brandon Thomas, had been sharing his ideas on bible prophecy with a small group of Black Jews in Richmond, Virginia, and with some members of his own Pentecostal Church in Raleigh, NC. Since the devastating war in the Middle East had occurred just as he'd foreseen, some of these men had suggested to the church leadership that Brandon should be invited to share with them more of his thoughts on prophecy.

The leaders were interested and a meeting was set up for a Friday night a week after the war ended. Brandon had researched the relevant passages and prepared himself for the sort of questions he expected people to ask. Because many had heard about how Brandon had got so much right, while others had not even considered these things before and were now curious, there was quite a turn-out on the Friday.

The pastor himself introduced Brandon and said some encouraging things about him, then handed over to Brandon to begin his talk. He referred to the war which had just taken place and then showed how the bible had accurately described the participants in that war and the kind of weapons that would be used.

When he finished – keeping his talk to three quarters of an hour – he then opened the meeting to questions. Most of these were about details of what he had been talking about, but one woman – known as a pretty committed member of the church – asked him, 'What do you expect will be coming next on the prophetic agenda?'

'Well,' said Brandon, opening his bible again 'we are told in Jeremiah that things will get better for the Jews and Israelites in *'their land'*, but that things will get worse for them in Babylon. Let me read you this passage from Jeremiah 50:33:

"This is what the Lord Almighty says: 'The people of Israel are oppressed, and the people of Judah as well. All their captors hold them fast, refusing to let them go. Yet their Redeemer is strong; YHWH Almighty is his name. He will vigorously defend their cause so that he may bring rest to their land, but unrest to those who live in Babylon."

'He will give rest to Israel in *'their land'* – well, that is happening right now. Israel are at rest from their enemies. But it also says, *'unrest to those who live in Babylon.'*

Before Brandon could add anything, the lady who had asked the question interrupted him, 'So, where is this Babylon, then?'

'Well, I was just about to say that it would take a whole other study to cover that subject. We would need to look at Revelation 17 and 18, Jeremiah 50 and 51, several chapters in Isaiah and also in Habbakuk. I can print out those passages for anyone who is interested,' he said.

'But do you believe – as some people do – that the Babylon in the Bible could be this here United States?' another man asked him.

'I do happen to believe that,' Brandon said, 'but, like I said, it would take at least another night to study those scriptures in any depth and see clearly what they are referring to.'

'So,' the man continued, 'do you not believe that the Rapture is about to take place at any time – before any of these other events can happen?'

Brandon answered carefully, 'I believe what Paul taught us about Yeshua's return. Let's look very quickly at 2nd Thessalonians Chapter Two:

'''*Concerning the coming of our Lord Jesus Christ <u>and our being gathered to him</u>, we ask you, brothers and sisters, not to become easily unsettled or alarmed ... Don't let anyone deceive you in any way, for <u>that day will not come until</u> the rebellion occurs and the man of lawlessness is revealed, the man doomed to destruction. He will oppose and will exalt himself over everything that is called God or is worshipped, so that he sets himself up in God's temple, proclaiming himself to be God.*

'''*For the secret power of lawlessness is already at work; but the one who now holds it back will continue to do so till he is taken out of the way. And then the lawless one will be revealed, whom the Lord Jesus will overthrow with the breath of his mouth and destroy by the splendour of his coming.*''

'Paul tells us that the coming of the Messiah – *'and our being gathered to him'*, which is where we get the word *'rapture'* – will not come until this man he refers to as *'the man of lawlessness'* is revealed, who will *'set himself up in God's temple'*. Well, we know who that man is, don't we?' Brandon continued. 'We usually refer to him as the Anti-Christ.'

Another man spoke up from the back of the room, 'But we will all be with the Lord by then. We won't *be* here when the Anti-Christ is revealed. That's what I've been taught all my life, anyway.'

'Well,' said Brandon quietly, 'I suggest you read carefully what Paul had to say in 2nd Thessalonians Chapter Two. I'm only quoting what Paul said, OK?'

He continued quickly, 'Now, if there are any other questions about what I've been sharing this evening, fine. But otherwise, I think we should leave it there for tonight. Bible prophecy is a huge subject, and we can't hope to cover it all in one night. Thank you all very much for coming.'

Brandon stepped down from the platform at the front of the building and some of his friends came up and thanked him for his talk.

'That was very interesting,' said one, 'we should have you back to share some more. People were obviously stirred by what you said – especially as so much of it has come to pass recently.'

'Thank you,' said Brandon, as they left the building.

That Sunday, as Brandon was about to leave after the service he noticed the pastor of his church waving him over. 'Brandon,' he began, 'We all enjoyed your talk on Friday evening. I wonder if we could meet up for a bit of a chat – perhaps tomorrow evening?'

Brandon was free and said, 'Certainly, Pastor, I'll be happy to meet up with you.'

They agreed a time and the next night he arrived at the Pastor's house and was shown into his study by his wife.

'Ahh, thank you for coming, Brandon. Please have a seat. As I said to you yesterday, we enjoyed your talk last Friday evening.'

'Thank you,' said Brandon again.

'But,' the Pastor continued, 'we were a little concerned about your theology afterwards.'

'Oh?' Brandon answered, wondering suddenly where this conversation was going.

'I know it wasn't part of your talk, but something was mentioned in the question time at the end – concerning the rapture. Now both I, and the denomination I represent, have always taught that Jesus can come at any moment. It focusses sinners on their need to repent, before it's too late, for one thing. Now, I'm sure if you think about it you will agree with me that *'God has not appointed us to wrath'*, so there is no way that us believers are going to go through the Great Tribulation, right?'

'Well, no, sir. Actually, Jesus taught us that we must *expect* tribulation – and so did Peter and Paul. Tribulation is the wrath of Satan against us who believe – NOT the wrath of God. Of course, I agree with you that we believers will not suffer *God's* wrath. Jesus is coming back for us before God's wrath will be poured out on the whole earth – when the sun and moon are darkened ..'

'Yes, yes, Brandon. My point really is this – in this denomination *we* believe that the Rapture is the next prophetic event to occur. Any time now, Jesus will return for his own and we will be caught up to meet him in the air, leaving many unbelievers baffled by our disappearance.'

'But how will they be baffled, sir, when the scripture says that *'every eye will see Him'*, and that *'all the tribes of the earth will mourn'*.

'No, no, Brandon,' the Pastor continued, 'that refers to the *Parousia* – the Second Coming. Jesus is coming for his bride before that, secretly, to carry us all away – *before* the Great Tribulation. Only the Jews will be left to repent during that time.'

'I'm sorry, sir, but that is definitely *not* in the scriptures. And there is no way I can accept a two-part return of the Messiah. I can see no 'secret rapture' in the word of God, sir.'

'Well, it doesn't matter whether *you* can see it, or not, Brandon,' the pastor's voice hardened. 'This denomination is not going to change its theology for your benefit – understand? I – and the other pastors in this denomination – have spent many years at theological college, being taught the fundamentals of our faith. We don't need to be corrected by someone who earns his living as a motor mechanic, you understand?'

Brandon was silent.

'Now, unless you can assure me that you will *not* speak any more about this nonsense of believers going through the Tribulation, I'm afraid we must part company.'

'How do you mean 'part company'?' Brandon asked, stunned.

'I mean that you will not be welcome in *Redeemer's Chapel* – or any other church within this denomination – if you insist on continuing with this teaching.'

'I afraid I can give you no such assurance, Pastor. I must adhere to what the word of God teaches,' said Brandon, beginning to assert himself a little.

'I don't wish to hear any more, Brandon. I'm afraid we must agree to disagree. I'm very sorry to lose you, Brandon, but there it is.'

The pastor rose and showed Brandon to his door.

'Goodbye, Brandon,' he said.

Brandon climbed into his car and drove home slowly in a state of shock.

Alyssa greeted him from the kitchen when he entered his home, but Brandon was so deep in thought – going over that recent conversation with the pastor – that he never heard her.

Alyssa came into the room and spoke more loudly, 'Brandon!'

'Huh?' he replied.

'What on earth is the matter with you? You were miles away. Did something happen?' she asked.

'You *could* say that,' he replied.

Brandon pulled himself together and began to share with Alyssa what had just transpired. When he had finished they sat looking at one another. Eventually, Alyssa recovered from her shock and said, 'Brandon, we must acknowledge God in all our ways. He has allowed this to happen for His own purposes.

'From what I heard from other members of the congregation on Sunday you were really great on Friday night. One friend of mine said you shared straight from your heart. She said she could have listened to you over and over again. She was hoping the church would ask you to teach a regular series on prophecy.'

'Huh, some hope!' said Brandon.

'Listen darling,' she said more softly. 'I know you have studied these things probably far more than the pastor has. He did all that *thee-oh-logical* training a long time ago. But you share the scriptures fresh from your study of them. You are always questioning and checking things. I know you Brandon.

'And I know this – God has a purpose in all this and He will make it known. He wants to use you – mebbe not in *Redeemer's Chapel*, but He will show you where. I'm beginning to believe that *He* is the one who has closed this door, so He will surely open another one. So, we just need to pray for our eyes to be opened to recognise that door when we see it. Right?'

'OK,' he agreed.

Alyssa prayed, 'Lord we are both hurting right now at this rejection of Brandon's ministry, but we know that You are the one in control, here. You have a purpose in this situation, Lord, and we submit to your will in it. Please show us where we should go from here. Amen.'

'Amen,' said Brandon.

'You know something, Alyssa?' he said mysteriously.

'What's that, honey?'

'You talk an awful lot of sense, sometimes,' he replied.

'Only sometimes?' she returned, raising an eyebrow.

'Well, a *lot* of the time, actually. Let's go to bed now, eh?

'Good idea,' she answered, smiling at him.

Brandon and Alyssa, together with their children, Hannah and Caleb, continued to pray about their future. Brandon discussed the situation with his partner, Josh, at their now jointly-owned garage business.

'He just told you that you weren't welcome at his church anymore?' asked Josh.

'Nope,' Brandon agreed, 'nor at any other church of our denomination.'

'Wow, that really sucks,' Josh commiserated.

'Well, we just believe that God has something else for us. I'm still meeting with the Black Jews over in Richmond, Virginia. *They* seem to enjoy my teaching, still, at any rate.'

Chapter 12 – Trouble in Raleigh

'Ain't there no black Jews in Raleigh, then?' said Josh. 'Couldn't you start a group here, maybe?'

'Only a few guys from the church who came with me to Richmond a few times – but they're just Pentecostal believers. They don't really think of themselves as Jewish, or even Israelite.'

'Remind me of the difference, again?' said Josh.

'Well, many of us black Americans have some Igbo background – from the Nigerian tribe. The Igbo in Nigeria have a history of religious practices which are basically derived from ancient Israel. But rather than being Jewish – i.e. from the tribes of Judah or Benjamin – they are Israelite, from the other ten tribes. Several thousand of the Igbo in Nigeria are now fully practicing Judaism, but the majority of the Igbo are just Christian, with a lingering knowledge that they have Israelite background.'

'So how do you think of yourself, then, Brandon?' Josh asked.

'I suppose I think of myself more and more as a Messianic Israelite. I'm not Jewish, as I'm *not* from the tribe of Judah, but I *am* Israelite – from the ten tribes – and I also accept Yeshua as the Messiah. I'm certainly not going to abandon my faith in Yeshua.'

'Yeshua is just Jesus, right?' asked Josh.

'Sure, it doesn't matter which version of his name you use, it has the same effect,' Brandon replied.

'Well, y'know I bin going to that there *Redeemer's Chapel* since before me 'n' Rochelle got married. But I don't like the way they've treated you over this. It don't seem like the Christian way to do things. Seems like they didn't even want to discuss it – like have a bible study and thrash out what the bible is saying, or anything. That pastor just laid down the law like he was Moses, or somethin'. I dunno if I wanna continue goin' to that church anymore.'

'Well, don't let me influence you, Josh. It's better to be in fellowship, than not, y'know. This just affects *us*, right now.'

'I know, I know, but it just don't feel right. I'm gonna have to think about it – talk it over with Rochelle.'

Brandon decided to drop the subject in the meantime, as he had no useful direction he could give his friend at the moment. He concentrated on repairing the truck he was working on.

The following Sunday Brandon and Alyssa had to explain to their children why they weren't going to their church any more.

Hannah wasn't pleased, 'But I like hearing all the stories about Jesus and King David, 'n' all,' she whined. 'And I like seeing my friends and singing and praying with them.'

Alyssa looked at Brandon over Hannah's head, raising her eyebrows.

'Well, we're still waiting for God to show us what we're meant to do,' said Brandon, 'but in the meantime, we can have our own little service right here. We can have church in our house – how does that sound?'

'Just the four of us?' Hannah asked, uncertainly.

'Well that's all the people I see at the moment,' Brandon chuckled.

'I guess …' she said slowly.

'Can we sing, *'Miracle in my heart'?'* asked Caleb.

'Sure, Caleb. Let me get my old guitar and we'll sing that and a few other songs, OK?'

Brandon retrieved his guitar from the den and began to tune it. 'I haven't played this for a while,' he said.

Brandon asked them all to close their eyes and he opened with a prayer. They sang *'Miracle'* and several other favourite songs of the children. Then Brandon asked Alyssa to pray and he began to share the story of Moses leading the Children of Israel out across the Red Sea.

'The Israelites had escaped from Egypt – does anybody know why they wanted to escape?' asked Brandon.

'It was too hot for them?' said Caleb.

'Well, that's nearly right,' Brandon said, 'but there was more to it than that.'

Hannah waved her hand, 'I know, I know. The Egyptians had them making bricks for them and they started to get nasty and told them they had to make bricks without straw. Isn't that right?'

'Pretty good, Hannah. The Israelites had become slaves and, be-cause they asked the king – who was called what?' Brandon asked.

'Pharaoh!' Hannah shouted.

Chapter 12 – Trouble in Raleigh

'Right Hannah. Because they asked Pharaoh the king for permission to go into the desert to pray and sacrifice to their God, he got annoyed and said they were just lazy and told them they must still produce the same amount of bricks, but now they would have to get their own straw. His men wouldn't deliver any more straw for them. So they had to work much harder to get enough straw and still make as many bricks as before. They cried to God to help them and he heard them.

'What did God do? Do you know?'

'He sent the plagues on the Egyptians, didn't he,' Hannah answered.

'Oh yeah, all them frogs and spiders and ants and lizards and bugs 'n' things – and rivers turning into blood – isn't that right?' said Caleb very enthusiastically.

'That's close enough, Caleb,' said Brandon. 'And there were flies and gnats and locusts, too. But did Pharaoh let them go, then?

'No,' said Hannah.

'So, what did God do at last to persuade him?' he asked.

'Mmm, he sent an angel to kill all their firstborn,' answered Hannah.

'He did,' said Brandon, 'He sent an angel of death. But how did the angel know which houses were the Israelites and which were the Egyptians?'

'They had to paint their doorposts, didn't they?' Hannah responded.'

'Yes, do you know what with?' he asked.

'With blood!' Caleb answered in a deep scary kind of voice.

'That's right Caleb, but where did the blood come from?'

'From a little lamb,' Hannah said. 'They had to kill a whole lot of little lambs.'

'They did, Hannah. Each household had to kill a lamb and take a bunch of a plant called hyssop – like a paintbrush – and paint some blood on the sides of the door frame and on the top. Then the angel of death knew he was supposed to pass over those houses and not kill anyone there.'

'But it's not fair,' cried Hannah. 'Why did all the little lambs have to die?'

'Well, the lambs weren't actually tiny little lambs – they were a year old and full grown sheep by then – but it was either be obedient to God and sacrifice the lambs, or the angel of death would take the firstborn in the house instead. Now, if it was our house, who would the firstborn be? Who is the oldest child here?'

'I am,' said Hannah.

'Well, if we had a lamb, would we kill it and sprinkle the blood on the doorposts, or would we let the angel come and kill Hannah, instead?'

'Then I wouldn't have a sister,' said Caleb.

'Indeed,' said Alyssa, 'and that wouldn't be nice, would it?'

'No,' said Caleb.

'The reason that God chose a lamb to be sacrificed was to show that someone innocent – just like the innocent lambs – had to die for our sins. But the real Lamb of God was a person – do we know who that person was?'

'Yes, yes,' shouted Hannah. 'It was Jesus, wasn't it – I mean, Yeshua.'

'Yes, and you can call him Jesus, *or* Yeshua, Hannah. He was *'the lamb of God who takes away the sin of the world'*. And do we know what that night was called?' asked Brandon.

The children shook their heads.

'It was called the Passover, because the angel of death passed over all the houses that had the blood of the lamb on their doorposts. But at each of the Egyptian houses someone died – even Pharaoh's oldest son. The next morning there was mourning all over Egypt and the people said to Pharaoh, 'Let these people go.'

'So Pharaoh called Moses and his brother, Aaron, and told them to take the people and leave. And Moses and Aaron told the Children of Israel to get all their belongings packed up and ready and they headed out into the desert. And some of the Egyptian people even went with them. And the others gave them presents of gold and jewellery and stuff like that.

'But after they were all gone, Pharaoh looked around and there were no more Israelites. And he thought to himself, 'I'm stupid. Who's gonna do all the work around here, if there are no Israelites?' And he changed his mind about letting them go.

'The Israelites meantime had travelled for three days across the desert, with a pillar of cloud in front during the day and a pillar of fire by night. And who was in the cloud and the fire?' he asked.

'God was,' Hannah replied.

'That's right, Hannah, and then they came through a large valley – called a wadi – with steep cliffs on either side of them and ahead of them was the Red Sea, where there was a big beach. And the pillar of fire moved behind them. Then some of the Israelites where very frightened and came to Moses and said, "We can see the Egyptians coming behind us, beyond the pillar of fire. What are we going to do?" And do you know what Moses said?'

The children both shook their heads.

'Moses said to the Israelites, "Well, have a really good look at them because, y'know what? You're never gonna see them ever again!" The pillar of fire stood between the Egyptians and the Israelites all night and Moses stretched his staff out over the sea and an east wind started to blow and it blew all that night. And the next morning there was a path right through the middle of the sea, and the water stood up like a wall on either side.

'Moses led the Israelites into the path through the sea and when they were nearly at the other side – it was a few miles they had to walk on a nice sandy path – the Egyptians started driving their chariots along the path through the sea and they had nearly caught up with the last of the Israelites, who were nearly at the other side, when guess what happened?'

'The sea rushed in,' Hannah and Caleb said.

'No, not yet. Remember some of the Israelites were still just reaching the other side, so *they* would have drowned, too. No, what happened was that the wheels came off Pharaoh's chariot and off all the other chariots. That gave the last of the Israelites time to reach the other shore and get onto dry land. Then Moses stretched out his staff again and then the water rushed in and drowned Pharaoh and all the Egyptians. Their bodies were washed up onto the beach in the land of Midian, on the other side of the Red Sea from Egypt.

'Then Miriam, Moses' and Aaron's sister, took a tambourine and danced and sang a song of victory. And you know what?'

'What,' the children asked.

'Those chariot wheels are still down there at the bottom of the Red Sea today – people have dived down and taken pictures of them with coral growing over them. There's even a shiny gold wheel from Pharaoh's own special chariot.'

'Wow!,' said Caleb. 'That was a good story.'

'Yes, Daddy, you tell stories really well. Maybe you should be a pastor.'

Alyssa looked at Brandon and said, 'Out of the mouths of babes and sucklings, eh?'

'Hey, I'm not a baby,' Hannah complained.

'Of course not,' said Brandon. 'Anyone fancy a trip to the park?'

'Yessss!' the children shouted.

'And maybe get us an ice-cream?'

'Yeahhhh!' they shouted again.

'Let's go, then,' Brandon said.

13 – Flight across Iran

Shaul and Rebekkah drove in a jeep to the former Basra International Airport at 07:45 the next morning, along with a CombatGuard APC containing medical personnel and supplies, and a second with mechanics and motor spares. Both APCs also carried as much bottled water as they could spare room for.

The giant *Sikorsky CH-53K 'King Stallion'* helicopter had arrived half an hour earlier and was just finishing refuelling from the airport tanks. Known in Israel as the *Yas'ur (Petrel) 2025* – the plane could carry five crew and two military size pallets or, as was the case today, two APCs – one inside the hold along with the jeep, leaving some room for the personnel, and one slung below the aircraft.

The jeep and first APC were loaded and Ben Ezra, Shaul and Rebekkah climbed into the cabin of the aircraft. The mechanics, medical personnel and drivers had to make do with the hold. The second APC was attached to the helicopter and the aircraft ascended vertically, first moving sideways over the APC slung underneath, then rising slowly until it also lifted off, and accelerated eastwards.

Shaul and company were treated to a panoramic view of western Iran. After three hours of flying the pilot informed them that they would be re-fuelling in a few minutes. As they watched, the long probe telescoped forwards from the front of the helicopter.

Then they observed the *Hercules C-130* tanker aircraft over-taking them, lining up ahead of the *CH-53K*, re-fuelling boom suspended, as the helicopter pilot closed the gap and made the connection. The two aircraft continued to fly in unison until the fuel tanks of the helicopter were fully replenished. The *Yas'ur 2025* then broke the connection and the *Hercules* banked away to the left and turned back.

'That was quite impressive,' said Shaul. 'And we do this four times on this flight?'

'Correct,' said the chief pilot.

'Wow,' Rebekkah murmured. 'Unbelievable!'

'We'll be passing over Sirjan in another ten minutes,' the chief pilot informed them. 'Then another forty minutes until we land at Kerman.'

'Beseder,' Shaul replied.

In another few minutes they could see the small town of Sirjan approaching on their right, in a wide valley almost surrounded by mountains – with the airfield to the north of it.

Half an hour later, over yet more mountains, they began to descend for their landing at Kerman Airport. The pilot descended slowly until the APC slung underneath was on the ground, then he extended the sling, moving up and sideways and landed the helicopter itself on the apron close to the terminal buildings, then lowered the ramp at the rear.

'Rebekkah watched as the second APC was slowly driven out of the huge aircraft onto the apron, then climbed in. Ben Ezra also drove the jeep out of the helicopter, then headed towards the main north-south runway, counting the craters and recording them in his notebook. There were two runways at Kerman and Ben Ezra also carefully examined the shorter east-west one, noting the damage there also.

Shaul wished Rebekkah and her crew a safe journey and the two APCs moved off east out of the airport on the divided highway towards a roundabout, then south past the airport where they then joined Highway 84. They were now travelling back west towards Sirjan and Shiraz, merging with the vehicles of the convoy, clearly visible on the main freeway. Shaul stood watching the APCs disappear until Ben Ezra returned in the jeep and then they investigated the airport buildings nearby, looking for BDRMs in particular.

'Quite a lot of damage to this airport,' Moshe reported. 'Let's hope some of them are a lot less affected. I haven't seen any BDRMs, though, but this is quite a large area. They may have them stored somewhere far away from the runways. That would be the wise thing.'

'Some of the airport buildings appear to be usable, at any rate,' Shaul remarked, pointing to some buildings separate from the main airport buildings to the south east, close to Highway 84. 'That looks like a hotel there, still intact. We could use that as a forward base at some point.' He made a note in his own notebook in turn. They took a last look around, then returned to load the jeep into the waiting helicopter.

Chapter 13 – Flight across Iran

'Did you guys notice anything as we landed here?' the chief pilot asked.

'No, anything in particular we should have spotted?'

'Ken,' the pilot responded, 'I'll show you now.'

As soon as they were strapped in their seats, the pilot took off, flying low and moving northwards. 'See all those circles, with roadways joining them?' the pilot asked.

'Yes,' they replied.

'Helicopter landing pads,' the co-pilot explained. 'And there are a lot of destroyed helicopters still there.' As they flew slowly over the maze of landing areas both Shaul and Ben Ezra could see the destroyed helicopters below.

'Might be some useful salvage among that lot,' Ben Ezra remarked, making another note in his book, as the helicopter rose and, turning to the south east, accelerated forwards.

They were now heading south east along a ridge of mountains, with what looked like arid desert beyond them to the east. The road below looked in good condition, a lot of it being divided highway. Forty minutes later they were flying low over the small town of Bam, and on the north eastern corner of a highly cultivated green area they found Bam Airport.

Although very small in terms of airport buildings, the runway appeared to be quite lengthy. This time Shaul accompanied Ben Ezra in the jeep out to the single runway. 'Hmm, this is a lot more like it,' Moshe exclaimed. Only minimal damage. We could probably get this operational in a few days, once we had our equipment out here. Let's check for BDRMs.'

But, although they drove all around the airfield, the essential mats were nowhere to be found. Apart from the runway and the few small terminal buildings, there was nothing but barren landscape in every direction except to the west, where the cultivated area was. 'OK, I guess we'd better move on,' said Ben Ezra.

They drove the jeep inside the huge machine and then moved into the cabin where they found the two pilots finishing their lunch. 'Hope you guys brought some food with you,' the co-pilot said.

'Sure,' replied Shaul, 'we'll eat as soon as we're airborne.'

The *Yas'ur 2025* took off and headed further east away from the highway, across a barren plain. After a while they crossed the highway again as it looped north east, before turning east and then south east through the mountains to Zahedan. The helicopter continued almost due east across the mountains and, just over an hour later, they flew over the town and landed at the airport east of it.

'That's Pakistan straight ahead, over those mountains,' the chief pilot proclaimed. 'With Afghanistan just beyond and to the north.'

As they jumped down from the helicopter Shaul remarked, 'Doesn't look as if there's much damage, does there?'

'No,' Ben Ezra replied, 'maybe it was too close to the Pakistan and Afghan borders for the Saudis to risk missiles out here – they are both Saudi allies, after all, being mainly Sunni. Good news for us, eh?'

'Indeed,' replied Shaul.

They extracted the jeep and continued to examine the airport. 'Even the buildings seem to be intact,' Shaul commented. 'Good spot for a base. You can see the convoy from Pakistan on the ring road, just to the south.'

'Yes, I see them,' Ben Ezra replied. 'There are buildings to the south west, there, possibly where BDRMs could be stored. He drove towards the buildings and they searched around and inside them, discovering a store of BDRMs in one of them.'

'Great!' said Moshe, making another entry in his notebook, 'we can use every one of those in the near future.'

'Indeed,' said Shaul, 'so, we've only Zabol to check now before we turn homewards.'

'Yes, it's almost due north of here, isn't it?' said Moshe. 'We fly along the Afghan border the whole way.'

The two men returned the jeep to the helicopter and the *Yas'ur* took off again. As they flew northwards they could see the runway below them still intact.

'Good news then?' the chief pilot asked.

'Yes, indeed,' Shaul replied. 'There appears to be no damage at all.'

'They seemed to be in the process of building a second runway – parallel, to the east of this one.' the co-pilot said. 'But they haven't finished it.'

'One runway will be all we'll need, anyway,' Ben Ezra added.

Chapter 13 – Flight across Iran

'It's only 220 kilometres to Zabol airport, but we need to re-fuel in about ten minutes,' the pilot said. Shortly afterwards the earlier procedure was repeated successfully and they were once again flying on full tanks. Half an hour later they were flying over Zabol – the furthest point of their journey east.

The airport lay well to the north east of the small city and about fifteen kilometres beyond it. The pilot flew over the runway, before turning south again and landing near the airport buildings. There was some bomb or missile damage to the surface but, to Shaul's un-educated eye, it was fairly limited.

Incredibly, an untouched airliner was sitting beside the airport building. We can take that one home with us one day soon, 'Ben Ezra remarked. 'Spoils of war!'

Moshe and Shaul exited the aircraft in the jeep and drove towards the runway. Ben Ezra had his notebook out and was scribbling in it. 'Don't even see any buildings capable of holding BDRMs,' he commented. 'There are some buildings to the south, but they seem too small – probably just houses.'

'How repairable is this one,' Shaul asked him.

'Oh I think we could sort this one out,' Moshe replied, cheerfully. 'How far is Basra from here?' he asked.

Shaul consulted his notebook, 'Just over thirteen hundred kilo-metres, I reckon.'

'Beseder,' said Moshe, 'Here and back is easily within range for a *Hercules C-130j*. All we've gotta do is get our equipment here. That will be the hardest part. Some of our machines are just too big to fit in a helicopter.'

'We've been offered this *Sky Crane* from Europe, to move and assemble our bridges. Would that be suitable to move your equipment?' Shaul asked.

'Are you kidding?' Ben Ezra exclaimed. 'An *Mil M1-26?* Those things can lift a 30-tonne tank! Then we could be in business.'

'Great,' said Shaul.

They took a last look around and returned the jeep to the waiting helicopter.

'Back to Sirjan, now, isn't that right?' asked the chief pilot.

'That's right,' Shaul answered.

'We'll re-fuel before we land there – in about two hours time. You guys can take a nap first, if you like. A good bit of the distance we'll be flying over flat empty desert. Not much to see.

'OK,' said Shaul. 'Might just do that.'

Taking a drink from his water bottle, he lay down on the cabin floor and was soon asleep, Ben Ezra mimicking his actions. Two hours and ten minutes later he was awakened by the co-pilot repeating his name. Ben Ezra was also awake and stretching his limbs.

'We've just finished refuelling and are about to land at Sirjan Airport,' the pilot told him.

'Beseder,' Shaul replied, coming fully awake.

The airport was about eleven kilometres north of the town, which appeared to be pretty badly damaged in the recent war. The airport itself, on the other hand, didn't appear too badly damaged as they flew slowly over the runway. The buildings consisted of one large shed, a small building with a control tower attached, and a smaller shed – possibly a hangar – some distance to the south east.

'This one has possibilities,' said Ben Ezra, as they rolled down the ramp from the helicopter. They drove to the runway and he made some notes, then they checked out the hangar to the south east.

'Nowhere else to store BDRMs that I can see. We'll have to search each of these airfields pretty thoroughly in the near future – see what we can salvage.'

They returned the jeep to the aircraft and the pilot took them aloft once again. 'Next stop, Shiraz,' the pilot told them. 'About an hour or so's flying.'

'Tov,' Shaul replied. 'We'll maybe eat when we get there.'

'I'd guess Shiraz could be pretty well destroyed,' Ben Ezra suggested. 'It's closer to Saudi Arabia and it *was* a major city of Iran.'

They flew away from the plain surrounding Sirjan and over mountains the rest of the way to Shiraz. About halfway they could see what had been a huge irregular-shaped lake, but was now mostly dried up. Only the western end retained some water. As they drew closer to Shiraz they could see another large lake to the south of the city.

The pilot flew quite close to its northern shore as he approached the airport. The city ahead looked totally devastated. A buzzer began to sound quietly in the cabin. 'That's a Geiger Counter you're hearing,' the co-pilot explained, as the captain concentrated on landing the aircraft. We carry a couple of hand-held ones that you'd better carry with you this time. The sound is self explanatory – if the buzzing gets angry you shouldn't hang about. If the needle goes near the red then you're in danger of radiation damage. Get out of there quickly!'

'Beseder, we'll be careful,' Ben Ezra replied.

As they flew along the parallel runways they could see that there was a considerable amount of damage to both of them. The pilot landed near the western end of the terminal buildings, where they could see their two APCs waiting for them. Shaul hopped down and made his way over to them, while Moshe exited the aircraft in the jeep and went to take a closer look at the runways. Rebekkah Bar-Ilan emerged from the nearest APC and approached him.

Her APC driver reversed carefully up the opened tail ramp into the hold of the aircraft. Several people exited the second APC, which then positioned itself near to the aircraft, under the direction of the co-pilot, and the slings were attached.

'How was your patrol,' Shaul asked, as they watched.

'Fairly eventful,' Rebekkah told him. 'We have several casualties in the first APC, plus some unhurt passengers in the second one. The mechanics dealt with a lot of breakdowns and we came upon the scene of another accident. The roads were quite good at first, but the closer to Shiraz the more damage we saw from missiles and bombs. We were glad we brought the *CombatGuards* and not Hummvees – those APCs take rough terrain in their stride.

'Quite near to the city the road passes between a small cliff and the lake. Rocket damage had filled more than half of the road with debris and traffic was slowed up trying to get past the obstacle. This pickup had hit a loose rock in the road – possibly knocked there by traffic in front – which bounced him sideways and he drove over the edge into the lake before he could stop. Two of the passengers were thrown from the back into the front and sustained moderate injuries. If they'd been wearing seat belts, of course, they'd have been OK.

'We've treated their injuries and the other APC towed the vehicle out again – still drivable. We managed to communicate to the driver that we had a hospital in Basra – using another driver as an interpreter. They will pick up the two injured passengers when they reach Basra. The other patients are suffering from heat exhaustion and dust inhalation – one elderly lady has difficulty breathing, so we've given her an inhaler.

'The remainder are the driver and passengers from another pickup which had totally broken down beyond repair. The vehicle had run out of oil and destroyed the engine, I think. So, we've had a busy enough day. How was your trip east?'

The first APC was loaded now and the ramp was ready to be raised into place so they moved towards the aircraft. Ben Ezra was there ahead of them and drove his jeep up the ramp into the machine, the ramp closing behind him.

'We had some good news and some not so good,' Shaul said. 'The two furthest away airports are in pretty good condition. Bam is also fairly easily repaired. Kerman is badly damaged, but Sirjan can be made usable. This airport looks to me beyond repair, plus the radiation level is fairly high …,' he pointed to the Geiger counter in his hand which had been emitting a continuous low level buzz all the time they had been speaking.

'It's not at danger level, at the moment, but the city itself has obviously been hit with a nuclear missile,' Shaul explained, as he helped Rebekkah aboard the helicopter, climbing quickly up after her.

When they were strapped in the pilot took off and circled well to the south west of the city – well clear of the irradiated area – then headed north west towards their next destination, the smaller town of Gachsaran.

'Well, the only good thing about Shiraz is they have a reasonable supply of BDRMs,' said Ben Ezra. 'Otherwise I think the airport is out of the question.

'So, it seems like the larger cities got the greatest onslaught, including their airports?' Rebekkah asked.

'Yes,' Shaul replied. 'We can rule out any forward base in Shiraz, I reckon. We can set something up in Sirjan and, possibly, in one of the places we've still to check out.'

He flicked through his notebook and scribbled for a minute, then looked up again. 'Zabol is the nearest airport to the Afghan border. It's way off the convoy route, but there's a small yard right where the border road meets the partly built ring road south of the city. It's walled around, with gates, and can be kept secure.

'It would be good for morale if the immigrants can meet with some Israelis early on in their journey. Also, we should have something in their own language to give them, explaining what to expect along the route and also when they arrive in Israel.

'Good idea,' Rebekkah agreed.

'From Zabol to Bam is normally just over a six hour drive – but a full day's run with the convoy conditions. From Bam to Sirjan is only a four hours fifteen minute journey under normal conditions – so a fairly easy day's drive, even with the slow convoy speed.

'From Sirjan it would normally be an eight hour journey to Gachsaran – another two hours at least to Omidiyeh – so that will be a long stretch for the *olim* and also for our patrols. So, it would be really helpful if this next airport is not too badly damaged. Even if it is, it would probably be worth trying to repair it soon to reduce the journey time between posts.

'Say we pick up someone really ill,' Shaul continued, 'or critically injured, just this side of Sirjan – a fourteen hour wait until we get them to an outpost, or an aircraft, is just too long. They could be dead long before then!'

'I see what you're saying,' said Ben Ezra. 'Let's hope for good news in Gachsaran, then.'

In another three quarters of an hour they saw Gachsaran ahead, with the airstrip immediately before them, to the south east of the town. As they cruised over the single runway they could see some damage. As they landed they could tell that this was not a major airport – the buildings consisted of a very small terminal building, plus a collection of hangars and sheds in a row. The terminal was right beside the main Highway 86, which was a divided highway all along this part of the route.

Ben Ezra exited the aircraft in the jeep, to note the damage to the runway, while Shaul walked over to check out the buildings. Rebekkah joined him a few minutes later.

'We could use this place,' he told her as she approached, 'It's so convenient to the highway and we can close the gates and secure this courtyard area. Even if the runway requires a lot of work, I think we should consider it. It's nominally five hours from Basra, on a road that is getting better every day, thanks to Tamari and his engineers.'

'Yeah, it makes sense to have a check-point every five or six hours – where it's possible,' Rebekkah agreed. 'What about Omidiyeh, then?'

'Well, we'll look at it and see what Moshe thinks. They were just out of sight now of the helicopter and the jeep and Shaul grabbed Rebekkah by her arm and swung her towards him, kissing her fervently.

'Wow,' she said, 'what brought that on? Not that I'm complaining, mind.'

'I just needed that,' Shaul replied, holding her close. 'But we really need to get back now. Two more stops. We don't want to keep your patients waiting any longer than we can help.'

As the helicopter came in sight again, they saw that Ben Ezra was just returning from his runway inspection. They watched as he boarded the aircraft, then joined him in the cabin.

'Well?' Shaul asked him.

'Not too bad, actually,' Moshe replied, 'Repairable, I think.'

'That's great!' said Shaul.

'Two more to go, then?' asked the chief pilot.

'Yes,' Shaul replied. 'Omidiyeh and Bandar Mahshahr – Mahshahr is a civilian airport, but I think Omidiyeh is an Air Force base, so it may well have been bombarded.'

'Well, it's less than half an hour away. We'll soon know. We'll refuel on the way, though. We're not low on fuel yet, but it makes sense to top up while we still have daylight.'

'*Beseder,*' Shaul replied.

A few minutes later the tanker aircraft drew ahead of them and the refuelling took place. As the two aircraft separated the captain spoke again, 'Omidiyeh coming up now.'

As they approached the airfield – on the west side of Omidiyeh – it was obvious it was not a civilian airfield. There was very little space for parking outside the terminal building, and the building itself was minimal. There was one large hangar nearby and, though the north end of the runway was quite near the highway, the access road required travelling through the centre of the town to reach the airfield.

'Not as ideal as Gachsaran,' Shaul commented.

Chapter 13 – Flight across Iran

'Looks like quite a lot of damage, too,' Ben Ezra added. 'We'll assess it, but I think Gachsaran is a better option.'

Rebekkah had by now succumbed to sleep on the rear of the cabin floor and Shaul avoided waking her. He and Moshe left the aircraft and did their separate inspections. They both reported back to the helicopter fairly quickly and boarded, as the pilot lifted off again. 'Only ten minutes to Mahshahr,' he told them, flying low over the highway, which ran straight as an arrow to Mahshahr.

'There was an enclosed yard area there,' said Shaul, but it was too small and too far away from the highway.'

'No sign of any BDRMs, unfortunately,' added Moshe.

As he spoke they could see the town of Bandar Mahshahr appearing ahead. The highway looped around the north and western sides of it, turning west again as it passed the airport, which was on the opposite side from the town. Again there was a single runway and the terminal buildings were accessed by about a kilometre of divided road.

'There's a fairly substantial terminal area, enclosed by a wall around the front,' said Moshe. 'Looks like you could close that gate and secure the front end at any rate. The runway looks like it's taken a lot of damage, though. I'd better have a closer look.'

Again Moshe drove the jeep out of the helicopter, doing his usual inspection of the runway, while Shaul walked over and entered the relatively large terminal building.

This has been a proper airport, originally, Shaul thought to himself, looking around the now empty building in the light of the setting sun. *If we need a base here, this would be quite a good setup. It's halfway between Gachsaran and Basra.*

He headed back out towards the helicopter and was picked up on the way by Ben Ezra. As they drove aboard the machine, Shaul asked him about the condition of the runway.

'Not good,' he replied. 'It would take quite a bit of work to make it operational. On the other hand we could easily move our machines over here – it's only two or three hours away by road. They have some BDRMs, though, which is good news.

'I'll sit down tonight and compare my notes. Then tomorrow I'll let you know what my thoughts are on where we should place our energies. Of course I'm only looking at the practical aspects of what is easiest to make operational. Your perspective will be quite different. How about if I join you tomorrow at your HQ and we can discuss it then?'

'Yes,' said Shaul, 'Join us for an Israeli breakfast. Our volunteers are getting quite good at preparing that.' Most of my staff will be there as well – you've already met *Segen Mishne* Bar-Ilan, here.'

In just over half an hour it was completely dark and they were landing at Basra Airport. The pilot quickly lowered the rear ramp allowing the jeep and APC to exit the hold. The driver of the second APC and the stranded passengers made their way to the vehicle, as the co-pilot detached the slings.

Shaul sent one APC – containing the injured – directly to the hospital. The other he sent via the University, where they dropped off the family who were stranded now without a vehicle, then returned to HQ.

Shaul – with Rebekkah now awake, but still drowsy – drove their jeep back up Highway 6 to the new road – now completely surfaced and still filled with traffic travelling west towards Israel.

'That new road cuts off about seven kilometres from the journey,' Shaul remarked.

'Tov ma'od,' Rebekkah said, yawning loudly.

'Beseder,' laughed Shaul, 'I get the message. No more shop talk, right?'

Rebekkah just nodded her agreement, as Shaul reached over and gave her a quick hug. Then he quickly drove the last couple of kilometres back to base via the newly surfaced road.

14 – Email from Kabul

When he returned to his office before heading to bed Shaul opened a new email from his friend Ali in Afghanistan:

Shalom, my brother,

Thank you for the news about the bank account. The other email had already arrived with the account details, so I will be able to transfer my money safely by Western Union.

Khaista is very excited by my marriage proposal and our planned journey to Israel together. Her parents, like mine, are deceased, so neither of us have any close ties to break. My uncle will be sad to see me go, but he says he understands my reasons. I'm not totally sure that I understand them myself, though.

It is becoming very difficult to purchase a decent vehicle here – especially one with four-wheel drive. But my uncle owns a Daihatsu truck which he has agreed to sell to me. It has four-wheel drive and is fairly new. He says he will be able to find another vehicle eventually, but he wants us to be safe on the journey.

He is also happy to know that I will be getting married when I get to Israel and has given me his blessing. My cousins want me to email them when I get there and tell them what it is like – so, they may want to come as well in the near future. My cousin, Elina, insists that Khaista sends her all the details of our wedding – she is even more excited about it than Khaista, I think!

I have talked to my superior officers about retiring from the Army. Surprisingly, they have raised no objections, so it seems as if I will become a civilian by the end of the week. Because I am leaving, they have asked me to stay here in Kabul and collect my discharge papers on Thursday. Until then I have some leave to take, so unofficially I am free of the Army already.

I will use the time to purchase some containers to fill with diesel fuel and drinking water, buy food that will keep and sleeping bags, a first aid kit, etc. My uncle has agreed to take care of renting out my apartment. He will take payment for his truck from the rent.

Friday, as you know, is our Muslim holy day, so Khaista and I plan to leave after that – on Saturday morning. That means we should be with you in Basra maybe by Wednesday or Thursday of next week.

I have purchased a notebook and some pens to record the problems along the highway – though Khaista has insisted on buying a tablet computer and says we can easily record everything on it. Anyway, it means we will probably have a dual record of everything.

This whole adventure seems to me very unreal. I no longer know whether I am a Muslim or a Jew – Brandon would probably tell me that I'm an Israelite! And I certainly feel very disillusioned with Islam, after the recent war and Islamic countries destroying one another in it. I don't speak any Hebrew – 'Shalom' is the only word I know – and I know nothing about Judaism, except that it maybe has some similarities to our Pashtunwali code? And your holy day is Saturday – Shabbat, isn't that right?

Khaista and I are beginning a journey to a very different life and we will need your help, brother, to learn new ways and customs. We do know, though, that Israel is a place of freedom and Kabul is not – so really we are very happy to be taking this journey.

Thank you very much for all your help, brother. We will see you face to face very soon. Please pray that we will have a safe journey through the ruins of Iran.

Your comrade,

Khan Ali Yusufzai.

Shaul typed a quick reply and sent it off:

Shalom, Ali,

Great to hear that you are on your way on Saturday. I have just been all the way to Zabol and the intervening airports by helicopter. There are some very remote and barren areas – particularly on the first part of your journey. So, be careful driving and take regular rests.

Chapter 14 – Email from Kabul

Can Khaista drive – if so, you can alternate the driving task with her and travel further and faster?

Surveying the roads will be of great help to us in the near future. Please make a note of the damage – especially where it means the road is partially blocked. Some of the roads seem very well made – divided highway in many places – but the devastation of the recent war may have changed the situation a great deal.

As you come into Zabol – the first town actually on your route – you will see a partly constructed ring road running from north east to south west and crossing the main road, Just to the left of this junction – south of the intersection – is a walled compound with its entrance facing north and a building in the center. There may be a few trucks parked inside it. Can you examine this compound and make some notes about it?

My second lieutenant, Rebekkah Bar-Ilan, travelled by APC from Kerman to Shiraz and found several bad sections – especially where exploded rocks had fallen onto the road going through the mountains and vehicles were forced to drive off the highway to get past. These are the sort of obstacles that we need to know about – where accidents can easily occur. I will tell you more about Bar-Ilan when you get here.

Also, please note any gas stations – petrol stations the Iranians call them – or places like truck compounds, where diesel fuel can be stored, and where our road repair machinery could be secured overnight. Places where vehicles can pull off the highway – especially on single highway sections of the road – would also be worth noting.

By the way, you can quit your survey once you reach the exit road from Kerman, as we already have Bar-Ilan's report on the road from there to Shiraz. From Shiraz airport onward you can start making notes again – as far as Bandar Mashahr.

We are praying that you both have a safe journey and we are looking forward to welcoming you both to our team and, eventually, showing you some of my new homeland – Israel.

Your comrade,

Shaul.

15 – Bridge Building

Shaul and his comrades were joined for breakfast next morning by *Seren* Moshe Ben Ezra – complete with his notebook – and the two helicopter pilots. Shaul introduced them to Peled and Katz – Tamari having left early with the tank transporters and extra men for dismantling and loading the bridge sections.

Shaul nodded to Moshe to go ahead.

'Well,' he began, 'Shiraz and Kerman are out of the question at the moment. Omidiyeh Airbase and Mahshahr Airport are also very badly damaged and, I believe, should not be a priority. Abadan is also badly damaged – according to my sergeant – and is also too close to Basra for our purposes, *ken?'*

'Ken,' Shaul agreed.

'So, out of ten airports in total, that leaves us with five that may be usefully made operational Zabol, Zahedan, Bam, Sirjan and Gachsaran. Some of my crew and machines will be available from today on to begin work at one of these. But very soon we'll need our heavy equipment moved over to that site also.

'Now, if we choose the nearest of these five and, to my mind the easiest to repair – Gachsaran – then we can take our equipment by road on our low-loaders. It's about a full day's drive from Basra and on the way we can do a thorough search of both Mahshahr and Omidiyeh for BDRMs and take any we find with us.

'We would also be in helicopter range from Basra – without costly refuelling – if we need to transport materials from Israel, or elsewhere. It depends what you think is the highest priority, *Rav Seren?'*

'Well,' Shaul began, 'I agree that Gachsaran should be a high priority. I guess it makes sense to progress in stages and bring in fuel and other facilities as we go. Have you any idea how long it will take to make Gachsaran operational for *Hercules* flights?'

'That depends on what we find at the other two airports. If we don't have what we need from those two, we could retrieve BDRMs from Shiraz, which is only three and a half, four hours away. Failing that, we'll have to transport in what we need by helicopter all the way from Israel. But at least the helicopter will be able to refuel at Basra, now – and again on the way back.'

'Beseder,' Shaul replied, 'I think we should go for Gachsaran and pull out all the stops to make it operational as soon as possible. Then we can arrange for a *Hercules* to be permanently at our disposal and begin to put Peled's plan into operation. Any other ideas, suggestions?'

'Ken,' said Peled, 'it seems the logical plan to me.' He looked at Bar-Ilan, Junbalat and Katz, who nodded their agreement.

'Right,' Shaul continued, 'We're minus Tamari and Gold for most of the day. Katz, you're in charge of breakdowns and fuel supplies today, right?'

'Ken, sir,' he replied.

'Peled, you're on your own as far as patrols today – I'll need Gold when he gets back with the first bridge sections. *Beseder?'*

'Ken, sir,' Peled replied. 'I used the two tank transporters to pick up broken down vehicles on their return journey, yesterday. That seemed to work well, sir – and it left the road clear for a while. Unfortunately, I can't do that today as all the transporters are in use up north.'

'Might I suggest,' Ben Ezra intervened, 'I'll be sending my sergeant with some of our machinery and trucks to Gachsaran, later today. The low-loaders can go directly there – maybe with one truckload of troops – to unload, operate and guard the machinery – with the other trucks picking up the BDRMs from Bandar Mahshahr airport. On their way back I could make our low-loaders available to Peled here for picking up any stray traffic?'

'That's a great idea, Moshe,' Shaul answered. 'But they wouldn't be coming back tonight, would they?'

'Lo. How about they meet you tomorrow – say at Omidiyeh at 11:00 hours?

'Make it 12:00 hours, 'Peled replied. 'It will take me longer to travel from here. Our checkpoint is just on this side of Omidiyeh – off the highway to the right at a large roundabout. You'll see our tanks near to the highway.'

Chapter 15 – Bridge Building

'Beseder,' Ben Ezra replied, making a note. 'By the way, I'm assuming you'll be taking the helicopter now from here to your bridge site, Shaul?'

'Ken,' Shaul answered.

'In that case can I beg a lift back to the airport?' he asked.

'Sure,' said Shaul, 'Bar-Ilan here will take you over.'

'Beseder, guys,' Shaul downed the last of his coffee and wound up their conference. 'These pilots and myself have got to go start on that bridge. Catch y'all later.'

The pilots led Shaul out to the parking area to the rear of the Shatt-al-Arab Hotel HQ, where the huge *Yas'ur/*Sikorsky helicopter sat, dwarfing the other vehicles there. They climbed aboard and the machine rose into the sky over Basra and flew south for forty kilometres. In a few minutes the craft had landed and Shaul hopped down onto the ground to begin the day's work of shifting men, machinery and a bridge onto the first island.

Two truck-loads of men arrived from the hotel shortly after the helicopter. The items to be transported the short distance included the Rapid Deployment Bridge sections, the men who would build it and their trucks; the engineer, Efraim Barkat, his excavators and road-laying machinery; and several truck loads of asphalt. The order of transfer was fairly important if the work was to continue smoothly.

Shaul decided to load the helicopter first with the engineer and his machine operators, the bridge-building team, and two jeeps for transport on the island, while also slinging the first of the excavators below the huge aircraft. Once unloaded the excavator operator went straight to work widening and straightening the small island road ready to carry the convoy traffic.

A second machine and driver were soon transferred onto the further island and soon both machines were busy under Barkat's supervision. Once the inter-island bridge was in position he, and his trucks and machinery, would be able to move freely from one island to the other.

Next the helicopter began to transfer the trucks and sections of the new island-to-island Rapid Deployment Bridge, setting them down on the laneway close to the location the bridge was to occupy. As soon as the first sections were transferred the team went to work bolting the sections together.

When all the bridge components had been safely taken onto the island, Shaul directed the helicopter crew to begin transferring the asphalt-laying machinery and the loaded trucks of asphalt. Here there was a problem, because the fully loaded trucks were too heavy for the helicopter to lift – its maximum payload was just under sixteen tonnes.

The solution arrived at was to lift the 'hot box' across separately, then carry the tipper truck over and load the hot box onto it again. This operation was repeated for each of the asphalt trucks. Eventually, all the loaded trucks had been transported to the first island and a couple of by then emptied trucks were lifted back from the island and were now standing in line back on the Iraqi side.

Shortly after noon the helicopter brought all Shaul's men – with the exception of the bridge-building team – over to the Iraqi side, before the crew returned with their machine to Basra Airport for refuelling. Shaul, Barkat and the rest of the men returned by truck to their base for some well-earned lunch. After half an hour they returned for another strenuous afternoon's work.

The bridge-builders had elected to work on while Shaul's team left for lunch and, by the time the helicopter returned, the new inter-island bridge was in place and fully operational. Its builders were now happy to be carried back to the Iraqi side, to be transported by road to the hotel in their turn. They would return in the morning to help with the off-loading of the main bridge sections from up north.

The first loaded transporters were due to arrive that evening, along with *Samal* Gold and one of the bridge engineers, Wolfson. Becker, the second bridge engineer, would remain up north supervising the dismantling. Meanwhile, Barkat and his machines and men worked busily on the first section of road. By late afternoon the road was finished as far as the new bridge and both excavators were now working on the larger island across the newly built bridge.

Late in the afternoon – after the helicopter had retired once again to Basra Airport – a team of Israeli Navy engineers arrived at the hotel in several trucks, complete with welding equipment, tankers of marine diesel and other equipment. Bar-Ilan radioed the news to Shaul and, leaving Barkat in charge at the site, he drove in an APC back to the Basra base.

The Navy team was led by a *Seren* Friedman. Shaul took him and *Segen* Karni, his assistant, across the River to Khorramshahr, to show them where the bridge was to be constructed. They could see and hear the machines still working on the large island across the river. Shaul pointed out the boats which Wolfson and Becker had marked for use as bridge pontoons. The two Navy officers examined several of these and planned to begin work the next morning on converting the selected boats to be used as pontoons.

While there, Shaul received another radio call from Bar-Ilan to inform him that Tamari and Wolfson had arrived with the first convoy of bridge spans from Baghdad and were now travelling on south to the bridge site. Shaul arranged to meet them there as soon as he had returned with Friedman and Karni, who offered to accompany him around to the Iraqi side to view the operation there.

By the time Shaul and the Navy men arrived at the Iraqi bridge site off Highway 6, a series of tank transporters were already lined up along the bank of the river channel. Shaul approached Tamari and Becker, who were standing at the end of the new road, viewing the location where the bridge was to be built.

'*Shalom,* Tamari, Wolfson,' Shaul greeted them. 'Have you everything you need to start in the morning?'

'*Shalom,* Shaul, 'Tamari answered. 'We brought some pontoons with us from the original bridge.' He pointed to the first transporter, loaded with bridge pontoons. 'We can't bring the rest until the bridge sections are lifted off them, but we should have them by tomorrow. Have the Navy arrived yet?'

'Just getting out of the APC,' Shaul answered. 'I'll bring them over.'

Shaul brought the two Navy officers across and introduced them to both Tamari and Wolfson. Barkat and the machine operators had now finished for the evening and were heading across the channel in a small power-boat. When they arrived Shaul introduced them to the Navy men.

'I see you've brought pontoons with you,' Friedman remarked to Becker.

'Yes,' Wolfson replied. 'And we'll have more here by tomorrow afternoon – enough to complete the bridge on this side. But we'll need a vessel to help position and anchor them in the morning.'

'No problem,' Friedman replied. 'We'll send a team around from the downstream side first thing. Karni, here, will supervise them. Meantime, I'll make a start on running up the engines on the other boats, checking them for fuel, welding on the brackets to hold the bridge sections, and sorting anchors and cables.

'Well,' Shaul addressed Tamari, the two engineers and the Navy officers, 'I think we've achieved quite a bit today. One road more or less complete, another well under way, and a new bridge connecting them. Let's go eat and plan our day tomorrow. We'll just catch Peled, I think – he's got to leave early in the morning to meet up with a couple of low-loader trucks at Omidiyeh and use them to pick up any broken-down vehicles between there and Basra.'

The men climbed into the APC and several trucks and headed north to the hotel HQ and some welcome food. Peled, Katz, Junbalat, Bar-Ilan and Lev were already there when they arrived. Shaul also introduced them to the crew who had assembled the Rapid Deployment Bridge and explained that they would be available to help construct the new bridge in the morning.

He also explained that the *Yas'ur* helicopter would again be at their disposal to lift the bridge sections onto the pontoons. 'You've got quite an engineering project going on here,' the Navy commander, Friedman, remarked.

'That's only part of it,' Shaul replied. 'We've got a hospital operating a few kilometres from here, a second airport beginning to be repaired 350 kilometres away at Gachsaran, and an ongoing *aliyah* to patrol, service and give medical aid to. There's something new to deal with every day. Tomorrow, for instance, we'll have the Army, Navy and Air Force all working – together with civilian engineers – on one project.'

'Well,' remarked Tamari, 'we're building an entirely new country. No one's ever seen this done before, so we're all pioneers.'

'Yes,' Bar-Ilan added, 'It's like the first days of Zionism once again – only on a much larger scale and with all the benefit of new technology.'

'I wonder what it's like back home at the moment?' Peled queried. 'It must be really strange to suddenly have totally new borders, no visible enemies and a huge influx of *Olim* who don't speak a word of Hebrew. There must be several hundred *Ulpans** being organised right now, for instance.'

---

*Hebrew language schools

'Yes,' said Bar-Ilan, 'and I imagine a whole host of construction projects and infrastructure being re-built in the captured territories – not to mention the Gaza Strip, Judaea and Samaria, and Israel proper.'

'Well, the good thing is,' Shaul added, 'we're a united country now – not two peoples fighting one another for one land. Even politically, things are so different. I mean, apart from having a National Unity Government, what does Likud, or Israel Beiteinu mean to someone just arrived from Nigeria, Afghanistan or Pakistan?'

'Right,' Tamari said, 'and we no longer need to look over our shoulders to see what the Europeans, or the Americans, think of us. *They* are dependent on *us* getting the oil to *them*. We're freer than we've ever been in our history. Egypt and Sudan are under our control. Saudi Arabia and Iran pretty much wiped one another out of existence!'

'Yes,' said Shaul. 'This *aliyah* is our biggest challenge at the moment. And we need to be single-minded about it. If we were to fail at this we would look so sad in the eyes of the whole world – even though we're taking on something which has never been done before – something unquantifiable.'

'Well,' said Peled, 'I reckon we should start with a good night's sleep. What about you, Tamari? Are you off early, too?'

'Normal time, tomorrow, for once' Tamari replied. 'I've got to set up a repair facility here in Basra – for all these broken down vehicles you keep bringing me, Alon. Nevertheless, an early night is definitely called for. *Leila tov,* lady and gentlemen.'

'Leila tov,' they replied, as both Tamari and Peled left for their rooms.

'Ken,' said Shaul, 'I think I'll join them.'

'Leila tov, sir,' they said, as the entire crew made their way to their quarters.

16 – Day Six: Shabbat in Basra

Friday

The next morning Peled had left early for Omidiyeh. Tamari set out to find a suitable location for a workshop where he could move the increasing number of vehicles needing repair. More mechanics were rumoured to be on their way, so he needed a base for them to operate from.

The Navy crew left immediately they had eaten for Khorramshahr and began work servicing and checking equipment on the boats reserved for the eastern bridge. Two boats were chosen and set aside as tugs, which immediately set off around the southern end of the two islands to help place the bridge pontoons into position and anchor them.

Shaul, the two engineers, the bridge-building crew, and several more men headed south to the Iraqi shore site. Shortly after they arrived the *Yas'ur* helicopter appeared and landed close to the bridge-head. After transferring the machine operators and road-building crew to the first island the pilot returned and attached slings to the underside of his machine. The first transporter moved up close to the western end of the proposed bridge and the helicopter, with slings now attached, took off and began the process of unloading and placing the pontoons into the river channel.

The navy team arrived and worked as two groups – the first of which quickly boarded the first pontoon as it was placed and began to anchor it in position, while the helicopter continued to place pontoons into the water. The second team began lashing several pontoons together and to the bank before manoeuvring the next one into position and anchoring it. Once enough pontoons were in the river the first bridge section was carried out and placed into position. The bridge-building crew secured it at the shore end and the first navy team fixed it to the pontoon.

By now the second Navy team had another pontoon ready to anchor and the helicopter carried another bridge section to link to this one, while the first team towed a third pontoon into place. After an hour or so a rhythm began to develop and the bridge gradually began to take shape. The total width of the span was about ninety metres and the bridge sections were six metres in length, so fourteen pontoons would be required in total – with fifteen bridge sections.

They broke for lunch and were back again within an hour and a half to continue the construction. The helicopter had returned to Basra Airport for refuelling and was back in time to meet them and carry on what had now become a routine. By late afternoon they had used almost all of the components so far delivered and, when the last bridge section was placed in position and secured, Shaul signalled a halt to the proceedings.

One bridge section remained, but there were no more pontoons available. It was lifted off by helicopter and placed close to the partly-completed bridge. The transporters would be travelling back north to Maidan that evening to be ready to load the components of a second bridge on Sunday morning.

One of the Navy boats collected Barkat and his road-building crew and brought them to the Iraqi side of the channel, both boats mooring on the Iraqi side. The convoy then travelled back to Basra for an early evening meal. Shaul had already warned the men that even though it was *erev Shabbat* they would be working late that evening – assuming the next transporter convoy arrived in time. The radio call came through as they were eating and Shaul sent two men in an APC to meet the drivers and direct them to the bridge site.

'*Shabbat shalom!* I guess we're working till dark, then?' Wolfson said, laughing.

'Indeed,' Shaul replied. '*Beseder,* men, let's get to it.'

The convoy of trucks and APCs headed south again, while the empty transporters made their way north on Highway 6. The helicopter reappeared and work continued until half an hour before darkness fell. It was now Shabbat and the roadway on the second island was well on the way to completion and the bridge on the Iraqi side was nearly three-quarters of the way to the first island.

Seren Friedman and the Navy engineers had arrived back just before Shaul and his men. They had prepared more than half of the boats required for the eastern bridge and had them moored side by side ready for manoeuvring into position once the construction of the eastern bridge commenced.

Shaul reckoned that Sunday morning would see the western bridge and both island roads completed. They would then be held up until the next delivery of bridge sections arrived, before they could transfer operations to the eastern, Iranian shore at Khorramshahr.

Peled arrived back late in the evening, having delivered the broken-down vehicles to the new repair workshop Tamari had selected – about two and a half kilometres south east of Ben Gurion Hospital – unloaded the vehicles and sent the low-loaders back to Basra Airport, where they would load up more of Ben Ezra's machinery for transport to Gachsaran Airport on Sunday.

Shaul greeted everyone with, '*Shabbat shalom,*' and they waited with interest to hear what he had to say. 'Men – and women – we've achieved quite a lot in just one week. It is now *Shabbat* and I propose – especially in the light of Israel's miraculous deliverance – that we will make more progress if we honour HaShem by keeping it as best we can. So tomorrow some of us, at any rate, will take a well-earned rest.

'Emergencies, unfortunately, will continue to happen, so we will still be sending out patrols with medics and breakdown crews, but the bridge-building will be suspended until after *Shabbat*. Those who do patrols tonight or tomorrow will be able to take the next day off in lieu. *Beseder?* Have a peaceful *Shabbat.*'

Saturday

Next morning a different atmosphere pervaded the breakfast table at their headquarters. For the first morning in what seemed much more than a week many of Shaul's forces had no tasks to perform. It was a welcome relief from the tensions and pressure of the past week.

The men and women of Shaul's team slept late, took time over breakfast and lounged about – some writing emails to their families or using Skype to contact girl and boyfriends. A queue soon formed, waiting to use the few computers available. Some played chess or cards inside the hotel building, while some of the more religious among them organised an impromptu synagogue service in one of the hotel function rooms.

Others played football in the car park, walked along the shore of the Shatt-al-Arab, or tried their hand at fishing in the River, where the low water level seemed to have concentrated the fish and made them much easier to catch. That evening freshly-caught fish definitely added some variety to their evening meal.

Shaul listened to the voices raised in praise of HaShem for awhile, until he was joined by Rebekkah, who raised her eyebrows to him in enquiry. By mutual consent they took a drive in one of the spare *Hummvees* and travelled west, temporarily joining the convoy route near the Sinbad Island bridge and carrying on west until they could break away from it northwards along Highway 6, passing the University site on the right – which they were now using for temporary accommodation – crossing the bridge over the Qamat Ali Canal and heading for the riverside.

Just past the ruins of the Al Hartha Power Station Shaul turned right, away from the highway, onto a narrow street which led to the river bank. Here they turned north onto a laneway which followed the Shatt-al-Arab waterway.

Eventually, they came to a pontoon bridge which would allow them to cross over the waterway to the eastern bank and turn east into another laneway which would eventually take them back towards Basra. Here Shaul parked the *Hummvee* on the southern side and he and Rebekkah walked hand in hand along the waterway beyond the pontoon bridge.

'Too far from the city to be of any use to the convoy,' he murmured, nodding back towards the bridge. 'There's another bridge even further to the north than this. Anyway, it's shabbat and we should forget about the aliyah for an hour or two.'

"I couldn't agree more,' said Rebekkah wholeheartedly. 'We've had a pretty eventful week – not to mention nearly a month of war we've just been through. It would be really silly for either of us to burn ourselves out at this stage.' She looked Shaul pointedly in the eye.

'You think I'm in any danger of that?' he smiled at her.

'I think you take your responsibility – and it certainly is a big one – very seriously.'

'Well, it's vital that we get this right. I don't want to be the one responsible for making Israel look bad in the eyes of the world. They're all just waiting for us to make a complete mess of this,' he said seriously.

'You're absolutely right, of course,' she replied, 'but we need to detach ourselves from the enormity of the task – at least for a short while – otherwise we'll end up being overwhelmed by it. I worry about the pressure this is putting on you – on all of us, really – but you're the one who has the ultimate command.'

'Well, I couldn't ask for a better team – most of us have been bonded together by our recent experience in battle together – and I'm trying my best to delegate as much as I can to them.'

'*Ken*, they are a good team. We all seem to work well together – even Lev and the various engineers. I think they've all quickly come to respect you. And you've already come up with some great solutions to the problems we're tackling. I don't think anybody could have achieved more in the first week of such a new situation.'

'Yeah, we've really been thrown in the deep end, haven't we?' said Shaul wryly.

'Israel has been given no choice, really. And we just happen to be in the right place at the right time – and all that. But that doesn't lessen the stress on you and it's you that I'm particularly concerned about. I'd hate to see you damaged as a result of such a weight on your shoulders.'

'Well, I'm glad you care so much about my well-being, Bekkah,' he looked her again in the eyes.

Rebekkah responded by putting her hands on his neck and caressing him. 'I guess what I'm saying is that in such a short time I've come to love you very much and I want to see you come out of this whole enterprise undamaged, so we can have a normal life together afterwards.'

Shaul gazed into her eyes and answered, 'I guess that I love you too, Bekkah. And I'm really touched at your obvious concern for me – especially with my parents both being killed not so long ago and my brother Reuben being so tied up in running the company that he doesn't really have any time for me.

'But don't forget that I believe in HaShem and I'm quite sure that he is looking out for me – for all of us here, really. I've begun praying to Him much more, recently – especially because of this responsibility I've been given. And I really think that helps with the pressure – it takes quite a lot of the burden off my own shoulders.'

'I really hope so,' she sighed, then was silent as Shaul kissed her passionately and at length. When they eventually parted they began wandering slowly along the waterside, still holding hands. Neither of them seemed to want to lose contact with the other.

As they walked on they talked quietly about what they hoped Israel would be like when they eventually got back there – about all the changes there would be. After some time they returned to the *Hummvee* and drove across the bridge, eventually re-joining the incoming convoy towards the Sinbad Island bridge. When they re-entered the city Shaul dropped Rebekkah off at Ben Gurion hospital to check on the medical team, while he returned alone to their hotel HQ.

17 – The Adventure Begins

Saturday

Ali drove up to the university in his newly acquired red Daihatsu pickup truck – loaded with containers of diesel fuel, two spare wheels, tools, water, tinned food and some fruit and bread, most of the furniture from his apartment, his clothes, etc. He was reminded of those early American pioneers he'd once read about, who crossed the United States in covered wagons with all their possessions and had to fight off hostile Indian tribes along the way.

At least we won't have to do any fighting off of hostile natives, he thought, hopefully – although as a precaution, he had acquired a rifle from one of his Army contacts and had secured it behind the driving seat. He also had a pistol, acquired from the same source, stashed under the dashboard.

Khaista was already waiting for him and they drove to her apartment and Ali loaded her possessions into the truck, which had already been filled up with fuel – the oil, water, screen wash, tyre pressures and wheel nuts all checked.

As they got back into the vehicle and closed the doors they both looked at one another. 'No regrets?' asked Ali.

'Definitely not,' Khaista replied. 'But it is hard to believe that we are really leaving Afghanistan for ever and going to a country we have never seen before, where they speak a different language.'

Ali reached over and took her hand, 'God of Ibrahim, we ask you to lead us and protect us on this journey, which we believe You have guided us to take. We trust ourselves to Your great mercy. *Amein.*'

'*Amein,*' Khaista added.

'Let's get this show on the road, then,' said Ali, 'as my American friends would say.'

As he drove Ali regaled Khaista with several more Americanisms he had picked up while working with the International Security

Assistance Forces (ISAF), or from TV shows, or the internet. She in turn told him about some of her experiences and conversations with students from the University of Maryland while doing her computer course.

As they drove west on Afghan Highway 1 (AH1) the road at first followed the Paghman River – a tributary of the Kabul river – up into the mountains, gradually turning south west and then south towards Ghazni. This road had been intended to be a tribute to the American and other foreign ISAF forces who had been stationed in Afghanistan but, unfortunately, it had turned into the most dangerous road in the country.

The Taliban had made a point of stopping vehicles and checking their drivers and passengers, opening fire on anyone they thought in any way suspicious. Many people had lost their lives along this highway and the evidence was littered along its length in burnt out trucks, cars and buses.

The atmosphere had, thankfully, changed recently, in the immediate aftermath of the horrendous nuclear war the Middle East had just experienced. The forces of Islam – previously in the ascendent – were now dispirited and shocked at the recent happenings. Both Sunni and Shi'a had forgotten their desire to destroy Israel, reverting to their centuries old rivalry for the leadership of the Islamic Caliphate, and destroying one another in the process.

The infrastructure of both southern Iraq, Iran and – to a large extent – Saudi Arabia, had been so undermined that none of those countries were any longer habitable – not to mention the devastation and radiation caused by the explosion of multiple nuclear devices. The obliteration of Mecca, the heart of Islam, had been the final nail in the coffin and the world of Islam was still reeling from it.

Many Muslims – Ali included – wondered how, if Islam was the only true religion, they had managed to prove its bankruptcy to the whole world so effectively. Because of this the road was now a relatively safe place to travel once again – at least for the moment. Ali was not sure that that situation would continue indefinitely. Islam would probably re-invent itself at some stage, as had often proved to be the case in the past.

Nevertheless, there were still those who lived only for the material and the rich pickings of a convoy such as this were bound to become an attraction to bandits and former Taliban turned outlaws.

Most of the obstructing vehicles had been removed by the Americans – or the British operating further south, in Helmand Province – or by Ali's late employer, the Afghan National Army (ANA). *It's really strange,* he thought, *to no longer be a soldier, after so many years training and operating as part of a military unit.* He supposed that his new job with Shaul's force would have some similarities to his previous role, but still he would be operating as a civilian – no longer as a soldier.

Eventually, after four hours driving behind the slow-moving convoy, they came out of the mountains and bypassed Ghazni to the south east – not even a third of the way to Kandahar yet. The road had levelled into a plain and continued that way, although there was a ridge of mountains always on their right hand side, to the north of the highway.

After another hundred kilometres, or so, the road began to follow the valley of the Tarnak River. Now and again there were some signs of cultivation along the meandering river but elsewhere, beyond the narrow confines of its flood plain, there was little sign of any.

Thirteen hours after they had left Kabul, they found themselves crawling through the streets of Kandahar. The sun had set just before they reached the outskirts and they were now driving with headlights on. They had snacked on fruit and drank bottled water as they drove – Khaista having handed the wheel back to Ali just a short while back.

'Do you want to stop for something more substantial to eat now that it's a little cooler,' he asked.

'Yes, OK,' she replied. 'But let's be fairly quick. I'd like to get out of Afghanistan this evening if at all possible.'

'Sure,' said Ali, 'I feel the same way. Now that we've started out I really want to keep moving.'

They found a small restaurant in a side street near the main road and ate quickly, before returning to the pickup, where Ali re-filled the fuel tank from some of the containers he had on board, also topping up the screen wash and checking the radiator. They re-joined the flow of traffic towards the border.

The convoy had split into separate routes through the city, but now merged again as they continued west – the merging only slowing things further – causing quite a few angry shouts and sounding of loud horns and klaxons from impatient drivers.

Ali and Khaista found themselves travelling behind a huge Afghani truck, decorated from front to back with colourful artwork and Afghan script. As the road passed through a large roundabout and began to head west out of the city, it became a divided highway and Ali was able to overtake the lumbering giant. On the front it had a large hand-painted sign saying, *'Israel'*, with a Star of David depicting a turbaned Pashtun above the front windscreen.

Another truck had *'Freedom'* painted on its front, while others had *'Shalom'* and *'Pashtuns cuming home'*, among many other similar slogans. One even had some Hebrew script.

'What did that say?' Khaista asked Ali.

'I think it was the Hebrew for 'Israel',' he answered. 'Hebrew script is written from right to left – like Pashto – and I could read the letter *yod, or 'I'*, a *shin*, which looks like the English letter *'W'*, and the next one, *resh* for *'r'* – only the *'r'* is written backwards. So, it probably said *'Israel'.'*

'Have you been learning Hebrew, then?' she said.

'Not really,' Ali replied. 'Just making myself familiar with the letters. There are only twenty two – half that of Pashto script.'

Khaista was quiet for a moment as she switched on her tablet and searched for the Hebrew alphabet. 'Yeah, I see what you mean,' she said a moment later. 'Much easier shapes to distinguish, as well.'

'*I* think so,' Ali agreed.

'By the way,' he continued, 'when we cross the border we'll probably have no internet or cellphone reception.'

'Oh, OK,' Khaista answered. 'I'd forgotten that – because of the war, you mean?'

'Yes,' said Ali, 'Civilisation has basically ceased to exist in what used to be Iran.'

Khaista thought for a few moments and Ali concentrated on driving in the fast lane. After about nine kilometres the highway became single again and Ali had to content himself with sitting in slow-moving traffic, only overtaking when it was safe to do so. At least there had been no accidents, or similar hold-ups so far. The slow speed of the convoy was the only hindrance.

They crossed the Arghandab River to the north side and then turned west again to follow its valley. At first the area along the river flood plain was well cultivated but, as they drove further west, the road drew away from the river to the north and they travelled through what Ali knew from his recent patrols here to be a desert area.

About one hundred and twenty kilometres out of Kandahar they crossed the larger Helmand River, heading west into more desert again. This area – Helmand province, patrolled by the British, whom Ali had only interacted with recently – was a renowned stronghold of the Taliban.

After they had crossed the river, Khaista – who had begun yawning several times already – climbed into the back seat and lifted some of her stuff into the front to make room across the back seat. She wriggled into one of the new sleeping bags Ali had bought, made a pillow of her coat, said, 'Good night' to Ali and was soon fast asleep.

Ali turned on the radio, which was still working and playing Pashtun music, to keep himself alert. After some time the road crossed the Khash River and passed through the small desert town of Delaram, with the joint US Marines and ANA 215th Corps Forward Operating Base nearby.

The convoy turned left in the town and left again just beyond it onto Highway 606. This road travelled south west parallel to the river towards Zaranj and the Iranian border, traversing an arid desert, with cultivation only visible where the road ran close to the river.

The road swung south east, crossed the Khash River again, then turned abruptly south west to follow the river on the southern side. Before they reached the Iran border the river had dwindled to a dry river bed some distance to the north. The sun had been up for some time as the convoy passed down the main street of Zaranj, an isolated Afghan town just east of the Iranian border.

In One Hour – Babylon will fall – *Raymond McCullough*

18 – Second week, a second bridge

Sunday

Late on Sunday morning the work was complete on the western bridge and Shaul and his crews loaded up the excavators and road-laying machinery on the now empty tank transporters and brought all the equipment back to base.

As they were finishing lunch the radio signalled the arrival of two transporters which had been sent on ahead from Baghdad as soon as they had been loaded. *Great,* thought Shaul, *now we can begin work on the main bridge this afternoon.* He passed the news on to the men, some of whom groaned good-naturedly in response to the continuation of their labour.

The excavators were unloaded at the base so that the convoy of now empty transporters could head north immediately, while the rest of the men and trucks, plus the newly arrived transporters, headed across the Sinbad Bridge for Khorramshahr, to begin work on the main, eastern bridge. The *olim* convoy was halted for several minutes while Shaul's vehicles crossed to the right hand side of the highway.

The helicopter joined them once again and the first boat was manoeuvred into position and then a bridge section lowered onto it. Although there was a stronger current and slightly more work involved, they also had the extra Navy men and so, after an hour or two, once again a routine was established – everyone knowing their job and getting on with it without much instruction needed.

By late afternoon the beginnings of a bridge was discernible. The helicopter returned to base to refuel both machine and pilots and Shaul's teams took a well-earned break, eating a meal sent down from the base by Junbalat. After they had eaten the helicopter returned and they continued working until dark.

When they arrived back at the hotel, Shaul consulted with the engineers and they decided on a plan to speed up construction. When the last bridge sections were on their way they would be able to call upon the help of the hired-in *Sky Crane* helicopter – the Russian-built *Mil Mi-26*.

With two helicopters they would be able to divide their men into two teams – one working as they had been, extending the bridge from the eastern bank towards the west, boat by boat and bridge section by section. The other team would begin connecting boats and bridge sections in a raft parallel to the dockside, with the boats temporarily moored to the shore.

When several boats had been linked in this way they would be driven into place – using two of the boat's engines – and joined to the existing length of bridge by another bridge section. Then those boats would also be anchored in position – the sluggish movement of the river facilitating this. In that way the bridge would progress almost twice as fast – taking, hopefully, about four days to complete instead of six or seven.

19 – Journey across Iran

Sunday

According to Ali's map the main road crossed another north-south road and continued north west across the border. However, instead the traffic turned south onto the other road – no continuation of the highway was to be seen westward. 'I guess they haven't gotten around to building it yet,' Ali thought to himself, not realising he'd spoken aloud.

'Whaa ..?' came a muffled grunt from Khaista. 'Oh, it's morning. Are we still in Afghanistan?' she asked.

'Just coming up to the border – if we can find it,' Ali said. 'The map shows a road that hasn't been made yet. So, I guess we just follow the traffic and see where it leads us.'

Khaista sat up and crawled out of the sleeping bag, climbing back into the front seat, after removing the stuff she had placed there. She took out a hairbrush and began brushing her long black hair. Ali, distracted by this, almost ran into the large truck in front as it slowed to turn sharply right towards the border, now only two kilometres away.

As they neared the border Ali could see a fence, and inside it were banks of earth partly obliterated by sand dunes. Close to the crossing point there were some trees along the north side of the road and a couple of buildings either side of it. Two American *Hummvees* were parked on the right side of the road, with a couple of men in uniform standing idle as the convoy continued across.

'Afghan Border Police,' Ali announced. 'They don't appear to be interested in stopping anyone.'

'That's good,' Khaista murmured. 'So, we'll be in what used to be Iran in a few minutes?'

'Yes,' Ali replied. 'Though all I can see ahead is a dried up river bed and some sand dunes beyond it. Doesn't look very appealing.'

163

The road had deteriorated into a sandy track, leading into the river bed at an oblique angle. There were sand dunes encroaching on the road on their left and a small lake – all that currently remained of the river – on their right. The road – or track – continued northwards for another kilometre and a half, then turned sharply left through what had previously been the Iranian customs post, but was now deserted.

They were now driving south, almost parallel to the track they had just traversed, joining a proper surfaced road again. Ali had caught a glimpse of the Iranian town of Milak as they turned south again, but the road was leading away from it. The map also showed an apparently non-existent road circling Milak to the north and west.

Ali pulled off to the right and allowed the convoy to flow past him. 'Duty calls,' he said, getting out his notebook and making some notes about the border crossing and the existing roads, as opposed to those shown on the map. 'I guess we should let Shaul know the map is wrong,' he said.

'OK,' said Khaista. 'Let me have your notebook when you've finished and I'll make a copy of your notes in my tablet.'

After about two kilometres the road turned north west and joined the main road out of Milak – about two and a half kilometres north east of the junction. The convoy turned south, passing close to the river bed – now on the other side of the border – and the border fence. After another three kilometres it turned westwards away from Afghanistan.

'Say goodbye to Afghanistan, my dear,' said Ali, 'We're heading across Iran now. The adventure begins!'

It took almost an hour to cover the forty kilometres to Zabol. As they crossed a canal and came towards the buildings, Ali asked Khaista to look out for a ring road being built, crossing the road they were on. After another three kilometres she pointed to a road crossing theirs.

'Is that it?' she asked.

'If it is there will be a walled compound on our left. Yes, I think I see it. Another couple of hundred metres and Ali pulled across the road towards the compound.

'The gates have been left open,' he told Khaista. 'How thoughtful of them.'

Chapter 19 – Journey across Iran

He drove the pickup inside and around the building in the centre. Behind the building were two long storage tanks – probably for petroleum. There was also a diesel tank in one corner, with a filler hose and nozzle. 'Time to fill up, if it hasn't been emptied already,' said Ali.

He pulled the pickup up close to the filler hose and got out to test it. 'Yes, there's still diesel in it,' he called. 'I'm going to fill the tank up. Means we will have more in reserve for any emergency.' A few minutes later he returned to the cab and climbed in, starting the engine – then he switched it off again.

I've been wanting to do this ever since I first met you,' he said, putting his arm around Khaista and pulling her towards him. He hugged her to him and began to kiss her fervently. At first she was taken by surprise, then she began to respond enthusiastically, putting her arms around his neck and pulling him tightly to her. After some time they drew apart again slightly.

'Well,' said Khaista, 'You took me by surprise – and a very pleasant surprise, I must say.'

'We've been restricted so much by the traditions around us. It's such a relief to feel free of all that and be able to express my feelings for once.'

'Yes, I think you managed to do that all right,' Khaista smiled at him knowingly.

He pulled her close and kissed her again. He felt like a thirsty man after crossing a desert and being allowed to drink pure water at last. The kiss lasted for some time but, eventually, they both had to breathe.

'Wow!' said Khaista, 'So that's what it's going to be like, is it?'

'Lady, you ain't seen nuthin' yet!' he quoted, with an obvious American accent.

'Oh, good,' she answered him, with another mischievous look.

He started the truck and drove out, stopping it again just outside the compound. He got out and closed the gates over. 'People might just think it's locked up and pay it no attention,' he told Khaista as he climbed in again. 'The fuel will be useful to our vehicles when they get to patrolling this far.' He got out his notebook again and wrote for a few minutes, then handed the notebook to Khaista.

'Shall we have some breakfast?' he asked her.

'Yes,' she replied, 'I seem to have worked up an appetite, somehow!'

They ate some fruit and bread and drank more of the bottled water, which was already getting warm.

'Do you want me to drive for a while?' she asked.

'Yes, if you don't mind,' said Ali. 'The road seems to be OK here. We're going left onto the partly made ring road until we hit the main road south.'

'Or I could just follow the convoy,' she said, wryly. 'It's not exactly difficult to do that!'

'Yes, of course,' Ali answered. 'Carry on, sergeant. I'm gonna try to catch up on some sleep now, OK?'

'You go ahead,' said Khaista, turning the vehicle onto the ring road and merging carefully into the convoy traffic, as Ali climbed into the back seat and was soon fast asleep.

After about three kilometres the road became a divided highway and Khaista was able to overtake a lot of the slower traffic. The road continued like that for about fifteen kilometres, until she bypassed Mohammadabad, then it became single highway again and once more she was slowed by the convoy.

The road was still wide enough for her to overtake on all the straight sections. There was no traffic coming in the opposite direction and some vehicles were continuing to drive on the left side even around bends. Khaista couldn't bring herself to do that, but pulled back into her own side before bends, unless she could clearly see around them.

The driver's window was open and Khaista luxuriated in the freedom of being able to drive with no hair covering, her hair blowing in the breeze from the window. Highway 99 joined the north-south Highway 95, driving across a flat, bleak and barren landscape. Some of the convoy traffic turned right here, but the majority turned left and Khaista – after checking Ali's map – followed them. Soon the road rose from this plain into the mountains. According to the map, both Afghanistan and Pakistan met together just over the mountain to her left.

Highway 95 joined Highway 84 and the convoy turned sharply right onto 84, merging at the roundabout with another convoy coming north from Pakistan on 95. Khaista stayed on the 95 south, now driving against the traffic on an empty highway, meeting the convoy from Pakistan and skirting Zahedan to the west. It had taken only three hours and thirty minutes to reach Zahedan.

She continued on around the south of the city, staying with 84 eastwards as Highway 95 veered south again. The road travelled through an almost featureless flat arid plain, with tall mountain ridges on either side. Khaista had brought a digital camera with her and took pictures occasionally as she drove. *Our children will one day look at these pictures and wonder how we travelled all this distance from such a strange land to Israel*, she thought.

After nearly an hour from Zahedan – with mercifully only a few hair-raising encounters with careless Pakistani drivers who had temporarily forgotten that, having crossed the border, they should now be driving on the right! – Khaista could see the Pakistan border fence approaching the road from the left, then turning at right angles and following the road. In another ten kilometres she was approaching the border post, with the Pakistani town of Taftan on the other side.

Across the border about three hundred metres along the Pakistan road she could see the trucks and cars crossing from the left to the right hand side of the road, before approaching the border post. She remembered that in Pakistan – with its British heritage – they drive on the left side of the road. She pulled into the Iranian border post, which was deserted on her side of the road, and woke Ali. 'We're now at the Pakistan border,' she told him.

'OK, do you want me to drive now?' he asked.

'No, I'm fine,' she answered. 'I'm enjoying myself, actually. I took a few photos. Want me to take some of the border here?'

'Yes, why not?' he replied. 'Then we can follow the convoy back to Zahedan and I can make notes on the way.'

'Fine,' she replied, taking several photographs. Then she started the vehicle and re-traced her course to the west of the border post, merging carefully with the convoy coming in from Pakistan. Several of the male drivers sounded their horns at her when they realised she was female, but they looked happy enough – probably just surprised to see a girl driving.

Ali was quite busy making notes about the border crossing and added to them from time to time as they journeyed back north west to Zahedan. They reached the city again at three in the afternoon and stopped to eat something from the tins they had with them.

Ali took the wheel for the next stretch as far as Bam, which turned into a six-hour drive, and Khaista typed his notes into her tablet. As they passed the road from Zabol at the roundabout inter-section, the road became divided highway again for about nine kilometres and Ali was able to overtake a lot of the slower traffic.

Beyond this was a long stretch of mostly straight road, which allowed him to overtake as well, although the traffic in the left hand lane was not going that much faster than the right hand lane. The road was traversing a huge barren plain, with no sign of vegetation in any direction.

In places the road had been hit by missiles, leaving craters that had to be circumvented by the convoy, causing considerable delays. Ali asked Khaista to make a note each time and checked his kilometre gauge to record their distance from Zahedan. As the road crossed a mountain ridge they came upon a section which had sustained major damage.

The missile had brought down part of the rock wall above the road on the left, leaving only a narrow lane for the vehicles to traverse. *This would need urgent repair work,* Ali thought, as he squeezed carefully past the obstruction in his turn. He asked Khaista to make a note of the damage and the gauge reading.

After crossing the mountain ridge, which had some other bad spots, the road then crossed an even larger barren plain, perhaps one hundred and forty kilometres across. At last they came to a valley which had quite a lot of cultivation going on, plus the road became a divided highway once again for another forty five kilo-metres.

Ali was able to gain quite a bit of ground on this stretch, which took them through the small town of Narmashir and on through Bam. It was now 21:00 hours – Ali still thought in military terms. He was becoming weary and pulled off the main highway at a huge round-about onto the road leading to the centre of Bam, then stopped for some minutes to top up their fuel tank from the jerrycans in the rear.

'How are you feeling?' he asked Khaista when he returned. 'Do you think you could drive for a while?'

'Yes, she said – maybe not all night, but for an hour or two anyway. If I start to feel sleepy I'll just find somewhere to stop. This looks like quite a good section of road. I hope it continues like this for a while.'

Chapter 19 – Journey across Iran

They helped themselves to some bread and food from the cans they'd brought with them, then Ali climbed into the back, made room for himself, got into his sleeping bag and fell asleep very quickly. Khaista pulled the vehicle into the main highway again at the round-about and sped fairly quickly down the outside lane of the divided highway. It continued like this for another thirty five kilometres, although there were parts of the road that had suffered severe damage, so that traffic had to transfer to the other half of the divided highway at several points.

Each time this occurred there were delays and Khaista tried to make accurate notes using the kilometre gauge to definitely locate the damaged sections. She was getting quite good at typing on her tablet with one hand while driving, although it was not always possible. Sometimes she found herself repeating the kilometre reading in her head for some distance before she found somewhere to stop and fill in the information.

The road then travelled through a mountain section, where there were more dangerous rockfalls, blocking half of the road, or more. Khaista took her time negotiating these and noted their location as soon as she could safely do so. After the mountain section the road became divided highway again all the way to Kerman, so she was able to make reasonably good time.

After three hours driving she began to feel fatigue overcoming her and decided to look for a suitable place to stop. Some of the best spots had already been taken by other vehicles, but she had seen the signs that told her she was getting quite close to Kerman. Ali had told her to look out for a place called Mahan, because that was where they were to bypass Kerman.

She successfully negotiated the complex intersection of highways south of Mahan and came to the large roundabout to the west of the town. The roundabout was marked *Seven Garden Big Square*. Here she turned east back towards Mahan on a single carriageway road and, before entering the town, found a turnoff on the right to a small enclosed industrial compound. Here she parked, switched off the engine and then crawled into her sleeping bag. She moved her stuff off the passenger side of the seat, stretched out along the front seat and within minutes she was asleep – despite gentle snores coming from Ali in the back seat.

20 – Tragedy Averted

Monday

Ali woke up first. The sun was shining into the pickup and he looked at his watch – it was 05:57 hours. He looked over the seat to find Khaista sleeping peacefully in the front seat. He stared at her beautiful face in peaceful composure for a while and thought how delightful it would be to wake up every morning to that sight.

Unfortunately, his urgent need to relieve himself cut short any further romantic thoughts and he slipped quietly out of the vehicle and found a suitable secluded spot in the small compound. When he returned Khaista was still asleep and he debated whether or not to waken her. He decided to refuel the pickup first.

When he had topped up the fuel tank he decided to nudge her awake. 'The back seat is now free, and it's more comfortable,' he said.

'OK,' she mumbled and proceeded to manoeuvre into the back seat with only one eye open and without getting out of her sleeping bag – a difficult procedure indeed. Ali watched with amusement until she lay down on the back seat and went straight back to sleep. He started the vehicle and tried to figure out exactly where they were. As he turned right onto the main road he saw a sign ahead, which read 'Mahan' when he reached it.

Ahh, he thought, *but I don't want to actually go into Mahan.* He drove right around the roundabout ahead and returned to the large roundabout on the bypass that Khaista had turned off at last night. *I think I know where I am now,* he thought. He took the most westerly route off this roundabout – opposite the road he had come from – and continued around the Kerman Southern Bypass Freeway.

The freeway continued for another forty seven kilometres and he covered the distance in less than an hour – after detouring onto the other carriageway several times to avoid damaged sections.

Kerman seems to have taken a considerable pounding in the recent war, if the bypass is anything to go by, he thought.

He made notes of all the damaged areas in his notebook and, when he reached the end of the bypass, turned south at the huge butterfly intersection onto Highway 86 for Sirjan and Shiraz. The first part of their official task was now done, as Shaul had told him that someone called Bar-Ilan – a girl, apparently – had already surveyed the next section.

He wondered how Shaul could have a female soldier with him. He had never experienced such a situation – neither the ANA nor the Americans had any female soldiers deployed. Of course, he enjoyed sharing his task with Khaista at the moment, but she was *not* a soldier, and never would be. Ali could not really imagine such a thing.

The road continued as divided highway, heading south across a plain and through a mountain section, then west across a smaller plain, bypassing Bardsir. Then came another long mountainous section, although the road was divided highway all the way to Sirjan.

There were several dangerous areas along this section and, because the carriageways were widely separated in places, it was not always possible to move onto the other half of the highway. It was on one of these sections that the accident occurred.

For part of the road ahead the fast lane was completely blocked with rock debris, forcing the traffic very close to the right hand edge of the road, where it sloped away quite steeply towards a deep river gorge on the right. Ali made it slowly past the obstacle, negotiating it safely, but a large and well-loaded truck was crawling in his wake.

The road edge began to crumble beneath the rear wheels of the over-loaded truck and the rear slowly slid off the edge of the road, leaving the truck suspended precariously above the steep slope.

Ali drove forward a few metres and stopped his vehicle and woke Khaista. 'Stay in the truck, he said loudly. It's not safe to get out, OK?'

Fully awake all of a sudden, she said, 'Yes, Ali. What has happened?'

'The truck behind us has gone partly over the edge,' he said. 'I've got a steel tow rope in the back. I'll use it to try to hold the truck in place so we can rescue the occupants. I'll go take a look first, though.'

'OK,' she replied.

A number of other drivers had stopped behind the stricken truck – unable to negotiate past it – and several of them approached it. The truck was very delicately balanced and the occupants – an extended family with several small children – were looking white-faced and terrified. The slightest movement in the truck cab caused it to see-saw dangerously above the gorge.

If one of the occupants were to jump to safety it would cause the truck to lose its delicate balance and plummet into the gorge, carrying the other passengers with it. Ali looked carefully at the vehicle. The first and essential thing was to try to get the family safely out of the cab. But they would first need to add weight to the front of the truck to tilt it towards the road.

Ali explained his solution to the men gathered around, 'We need poles or something similar, to place into the engine compartment, that we can then place large rocks on, to balance the truck.' Some of the men nodded and began to discuss the idea with others in front and behind the accident.

Ali moved closer to the cab of the afflicted truck. The driver had his window open, but was looking terrified and panicky. Ali spoke quietly and calmly to him, 'Try not to move around in the truck. Tell your family that we will soon be able to get you all to safety. Do you understand?'

The man nodded, 'Yes, yes, I understand – but how?'

'We need to re-balance the truck – add more weight to the front. We just need to add more weight than the weight of you and your family, OK?'

'Yes, I see,' the driver said, 'but how will you do that?'

'I need you to pull your bonnet release,' said Ali. 'Can you do that for me now?'

The man nodded and reaching down pulled the release for the front hood. Ali stepped to the front of the truck and opened the bonnet, propping it open on the rod provided. A large man approached Ali. 'There is a truck behind which is carrying some steel scaffolding poles. The shorter ones are about one and a half metres long. Would those work?' he asked Ali.

'I think so,' he replied. 'Can you bring them now?'

'Yes,' said the large man, beckoning some of the others to come with him. In a few minutes they returned carrying about a dozen steel poles, all about 1.5 metres in length. Ali took one from one of the men and pushed it into the open engine compartment, wedging it securely as far in as he could manage. Another man did the same with another pole. Ali grabbed another one and found a spot to wedge it securely. Soon there was nowhere else to wedge another pole into.

'I think that's enough,' said Ali. 'Now we need some large rocks – preferably long flat pieces, rather than round shapes. The men behind him nodded and began to search for suitable rocks in the pile of debris. As they brought the rocks, Ali placed them on top of the steel poles, building a sort of shelf of rocks on top of the poles, so that more rocks could be placed on top of them.

After some minutes work the front of the truck had a large pile of rocks built onto it. The truck had now stopped swaying so dangerously.

'OK,'; said Ali. 'Let's try to get you out of the truck – one at a time, and very slowly, OK?'

'Yes,' the driver replied. 'Thank you.'

Ali walked to the driver's side of the truck, which was closer to the road. 'Open your door, carefully,' said Ali. 'Then hand out the smallest of the children.'

The driver did as Ali asked and a small boy of about three was handed out to him. The child looked terrified, but allowed Ali to take him from his father and hand him to one of the men behind. He passed him on to a woman – probably his wife – who spoke soothingly to the small child.

'OK, now another of the children,' Ali said to the driver.

Another, slightly older boy was handed out and Ali passed him to the others. Next a young girl was passed down to Ali, who set her down onto the roadway. She ran over to her brothers and held them in her arms, weeping.

'OK, we're doing well,' he told the driver. 'Are there any more children.

'No,' he replied, 'Only my wife and my sister.'

'OK,' said Ali, 'Let your wife climb past you carefully and then down from the truck slowly. Right?'

Chapter 20 – Tragedy Averted

'Yes,' the man replied. The wife managed to get past her husband and stepped slowly down from the truck. She collapsed, weeping and some of the other women had to help her over to her children.

'Now, can your sister get past you and climb down slowly?' Ali asked.

'OK,' the driver answered.

'Very slowly, now,' Ali told him.

As the man's sister climbed down she jumped the last bit and the truck swayed dangerously with the change of balance. There was a gasp from the crowd that had gathered – either to help, or to watch. The girl ran across to her sister-in-law and took hold of one of the children.

At this point another driver approached Ali. 'I have a pretty heavy truck,' he said. 'I might be able to pull this one to safety, but I don't have a tow rope.'

'That's OK,' Ali answered, 'I have a strong steel tow rope. Can you back your truck up to this one?'

'Yes, yes, I'll do it now,' the man replied.

There was a short delay while other vehicles were manoeuvred out of the way to give the truck room to move into position.

Ali explained to the driver of the stricken truck what they hoped to do. He then went to the back of his own truck and retrieved the steel rope he had bought from the bed of his pickup truck, attaching it to a towing eye on the front of the stricken truck. He threaded the rope through the eye and then the rest of the rope through the loop on the end. He waited for the other truck to slowly back up, then attached the loop on the other end to the towing hitch, replacing the pin.

Ali signalled to the towing truck driver to take up the strain on the rope. The truck moved slowly forward and the rope tightened. Ali signalled the other driver to restart his engine and put it into gear. As he released the clutch the rear wheels spun uselessly.

'Not yet,' Ali shouted to him. 'Wait until I signal you.'

The driver nodded in understanding. He still looked pale and scared.

Ali signalled the towing driver to pull slowly forward. This was a much heavier truck and might be able to pull the first one out of trouble. As the larger truck moved slowly forward the other truck slid sideways a little, but also moved forward as well. Ali signalled the first driver to keep pulling and the truck behind slid a little further sideways, but also forward a little more. Ali could see that there was some ground beyond the road edge and the wheels might be able to get a purchase as they moved sideways.

Ali signalled the first driver to keep going steadily and then to the other driver to slowly let his clutch out. The rear wheels spun again, but were now in contact with the ground. A little more sideways movement might allow them to grip. Sure enough, after a little more pulling from the larger truck the rear wheels caught and the truck suddenly lurched forward into the roadway. There was a cheer of relief from the gathered crowd.

The first truck kept moving slowly forward until the rope tightened again, making sure the truck behind was far enough away from the edge. The towing truck applied his brakes and the driver behind moved his truck forward a little more to slacken the rope again and there was a loud whoosh as he also applied his air brakes. Ali moved forward and removed the pin from the hitch of the towing truck, releasing his tow rope. Then he undid the other end and rolled up the rope again, placing it back into his truck.

The other men then moved forward and began to remove the rocks piled onto the front of the truck, pitching them with satisfaction from the edge of the road into the gorge. When all the rocks had been removed they extracted the steel poles and carried them back to the man who had provided them.

The driver of the rescued truck had now climbed out of his vehicle and came over to grasp Ali in a bear hug.

'Thank you, thank you,' he sobbed, overcome with emotion.

His wife and sister also came over and hugged Ali, thanking him and saying, 'We owe you our lives.' The children also came to him, hugging him with tears in their eyes. Then they hugged their mum and dad and their aunt.

Ali pointed out that the roadway was still very unsafe and asked if the men would help remove some more of the rocks from the edge of the debris pile, to allow more room for vehicles to pass. Some of the men agreed and began to help – including the rescued driver – but others slipped away, especially those whose vehicles had already passed the obstacle.

Eventually, the enthusiasm of even those still to negotiate the bad section waned and the rest of the men returned to their trucks, waiting patiently to renew their journey. *At least the roadway is a little bit wider and safer now,* thought Ali.

The rescued family had by now climbed back into their truck and were joined by the driver and father, who waved a final thank you to Ali and started his truck, moving off down the highway. Ali returned to his own pickup, started it and rejoined the convoy.

Khaista turned to him and said, 'That was amazing. You stayed so calm and collected, but so authoritative. Everyone followed your lead and your calmness helped the family to lose some of their panic. You literally saved their lives today. I'm very proud of you.'

Ali, embarrassed, didn't know how to reply to this, so he said nothing, just smiled at Khaista. They had lost about an hour because of the rescue and had another seventy kilometres to cover before reaching Sirjan. They were still travelling through mountains and there were more damaged sections to negotiate but, thankfully, they experienced no more mishaps.

About two hours later they reached Sirjan and drove through the damaged centre of the town – manoeuvring around the rubble from fallen buildings – until they reached the large roundabout on the south western Sirjan Ring Expressway. They turned right along this to the butterfly junction leading back onto the continuation of Highway 86 for Shiraz.

'Time for some lunch – or breakfast, even,' said Ali.

'Yes, it's after eleven,' said Khaista, 'no wonder I'm starving – not to mention the nerve wracking experience we just had. Let's stop somewhere soon.'

Ali pulled off to the right into a lane beside a walled compound. They drove down it until the track turned left along the back of the lot and stopped.

'Well, we have plenty of tinned food, some dry bread and some fruit left,' he told her.

'Yes, I haven't seen any restaurants open along this highway,' Khaista joked.

'Yeah, not even a gas station open,' Ali replied.

They opened a tin of tomatoes and ate it with the bread, finishing with some fruit each and some bottled water. Khaista slipped around the side of the truck for a minute and when she returned Ali drove the pickup back out to the main highway.

The road was single carriageway from here, so progress was slow, Ali overtaking where he could. There was more damage to the highway, so often there was only one lane available.

'I reckon we ought to reach Shiraz around 18:00 hours – six o'clock this evening,' Ali said. Shaul recommended we spend as little time there as possible. It was hit by at least one nuclear missile and there is a lot of radiation in the area. Thankfully, the highway bypasses it on the west, so we do not have to pass through the centre.

'We could stop at Nourabad – maybe three hours past Shiraz, but it will only take at most another couple of hours to reach Gachsaran, where the Israeli Air Force are repairing the runway. We can make contact with Shaul by radio from there and probably spend the night in accommodation there.

'OK, that sounds good,' Khaista responded. 'It would be so nice not to have to sleep in this truck again.'

Most of the afternoon was spent driving across a large desert plain, stretching for over one hundred and thirty kilometres, until they passed through the small town of Qatruyeh – surrounded by cultivated fields. The road then climbed into more mountains, crossed a large valley and entered a longer stretch through mountains, where the road followed the side of a gorge.

Where there was no damage the road was safe, hugging the mountains on their right – unless you tried to overtake, which brought you close to the edge of the gorge on the left side of the road. Ali decided to play it safe and stayed in his lane, unless the road was clear for some distance. Even then he accelerated only a little to get past some of the slower, heavier trucks.

At last they came out of the mountains and crossed a cultivated plain, bypassing the town of Neyriz on its north western side. The road became divided highway as it passed Neyriz and continued at first parallel to the mountains to the south of the road, then eventually turned towards them and passed through several winding stretches into a large valley, which brought them to an east west plain containing the town of Estahban. Ali was able to overtake continually on this divided highway and they made quite good time. Beyond Estahban the road continued to be expressway, although damaged in places, which slowed the convoy each time.

Although there were mountains all around them, the road travelled along the plains and valleys in between, remaining a divided highway and eventually passed between mountains to the south and a partially dried up lake immediately north of the road. Here there were some badly damaged sections of road and at one point they could see where a vehicle had broken through the barrier and been removed from the edge of the lake. Unknown to him this was the spot where Rebekkah and her team had recovered a pickup from the edge of the lake just a few days earlier.

They were approaching the city of Shiraz now, and Ali negotiated the complicated intersection onto the western Shiraz Ring Expressway. This also had damaged sections requiring careful driving, but in between was a good road. To the north they could see the airport runways, which appeared to have suffered a lot of damage. Then they passed through the western edges of the city and could see many destroyed buildings further north and east of the road.

Ali remembered to begin making notes again after they had passed Shiraz Airport. They were quite glad to see mountains ahead along the west side of the road and, when they came to a butterfly junction Ali turned west onto Highway 86, leaving the city quickly behind. The divided highway for the most part continued for another thirty five kilometres.

'Only Nourabad and Gachsaran and then we can stop for the night,' said Ali. Do you want to drive for a bit – it's quite a good road here.' He pulled in and hopped out of the truck, while Khaista slid across to the driving position. Ali climbed in the other side and Khaista set off again, overtaking where at all possible. She looked across to find Ali already asleep in the passenger seat.

The road continued roughly north west and then turned west to follow the valley of the Qareaghaj River, crossing the river at one point to the south side. Eventually, the road swung almost due south away from the river into a narrow side valley, which later widened out, eventually becoming a plain around the town of Dasht Arjan. The other half of the highway had disappeared, taking a different valley route, and they only rejoined it shortly before bypassing Dasht.

To the south east now was a huge lake – Arzhan Lake – and beyond it the two halves of the highway separated again for a couple of kilometres, before becoming single carriageway after only another two kilometres. They were travelling now along the side of a large valley with lots of trees growing around them, regularly crossing side streams.

After travelling north for some time, the road looped right around to the west and then travelled south along the the other side, close to the mountain ridge for some time. At a gap in the ridge it suddenly turned west through a narrow pass in the mountains and into another large valley running north west, where the highway became divided again.

Khaista was able to travel in the outside lane for most of the way now – except where the highway was damaged. They were passing small towns and cultivated areas as they progressed north west. As they skirted along the south edge of Qaemyeh the road ended at a roundabout. Khaista turned north onto the next section of Highway 86. As they left Qaemyeh the road became single again, travelling almost due north now.

Mostly the road was straight, so she travelled mainly in the left hand lane – except where one lane was blocked. As they approached Nourabad the road became divided highway again and continued generally north through cultivated valleys, crossing the Fahliyan River.

After Baba Meydan the road turned more north west through another large cultivated valley. At Akbari it turned south west, following the Tang Shiv River downstream for a short distance, then crossing the cultivated valley of its north south tributary, before entering the mountains again, heading west through a narrow valley.

As the dry river turned south, then west, the road followed it, then turned north west through another wide cultivated valley. Here the road became divided highway once again and Khaista kept in the outside lane as much as possible.

As the road approached Gachsaran she came to a roundabout, with the airfield visible to the south. Beyond the roundabout she kept to the outside lane, turned left across the central divide, crossing the other half of the highway and stopped at the airport entrance, where she could see the blue and white flag of Israel flying.

'Gachsaran,' she announced. 'And it's just after eleven o'clock – or 23:00 hours, as you would say.'

Ali was instantly awake and gestured for Khaista to drive on into the airport. They were stopped in front of the gate by an armed sentry, who asked in English what they wanted.

'Sergeant Khan Ali Yusufzai of the Afghan National Army, for Captain Ben Ezra,' Ali said with authority. 'I need to make radio contact with Major Levine in Basra.'

'OK, sir,' the guard replied. 'Please wait here while I contact *Seren* Ben Ezra.'

'Thank you,' Ali replied.

The guard spoke into his radio. A few minutes passed and he returned. 'You can go through, sir. Turn right just inside the gate here and park in front of the terminal building. Captain Ben Ezra will meet you inside.'

'Thank you and *Shalom*,' said Ali.

'Shalom aleichem,' the private replied, as he opened the gate for them.

Khaista drove inside, turned right and parked in front of the building.

She and Ali got stiffly out of the pickup and walked to the entrance of the terminal building. The door was open and as they went through an olive-skinned man in IAF uniform approached them. *'Shalom aleichem,* welcome. I am *Seren* – Captain – Ben Ezra. You are a friend of Major Levine, I am told?'

'Yes,' said Ali, 'Sergeant Khan Ali Yusufzai. We served together in Kabul for four years.'

'Ahh, the bonds of military service – sometimes last a lifetime, eh? ' Ben Ezra replied. 'And who is this beautiful young lady, Ali?'

'This is my fiancee, Khaista Afridi.' Khaista smiled shyly at Moshe.

'You are very welcome, my dear. Have you travelled all the way from Kabul? How long have you been on the road?'

'We left Kabul on Saturday morning,' Khaista answered.

'Now, I believe you need to contact Major Levine?' Ben Ezra turned to Ali.

'Yes, if that is convenient,' Ali replied.

'Certainly, come this way. My sergeant – Allouf – is already making contact with their HQ in Basra.' He showed Ali and Khaista into a small office with a radio transmitter. Sergeant Allouf stood up and beckoned Ali over. I have *Rav Seren* Levine for you. Please go ahead.'

Ali took the mic from Sergeant Allouf and spoke to Shaul. 'Hi there, comrade – or should I call you *Rav Seren?* We have arrived in Gachsaran, as you can gather.'

'Ali, it's so good to hear your voice. How was your journey? You have arrived safely?'

'Yes, we are both safe and well. I will give you my report tomorrow when we arrive. I'm hoping we can stay here tonight.'

'I would think so, Ali. Let me talk to *Seren* Ben Ezra about that. I'll see you tomorrow evening, then. Have a safe journey home. *Shalom.'*

'Shalom, Shaul. and thank you,' Ali answered, handing the mic to Ben Ezra.

He waited beside Khaista as Ben Ezra spoke to Shaul in Hebrew.

When the radio call finished Ben Ezra came over to them. 'We can only offer you a mattress on the floor,' he apologised to Khaista. We have a small office that Khaista can use – we'll put a mattress in there for you. Ali, I'm afraid you'll have to bunk with the rest of the guys, OK?'

'Sure, said Ali, 'It's no problem. More comfortable than in the truck, where we've slept for the last two nights. We both have sleeping bags with us.'

'Ahh, good,' said Ben Ezra. 'Would you both like something to eat? We don't have any hot food at this time of the evening, but we could heat you up a pizza?'

'That would be great,' Ali answered. 'Yes, thank you,' agreed Khaista, smiling.

'OK,' said Ben Ezra. 'My sergeant here will organise that for you. Take them into the dining room, Allouf. *Leila tov* – good night. I'll see you both for breakfast in the morning.'

Allouf waited with Khaista while Ali retrieved their sleeping bags from the truck, then beckoned for them to follow him. 'My English not so good,' he explained. 'You like coffee, or tea?'

'Do you have de-caff coffee?' Khaista asked.

'I think so. Check in that cupboard' – he pointed. 'I will put the kettle on and then get the pizza.'

He filled the kettle and switched it on and walked to a large freezer. You like mushroom, eggplant, or tomato?' he asked. Ali looked at Khaista, who shrugged.

'Anything will do,' said Ali, 'er, eggplant.'

'In Israel is no meat and cheese together. No pepperoni pizza. No beef, no chicken. Only vegetable with cheese. *Kosher*,' he explained.

'No problem,' Ali assured him.

In a few minutes Ali and Khaista had made their own coffee and the pizza had been microwaved and was served on a large plate. Allouf handed them cutlery, then produced some coleslaw, salad and bread. 'Enjoy,' he said with a grin.

'Thank you,' they both said at once, tucking into the meal.

'My name is Yusuf,' he explained.

'Thank you, Yusuf,' Ali said. 'This is great.'

'You have come a long way?' he asked.

'Yes,' said Ali, his mouth full of pizza. He washed it down with some coffee. 'We drove here from Kabul – about two thousand seven hundred kilometres.'

'My family came to Israel from Morocco – many years ago. I think it was about five thousand kilometre. But I was born in Israel – a *sabra*. In Israel you will find people from every part of the world – from New Zealand, South Africa, the Middle East, South America, Europe. But now we are all Israelis. It is good that you come. You are Pashtun, yes?'

'Yes, we are both Pashtun – both from the tribe of Yusuf,' said Ali. My surname is Yusufzai. It means children of Yusuf. And Khaista's surname is Afridi, which means Efraim.'

'You are very welcome to Israel,' said Yusuf. 'We will finish here tomorrow, I think. Then we will go to another airport and repair it. We are helping to make the road safer for your people to travel home to Eretz Israel. After tomorrow transport planes will be able to land here and bring repair vehicles and ambulances to help your people.'

'Yes,' said Ali, 'And I'm going to be working with those patrols. As soon as we get to Basra we will be working with Major Levine and his staff to make the road safer.'

Ali and Khaista had now finished all the pizza and other food. They drained the last of their coffee.

'You would like to sleep, now?' asked Allouf.

'Yes,' they both replied, nodding.

'Beseder, OK, I show you where to go.'

Yusuf showed them where the washrooms where, then led them to the small office where Khaista was to sleep. He showed her the key in the door, so she could lock the door, if she wanted.

'Thank you very much,' she told him with a smile.

'No problem,' he said. *'Leila tov* – good night.

'OK, *Samal* Yusufzai, come with me.'

Ali said good night quickly to Khaista and followed *Samal* Allouf to his quarters.

21 – Caught Up, or Caught Out

Brandon had spent some time praying while he worked. Working with his hands he found freed his mind to pray and contemplate. Apart from his partner, Josh, several of the other men from his former church had come to see him and tell him they would like to hear more about end-time prophecy.

Finally, he made up his mind. Why not set up a couple of meetings in a local hotel and invite those who had shown an interest to come? If, after a week or two interest had waned, then the idea could easily be abandoned.

He shared his thoughts with Alyssa who, after they had prayed together, encouraged him to go ahead. The first meeting was arranged for a Thursday night – so as not to clash with any of the meetings of their former church. The topic he had decided to speak on was entitled, *'Caught up, or caught out! What is the Rapture?'*

Alyssa had organised a babysitter so she could be there to give moral support to her husband. When they arrived at the hotel function room almost fifty people had gathered. Brandon was pleasantly surprised. He had brought his guitar with him and led the group in a couple of well-known modern hymns before starting his talk.

Brandon had researched thoroughly for the meeting and spoke clearly from his prepared notes. The audience were attentive and several could be seen looking up the verses he quoted as he announced them. The gist of his talk was that yes, we would be caught up to meet Yeshua in the air when he returned, but that this would certainly NOT be a secret event.

'Look, he is coming with the clouds,' he quoted from Revelation 1:7, *'and every eye will see him, even those who pierced him; and all peoples on earth will mourn because of him. So shall it be! Amen.*

'Now how on earth can that be a secret?' he asked. 'Every eye will see him. All the nations will mourn. That's about as public as you can get. This is no 'secret rapture.' It's not even called the rapture – Yeshua called it the resurrection. When will this happen? When will all the nations mourn? Yeshua tells us himself in Matthew 24:29-31:

'Immediately after the distress of those days,' he read, *'the sun will be darkened, and the moon will not give its light; the stars will fall from the sky, and the heavenly bodies will be shaken.*

'Then will appear the sign of the Son of Man in heaven. And then all the peoples of the earth will mourn when they see the Son of Man coming on the clouds of heaven, with power and great glory. And he will send his angels with a loud trumpet call, and they will gather his elect from the four winds, from one end of the heavens to the other.'

'Immediately after the great distress – the tribulation, that is – the sun will be darkened. When will we be caught up? When we see the sun darkened and the moon turned to blood – at the same time. This is not a solar eclipse, or a lunar eclipse, because it is impossible for those two things both to happen at the same time. This is something else – a unique supernatural event.

'All the peoples on the earth will mourn – why? Because they see the Son of Man coming on the clouds of heaven. There will be a loud trumpet call – again there's no secret about this. A *loud* trumpet call! And then the angels will gather his elect from the four winds. *Only then* will we be caught up – gathered up – to be with him as he returns to earth to reign.

'Paul tells us the exact same story, in 2nd Thessalonians 2. *'Concerning the coming of our Lord, Yeshua the Messiah and our being gathered to him',* he says. What's he talking about here? Our being gathered to him – to Yeshua. That's the same thing Yeshua himself told us – when the angels will gather us up.

'But Paul goes on to tell us, *'That day will NOT come until the rebellion occurs and the man of lawlessness is revealed, the man doomed to destruction. He will oppose and will exalt himself over everything that is called God or is worshipped, so that he sets himself up in God's temple, proclaiming himself to be God.'*

'When will we be caught up? *After* the sun is darkened. *After* the man of lawlessness is revealed. *After* the temple is built. *After* the distress of those days – great distress, Yeshua says. Great tribulation! After, after, and after!

'So, could Yeshua return at any moment? Definitely not! Not until *after* – after what?' Brandon waited for a response. 'After what?' he shouted.

Chapter 21 – Caught Up, or Caught Out

One man answered, 'After the sun is darkened.'

'Yes, indeed,' said Brandon. 'After what?'

'After the Son of Man appears in the clouds,' another man replied.

'Yes, correct. After what?' he asked again.

'After the man of lawlessness is revealed,' said another.

'Yes,' replied Brandon. 'After what?'

There was silence for a minute and then a young man put his hand up. 'Go ahead,' said Brandon.

'After the Great Tribulation?' he said hesitantly.

'Yes, again,' said Brandon. 'So, when will we be caught up – *after* the gospel is preached to every nation, *after* the new temple is built. *after* the falling away, *after* the man of lawlessness is revealed, *after* the Great Tribulation, *after* the sun is darkened, and *after* the Son of Man appears in the clouds. *Then* – and only then – will he send his angels to gather us up. *Then* we will be caught up to meet him in the air. *Then* we will be with the Lord forever.'

'In Revelation 7 we read about 144,000 Israelites who are sealed by God, and then we read about another *'great multitude that no one could count, from every nation, tribe, people and language, standing before the throne and before the Lamb. They were wearing white robes and were holding palm branches in their hands. And they cried out in a loud voice: 'Salvation belongs to our God, who sits on the throne, and to the Lamb.'*

' *"Who are these people?"* John is asked by one of the elders. He doesn't know, but he is given the answer. The elder said, *"These are they who have come out of the great tribulation; they have washed their robes and made them white in the blood of the Lamb."*

'There is no *other* great multitude mentioned – the great multitude who were caught up in the secret rapture, for example? Where are they? They are not mentioned – because they don't exist! There is only *one* great multitude – those who came out of great tribulation.

'In Revelation 20 John says, *'I saw thrones on which were seated those who had been given authority to judge. And I saw the souls of those who had been beheaded because of their testimony about Jesus and because of the word of God. They had not worshipped the beast or its image and had not received its mark on their foreheads or their hands. They came to life and reigned with Messiah for a thousand years.'*

'Only one great multitude – who come out of great tribulation, who were beheaded for their testimony of Yeshua. Brothers and sisters we need to be prepared for trouble. We need to be prepared to lose our very lives for Yeshua's sake. And we need to stop believing in this fantasy, this powerful delusion – of a secret rapture!

'Back in 2nd Thessalonians 2 Paul tells us that, *'The coming of the lawless one will be in accordance with how Satan works. He will use all sorts of displays of power through signs and wonders that serve the lie, and all the ways that wickedness deceives those who are perishing. They perish because they refused to love the truth and so be saved. For this reason God sends them a powerful delusion so that they will believe the lie and so that all will be condemned who have not believed the truth but have delighted in wickedness.'*

'Because people – yes, even God's people – refuse to love the truth, God will send them a powerful delusion so they will believe the lie. What is the lie? Well, one of the lies is this teaching of a secret rapture. There will be other lies, no doubt, but this is an important one for us at this point in time. Instead of trusting in a lie – a delusion – that we are about to be 'beamed up' out of all trouble on earth, we should be preparing our hearts and minds to stand strong in the day of trouble.

'We have seen our brothers and sisters in the Middle East, in Iran, in various parts of Africa, in China, North Korea and Vietnam – shot, crucified, burned and beheaded for their faith in Yeshua. Why do we think *we* in America ought to be different? Trouble is coming to the whole world. And trouble is coming to America.

'We want to be 'caught up' on that day, but we don't want to be among those who believe the lie and end up being 'caught out' – do we?'

Brandon allowed the pause to lengthen and his words to sink in.

'Next week I'll be talking specifically about the trouble that is coming to America and how we should respond to it. In the meantime, if you have any questions about tonight's topic please feel free to ask them now.'

With difficulty, Brandon managed to keep the questions 'on topic', by firmly refusing those that were about other subjects relating to bible prophecy.

Chapter 21 – Caught Up, or Caught Out

Several people came up to him afterwards and thanked him for presenting things so clearly, saying they would definitely be coming back next week to hear more.

Brandon turned to Alyssa as they climbed into their car to go home, 'Well, I think that went OK?'

'I think you presented it very clearly, darling. You really made people think. They are not used to someone really spelling it out from scripture like that – it was refreshing. Well done!'

'Well, darling, all I can do is fill myself with His word and then let it out, in the expectation that the Holy Spirit will anoint my words and really bring the truth home to people's hearts.'

'Well,' she replied, 'I think you achieved that tonight.'

In One Hour – Babylon will fall – *Raymond McCullough*

22 – Home Run

Tuesday

Ali and Khaista joined Ben Ezra, Allouf and the other IAF men for breakfast. 'You are welcome to fill up your tank before you leave,'Ben Ezra told them. In fact, if you wait another day, you could get a lift back by *Hercules*? The first one could be coming as early as tomorrow morning.'

Ali looked at Khaista and answered, 'No, thank you, I think we'll complete the journey in the truck. That way we'll be familiar with the whole route. But we'll be happy to fill up with diesel, thank you.'

Ben Ezra wished them good luck and left Allouf to show them the diesel pump. Ali filled up the tank and the empty jerrycans and they said goodbye to Sergeant Allouf and set off towards Basra. As they drove into Gachsaran, some of the convoy turned left at the first roundabout onto the Belt Way which bypassed the rest of the city on the south west. Ali opted to drive straight on and took the left half of the divided highway until they reached the next roundabout, north of the city.

From here on the road was single carriageway, though straight, and Ali kept in the outside lane wherever possible. Gachsaran was enclosed by mountains and these drew closer as the road led north. The road wound through them, emerging into a valley, narrow at first, but widening into a wide cultivated area which they followed north west, until the hills closed in once again.

The road continued straight and Ali was able to make reasonable time. After an intersection the road turned west into a wide valley, eventually crossing it and heading north into hills once again. As they came out of these they descended into another cultivated plain surrounding the city of Behbahan. Ali followed the Ring Road around the north east of the city and continued across the plain into mountains once again.

There were too many bends on this section of road for much overtaking and progress was slow for the next twenty kilometres, or so.

Eventually, the road left the mountains for the last time, travelling north west in a straight line, heading for Omidiyeh. The highway became divided again just south of the city and skirted it to the east, then the north as Ali turned west at the roundabout.

At the next roundabout – on the western edge of the city – Ali spotted Peled's checkpoint on the right hand side, just off the roundabout, with an Israeli flag flying from the building behind. He pulled in to the right and stopped beside the first of the two tanks.

'*Shalom aleichem,*' he greeted the soldier on duty. Ali explained who he was and what his duties would soon be. The soldier, thankfully, spoke good English and chatted to Ali about the problems they had experienced with members of the convoy – communication being one of the prime concerns.

After a few minutes, Ali indicated that they needed to move on and asked Khaista if she wanted to drive for a while. 'We've left the mountains behind, now,' he told her. 'It's all flat land from here to the River, and the roads should be pretty straight.'

Ali jumped down from the truck and got back in on the passenger side, while Khaista slid into the driver's seat, started the engine and pulled out carefully into the convoy again. For most of the way she was able to keep to the left hand lane, overtaking the slower vehicles. The surroundings were now completely flat and barren. As Khaista drew near to Bandar Mahshahr she noticed the convoy was moving onto the other half of the divided highway. As they got closer she could see cones and an Israeli soldier waving the traffic across laconically.

'Roadworks,' she said to Ali, 'Your friends at work, presumably?'

'OK,' he replied. 'maybe we should stop and introduce ourselves.'

As they came up to the soldier, Khaista indicated right and pulled over beside him. '*Shalom,*' she greeted him.

'*Shalom,*' he replied. 'Are you in trouble?'

Ali leaned over and entered the conversation. 'No, no trouble,' he said, 'But we'd like to speak to the engineer in charge of the repairs.'

Ali quickly explained who he was and what his role would be from tomorrow. The young soldier nodded and allowed them to continue down their own side of the highway until they came up to the machines working on the road. They stopped again and asked the men for the engineer. One of the soldiers pointed a little further down the highway and they thanked him, driving on for another few hundred metres.

The engineer – Abrahams – was happy to explain what they were doing, once he understood who Ali was and what his future role would be in the operation. 'This section has several missile damage craters. We just fill in the craters and compact the material with a vibrating roller, then we put down a layer of asphalt and roll it in.

'Any excess material we collect and take to our storage depot – which right now is beside Bandar Mahshahr Airport. That's were we store the machinery at the end of the day for the moment as well. There is very little stone in this area, so we collect up what we don't need for future use.

'We work from dawn until dusk, six days a week. It's maybe three hours, or more, back to base so we only go back there now on Friday for Shabbat – we'd lose too much time otherwise. In the near future, the plan will be for patrols to bring us supplies by air to Gachsaran, then drop it off to us as they pass back this way.

'Our main problem is getting asphalt way out here. At the moment it comes all the way from a plant in Jordan – until we can get an asphalt plant working closer to here. The trucks are tippers, fitted with hot boxes – which have gas heaters to keep the asphalt hot. Anyway, I'll look forward to seeing you in the future. Welcome to Israel, my friend.'

'Thank you,' said Ali as he returned to his truck and Khaista negotiated her way past the other machines and soldiers working on the road. At the end of the repaired section she merged with the convoy traffic returning to the right hand side of the highway and moved into the left hand lane again.

'Well,' said Ali, 'that gave me an idea of what they are doing to repair these roads.'

'Good,' she answered, concentrating on overtaking a large truck ahead.

As they approached Bandar Mahshahr, more convoy traffic merged from Highway 43 to their right. The divided highway continued around the north and west of Mahshahr and passed the airport to the north of the road. Ahead a truck loaded with waste road spoil was turning off to the right. Ali pointed to the Israeli flag. 'Looks like that's where they have their depot,' he said. 'We don't need to follow the truck but we could stop here for some lunch.'

'OK,' said Khaista, turning off to the right and parking. They opened a tin of curry and ate it with some fresh pitta bread – provided to them earlier by Ben Ezra and Allouf – finishing with some fruit and drinking the once again warm bottled water. The empty truck, meanwhile, re-emerged from the depot and merged back into the convoy, moving into the outside lane and turning left across the central reservation to return to the repair site.

Ali took the wheel again and they rejoined the highway. '13:30 hours,' he remarked. I think we'll arrive in Basra in about another four hours. The highway has been repaired from here on – no more craters to dodge around – so we should be able to make good time in the outer lane.

After they passed through the centre of Sarbandar they were on an open highway heading west again. Ali noticed a convoy of three Israeli *Hummvees* ahead on the other side of the highway. Ahead, on his own side, a pickup truck had stopped at the side of the road and the convoy was manoeuvring around it. The Israeli vehicles had now pulled up opposite the parked vehicle on the empty side of the highway. Ali pulled in behind the pickup and joined the Israeli soldier at the parked truck.

It turned out that none of the occupants of the vehicle spoke any English – apart from the driver saying, 'Help us, please.' The Israeli soldier tried to ask in English what the problem was, but his lack of a common language defeated the driver, 'No English, no English, ' he repeated.

Ali approached the officer. 'Perhaps I can help?' he asked.

'You speak English? Good!' the soldier replied. 'Ask him what the problem is, please.'

Ali spoke to the driver in Pashto, asking what was the matter. It appeared that the vehicle had simply run out of diesel. There were jerrycans in the back of the pickup, but apparently they were all empty. Ali explained to the soldier.

'Unfortunately, we don't have any more fuel with us,' the soldier replied. 'We used the last can half an hour ago. We have a fuel depot down the road in Abadan, but we'll have to tow him there and fill him up then. Can you explain that to him?'

Chapter 22 – Home Run

'I can do better than that,' said Ali. 'We have extra fuel in our own pickup. We can let him have a can.'

'That's great,' the soldier replied. 'Can you get the can and put it in, while I get one of our mechanics over. We'll probably have to bleed the fuel system before it will start again.'

'No problem,' said Ali, explaining first to the driver, then returning to his own truck for a can of diesel, while the soldier went to get his crew organised.

By the time Ali had returned with a can of fuel, and began to pour it into the filler, a mechanic had arrived. 'Tell him to open the hood,' he asked Ali. Ali repeated this and the driver opened the hood of the vehicle. The mechanic set down a toolbox and began to work at the fuel line for several minutes.

'Tell him to try starting it now,' he said to Ali. Ali spoke again to the driver, who turned the key. Thankfully, the engine spluttered into life and then ran smoothly.

The driver offered his thanks to Ali and the mechanic.

'Tell him that it is another seventy kilometres to Abadan. He will need to fill up when he gets there.'

Ali repeated this instruction.

'The mechanic continued, 'When he comes into Abadan there is a very large roundabout. Take the second exit and, past a row of small trees, he will see the depot on the right. OK?'

Ali repeated these instructions to the driver, who repeated them back to him carefully. 'Yes,' Ali told him. *'Salaam alekum, Shalom!'*

He told the mechanic that the driver understood.

'Shukran!' the driver said as he filtered back into the convoy.

'Thank you,' the mechanic said to Ali, 'I'm Shlomo. You've been very helpful.'

'Actually, you'll probably be seeing more of me in future,' Ali confided. 'I'll soon be joining your patrols. I am a friend of Major Levine, from his time in Kabul. My fiancee and I will be based with you in Basra.'

'Ahh,' the soldier's face lit up. *'Tov ma'od* – very good! I'll see you soon, then. *L'hitraot!'*

The soldier followed his mechanic back to their *Hummvee* and the Israeli patrol headed on down the empty right hand side of the highway.

Ali followed the now mobile pickup into the traffic flow again. 'I guess that's the sort of thing I'll be doing a lot more of,' he said, as he accelerated past it. 'None of those guys spoke any English at all.'

'Well, it's great you were able to help, then,' she replied.

In another hour and a half they were approaching the same roundabout that Ali had been describing to the driver. He took the second exit, following the convoy, then turned right into an enclosed yard area. At each side of the entrance a tracked APC was parked. The pickup that Ali had helped earlier arrived shortly after to fill up with diesel.

Ali once again explained who he was to the enquiring soldiers, receiving smiles in return, once they understood. One of them offered to show him around the depot and pointed out the fuel hoses. A tanker arrived at that point and pulled into the entrance.

'More diesel arriving,' the soldier explained. 'Who'd ever have thought we'd be exporting diesel to Iran, eh?'

Ali laughed and thanked him, *'La-hee-tra-oh?'* he tried out in Hebrew.

'L'hitraot!' the soldier repeated, with emphasis on the last syllable.

'L'hitraot!' Ali repeated, getting back into his truck.

The road took them through the middle of Abadan, which obviously had seen a lot of damage – though the rubble had now been bulldozed into the side streets. They crossed the bridge over the Bahmanshir River and drove past more piles of rubble which had been bulldozed to one side to leave the roadway clear. The road took them north west, close to the huge Shatt Al-Arab River. In a couple of kilometres they were in Khorramshahr and crossed the Bahmanshir River once again in the middle of it.

Four kilometres on they came to another Israeli checkpoint, where a road led off to the left, towards the River. Two soldiers were directing some of the traffic down this road, then some straight on.

'Let's try out this new bridge that Shaul has been building,' said Ali. 'I think this must be the way to it.'

Chapter 22 – Home Run

'OK,' Khaista replied.

As Ali approached the junction he indicated to the soldier on duty that he wanted to turn left. The soldier waved him on. The convoy had slowed to a crawl, proceeding slowly for two kilometres to the River, where they could see the traffic crossing the wide expanse of water on a pontoon bridge.

'It must have just opened, I think,' said Ali.

'It looks like quite a feat of engineering,' Khaista remarked.

They drove slowly onto the bridge, which seemed quite secure. At the other end a newly surfaced road led across the island to a metal bridge formed of two tracks.

'This looks a bit less secure,' Khaista said, as they drove onto it.

'No, it's solid as a rock,' Ali commented.

Another stretch of newly surfaced road led to a second pontoon bridge – only about a third of the length of the huge one they had just crossed. After they crossed another short section of new road led to the existing highway running west and then north west. In less than an hour they were in Basra and coming to the Highway 31 junction.

'We need to head east now, I think – towards the northern bridge that Shaul told me about. His email should be with the maps.' Ali swung north east at the butterfly junction ahead, onto a much less major road. It was obviously the right one as there was now a continual stream of traffic coming towards them, merging behind them with the north-bound traffic from Highway 6.

'Yes, found it,' said Khaista, producing a printout of Shaul's instructions. He says to cross the Sinbad Island bridge – I presume we are heading towards it?'

'Yes,' said Ali. 'But we turn right just before it I think?'

'Yes, only it obviously says left here, being from the opposite direction. He says, *"When you cross the bridge you cross over Dinar Street and then turn left out of the flow of traffic."*

'OK,' said Ali, 'we're approaching a small bridge now – I think this is the new road Shaul was making. I don't think there's room for traffic from our direction, but look, there's another small bridge ahead, beyond the convoy. Ali indicated left and waited for a driver to let him through. He drove another couple of hundred metres along what was now a dirt road, then turned right and, after another hundred metres, crossed a small bridge.

'OK, this brings us back to the main route. There's a turn to the right here, if we can get straight across the convoy traffic.' He edged forward and managed to get across the convoy flow once again.

Khaista read from the email again, *"'About one kilometre south east the road turns north again. Keep going north (do NOT turn right, or cross the small waterway)."'*

Ali kept driving until the road turned sharply left. He rounded the corner and kept straight on, forking to the left as the road approached a right hand turn. 'What else does it say?' he asked.

"'Our HQ is the Shatt Al-Arab Hotel just a few hundred metres along the waterway. You will see trucks, Hummvees and APCs parked at the rear entrance."'

'OK,' said Ali, 'I see some trucks, *Hummvees*, buses … this must be it.'

Ali turned left, parked the pickup beside a *Hummvee* and switched off the engine.

'We're here. We made it! 3,103 kilometres we've covered,' he said, looking at the gauge. Ali reached over and pulled Khaista towards him and kissed her, Khaista responding enthusiastically.

'I could get used to this,' he told her quietly.

'Me too,' she said, looking at him from under her dark eyelashes. They drank in one another for a few minutes, then Ali said, 'I suppose we'd better report in.'

Khaista sighed, 'I guess so.'

'Just think,' Ali said, 'We'll be married, soon.'

Khaista looked at him and smiled again, 'Yes, Ali. Very soon.'

23 – Riverside Reunion

Tuesday evening

As they left the pickup truck Ali took Khaista by the hand and they entered the back door of the Shatt Al-Arab Hotel. They approached the reception desk and found a young girl in IDF uniform there.

'*Shalom,* hello,' said Ali, continuing in English, 'I am Sergeant Khan Ali Yusufzai, from Kabul, Afghanistan. I need to report to Major Levine. Is he here?'

'Just a moment,' the girl answered, lifting a phone. 'She spoke in Hebrew, but Ali made out the words *'Rav Seren',* 'Yusufzai' and 'Kabul'.

She put the phone down and asked Ali and Khaista to follow her. Ali looked at Khaista and they walked after her, Ali still holding Khaista's hand. Ali was still trying to get used to the idea of a girl being a soldier. *Yes, they really do things differently in the Israeli Army*, he thought.

The girl stopped at an office and smiled at them, directing them to enter. Khaista saw a larger man in uniform grab hold of Ali and embrace him.

'Ali, my old buddy,' Shaul said. It's so great to see you again.'

He let go of Ali and turned to Khaista, 'And you must be Khaista,' he said smiling, as he shook her hand.

'Well, Ali, you sure picked a beautiful one,' he said.

'I certainly did,' Ali replied. 'Even her name – Khaista – means 'beautiful'.'

'Well, Khaista,' said Shaul, 'Welcome to Basra. This is my office – and now it will be yours, too. We'll have to find a desk for you and a computer. But enough about work. I'll introduce you to the guys tomorrow at breakfast. We usually plan the day then. I expect you could do with a day's R&R, though – after such a long journey.

'Yes, that would be good,' Ali answered.

'Well sit down, both of you. There's someone I want you both to meet. Excuse me for just a minute. Would you like a cold drink, a beer, coffee?'

'Er, a soft drink for Khaista, I think,' said Ali, looking at Khaista, who nodded, 'And I'd really welcome a cold beer, thanks. For some reason all the bars were shut on the way here from Kabul!'

'Imagine that!' said Shaul, 'Coming right up,' and he disappeared through the door.'

In a few minutes he returned with the two drinks, followed by another female soldier, carrying another two beers. This one was a little older than the first and quite striking looking – even in the khaki IDF uniform.

Shaul handed the drinks to Khaista and Ali and closed the office door, Bekkah handing him a beer for himself. 'Ali, Khaista, this is *Segen Mishne* – Second Lieutenant – Rebekkah Bar-Ilan. Bekkah, this is my friend and former ANA sergeant, Khan Ali Yusufzai, and his fiancée, Khaista.'

They greeted one another enthusiastically.

'What you don't know, Ali, is that Bekkah and I are what we in America would call 'an item'. We've been seeing each other on leave, but none of my other staff are aware of this. So, you both have to swear to secrecy.'

'That is wonderful,' said Khaista, 'I wish you happiness, both of you.'

'Yes, congratulations, comrade,' said Ali.

'And congratulations on your engagement, Khaista and Ali,' said Rebekkah.'

'Yes, indeed,' Shaul agreed.

'When we get some leave – in a few weeks, I hope – Bekkah and I plan to show you a little bit of Israel. Oh, that reminds me,' he said, pulling out a drawer of his desk, 'Here is your new bank card and a check book. Welcome to Israel, buddy.'

'Thank you,' Ali said.

'Yes, thank you indeed for all you have done for us,' said Khaista.

'Well, you two are a part of Israel from now on. Tomorrow we'll get you to fill in a few forms for the *New Israel Plan* and the Interior

Chapter 23 – Riverside Reunion

Ministry, but we'll forget about all that for now. I take it you both must be quite hungry by now?'

'Yes, we could maybe eat something,' Ali replied.

'OK, how about we take some food and beer – juice, if you prefer, Khaista – and we'll have a picnic meal away from all this *aliyah* business, just for tonight? Rebekkah, could you organise something with Junbalat, maybe?'

'Sure,' Rebekkah replied, smiling. 'Not often I get such an offer around here,' she winked at Ali and Khaista.

She left the office again and Shaul sat down behind his desk, encouraging them to be seated also.

He told Ali a little of what they had been doing. 'You know, just this afternoon we finished the new bridge we've been building.'

'I know,' said Ali, 'We decided to come over it. It is an excellent job.'

'Ahh, OK, so you didn't come over Sinbad Island, then, obviously. Well, that means a quick change of plan, then. Instead of going downriver, we'll go upriver. There are two more bridges – both pontoon ones – but they're really too far away to be of use to the convoys. One would mean a diversion of about forty five kilometres and the other about eighty kilometres.

'But we've kept them intact in case an emergency situation arises – a problem with one of the other bridges, for instance. Anyway, I thought we'd take a trip along the river and find a quiet spot to eat and talk.'

'So, how did you build such a complicated bridge so quickly,' Ali asked.

'Well, we had the co-operation of both the Israeli Navy and the Air Force. The Air Force supplied us with two huge helicopters – one operating up north to dismantle the original bridges. The other helicopter – the one we travelled across Iran on – we used to carry our machinery across, including the smaller bridge between the islands. A team were building that bridge while we were building the pontoon bridge on this side.

'Then, when all the sections had been loaded from up north, the second helicopter joined us down here and we built the eastern bridge in two places – using both helicopters – motoring rafted sections across to connect into the bridge as they were assembled, then anchoring them in place. A team will have to run the boat engines every day to keep the batteries charged and the bilges pumping out.'

'It sounds like a great example of co-operation. In most countries there is not so much liaison between the different forces.'

'Ahh, but in Israel there is really only one force – the Israeli Defence Forces. Since this war started there has been a lot of co-operation between Army, Navy and Air Force.'

At this point Rebekkah re-appeared and told them she had organised some food and drinks, thanks to Junbalat and his volunteer cooks. 'He's getting it carried out to a *Hummvee* as we speak,' she told them.

'Great,' said Shaul. 'Well, I vote we celebrate this evening – Ali and Khaista's safe arrival, the completion of the bridge and being able to share our relationship with someone.'

'You may be able to add another item to that list,' Ali said. 'Sergeant Allouf told us this morning that they were hoping to have the repairs to the Gachsaran airport completed today. Of course, they might have had a last minute hold-up.'

Just then the radio crackled and Shaul answered the call. *'Ken,'* he said. *'Tov ma'od, Seren, tov ma'od. Toda.'* There was some more conversation, then Shaul ended the call with *'Beseder, l'hitraot!'*

Shaul turned back to the others, 'Well, you were correct, Ali. That was *Seren* Ben Ezra reporting that Gachsaran airport is now operational. A tanker aircraft of aviation fuel is on its way to fill up the tanks, there. So we can start using the airport from tomorrow.'

'That is good news,' said Ali. 'You will be able to do more patrols now, yes?'

'Yes, Ali. Our patrols will spend less time getting out there and will have more time available to help those *olim* in need. Sorry, *olim* means immigrants – like you and Khaista.'

'Olim,' Ali repeated. 'I understood the the phrase, *'L'hitraot!'* – 'see you' and *'Seren'* means 'Captain', I think?'

'Yes,' Shaul answered.

'And *'beseder'*, this means 'Yes'?' he asked.

'Actually, it means, OK,' said Shaul. The word for yes, is *Ken.'*

'Ken,' Al repeated again. 'And how do you say, 'No'?'

Chapter 23 – Riverside Reunion

'Lo,' Shaul answered, 'similar to the Arabic, *'la'.'*

'Ahh, *ken,'* said Ali. 'Thank you – oh, how do I say that?'

'Thank you is *toda,'* Shaul answered, 'Or *toda rabah* – thank you very much.'

'Beseder, toda rabah,' said Ali, smiling.

'Listen, you guys have had a very tiring journey. How about we just use English, tonight. We'll go for a drive, have our picnic, then have an early night. You can both join our team for breakfast and take the day off after that, OK?'

'Beseder,' said Ali, determined to learn these new phrases.

'OK, said Khaista.'

Shaul led them out to the *Hummvee* and gestured for Ali to get in the front beside him. Rebekkah and Khaista got into the back and immediately began chatting. Next to the *Hummvee* was one of the new *CombatGuard* APCs.

Ali asked, 'What is this vehicle? I have not seen one before.'

Shaul gave him the details of the Israeli made vehicle as they drove towards Sinbad Bridge, crossing the convoy. The traffic was still coming towards them, but on the island they were able to use the small roundabout to cross through the traffic and drive onto the northern pontoon, which was empty.

'We use this bridge for our own use, for travelling east *and* west,' Shaul explained. 'That leaves the other three bridges for the convoys going east to west.'

'Were the original bridges destroyed in the recent war,' Ali asked.

'No, the Brits destroyed them in 2001, when the US-led coalition forces invaded Iraq. I think the Brits built the pontoon bridges. I heard a story that they had help from a local Iraqi who owned a large mobile crane.

'When the bridge was completed and newly opened the crane driver then brought his crane over from east to west, but the weight of it collapsed the bridge at the western end. Apparently they had to use cutting gear to dismantle and then repair the bridge!'

'I don't think that crane driver would have been popular, eh Shaul?'

'Definitely not,' Shaul agreed.

They crossed the convoy into the right hand lane, with the help of the soldiers on the check-point, and drove rapidly north east. After crossing a small waterway Shaul slowed down and indicated to turn left, sounding his horn. A truck driver obligingly slowed and allowed them to cross through the convoy traffic again into a side road heading north parallel to the river.

The road was some distance from the Shatt Al-Arab Waterway, but as they travelled north, crossing another small water channel and then a new road that had been once been under construction, it drew quite close to the river. It followed the river as it curved westward then, as it separated from the river again, just across another water channel, Shaul turned left into a small lane, leading almost to the water's edge and turning to follow the River, separated from it only by small fields.

Eventually, the track led to a road running east-west, crossing the River on a pontoon bridge. Shaul drove across this bridge and turned south into a road running along the riverbank. He pulled up close to the water and switched off the engine.'Let's eat,' he said.

Rebekkah opened the hamper which Junbalat had provided for them and shared out chicken, salad and bread, along with cold beer from a cooler. Khaista, who had never drunk beer before, decided to try it.

'It's an acquired taste,' Rebekkah warned her. 'You probably won't enjoy it at first – but it *is* cold. I acquired the taste from my two brothers when I was a lot younger,' she said. 'If you don't like it there's grape juice and other stuff in there.'

Khaista took a drink of the Israeli beer and made a face, but continued to drink, 'The best thing about it is as you say, Rebekkah – that it is cold.'

Shaul and Ali ate and drank heartily and they watched as the shadows lengthened from the trees and buildings behind them. Soon all the food had gone and they relaxed, drinking more of the beer.

Ali asked Khaista if she would like to walk along the bank a little way and she agreed, 'Not too far, though.'

As she climbed down out of the vehicle she stumbled into Ali's arms, 'Oopsh!' she cried. Ali took her hand and they walked slowly along the bank southwards, away from the bridge.

'I think maybe Khaista is a little tipsy from the beer,' said Shaul, laughing, as Rebekkah climbed into the front beside him.

'I think they're really cute, actually,' replied Rebekkah, snuggling close to Shaul. 'They're both so innocent, coming from such a religious Muslim country.

'Yes,' said Shaul, 'they're gonna find things very different in Israel when they eventually get there. It'll be a bit of a culture shock.'

'It could be a culture shock for us, too, when we see how much things must have changed already,' Rebekkah said thoughtfully. 'A lot more black and swarthy people around, I would think.'

'People will just have to get used to it,' Shaul said, pulling Rebekkah close to his side and kissing her enthusiastically.

Their conversation dwindled.

After a while Ali and Khaista returned, holding hands, and got into the back seat. Shaul started the *Hummvee* again and turned it around, turning west into the road that crossed the bridge. The main road south – connecting to Highway 6 – was less than a kilometre away and soon they were speeding down a completely empty highway, slowing only where there was damage and then accelerating on.

Ali spoke up from the rear seat as they were driving into Basra, 'It has been so strange to drive through cities where there are no lights, at all – and no people.'

'No power, no infrastructure, whatsoever,' Shaul agreed.

When they arrived back, Rebekkah showed Khaista to a room already occupied by two Israeli girl soldiers, both of whom spoke English, and Shaul led Ali to his quarters – sharing a room with Junbalat, Lev and Gold. 'See you in the morning, Ali. *Leila tov* – good night,' he said.

'Leila tov,' Ali repeated.

24 – Good News in Triplicate

Wednesday

At 07:00 on Wednesday morning Shaul called a meeting with his staff over breakfast. A smallish dark-skinned man was seated with Shaul and beside him a beautiful olive-skinned woman, with long dark hair and dark eyes. Most of the men were were trying to avoid staring at her too obviously – she was certainly noticed.

'Comrades,'Shaul began in English, 'you've heard me mention my friend Ali Yusufzai, from Afghanistan – this is Khan Ali, otherwise known as Zai. And this beautiful lady – whom I met for the first time last night – is his fiancée, Khaista Afridi.'

There were handshakes and greetings all around the table, Khaista smiling shyly at all the attention she was receiving.

Shaul continued, 'Both Ali and Khaista will be joining our team here. Neither of them speak Hebrew, although they will start learning it soon, but they both have good English. Khaista will become my personal assistant and computer operator. Although Ali obviously has no official standing with the IDF, he was only discharged a few days ago from the Afghan National Army, where he was a sergeant – so, perhaps we could treat him as an honorary sergeant?

'Ali will be useful as a translator – as he and Khaista speak both Pashto and Dari. I'd like him to get up to speed with our operation here as soon as possible, so he will be sitting in on our meetings and also going out on patrols. They just arrived by pickup truck last night, so I think we'll give them both a day to recuperate before putting them to work.

'By the way, remember a guy called Daoud? He was the guy who translated for us on our way here from Amman? Command say they're sending him to us on a plane today, so we'll have two translators – actually three, counting Khaista here, whom I soon hope to get designing some leaflets in Pashto and Dari that we can hand out to the convoys.

'*Beseder,* the next good news is that our new bridge was completed yesterday afternoon. Peled has already set up a checkpoint which is directing part of the convoy traffic towards it.'

'Yes, sir,' Peled replied. 'I've moved a couple of *Namer* APCs to Khorramshahr, where they can steer part of the convoy towards the dock and the new bridge.'

'And once across,' Shaul continued, 'the convoy can move north on Highway 6, then onto Highway 31 past Basra Airport – bypassing the city altogether. With three bridges now allowing traffic east to west, that effectively speeds up convoy movement by about fifty percent.

'And we have more good news today,' Shaul added. 'Gachsaran Airport is now operational. I received word from *Seren* Ben Ezra yesterday evening that his team have completed the repairs to the runway and a tanker aircraft carrying aviation fuel was on its way to replenish the tanks at the airfield. They sent a team out to man and operate the airfield on the same plane.

'The patrol helicopters will also be able to operate from Gachsaran from now on – instead of Basra – but we'll have to bring any casualties back from there in our plane. So, we'll need a couple of medical personnel on hand there to take over from the helicopter crew, until our next plane arrives. Bar-Ilan, can you organise that?'

'*Beseder,*' Rebekkah answered. 'We'll need someone out there on the first plane, really.'

'Yes,' Shaul agreed. 'I've contacted Southern Command with the news and requested that a *Hercules C-130J* transport aircraft be made available to help us patrol the convoy. It will arrive this morning. So, everything is ready for the next stage. Peled's idea is about to be put into operation.

'And with the new bridge now speeding things up at this end,' he said, 'we can move our whole operation forward a step. Eventually, I believe, we will end up being responsible for patrolling from the Afghan and Pakistan borders all the way back here to Basra. Ben Ezra is ready to move his team and equipment to another airport, so we need to decide which one we want him to concentrate on first.

'We have four options,' he continued, moving to the map of Iran on his office wall. 'From west to east we have Sirjan, Bam, Zahedan and Zabol.' Shaul pointed to the four locations on the map.

'In terms of time to repair I believe from Ben Ezra that the three furthest airports will be the easiest to make operational. However, if we choose to make Sirjan operational first, we can then extend our operation a logical step further.'

'What is the distance from Sirjan to Gachsaran, sir?' asked Tamari.

Shaul consulted his notebook, then replied, 'Just over six hundred and fifty kilometres – normally an eight hour journey without the convoy slowing you down.'

'So, a pretty long day's patrol for us,' Peled observed. 'We'll need extra fuel with us, too.'

'Yes,' Shaul agreed. 'Quite a long day. So we won't be able to send the same patrol out two days in a row – we'll need to alternate the patrols.

'I think the plan should be to drop off three vehicles per plane – probably *Hummvees*, rather than APCs – at Gachsaran. One would be loaded with water and fruit, etc.; one as an ambulance with medics and the third with mechanics and spares – similar to our present operation. For this first leg our patrols will be returning to base here in Basra.

'I'm proposing we use one transport aircraft, which will return to Basra and load up a second patrol – probably a minimum three hour round trip, plus a bit of time for refuelling and loading up. Let's say we can have a patrol heading out every four hours. That should give us a good deal more control of the situation.

'I've also asked for a second Hercules. When that arrives we can extend our operation to Sirjan. The second plane will carry three vehicles, same as the first, but the patrols will travel onwards to Sirjan, rest overnight, then patrol the convoy back to Gachsaran and will then need to rest before being flown back to Sirjan again. We'll need a proper base set up at both Sirjan and Gachsaran, where our men can be rested and fed. Tamari, I'm tasking you with setting those up.

'Peled and Gold can handle the patrols – although there will need to be more delegation from here on, with so many extra patrols. We have new personnel coming in to help carry the extra load. Lev, I'm putting you in charge of stores from now on. We need to make sure we have everything we need well in advance – food, water, fuel, spare parts, medical supplies. The others will be reporting to you from now on with their requirements. It will be up to you to order what we need from Command. Khaista can assist you where necessary.

'*Beseder,* sir,' replied Lev.

'Also, I think you could look after the catering supplies as well, which will free up Junbalat for other duties – he's being under-used at the moment, I think.' Shaul grinned at Junbalat, who grinned back.

'Once we have enough vehicles at Gachsaran the second plane will mostly be re-supplying the vehicles, but it can also bring back personnel who've done say three patrols in a row. Obviously the aircraft will also bring back any sick or injured *olim*, when required.'

'When we go to stage two – when Sirjan Airport becomes operational – the second transport plane will be fully occupied with moving our vehicles from Gachsaran back to Sirjan. We will have the added problem of getting supplies to Gachsaran and our personnel back from there. So, not only would we need a second transport plane, but we'd also need another smaller plane to transport our men back and take fresh patrols out. Each leg we add to this from now on – each new airport added – will increase the complexity of the operation.'

'Yes,' Peled answered. It will start to get quite complicated indeed – especially if we have all five airports operational. And each additional airport will take that much longer to reach, before a patrol even starts.'

'Exactly,' Shaul replied. 'At the moment it will be fairly simple and one transport plane will be sufficient, I think. The plane can also load up any casualties arriving in Gachsaran and we can ferry them to the hospital here in Basra. Can we move your checkpoint also to Gachsaran, from Omidiyeh, Alon? We'll be able to drop your people there by plane now.'

'OK,' said Peled, 'That will actually be easier to operate. The tanks will have to drive there first, of course.'

'As far as broken down vehicles are concerned,' Shaul continued, 'the only way we can deal with those is by road, as before. There's no way we can ferry a tank-transporter or low-loader by plane. We could possibly take a mini-bus, though, for the stranded passengers.

'So, I believe the best option is to advise Ben Ezra to move on to Sirjan next. He can transport his equipment there by road and the Air Force can supply him from Gachsaran, with only one mid-air refuel on the way back. Anyone have anything to add?'

'Yes, sir,' said Bar-Ilan. 'Now that we have the new bridge, do you think we could use the *Yas'ur* helicopter again to take a team as far as Zabol? I'm thinking maybe one *Hummvee* and trailer of equipment inside and a bulldozer slung below. The excavator and team could work their way from the border back all the way, filling craters and clearing obstructions – like the one that caused that accident last week, and the one we dealt with just east of Shiraz.

'There are going to be more accidents if traffic has to detour partly off the road to get around those obstacles. That way the road might not be perfect, but it would be much safer. If we wait until we can fly out by transport plane we may lose lives.'

Ali cleared his throat and Shaul nodded for him to speak. 'We had to rescue a family on Monday in a mountain gorge.' He consulted his notebook, 'It was about halfway between Bardsir and Sirjan. Although it's a divided highway, the two halves of the highway are widely separated at this point and the lower carriageway was blocked more than halfway across with rock debris fallen from above.

'The large truck behind us was well overloaded and the edge crumbled under its rear wheels, leaving the truck balanced on the edge of the gorge. We couldn't get any of the family out because even with one person less the truck would have become unbalanced and then tipped over the edge.'

'So what did you do, Ali,' Shaul asked, intrigued.

'We used some steel poles from one of the other trucks and inserted them into the engine compartment, then we put large rocks on top of them and re-balanced the truck enough to get everyone but the driver out safely. I was carrying a steel towrope in my truck, so we were able then to pull the truck to safety using a heavier vehicle. After the truck was safe I managed to get some of the other drivers to help clear some of the rock pile away by hand. Unfortunately, they lost their enthusiasm after only a short while.'

'So, the road has been cleared just a little – it's safer than it was?' Shaul asked.

'Yes, sir, but it really needs that rock cleared away completely – even diverting the convoy onto the other carriageway a kilometre further back would by-pass it in the meantime,' said Ali. I actually thought of doing that, but I had no authority and no cones or signs to make it effective.'

'Well it certainly sounds like the family owe you their lives, Zai,' Shaul said. 'Well done, sergeant.' Ali smiled briefly.

To Rebekkah he said, 'Well, I think your's is an excellent idea, Bar-Ilan. 'I'll take it up with Command and see if they will let us have the *Yas'ur* for another day. We're using helicopters along the route anyway, so it shouldn't be a problem, I hope. I think Tamari would be the man to take charge of that team – once you've set up the two bases – *beseder*, Musa?'

'Ken, Rav Seren,' Tamari replied.

Peled had his finger lifted. 'Go ahead, *Seren*,' Shaul said.

'When Sirjan does become operational,' Peled began, 'could we use one transport plane to drop off a patrol at Gachsaran, but have the personnel and equipment for a second patrol on board, pick up the vehicles which have come from Sirjan and take both them and the new personnel to Sirjan to start a new patrol? The smaller plane can then be used to transfer any casualties, plus the team who've just finished their shift, back here.'

'Beseder,' said Shaul slowly, 'that might work. But we'd still need another transport plane, to keep up our schedule of a patrol every four hours from Gachsaran. Any ideas how we can maintain such a schedule when it takes three hours and twenty minutes to get to Sirjan? A round trip would take nearly eight hours, if we count loading and refuelling time.'

'Another thing,' Tamari added, 'the plane will also have to carry new supplies of water and other supplies, as well as fresh personnel. There's no point in bringing back the vehicles – they can refuel at the further airport – but they will need to be re-stocked for each trip.'

'Also,' said Tamari, 'I'm assuming we can also fly diesel fuel and gas to these airports. We could just use one or two tankers at each airport, then, to transfer the fuel to a gas station or truck depot near the highway.'

'That's a good idea, Tamari,' said Shaul, making a note, 'station a tanker at each airport, once they're operational. We can start by sending a full road tanker to Gachsaran, then top it up using tanker aircraft in future. I'm assuming the aircraft can only carry one type of fuel at a time?'

'Beseder,' said Shaul. 'At the moment the job is simple. We can handle one patrol every four hours, which gives time for loading and for refuelling the aircraft. I'd like you all to ponder what we need to do to handle two sections – and then three, four five. It's quite

a complex problem – both in use of the aircraft and as regards our personnel.

'For instance a straight flight to Zabol' – Shaul consulted his note-book again – 'would take six hours and twenty minutes. Imagine starting a patrol after flying that length of time first – actually, the crew would need to sleep on the aircraft.'

'How far from Zabol to Zahedan?' Peled asked, looking at Shaul's wall map.

'Actually they're quite close – only two and a half hours under normal road conditions. But remember, a patrol arriving at Zabol would first have to drive to the Afghan border and patrol back to Zabol, then travel on again to Zahedan. The border is only half an hour away – so an hour's driving, plus stops for servicing, medical help, etc.'

'And from Zahedan to Bam, sir?' Peled asked again.

Shaul again checked his figures, 'Three hours and thirty eight minutes under normal road conditions. Again, the patrol would need to take a trip, first – this time to the Pakistan border and back– about an hour and ten minutes each way.'

'But it would be possible for a patrol to start from Zabol and finish at Bam, wouldn't it?' Peled continued. 'What I'm getting at is that we could leave out Zahedan, in favour of Zabol in the meantime, couldn't we?'

'Let's see,' Shaul began scribbling in his notebook, 'OK, the total trip would be roughly ten hours under normal road conditions. With stops to help, as we all know, it will be several hours more than that – fifteen, sixteen hours.'

'Yes, sir,' said Peled, 'but we're already out that long at present – only going as far as Omidiyeh. When we start flying to Gachsaran I imagine the day will be just as long, only we'll be covering a greater distance in the time.'

'Ken,' agreed Shaul, 'I see your point Alon. So we could effect-ively eliminate Zahedan until we have Zabol operational? Or vice versa? After that it might be useful to have both operating.'

'Yes, sir,' Peled replied, 'And from Bam to Sirjan is how far?'

'Three hundred and seventy seven kilometres – about four and a quarter hours, nominally.'

'Then I suggest, sir, that when Sirjan becomes operational we focus on Zabol next, before Bam, and leave Zahedan until last. It would be a long patrol, sir, but it would mean we would actually be covering the whole route from then on.

Ali spoke again, 'I understand you are talking about Zabol and Zahedan, he asked?'

'That's right,' replied Shaul in English.

'We've just driven through there. The roads need some repair, but are not as bad as some of the roads further west. We crossed the border about 08:00 hours on Sunday and – after travelling to the Pakistan border and back – arrived in Mahan, outside Kerman, by … midnight?' He looked at Khaista for confirmation.

'Yes, midnight,' she answered quietly.

We left Mahan again shortly after 06:00 hours and arrived in Sirjan just after 11:15 – though we were delayed by about an hour due to that accident. So, our journey took us just over twenty hours – not counting the delay caused by the accident.'

'So,' Shaul brought the conversation back to the original problem, 'according to what Ali has just told us, a trip back from Zabol would take around twenty hours – plus say an hour to get from the airport to the border. Then we need to add in time for the patrols to aid the convoy – repair vehicles, give medical aid, food and water. It could add up to thirty hours, or more, for each patrol.'

'Maybe if we sent patrols out in twos, it would reduce the workload on each team?' Peled suggested.

'How do you mean, *Seren?* ' Shaul asked.

'Well, we would send two planes, then. Patrol *Alef* would head to the Afghan border first, while patrol *Bet* would go straight for Zahedan – helping *olim* on the way, of course. Patrol *Alef* would now be maybe two hours behind when they move on to Zahedan and they would travel straight there – unless there's a new emergency – as patrol *Bet* would already have taken care of most emergencies in that sector.

'When patrol *Bet* get to Zahedan, they would turn off to the Pakistan border and work back from there, then travel on to Bam, where again, they would have less cases to deal with as they've now been overtaken by patrol *Alef*. Both patrols would then continue on to Sirjan – probably overtaking one another and so sharing the load.'

'That sounds like it might work, sir,' Rebekkah commented. '*Alef* would patrol to the Afghan border and the road from Zahedan to Bam, while *Bet* would patrol the road from Zabol to Zahedan and the other border – both of them sharing the remainder of the journey from Zahedan to Sirjan.'

Tamari interrupted, 'There's actually another way to do it. If we use Zahedan airport, instead of Zabol, we'd then have a patrol of normal length to Sirjan – how far would that be, sir?'

Shaul consulted his notebook again and answered, 'From Zahedan to Sirjan would be seven hours and fourteen minutes under normal conditions.'

'So,' Tamari continued, 'Less than the distance from Sirjan to Gachsaran, which is nominally eight hours. So, we would still have two patrols, but the second patrol would cover both borders – travel to the Pakistan border first, and patrol back to where the two convoys meet. Then drive north to the Afghan border and patrol back via Zabol to Zahedan. That should only be a nominal five and a half hours by my reckoning.'

Shaul calculated in his notebook again, 'Yes, that's about right,' he said.

'The second team will not need to be airlifted once they are in position,' Tamari continued, 'but they *will* need a base to work from. The other advantage, I think, would be that we could set up a permanent checkpoint/fuel depot/medical station where the two roads meet and cover the whole migration that way. It would be simpler than two separate checkpoints.'

'Tamari has a point there, sir,' added Peled. 'Only one transport plane at a time, normally. We could use a smaller plane to ferry the teams, plus supplies, there and teams and casualties back.'

'Yes,' said Shaul, 'Or the plane that delivers the other patrol – the one going to Sirjan – can bring supplies and take back casualties. I'm beginning to like that idea. Yes, I like it indeed. As soon as we have airports operational at Sirjan and Zahedan we can implement that. Good work, team!' Shaul smiled at his staff and they grinned back at him.

'*Beseder,*' he summed up, 'so we'll ask Ben Ezra to make Sirjan his next priority. When he's finished there we can airlift his equipment to Zahedan – followed by Zabol and, finally, perhaps, Bam.'

His men – plus Rebekkah and Khaista – all nodded in agreement.

'And once we do have Zabol operational, one plane can drop off at Zahedan, pick up the patrol for Zabol and drop it back, before flying home with casualties. The logistics will be tricky at times, but it looks like it should work.'

He continued, 'Now we need to organise our four-hourly patrols from Gachsaran. Peled, Gold, Katz and Junbalat – can you each take a patrol for now? We'll need at least two more team leaders – preferably four – to make this work in future, because you obviously can't each do a patrol every twenty four hours. We'll need five, or better six, teams in sequence. With eight teams in total, that will hopefully give each team a little time to rest and recover. It would also mean each team will then be alternating day and night patrols. Perhaps each of you could delegate another team leader?'

'Right, Peled – I'll leave you to work out a new schedule. We need a team at the airport by 09:00 hours this morning, so they'd better get moving. We will still need a bus and transporter travelling to Gachsaran every other day or so, I expect. I'll contact Command now and let them know what we need, including the helicopter. I'll also ask Ben Ezra to start repairs on Sirjan airfield next, then to move on to Zahedan.'

'Beseder, sir,' said Peled, beckoning Gold, Katz and Junbalat to come with him.

'Tamari, when you get the new bases set up you'll need to sort out a team and bulldozer to travel to Zabol and work back to Gachsaran. You could probably tow one of those vibrating rollers on the trailer behind the *Hummvee,* do you think?'

'Yes, sir,' replied Tamari, 'Then we could compact all the craters we fill. They'd last a bit longer then. We'll not be travelling fast, anyway – keeping pace with the bulldozer. We have the machines we were using for the roads down at the new bridge – they're both outside at the moment. I'll take one of those and a roller over to the airport so it's ready to load when we get the go ahead. I'll take one of the bridge engineers with me as well. We'll need to take a lot of extra fuel, also – for the *Hummvee* and for the bulldozer. Even so, we may still need fuel airlifted out to us eventually.

'I'd better radio the engineer working on the road repairs as well. Let him know I won't be over for a few days yet. That's another thing, sir – as we get further and further from base we'll need air transport to bring the road crews back and forth. At the moment they're camping out where they can, but they need to come back to base for re-supply and rest, sir. Also, once we have Sirjan and then Zahedan operational, we could airlift out a second and then a third road repair crew.'

'Right, Tamari,' Shaul replied, 'We might need that second aircraft sooner than we thought. I'll bring that up with Command as well. *L'hitraot.'*

Tamari, Lev and Rebekkah departed to their respective duties.

Shaul asked Ali and Khaista to give him about fifteen minutes to make some radio calls and then to join him in his office.

Meanwhile, Shaul first contacted Ben Ezra in Gachsaran, to get his team moving on to Sirjan. He suggested sending a couple of his own men with the first patrol, who could accompany the drivers on their way back to Basra, collecting abandoned vehicles on the way. Ben Ezra agreed to release his drivers to Shaul once they had finished unloading.

Next he contacted Southern Command and reported the various items of good news that had coincided that day.

'Looks like we picked the right man for this job, Levine,' said his commander. 'We're planning to use some of your ideas already on the northern Iran route, Herat to Baghdad, and also on the African routes. We don't need to repair airfields in Africa, thankfully – just get permission from the countries involved to land patrol vehicles at their airports and, if possible, to set up our own depots at those airports, also. The main route there – the one from Nigeria – is around seven thousand kilometres in total.

'*Beseder*, Levine, anything you need at the moment?'

'Yes, sir,' Shaul replied. 'We may need another aircraft – not a *Hercules*, just a normal airliner capable of carrying personnel, stretchers and some materials like bottled water, vehicle spares and so forth. Secondly, we'll need to transport diesel fuel and gas to Gachsaran and, when its ready, to Sirjan, also.'

'Anything else?'

'Yes, sir,' Shaul continued. 'Would it be possible to transport a truck full of asphalt to Basra by air – slung underneath, of course? The journey is getting very stretched out now, sir. It's a material that needs to be kept hot until it's used. Obviously, we can only load the truck with whatever the plane can carry – about twenty tonnes, total, I think it is, sir. If we are able to do that then we can transport asphalt further afield once we have another airport functioning.'

'OK, we'll get back to you on that one. Is that it?'

'One more request, sir. We could use the *Yas'ur* helicopter for one more task, sir. We'd like to fly a bulldozer slung under the aircraft, plus a *Hummvee* and trailer, with crew, inside – to Zabol. I know that will involve mid-air refuelling four times, sir. But we can then have that team travel back down the route removing the most serious obstacles on the highway, filling in and compacting craters.

'Until our road repair crews make it out that far this will have to suffice, sir. We've had some quite near misses so far. One accident nearly took a whole family over the edge into a gorge on Monday. We'd probably be saving a few lives, sir.'

'*Beseder*, Levine. Do you have a team standing by?'

'They are on their way out to Basra Airport at the moment, sir. They will be ready to go as soon as the helicopter is available.'

'Well, the helicopter is still at Basra, so as soon as we can authorise the mid-air refuelling we can give the go-ahead for the flight. We'll let you know as soon as, *Rav Seren.*'

'*Toda*, sir,' said Shaul. 'That's all we need at the moment.'

'*Tov ma'od*, Levine. We'll be in touch.'

Shaul settled back into his chair as there came a quiet knock on his door. 'Come in, Ali,' he called.

Ali and Khaista came into the office.

"I just need you to fill in a couple of forms so we can get you re-gistered as new *olim* and start things moving back in Israel – like your future accommodation, for instance.'

He walked over to a filing cabinet and found the necessary forms, handing them to Ali and Khaista.

After you've filled those in you can relax for the rest of the day. Walk along the River, take a drive around the city. I can tell you where everything of importance is. In fact, if you like, I can get Bar-Ilan – Bekkah, that is – to give you a tour?'

'Yes, that would be helpful,' said Ali. 'I think we'd like to get fam-iliar with everything as soon as possible and then get straight to work. There's not much else to do in a city which is emptied of its population after a war.'

'That's very true,' Shaul agreed. 'It's a lot different from Afghanistan when we were both with ISAF, isn't it?'

Ali grinned, 'It is indeed, sir. But I'm looking forward to going out on patrol tomorrow. Yesterday we stopped with one of your patrols and I was needed to interpret, as the driver had no English. I'll be happy to be useful in that way, but I need to be familiar with everything – where the fuel supplies are, for instance – so I can give the right information.'

'Yes,' said Shaul, 'and I must get a desk and computer set up for you, Khaista – one for Lev, also. I'd like to get you started tomorrow on a leaflet giving basic information, that we can give out to the drivers. I'll spend some time today drafting it in English. Then tomorrow you can make a start translating it into Pashto and Dari.'

'I enjoyed sitting in on your staff meeting,' said Ali. 'It was very informative – very different attitude from ISAF or the ANA. Much less formal. And yet, it is obvious that all your men respect you, sir.'

'Yes, the IDF does things a little bit differently. The training is very rigorous, but the relationships are more informal.

'Well, I'll let you take these and fill them in,' he said. 'When you are ready, just give me a shout and I'll get Bar-Ilan to show you all the facilities. Are your quarters comfortable enough? When you are married I'll probably be able to organise for you to have a room of your own. Do you need help bringing any of your stuff in from your truck?'

'Yes, everything is fine,' said Ali. 'And we can bring our own stuff in – no problem. But I still have some containers of fuel in the truck, plus some furniture from my apartment and Khaista's that we brought with us.

'OK,' said Shaul. 'We'd better find somewhere safe to store your stuff in the meantime – until we can transfer it to Israel. 'I'll ask Junbalat if he has any ideas – he knows this building better than I do. Come with me and I'll ask him now.'

Shaul took him to meet Junbalat and explained the problem. 'I'll leave you with Samir, then,' he said.

'Beseder, said Ali, 'we will get back to you soon.'

'Beseder,' said Shaul, *'L'hitraot.'*

'L'hitraot!' Ali replied, grinning again.

Shaul sat down again at his desk and switched on his computer. He would need some time to draft the information he needed to convey to the incoming *olim*. It would probably also be best to send a copy to the *NIP* – the *New Israel Plan* – office.

The leaflet needed to inform the immigrants of what services the Israeli forces were already providing – breakdown and medical patrols, fuelling points, hospital in Basra, picking up broken-down vehicles, etc. It also needed to give information on what to expect when they arrived in Israel – for that he would need to consult with *NIP*.

An hour later Rebekkah knocked on Shaul's door and came in. 'I've brought you someone,' she announced. 'Remember Daoud? Well, he's now David.' She turned to the door and said, 'Come on in, Daveed.'

Turning back to Shaul she added, 'I'll leave you two to get acquainted, then. *L'hitraot.*'

'Come on in, Daveed,' Shaul smiled at the young man. 'Welcome. You're just what we need at the moment. We have thousands of people travelling on dangerous roads and we need translators to communicate with the convoys. We have two other Pashtuns like yourself who have just joined us – Ali Yusufzai and his fiancée, Khaista Afridi. They're having a day to rest from their journey across Iran, so I'll introduce you to them both later.'

25 – Smooth running

Ali began the next day accompanying Peled on a routine patrol from Gachsaran back to Basra. They flew out first thing in the morning at 06:00 hours – the whole team catching up on their sleep during the flight. The Hercules jet carried three *Hummvees* loaded with food, bottled water, medical supplies and spare parts.

When the plane landed in Gachsaran the patrol began their journey back alongside the convoy moving west. Ali was assigned to the repair squad and translated for the mechanics from Dari and Pashto, using his quite reasonable English also – while some of the Israeli mechanics had good English, others did not.

He soon became familiar with the most common types of problems they were faced with – overheating, punctures, dead batteries and vehicles running out of diesel or gas. He was also able to answer many of the questions the new *olim* were asking about Israel and what they should expect to face when they finally arrived there.

After his first week on patrol he had worked with the medical and food and water teams and was becoming pretty familiar with all the common questions being asked and ailments needing treatment and was able to pass this information on to Shaul and Khaista to be included in the information leaflet being prepared for handing out to the convoys.

On the second week Peled put Ali in charge of his own patrol – mostly made up of personnel with less fluent English than most, although one good English speaker was still required in each team in order for Ali to communicate to his own men effectively.

Although not a member of the IDF, Ali's military experience with the ISAF forces and Afghan National Army was generally accepted and he was treated by most personnel as if he were actually a sergeant in the IDF. Many of the mechanics, medical personnel and others by now were not members of the IDF, but volunteers from many walks of life in Israel – especially students – willing to play their part in facilitating the aliyah.

There were also more and more fellow Pashtuns who had by now arrived in Israel and they and their families been settled, who were keen to be employed in giving back something to the aliyah effort. These men – and a few women, too! – were of course spread around the different patrols in order to facilitate better communication with the convoys.

Shaul and Khaista worked hard on the wording of the Pashto and Dari information leaflets (also in English, of course), in conjunction with the *NIP* office back in Israel, and soon these were finalised, printed and delivered to Basra ready to be sent out with the patrols.

The *olim* were now met with Israeli personnel shortly after they had crossed the Afghan, or Pakistan, borders. They received information in their own languages welcoming them in their aliyah to Israel, briefing them on what to expect along the route, how to get help and communicate their medical and other needs, what to do if their vehicle broke down and what would happen if it was found to be beyond repair.

They were also informed on what to expect when they reached Israel itself and what services and options they would be offered there. The leaflet soon also became the basis for other information leaflets later translated into Igbo, Lemba, Kashmiri, Menashe and other *olim* languages.

Having set up permanent bases at Gachsaran and now also Sirjan, both being supplied by air from Basra, Tamari put together a team to be flown out to Zabol and begin to sort out the worst road damage along the convoy routes.

This team first travelled as far as the Afghan border and then began to travel back towards Zabol and then Zahedan, sleeping in tents when they had finished the long working day. The repairs they were able to carry out consisted mostly of clearing rubble and filling in craters, which were then compacted roughly to give a reasonably passable, though certainly not perfect, road surface.

The repaired roads, though still not top class, were much safer and faster to travel than they had been previously. The number of serious accidents reduced considerably as they progressed. As the number of air bases increased new road repair teams with asphalt would be sent out to complete the repairs, restoring the roads to a normal condition again.

Chapter 25 – Smooth running

Tamari's team personnel were swapped out after a couple of weeks, and a second team set up with a young engineer, Kaplan, in charge, but Tamari insisted on carrying on in control of the original team – arriving back at the Basra base after three weeks of exhausting work, but with a much safer route overall than had existed earlier.

Ali – who was thinking seriously of changing his name to a Hebrew one, to complement his new life in Israel – Khaista, David and other Pashtuns involved with Shaul's forces, were now taking regular Hebrew lessons, which Ali took to enthusiastically – using Hebrew whenever he possibly could. He even began to speak Hebrew when alone with Khaista, who was at first a little resistant but, as her understanding of the language grew, began to be more enthusiastic.

Sirjan airfield was soon repaired and Ben Era's team moved on to rehabilitate the Zahedan Airport. When it too became operational the number of Hercules transports increased, two aircraft regularly flying patrols – one to cover both the Pakistan and Afghan border routes, the other to travel back towards Sirjan.

After Zahedan, it was decided next to repair the Bam airfield, leaving Zabol to the last, as the plan using Zahedan was working so well and the distances to be covered were less exhausting for the personnel. Eventually, even Zabol became operational and Ben Ezra's team was reduced to maintaining the six operating airfields, though some of his personnel opted to continue helping the aliyah effort, being allowed to transfer to Shaul's forces.

More and more Shaul's team became a mixture of IDF and civilian personnel, with many volunteers coming from abroad – and from the aliyah itself – to help spread the load. The pace of the aliyah, if anything, had increased – not least due to the improvement in the roads and the increased patrols made possible by the newly repaired airports.

The pressure on the leadership was relentless and so Shaul and Rebekkah planned to take some much needed leave and accompany Ali and Khaista in their first actual visit to Israel, where the couple planned to get married in Jerusalem – a city they'd only heard and read about until now.

On Ali's behalf, Shaul had already contacted his old comrades, Brandon and Dev, inviting them to join them in celebrating Ali and Khaista's wedding.

26 – Reunited in Jerusalem

Shaul and Rebekkah, Ali – now definitely planning to change his name to the Hebrew, *Aviv*, meaning *a spring* – and Khaista, arrived in southern Israel early in the morning on a Hercules transport – the plane also carrying Aviv's truck and possessions in the hold.

Shaul drove them in the truck to his home kibbutz and – after an enjoyable Israeli breakfast in the kibbutz dining room – they transferred Aviv's baggage to a pre-arranged secure store and picked up a new set of Israeli licence plates, which Aviv quickly attached to his truck, while Shaul used the phone in the kibbutz office to order a hire car to be delivered to their hotel in Jerusalem later that morning.

The two couples then continued in the truck north along the Highway 6 freeway and then via Highway 1 to Jerusalem, where they had rooms reserved at the Leonardo Plaza Jerusalem Hotel – formerly the Sheraton Plaza. After their honeymoon Aviv and Khaista planned to return the truck to Shaul's kibbutz to be looked after there until such time as they should move permanently back to Israel.

Dev and Niamh were flying in from Boston in the afternoon and Brandon and his wife, Alyssa, were due in from Charlotte, North Carolina, that same evening. A room was reserved for Brandon and Alyssa in the same hotel, while Dev would share a room with Aviv, and Niamh with Khaista, until the wedding – both couples for similar reasons having agreed to wait until marriage before sleeping together.

When they arrived and had stored their luggage in their respective rooms Shaul and Rebekkah gave Aviv and Khaista some simple directions to the nearby city centre area, so they could explore the city on their own for a while. Shaul and Rebekkah would meet up with them for lunch and show them around for a bit after, before collecting their American friends.

As they watched the soon-to-be-married Afghan couple walk down the drive leading to King George V Street hand in hand Rebekkah sighed.

'A shekel for your thoughts, Bekkah?' Shaul said.

'I was just envying them, I suppose.' Rebekkah replied. 'Anyway, let's get back up to our luxurious private room, Solly boy.' she added with a mischievous twinkle in her eye.

'I hear and obey, *Segen* Bar-Ilan,' Shaul replied with a grin.

They walked back into the lobby of the hotel and took the lift to the tenth floor.

Half an hour later Rebekkah wandered out to the balcony of their room to appreciate the great panoramic view of the Old City walls to the east. Shaul donned a pair of shorts and joined her.

'Beautiful isn't it,' said Rebekkah.

'Yes, indeed,' Shaul replied, 'and that view of the Old City is great, too!'

Rebekkah looked at him and smiled. 'You after something more, Mr. Levine?'

'*Lo*,' Sol replied. 'I think I've had enough sex for a little while anyways. Mind you it's been a long time without. This military discipline has been killing me, if the truth be told.'

'Me too,' Rebekkah said with feeling.

'Well ... I've been thinking,' said Shaul. 'We could do something about that.'

'What? One, or both of us resign from the IDF?' she suggested.

'Nothing quite as precipitate,' Shaul replied. 'We could simply take a leaf out of Aviv and Khaista's book. Whadddya think, Bekkah?'

'Just what is it you're trying to say, Mr Levine?' she asked, looking up at him searchingly.

'Well, I guess I'm asking you if you'd consider marrying me, Miss Bar-Ilan?'

'Seriously?' Rebekkah asked, her mouth now open in surprise.

'*Ken*, seriously!' Shaul confirmed.

'Well, in that case the answer is *Ken*.' she replied, continuing to look Shaul in the eyes as he lifted her in his arms and they embraced.

'*Ken, ken, ken*,' she whispered in his ear as he carried her back to the king-size bed they had so recently vacated.

An hour later – after being disturbed once by a call from reception to inform them that their hire car had arrived, an eight person MPV – they joined Aviv and Khaista at the bottom of Hillel Street, near Zion Square, where they had agreed to have lunch at a shwarma stand. When they had ordered and taken their food to a table on the street, under the welcome shade of a tree, Khaista remarked, 'You too seem abnormally quiet? Is there something we should know?'

Aviv added, 'Yes, Bekkah keeps smiling to herself and Shaul looks like the cat who stole the milk.'

'I think you'll find that's 'the cat that got the cream', actually.' Shaul answered, smiling broadly.

'*Beseder*, so what gives, as you Americans are always saying? Something is up, I think?'

'OK, you got us,' said Shaul, 'shall we tell them then, Bekkah?'

'Go ahead, Mr Levine.'

'*Beseder*, it's only that Bekkah here has just agreed to become Mrs Levine in the very near future.'

'You are getting married?' Khaista asked, with a joyful, but surprised, expression on her face. 'That is truly amazing news. Congratulations!'

'Yes, congratulations, both of you,' Aviv added, grinning widely and looking from Shaul to Rebekkah and back again to Shaul. 'Now we must celebrate this tremendous good news.'

'I guess we should,' said Shaul. 'How about a cold beer apiece, then?'

'I don't think we're going to get champagne in Zion Square,' said Rebekkah, smiling, 'so beer it'll have to be.'

Shaul got four cold beers from the cooler at the shwarma stand and paid for them and they all drank a toast – proposed by Aviv – to Shaul and Rebekkah.

The happy foursome spent some time discussing the good news as they ate their food. Eventually, Shaul indicated that they'd better get a move on if they wanted to see anything of the city before they had to pick up Dev and Niamh, Brandon and Alyssa.

'Mebbe just a brief wander through Mamilla Mall as far as Jaffa Gate?' suggested Rebekkah. 'It will give Aviv and Khaista a taste of the Old City and the new, then we can give them a proper tour of it when the others join us.'

'*Beseder*,' agreed Shaul, 'Let's go then.'

They walked across Zion Square and along pedestrian Jaffa Street for a couple of hundred metres, avoiding the Jerusalem Light Rail trains as they passed in either direction. Rebekkah led them into Queen Shlomziyon Street to the right off Yafo Street, then across Bush Square and into the beginning of the mall.

'This area was badly damaged in 1948,' Rebekkah explained, 'It was the front line then with Jordan. It remained a danger zone for many years, because of snipers shooting from the Old City walls. Eventually, it became a run-down neighbourhood of workshops and car repair garages – until we liberated Jerusalem in the Six Day War in 1967.

'Ten of the original buildings have been preserved – some of them taken down brick by brick and rebuilt in the mall. The Clark House, the Stern House and the Convent of St. Vincent de Paul are still on their original sites, incorporated into the new construction by the architect, Safdie.'

Rebekkah pointed out these buildings as they passed them. 'It took nearly thirty seven years to complete the project,' she added.

'Why so long?' asked Aviv. 'I thought Israel was a go get 'em kind of country. Surely it doesn't take that long to build a mall?'

'There were many disputes about the construction – lawsuits, protests and so forth. Eventually, they sorted it out and it was completed in 2007,' she said.

Aviv and Khaista were amazed at the shops and stores they were passing, and the expensive goods available in many of them.

'I think you would need a lot of shekels to do any shopping here,' Aviv remarked.

'Indeed!, Shaul agreed. 'But there's something I really need to buy, and this is probably the right place to find it. He led Rebekkah into a classy jewellery shop on the mall and they spent some time looking at rings. Aviv and Khaista looked at one another and joined them. Before long both couples had purchased the ring of their choice – Aviv using his new bank card for the very first time.

'I feel more like an Israeli today – using my Israeli bank card to buy an expensive ring here in Mamilla Mall.' he said.

They continued along the length of the mall, approaching Jaffa Gate, where a flight of steps led up to a park bridging Highway 60, which ran north-south, parallel to the city wall, then disappeared into a tunnel further north, travelling underground as far as Damascus Gate.

'We can take a quick walk through the souks,' Rebekkah suggested. 'Get a flavour of the Old City, then catch the Light Rail at Damascus Gate, which will take us back up to King George Street, near our hotel?'

The others agreed, Shaul mumbling, 'You're the tour guide. Lead on.'

They walked through Jaffa Gate, where they were met by a mix of tourists in shorts, jeans and short skirts, Arab boys on camels, Israeli police on horseback, Orthodox Jews in black hats and long coats, Orthodox women in conservative dress, with scarves covering their hair, soldiers in uniform, Arab women in the full traditional burka and Arab men in kaffiyas.

Aviv and Khaista were amazed at the diversity around them, as they passed the deep dry moat around David's Citadel and the Arab shops and restaurants – with men selling bread, fresh orange juice and all kinds of tourist trinkets.

'I guess the whole world must meet here, eh?' commented Aviv.

'Pretty much,' Rebekkah answered. 'The Christian Quarter is on our left and the Armenian Quarter is on our right – the descendants of those who survived the Turkish genocide in 1905. Many of these jewellery and clothes shops are owned by Armenians.'

They were entering David Street – the Street of the Chain – which descended into the bowels of the city in a series of steps.

'So many people,' exclaimed Khaista, as they squeezed through the throng of tourists and locals, passing Bedouin carpet shops and clothing stores, shops selling olive wood carvings, pottery and expensive jewellery.

Rebekkah turned left into The Muristan, a more open area with wider streets, colourful shops and stores. In its centre was an ancient fountain.

'We could be back in Kabul,' Aviv commented.

At the far end Rebekkah led them to the left, into an open court-yard in front of an ancient church.

'The Church of the Holy Sepulchre,' she explained. There were various monks and nuns in black, brown, dark blue and grey habits, Orthodox priests with huge bushy beards and camcorder-toting tourists of every nationality in groups like flocks of sheep, each led by a tour guide waving a flag and talking loudly in different languages.

'These are Christian tourists from every part of the world,' Rebekkah said. 'Different Christian denominations control separate areas of the church building and hold separate services. Sometimes they disagree and have even been known to come to blows.'

'Very curious,' said Aviv.

Khaista was looking all around and drinking in all the sights. A young boy came up and, hearing them speak English, offered to guide them around the Old City, but Rebekkah spoke to him firmly in Hebrew and he left them again, shrugging.

She led them down a tunnel-like street, passing a Coptic Church with carved dark wooden doors on the way, entering the narrow alleys of the souks, where every kind of food, spice and fruit was on sale from small shops. They then turned left again emerging onto Al Wad Street, thronged with people of every hue and dress, more shops selling leather goods, trainers, clothes and stalls selling sticky honey-covered nuts and sweets. The throng increased as they approached the Z-shaped area of Damascus Gate.

As they exited through the huge gateway they came out into bright sunlight lighting a theatre-like set of steps leading up towards Highway 1 and the Light Rail system nearby.

'Across there is the Arab bus station,' Rebekkah pointed, 'and next to it is the Garden Tomb, which is actually quite a nice garden area.

'If we walk just a little way we can catch the Light Rail back to the city centre.'

'Thank you for showing us around,' Khaista said, smiling, as they waited for the sound of the bell signifying an approaching train.

'No problem,' said Rebekkah, adding, 'The Light Rail heads north and east into poorer parts of Jerusalem – both Arab and Jewish. In the other direction it leads to the Central Bus Station, the new underground Railway Station and the western part of the city around Ein Karem.

As she spoke a train approached slowly and stopped and they and the other people waiting boarded. The train made its way up the steep hill alongside the northern wall of the Old City.

'Tonight, or tomorrow, we can take the others with us and see some other parts of the Old City,' Rebekkah suggested.

'That's an idea,' agreed Shaul, holding her by the hand. 'It would be nice to show them the Western Wall by night. I remember being brought there when I finished my army training,' he mused.

'Yes, the Kotel is an amazing place by night,' she agreed. 'The wall is lit up by floodlights and there are always crowds of people there. And I believe Jews are now free to go up onto the Temple Mount itself – even pray there – now that there is no more Jordanian *Waqf* controlling it.

'Of course there are still restricted areas around the ruins of the two mosques, which were hit by missiles during the war and badly damaged. There was a lot of discussion recently among religious Jews about the possibility of demolishing the Dome of the Rock so they could begin construction of the new Third Temple, but when they brought in the experts – archaeologists, historians and so forth – they came to the conclusion that the actual temple site should be in the City of David area, just south of the Temple Mount.'

'So what do they reckon the huge Temple Mount area was for if it wasn't the actual site of the temple,' Shaul asked in puzzlement.

'Apparently, according to historic records, that was the site of the Roman Antonia Fortress, which held maybe 10,000 people – soldiers and ancillary staff included. The temple was completely destroyed by Titus's army in 70 AD – didn't even Jesus prophesy that there would not be one stone left upon another?' Rebecca replied.

'Wow!' said Shaul, 'I just assumed it was called the Temple Mount for the obvious reason!'

'Well, when we go back to the Kotel this evening we'll be able to see the construction site beyond the Dung Gate where they have already begun building the Third Temple,' Rebekkah replied.

The train had passed City Hall and through Zion Square and now stopped close to the beginning of King George Street and they disembarked.

'Do you guys want to rest and freshen up before we eat, while I go collect Brandon and Alyssa from the airport?' Shaul added.

Aviv and Khaista looked at one another and Aviv said, '*Ken*, that's a good idea. What about you, Bekkah?'

'I think I'll trail along with Sol here. Keep him out of mischief,' she replied. 'Besides, we might just have a few things to discuss.'

'That's true,' said Shaul. 'I imagine Dev and Niamh will have made it to the hotel by now. We'll ask at reception.'

They walked back from the Light Rail along King George V Street and into the hotel lobby. Aviv, Khaista and Rebekkah relaxed on some comfortable chairs while Shaul spoke to the receptionist. Soon he turned towards them giving them a thumbs up signal.

'They're here,' he called to them. 'Dev's coming down in a minute. Niamh's apparently already in your room, Khaista – but Dev reckons she'd be asleep by now. Jet-lagged.'

In a few minutes the lift doors opened and a big dark-haired American walked into the lobby.

'Lieutenant Levine – I mean Major now, I suppose – Solly, as I live and breathe,' the loud Irish American voice boomed. 'And Sergeant Yusufzai – hi there Zai, me oul' mate!' he added.

Dev strolled over to Shaul and crushed first him, then Aviv in a warm hug of welcome.

'OK, OK, you can let me go now,' said Aviv.

Dev released him, then noticed the two girls.

'Whadda we have here, then?' he said – 'no don't tell me. This tough blonde beauty must be Rebekkah, right? And the sultry brunette with the smoky eyes must be Khaista – did I pronounce that right?'

'Correct,' said Rebekkah, reaching out her hand as Devlin took it in his huge paw and kissed it. He then reached for Khaista's hand and kissed hers also.

Khaista smiled at him and said, 'You pronounced it perfectly Mr Devlin – Dev. I'm looking forward to meeting your friend, Niamh – did I get her name right?'

'You sure did, Khaista. So how did you meet up with my buddy, Ali, here? In Kabul, I take it?'

'Yes, we met at his uncle's. I used to work for the government there, along with his cousin Elina. But you'll have to get used to calling him Aviv from now on. Ali has decided to change his name to a proper Israeli one. It's Hebrew for *spring* – like in a well?'

'OK, I'll probably forget that a few times, so remind me if I manage to get it wrong, Ali – I mean, Aviv. Maybe I'll just keep on calling you Zai to avoid any confusion, eh?' he grinned.

'Bekkah and I are about to head to the airport to collect Brandon and Alyssa,' said Shaul. 'You're welcome to join us. Or maybe you'd prefer to catch up with Aviv, here, and Khaista?'

'Yeah, I think I'll do that – just for a short while – then I'm gonna crash for an hour or two. Niamh had the right idea, I think. Wake me up when you get back with Brandon and his missus. We've all got a lotta catchin' up to do – over some beers, I'd suggest. See you guys later.'

Dev joined Aviv and Khaista while Shaul and Rebekkah collected the hired MPV outside for the trip to the airport.

'Take it aisy, now,' shouted Dev as they parted. 'Drive safely.'

'Sure thing, buddy,' Shaul shouted back. 'See you guys later.'

As they headed out of the city on Highway 1 Shaul turned to Rebekkah in the passenger seat and asked, 'So, what were you and Khaista whispering about on the train, then? You had your heads together a lot.'

'She was suggesting that if we wanted to have a joint wedding she and Aviv would have no objection. In fact, she said they would love the idea. What do you think of it? Mebbe it's too soon for you?'

'Too soon!' Shaul exclaimed. 'As far as I'm concerned it can't be soon enough. As long as *you're* still sure about the whole idea?'

'Of course I am. I think it would be great to have a joint wedding. It would mean just one bout of organising – and Khaista and I can work together on it – Niamh and Alyssa and my friend, Ilana, would help too. I don't imagine either you or Aviv are going to be that much help?'

'Well, tell us what you want done and we'll get to it. We are both military men, after all – so are Brandon and Dev, for that matter.'

'OK then, so you're happy to go ahead with this?'

'Sure,' said Shaul, 'you and Khaista get your heads together – mebbe after breakfast tomorrow morning? Then let the rest of us know what you want done and the military will swing into action.'

'OK, we'll do that, then,' she replied, drifting off into possible wedding plans in her head.

'What about your family, then?' she said after a few minutes. 'Don't you want them to be there? It might be very short notice for them, don't you think?'

'There's only my brother, Reuben. His head is always full of business, but if I start by telling his wife, Leah – get her enthusiastic about it – then she can work on him. I'll give her a ring this evening – start the ball rolling. Never underestimate the moving force of the Jewish wife – a power to be reckoned with!'

'You better believe it, Shaul Levine. You're about to have one of those of your very own, so I hope you keep those words in mind.'

'Yes, *Segen*,' Shaul replied, giving a brief salute.

'Hands on the wheel, ' said Rebekkah, smiling.

Shaul drove on in silence for a while, the miles to Ben Gurion being eaten up rapidly by the fast-moving MPV as he moved from lane to lane pretty much on auto-pilot.

Brandon and Alyssa's flight was more or less on time and Shaul and Rebekkah had only a short wait after they parked the MPV, before the Thomases appeared.

Brandon and Shaul embraced one another with mutual greetings of *'Shalom aleichem,'* and then Shaul introduced Brandon and Alyssa to Rebekkah.

'Segen Bar-Ilan has agreed just today to become my wife,' he said proudly.

'Congratulations to you both,' Brandon responded. 'Are we having a joint wedding, then?' he queried.

'Looks like it,' replied Shaul, 'if we can organise it in time. The girls are going to put their heads together in the morning and make plans. Alyssa, you are welcome to join them.'

'Thank you, Shaul, and my congratulations to you both,' said Alyssa. 'It's really great to meet you after hearing about you for so long.'

Chapter 26 – Reunited in Jerusalem

Shaul took Alyssa's suitcase and led the way out of the terminal to where their MPV was parked.

'It's pretty warm here – just like North Carolina at the moment,' commented Brandon.

'Not as warm as it was just a month, or so, ago,' Shaul chuckled, referring to the recent *Six Hour War*. 'By the way, you sure got that one right, brother!'

'Well, if you study the prophecies in the Tanakh and ask Yahoweh for enlightenment as you study, things begin to fall into place. There are many more prophecies soon to be fulfilled – and not just regarding Israel. Shaul, I believe you still have family in the US?'

'Sure, my brother and his wife and their two kids are in New York. He goes to synagogue, but I don't think he has much interest in the Tanakh, or in prophecy.'

'Try to get his interest aroused, Shaul,' Brandon said, with a serious look on his face. 'Many Jews are going to be taken by surprise when the backlash comes. The US is getting more like Nazi Germany every day – especially since the change of government. There is a lot of bad feeling against Israel – a lot of it because your politicians have been proven right and ours so badly wrong about Iran and so forth. It's also to do with repressing guilt over US responsibility for this war.'

'Yes, there's little sign of the US apologising to Israel for the hundreds of thousands of deaths and injuries we've suffered as a direct result of their so badly mistaken policies,' agreed Shaul.

Rebekkah and Alyssa sat in the rear of the vehicle, discussing the coming wedding plans and the stresses of serving Israel in the current post-war aliyah crisis.

By the time Shaul was entering Jerusalem and turning into King George V Street towards their hotel, it was dark and they were all beginning to feel hungry. The others were all awake by now and – after Brandon and Alyssa had had a little time to settle in and refresh themselves – they all gathered in the foyer of the hotel again.

Shaul took charge: 'Welcome to Jerusalem, all of you. I've booked a meal for the eight of us at the *Piccolino* Italian Restaurant near Zion Square. We can easily walk there from here through the park, so maybe we should head out now, *beseder?'*

'Sure,' drawled Micky, the others muttering *'Beseder'*, or 'OK' more or less in chorus.

They made their way along the drive towards King George V Street, but turned right instead of left, into Independence Park. They crossed the park in a few minutes and walked north to cross over Hillel Street into the narrow Yo'el Moshe Salomon Street, which led up to Zion Square. Halfway up on the left they entered a typical old cream Jerusalem stone building which housed the *Piccolino* Restaurant.

They walked through the almost empty interior of the building, housing the bar and kitchens, and into the courtyard behind, which was well-filled with customers and tables. A young man playing a fiddle and an older man with a keyboard, were performing classical music plus some jazz, facing away from the building and towards the customers.

'This is beautiful,' commented Niamh.

A waiter led them to their reserved table to one side of the court-yard and took their orders for drinks – the men preferring cold Is-raeli beer, while the women opted for a bottle of Pinot Grigio white wine between them. The waiter returned shortly with their drinks and menus and they each decided on their meals.

The atmosphere was relaxed as they ate, listened to the soothing music and discussed old battles – in the case of the men – and the im-minent wedding – in the case of the women. When the main courses were cleared away they all opted to try the delicious range of deserts available. No-one was disappointed.

Eventually, after Shaul had discretely paid the bill, he suggested that it was time to walk off all that food and to see a little of the city.

'We're only a short distance from Zion Square and Yafo Street, then we can wander down towards the Old City and we'll show you the Cardo, some of the Jewish Quarter and the Kotel – the Western Wall.

The eight friends wandered slowly to Zion Square, where the newcomers were shown the Light Rail trains for the first time. They turned right along Yafo Street in the wake of a train and joined the crowds walking this pedestrian thoroughfare.

'It was certainly a great idea to pedestrianise this area,' commented Micky Devlin. 'It makes a great feature of the city centre – especially with all these restaurants, bars and stores.'

'It's even better just after the end of shabbat,' Rebekkah added, 'when everybody comes out onto the streets in their best clothes and there are many more musicians playing.'

At the end of Yafo Street they could all see the floodlit walls of the Old City ahead, though they had to wait until the lights changed, halting the surging traffic heading towards Damascus Gate.

'That's Highway 60 down there, leading to Highway One and Tel Aviv.' Rebekkah explained.

They crossed the street and walked outside the city walls until they came to Jaffa Gate, where the crowds of people increased. They walked through the stone arch forming the gate and Rebekkah pointed out David's citadel, floodlit on their right and built into the city wall.

'The gap in the wall where the traffic enters was made for Kaiser Wilhelm, when he visited Jerusalem – he drove through that newly made gap in his Daimler. At least when Allenby, the British general, came he chose to walk through the gate on foot.

'We'll let you see a little of the souks, but then we'll turn off into the Jewish Quarter and head towards the Kotel. This is the Armenian Quarter on the right – survivors of the 1905 Armenian Genocide made their way here and settled in Jerusalem. On the left is the Christian Quarter. The Jewish Quarter is beyond the Armenian Quarter, and the Muslim Quarter, and the Temple Mount, are beyond the Christian Quarter.

'This is the Street of the Chain, or David Street,' she said, as they entered the narrow, thronged street straight ahead of them, which stepped downwards into the bowels of the Old City.

'Be careful of the steps, they can be slippy and there are unexpected ramps on each side for the little tractors which supply the shops here.'

They made their way slowly downwards through the throng of tourists, soldiers, Arabs and Orthodox Jews, until an opening appeared on their right. Rebekkah led them into it. A small sign said Habad Street.

'Just below are the main shuks,' Rebekkah explained, pointing in the direction they had originally been travelling. This street will take us to the Cardo, in the Jewish Quarter. The Cardo was the main street of the old Roman city, Aelia Capitolina, which the Romans built after destroying the original Jewish city in 70 AD. The Cardo was pretty much the Roman predecessor of our modern shopping malls – paved with stone slabs, roofed over with columns supporting the roof and shops all the way along it.

'Here we are,' she said, as they turned left down steps leading towards an open square with trees, with an open space far below them on their right.

'That down there is part of the old Cardo, the continuation of it is underneath the shuks we were talking about, underground.'

Rebekkah led them down into a brightly lit mall, which continued from the open air section of the Cardo. It was like a typical mall, except that the buildings were obviously ancient, with well-worn slabs of limestone paving the street. There were high end art shops, a Bank Leumi, jewellery stores, Judaica for sale, as well as clothing boutiques, shoe stores, etc.

They wandered along it for a short distance. Rebekkah commented, 'This is where the Golden Menorah used to be on display, but it was moved some years ago to an open square nearer to the Kotel and the Temple Mount. We'll pass by it on the way.'

They retraced their steps and back into the open air, where there were signs pointing to several synagogues and yeshivas. They headed east through the square with trees and sculptures – Jewish Quarter Street, a sign said – through narrow streets with fairly new apartment buildings built in the same honey-coloured stone as the rest of the Old City.

'The whole Jewish Quarter was pretty much destroyed during the Jordanian occupation,' Rebekkah continued, 'from 1948 until it was liberated in 1967, during the Six Day War. It has all been rebuilt since – including the old Hurva synagogue.'

They wandered through more narrow streets – with modern apartments leading off – plus yeshivas and synagogues – until they came to steps leading down in the direction of the Kotel plaza. Just off the main route a small square housed a cylindrical glass structure, containing the Golden Menorah, destined for the new Third Temple. They admired the beautiful golden piece, created from 45 kilograms of pure gold, modelled on historic drawings of the original from Hadrian's Arch in Rome, and other sources. According to the sign, the Menorah was worth around three million dollars.

Rebekkah led them on eastwards and they stood at the top of a steep stone staircase, leading down to the Kotel Plaza and the Wall itself. The whole area was brightly floodlit and many Jews – of all colours and former nationalities – were milling around. Some were queueing to approach the wall to pray – the women in a separate area to the right.

The wall itself was also brightly lit, with the now damaged Dome of the Rock mosque visible above it to the left. Next to the staircase was a large display depicting an artist's impression of how the new third temple would look when completed and describing its imminent construction.

'Soon the Third Temple will be built on the site of the previous temples of Solomon, Zerubavel and Herod,' explained Rebekkah, 'but apparently there has been a whole dispute going on as to the exact location. That has yet to be determined – hopefully as a result of the recent excavations – and eventually it will have to be agreed upon by all the Jewish authorities. '

'Oh,' queried Niamh, 'Is there some disagreement about it then?'

'Oh yes,' Brandon replied, 'there's quite a difference of opinion on where the site of the Temple is located. Quite a few people now believe that the so-called Temple Mount was really the Roman Antonia Fortress – which would explain why the Romans didn't destroy it along with the rest of the Jewish city. In which case the real Temple site would have been just south of the fort, in the northern part of the City of David.

'Remember that Yeshua prophesied that *'not one stone will remain upon another'*? Ancient records – Josephus in particular – bear out the fact that that is exactly what happened. Apparently, the Romans dug up even the foundations in order to get at melted gold and silver from the fire which destroyed the building.

'There have actually been five temples – Simon Maccabee, the Hasmonean ruler of Jerusalem in the first century BC, decided to rebuild the temple twice its original size. Later, Herod came along and decided to double the size again, making the temple court a perfect square, 600 feet across. It was Herod's temple that the Romans destroyed, so we shouldn't expect to find any evidence of that – but the original site of both Solomon's and Zerubavel's temples would have been further south, so some evidence of those may have been preserved.

'Also, in 313 AD the Jews still living here commenced building a new Temple after the Edict of Milan – when they were still aware of exactly were the original Temple had been. That work was stopped again only twelve years later by Constantine, and so it fell into disrepair, leaving just the 'western wall' of the Holy of Holies for Jews to worship at. Eventually – only twenty years or so before the Crusaders arrived in Jerusalem – an earthquake caused the Gihon spring to become bitter and the Jews were so discouraged that most of them relocated to Tyre, and then to Damascus.

'By the time Jews returned again to Jerusalem – in the thirteenth century – the tradition had already become established that the Dome of the Rock was where the Temple had previously stood and the original 'western wall' was replaced by this current one here at the Kotel.

'If the archaeologists do determine that the Haram was merely a Roman occupation fort and if those at the lower excavation can discover conclusive evidence of that new temple – Josephus recorded exactly where it should be found – then the City of David site will be confirmed and a new temple can be built without incurring any serious objections from Muslims. In fact, I believe local archaeologists have already found some evidence of a worship site.

'So you're really saying, Brandon,' Shaul began, 'that the Jews we see so fervently praying here at the Kotel – are really praying at the site of an ancient Roman fortress, something which would actually have been completely anathema to our ancestors – and that the real 'western wall' is probably a few hundred yards away, outside the gate there?'

'Exactly!' Brandon agreed.

'Yes,' added Rebekkah, 'and the stones for the new temple are already being quarried near Eilat, which is also where the Temple Institute have discovered a large quantity of gold – the gold is being used to create new temple vessels, and also to help pay for a large part of the soon coming construction.'

'Amazing, said Niamh. 'So, prophecy is about to be fulfilled right in front of our eyes?'

'Indeed,' agreed Alyssa, 'we are very privileged to witness it. One day soon all the nations of the world will come here to worship YHWH. The prophet Zechariah said that *'the survivors of the nations –* after the final battle for Jerusalem and the coming of Messiah – *will come up to Jerusalem year after year to this temple, to celebrate the feast of tabernacles."*

Chapter 26 – Reunited in Jerusalem

'Amazing!' said Niamh, as they stared for a while down at the worshippers below them.

When they descended into the Kotel plaza, they walked outside the Dung Gate entrance to briefly view the greatly extended archaeological site below, before walking across the plaza again towards the Western Wall tunnel, which led them back northwards through the centre of the Old City.

'During the day,' Rebekkah began again, 'we would be able to go up onto the Mount, but it is closed at night. Jews and Christians are now free to go onto the Mount and pray whenever they want. Before the recent war the enemies of Israel made that almost impossible and for some reason our government tolerated that situation.'

'If they start work on the new temple in the City of David, the Haram would be a great place to view the progress of the construction,' said Brandon.

They made their way uphill towards Jaffa Gate through the sparsely lit, tunnel-like narrow streets. Shaul led them across the plaza outside the city walls and down the steps into the bustling Mamilla Mall. The girls stopped frequently to look at potential bride outfits – planning to return the next day – while the men reminisced over their Army days together in Kabul.

By the time they had made their way through the city centre and back to the hotel, they were all ready for a good night's sleep. However, before Shaul could fall asleep he was aroused by a return call from his older brother, Reuben.

'Well, he said presently to an almost asleep Rebekkah, 'Reuben and Leah are on their way. They should arrive tomorrow evening. I knew Leah would swing it.'

'Great,' mumbled Rebekkah, 'and my parents and brothers are coming up tomorrow as well.

'I don't want to keep you up, but I've been thinking, this hotel is not the ideal wedding location. I was having a look online earlier and the Ramat Rachel Kibbutz Hotel seems a much better bet. They have beautiful gardens and are used to hosting weddings. They can handle the meal and mebbe even provide some entertainment afterwards. We can book my brother and your family in there and move ourselves and the others there on the wedding day. What do you think.'

'Sounds good. Mebbe we should take a trip over there in the morning, then, before we start organising all the dresses and stuff. See if Khaista and Aviv feel the same way. *Leila tov.*'

'*Leila tov.*' Shaul replied, climbing back into bed and rapidly falling asleep.

27 – Preparations and conversations

Next morning they all congregated for breakfast in the hotel dining room. The girls elected to sit together and make more definite plans, involving a major shopping trip that afternoon, of course. Aviv and Khaista had been looking at the details of Ramat Rachel Hotel and wanted to take a trip there immediately after breakfast.

They just managed to all fit in the MPV and travelled the short distance to Ramat Rachel – in the south of the city, overlooking Bethlehem and the remains of the former 'separation wall' – in a short time. The views from the kibbutz on the hill were spectacular and everyone agreed it would be a great venue.

After a discussion with the events manager – a young man only too glad to accommodate them – they managed to book the hotel for both the actual wedding ceremony and a celebration meal afterwards. The hotel also had enough rooms free to take Shaul's present party and he and Rebekkah's other guests. They sat down at a table in the garden and ordered coffee, while deciding what next.

The men were given instructions to accompany the girls as far as a men's hire store, to be measured for suits, etc. Other than a promise to comply with that task and to organise cars to take them from their present hotel to Ramat Rachel, plus a photographer to film the event, they were free to spend some time together discussing old times.

Rebekkah had been in contact with her ex-IDF comrade about the venue and had informed her of the now changed circumstances. Her friend – Ilana – was overjoyed to hear that the wedding would now include Bekkah and Shaul, and promised to contact a friend of hers, who was a Reform rabbi.

An Orthodox wedding was out of the question in Israel, where non-Jews (as the Orthodox would see it) like Aviv and Khaista were frowned upon, unless they had completed a full Beit Din conversion process, which there was no time for anyway, at present.

Although Aviv and Khaista no longer really considered themselves Muslim, and were intrigued by their Israelite backgrounds, they were not yet convinced they wanted to officially convert to Orthodox Judaism – in fact, both of them – especially Aviv – were also interested in the whole Messianic/Christian question, and wanted to learn more of that, also. As former Muslims they already regarded Yeshua – Issa Al Masih to Muslims – as a prophet to be revered. And even the Quran had a high regard for Issa, depicting him as the saviour, who currently resided in heaven, but was coming back again to earth one day.

The four couples drove back to the city centre, the men heading for one of the few formal hire stores for men in the city – where they were measured for suits, shirts and shoes for the occasion. After that ordeal was finished and Shaul had paid for the outfits – plus extra outfits for his brother and Rebekkah's father – and arranged when they were to be collected, they headed to a nearby *Aroma* coffee shop and sat down with beers apiece at a table in the shade.

Dev had already agreed to act as Shaul's best man and Aviv had since asked Brandon to perform the same service for him. Niamh, Ilana and Alyssa were happy to act as bridesmaids/matron of honour to both girls.

Armed with credit cards the four girls – joined also by an excited Ilana – began a tour of boutiques in the city, shopping for suitable dresses and shoes for the event. The wedding itself was to be held in two days time.

Shaul had also arranged for two cars to pick them and their families up at their hotel and take them to Ramat Rachel. Shaul's brother had been persuaded to take time off with his wife and was expected to arrive the next day. Rebekkah's brothers and wives, plus her parents, planned to travel up to Jerusalem on the same day.

Several of Bekkah's friends and former army buddies were planning to attend, as were representatives from Shaul's kibbutz in the south. Even so it would not be an extravagant affair – Aviv and Khaista were obviously unable to have either of their families join them, and Shaul only had his brother and wife attending.

The men relaxed in the warm atmosphere.

'Well,' began Dev, 'we agreed back in Kabul to meet up again in Jerusalem after the *Six Hour War* – assuming that Brandon had that right – and here we all are. That war is over and we are sitting at peace in the middle of Jerusalem. You got that one spot on, Doubtin',' he said, deliberately using Brandon's old nickname.

'Yes,' agreed Shaul, 'you sure got it right, Brandon.'

'I can't take any credit for reading what the prophets have told us and simply believing it,' answered Brandon.

'Well, one way or another you've managed to influence all of us, bro,' said Dev. 'What else have you sussed out from all your study of the prophets, then? I seem to remember you talking quite a bit about America being the Babylon spoken of in the bible?'

'Yes, Micky,' Brandon replied, 'and I think that's going to become more and more obvious now. Already there are attitudes developing in the States since the recent war. Far from apologising for our disastrous foreign policy – in allowing Iran to develop nuclear weapons – our government seem determined to keep on blaming Israel. Many people in our nation seem to be agreeing with that attitude – blaming the Jews and/or Israel for every American misfortune. We're very much dependent upon Israel now for oil supplies, for instance.'

'Well, we've landed on our feet, here, that's for sure,' said Shaul. 'Even with all the pressure and economic stress of the war and now this unprecedented aliyah, the future looks bright for Israel. We are becoming more and more a world power to be reckoned with – especially now we don't need to focus nearly so much of our resources on defence.

'Once the country settles down we will begin to grow economically, as well as in population. The government and the *New Israel Plan* are working hard to get agriculture and industry up and running again in the captured territories. At the moment we are importing a lot more food and commodities than we would like, but that will gradually change. Some reckon the total population of Israel could end up more than one hundred million – much more than ten times her size before the war.'

'Yes, well Jeremiah 50 says of the sons of Israel that YHWH will *'bring rest to their land, but unrest to those who live in Babylon.'* So, things will get better here, but for Jews – and others – in America, things will get worse. The verse before that one says that *'the people of Israel and the people of Judah are oppressed. All their captors hold them fast, refusing to let them go.'* I believe that will begin to happen soon in the USA.'

'Brandon, when I met Niamh over in Ireland, we discussed some of these things that you first told us about. Niamh had heard similar teaching on prophecy from the pastor of the church that my cousin and her new husband attend. We decided to have a bit of a talk with him and he talked about Yeshua – Jesus – and offered to pray with us. That was a really strange experience and we both prayed with him to commit ourselves to Yeshua. Since then I've been reading the bible quite a lot – so has Niamh – and I'd really be interested in what you believe will happen next?'

'Yes,' agreed Shaul, 'I was going to ask you something similar.'

Aviv also nodded enthusiastically, adding, 'Khaista and I have also discussed some of these things. We are still confused about a lot of stuff we've read, but we really want to learn more about these things.'

'That's amazing, Michael' said Brandon, 'a real answer to prayer. My congratulations to you both. And Shaul and Aviv, I really appreciate your interest, too. Though, after the events we've all witnessed in the past few months I think you'd be really thick-skinned not to have developed an interest in bible prophecy.

'Well, the prophets spent a lot of time telling us about the last days – which I think you'd agree is definitely where we are now. Some of their words concerned Messiah's first coming, which most Jews still reject – although I think when they open up this tunnel beneath the Temple Mount, there could be a great shock in store for current-day Judaism.

'I agree that things are going to consolidate here in Israel. Israel will prosper and all the talk among other nations about the land Israel now occupies will die down. There are still many enemies of Israel out there – and their intention will still be to see the destruction of Israel – but they are scattered and very disorganised at the moment. The shock of their defeat and the destruction of Iran, Saudi Arabia – and the other Muslim countries that no longer exist – will mean that it will take quite a long time for them to re-group and to re-organise.

'An interesting thing here is America's willingness to allow so many refugees – from Iran, in particular – to come to the USA. Many people have warned that these may become a Trojan Horse, bringing potential destruction to the US, but they are once again being ignored. This influx can only add to the anti-Israel, anti-Semitic – and increasingly, anti-Christian – sentiments, that are becoming more widespread now across the country.'

'Yeah,' added Micky, 'I've been noticing a lot more negative comments about Israel, and about 'Jews controlling the world', etc. – even in my Dad's pub! You reckon that's only gonna get worse?'

'Yes, I think so,' agreed Brandon. 'Eventually, the whole world – every nation included, which means the UN, of course – will join together and send their armies to Jerusalem to destroy Israel once and for all. There will be some destruction, but Israel will NOT be destroyed – and after that will never be insecure again, we are told. But, long before all that happens, I believe America will be taken right out of the picture.'

'That's this 'Babylon' thing, right?' asked Shaul.

'Yes,' said Brandon. 'One thing I did some time back, was to take all the unfulfilled prophecies about Babylon – *mega-Babylon*, or the daughter of Babylon – and put them end to end in one document. Then I colour-coded different sections and printed it out so I could study it over and over.

'A lot of things began to link up when I did that. You see, I believe that YHWH God has hidden all the truth that we need to know in the Tanakh, with the New Testament being a key that helps us unlock the truth. Pieces of the puzzle are hidden in different prophecies and, until we put them all together we don't really begin to see the whole picture. That's how I approach it, anyhow.'

'So, you're saying that we can only find these things out if we really study *all* the prophecies?' asked Dev.

'Yes. Moses told us this when he prophesied that Israel would one day be scattered among all the nations – he promised that, *"if from there you seek YHWH your God, you will find him if you seek him with all your heart and with all your soul."* So, if we keep sincerely seeking to discover the truth, I believe God will show us more and more truth that He has hidden in these prophecies.'

'So, what are the main things you have learned so far?' asked Shaul.

'Well, there are two main things to bear in mind, I suppose – Babylon, which I already mentioned, and this guy the New Testament refers to as the *'man of lawlessness'* – or the *'man opposed to the Torah'* – and also as *'the beast that rises from the sea'*. Evangelical Christians often refer to him as the anti-Christ – the anti-Messiah'.

'The Tanakh speaks of him in different ways, too – *'the prince that will come'*, it says in Daniel, or *'the king of the north'* – which has led some people to think that Daniel is talking about Russia, but it could equally well mean Turkey, which *is* directly north of Israel.

'Do you think he will be Islamic?' asked Dev.

'I think that's a strong possibility – or perhaps just cynically making use of Islam to build a strong following. It may become clear afterwards – when it will be too late, probably – that he only believes in himself as God, because he will come to this new temple – the one Israel is about to build – and declare himself as God there.

'Now those two things tie together like this. The beast will be the one who will destroy mega-Babylon – this great trading mega-city, and the nation she represents. He will work along with Babylon for a while – Babylon is depicted as a woman riding upon the scarlet beast – but then the beast will turn against her. He will form a coalition of ten strong nations – possibly some of those we refer to as the G8, or G20, today – and persuade them to attack and destroy Babylon.

'Habbakuk described their motivation as calling in a debt. *"Woe to him who piles up stolen goods and makes himself wealthy by extortion!"*, he says, *"How long must this go on? Will not your creditors suddenly arise. Will they not wake up and make you tremble? Then you will become their prey."*

'Now what nation has a huge debt to other strong nations and has really no foreseeable hope of being able to repay it? America owes more than twenty trillion dollars to other nations. Who holds the bulk of that debt? China, with Japan a close second, Taiwan, Hong Kong, the UK, Russia, and several other countries – including the main oil exporting countries and the Caribbean banking states.

'Ten nations are going to plot together to destroy America, attack her and destroy her *'in one hour'* – probably with nuclear weapons. Many of those weapons may already have been smuggled into the United States and could be in position now in our major cities. When the destruction comes, it will impact every nation – Jeremiah says, *"At the sound of Babylon's capture the earth will tremble; its cry will resound among the nations."'*

Dev queried, 'When you say 'destroyed', what exactly does that mean? Does it say how final this destruction will be?'

'Yeah, I was wondering that, too,' said Shaul.

'Well, Jeremiah refers to survivors, but they will have to *"return to their own countries",* because there will be no water or food – and presumably a lot of dangerous radiation about. He also says that *"neither people nor animals will live in it; it will be desolate forever."* Jeremiah and the other prophets talk of Babylon becoming desert and swamp and even of the sea covering part of it.

'So, all these survivalist guys – preppers, living in cabins in the woods – they're really just wasting their time then, aren't they?' said Dev.

'Yes, they are indeed,' Brandon agreed. 'The only solution will be to flee – Jeremiah clearly tells us to – before the destruction comes. But many Jews and others will ignore the warning – just like in Germany in the '30s – and remain and be left destitute afterwards, saying, *"Show us the way to Zion."* There won't even be an obvious way to get out of America by then – presumably others, who have prepared for this beforehand, will be able to come in and help them get out and across to Israel.

'Meanwhile, those same ten rulers will have an immediate solution to the world economic crisis that will inevitably follow on from America's destruction. The whole world will be waiting for an answer – and they will have one ready prepared, their chosen leader, the beast, or anti-Christ.

'Of course, he won't be presented in any such terms. He will appear very plausible and sophisticated and, The Revelation says, *"the whole world will wonder after him"*. This guy will be a very acceptable, very charismatic person. Everyone will welcome him as a saviour – a false Messiah.'

'A bit like the reception Barak Obama got after winning the election in 2008 and replacing George Bush?' said Shaul.

'Exactly like that. The reception Obama got then was totally unprecedented – everybody loved him. And we all know how that turned out, and just how much damage he did to our country. This guy will be very similar – only we're talking about ruling the whole world, now. Initially, he will rule over what is referred to in The Revelation as *"the kingdom of the beast"* – the ten nations who appointed him, but he will extend his control to worldwide domination. The Revelation says, *'Who is able to make war with him.'* Obviously, the expected answer is 'No one!'

'And if he's already backed by China, Japan, Russia, and goodness knows who else, and the US is out of the picture ...' said Dev.

'Yes, not a lot of nations that could oppose that line-up.' Shaul agreed.

'The good news is that – according to Daniel – he only has seven years to rule until the real Messiah comes. He'll probably spend the first three and a half years consolidating his power over the whole world, including appearing to be a good friend to Israel. But then he will show his true colours, by setting himself up in the temple and

proclaiming himself to be God. Then people will have to flee Jerusalem. That's referred to as the time of *"Jacob's Trouble"*, or the
Great Tribulation.

Aviv spoke for the first time, 'I find all of this very interesting.
Brandon. You told us back in Kabul about the coming *Six Hour War*
– and now we know that what the bible prophesied was true. Also,
Islam has been dealt a terrible blow by Israel winning this war –
and by the destruction of Mecca. I used to be a faithful Muslim, but
now I have lost all confidence in Islam. Now I am somewhere in between
– a bit of Jewish, bit of Christian, bit of Muslim – but I would like to
know much more!

'Khaista and I have been reading some of these prophetic books
in a Dari translation bible app on our cellphones – only a few
books are in Pashto, and none of them the prophets. Hopefully, in
the near future I will be able to read in Hebrew and then I can read
all of it in the original language.'

'That's great, Aviv. You are a perfect example of that scripture
I quoted earlier – when Moses said about the scattered Israelites that
if we seek YHWH with all our heart we *will* find him. Keep reading
and searching, bro. And it sounds like Dev here has already found
that path.'

'I hope so, Brandon,' Dev said, quietly.

Just then Shaul's cellphone chirped and he answered to find Rebekkah and the girls were ready to meet up with them. Shaul told
them where to find them and ended the call.

Shaul turned to his comrades, 'The girls will be joining us in a
few minutes. Apparently they've completed their shopping spree.'

'On another subject, Shaul – you too, Aviv,' Dev began, 'Niamh
is a realtor back in Ireland and I'm getting involved with her in
selling homes there – to Irish Americans who want to leave the US. I
was just thinking, surely property in Israel must be getting extremely
scarce now – with all the new immigrants – so prices for existing
houses and apartments will start to go up and up. Shouldn't you both
be buying a place to live in before they become totally unaffordable?'

'That's a very good thought, Dev. What do you think, Aviv?'
Shaul responded.

'Yes, I've been thinking about it a little – Khaista and I have
some money saved, which we transferred from Afghanistan into an

account here in Israel. Actually, yesterday was the very first time we used our new bank card. I was surprised when it actually worked. But I don't know what prices are like, or even what part of Israel we want to live in.'

Just then the girls arrived to join them, weighed down with a collection of parcels.

'To be continued,' commented Dev.

'Yes, indeed,' Brandon agreed. Aviv and Shaul both nodded.

'Successful expedition?' Shaul asked, as the girls got seated.

'I think so,' said Rebekkah, with an exhausted sigh. 'But my feet are killing me, now.'

Soon an assortment of beers, coffees and glasses of wine had been ordered and the girls began to relax as their drinks arrived.

'So what've you guys been up to?' asked Niamh.

'Well,' Shaul began, 'we've sorted out all the suits, hire cars and a photographer. Since then we've just been relaxing here and chatting.'

'Oh yeah,' said Rebekkah, 'What were you all discussing, then?'

'Well, just before you arrived we were talking about property in Israel going up in price and the need to buy somewhere to live very quickly.'

'Yes, indeed,' Niamh agreed, 'You are going to see prices go out of reach now that you have all these new immigrants arriving in such numbers. You should seriously consider choosing somewhere now, while you have the chance.' She looked at Aviv and Khaista, 'You, too, Aviv and Khaista.'

Niamh thought for a minute, 'I'm not an expert on the Israeli market, but I'd be happy to offer my expertise, such as it is.'

'That's great, Niamh,' said Rebekkah. 'I really don't feel like running around looking at properties right now, but maybe we could do something in the morning?'

'Tell you what,' said Niamh, 'You guys tell me what you have in mind, and where you'd like to live and Micky and I will contact a couple of local estate agents – sorry, realtors – this afternoon and see what is available and just how expensive it is going to be.'

'Beseder,' said Shaul. 'How about we order some food, then, and we can discuss it?'

Everyone agreed and soon they were eating and talking all at once.

The consensus eventually seemed to be to that Aviv and Khaista would be keen to live near to Shaul and Rebekkah, and also that an apartment in Jerusalem would seem the best option for now – seeing they had a limited time window.

'All you really need is to be in the game,' advised Niamh. 'You can always sell again and move somewhere else, once you have a better idea of what you want. If the prices go up, so will the amount you can expect to get if you sell. The main point is to get on the ladder.'

Shaul and Aviv looked at one another and nodded.

'That sounds like good advice,' said Shaul. 'If you guys are happy to check out the market for us. Somewhere with a good view would be good – and mebbe close to the Light Rail, with parking included. One thing for sure, we won't need a secure room any more.' He smiled.

'OK,' said Niamh, Or *beseder*, as you guys say. Come on, Dev, we've got work to do.'

'See you guys later – back at the hotel, OK?'

The others agreed and Niamh and Micky left on their self-appointed task.

That evening the four couples gathered again in the hotel foyer. Rebekkah's parents – Yuval and Ronit – had arrived from northern Galilee and her eldest brother, Yoel, with his wife, Batya, from Petah Tikvah. Shaul had already taken both couples over to Ramat Rachel to check in and leave their luggage in their rooms, bringing them back in the MPV to the Leonardo Plaza to join the others. Dev and Niamh had arrived back from their tour of properties and were armed with a sheaf of property details.

'*Beseder,*' said Shaul, 'We can discuss the possibilities over a good meal. How about something more Middle Eastern tonight?'

'What do you have in mind?' asked Dev.

'I was going to suggest a Yemenite restaurant – there's one not far from the city centre. You guys will probably never get the chance to try Yemenite food outside of Israel.'

'*Ken,*' said Yuval, Rebekkah's father, 'it is an experience not to be missed.'

'OK – *beseder,* even – let's go for it, I'm starving!' said Dev.

The others agreed wholeheartedly and Shaul made a call to reserve a table for twelve before they headed out to the MPV and Aviv's truck and drove to the German Colony, a couple of kilometres south of the city centre.

When they arrived at the restaurant Shaul received a text from his brother, Reuben, to say they had just arrived in Jerusalem. Shaul gave Reuben directions to take a taxi to join them, transferring their luggage to the MPV when it arrived. Shaul made introductions all around and the proprietor bustled over with a huge grin and added another table, welcoming the newly arrived couple enthusiastically.

'Well, the owner recommended the stuffed plate and I went for it. Now I'm definitely stuffed! That was a great meal.' said Micky, enthusiastically.

The others all nodded in agreement.

'I also had the stuffed plate,' said Yuval, rubbing his stomach and grinning.

'Well, I had the chicken schnitzel, and it was delicious,' said Niamh.

Even Reuben and Leah agreed that the meal had been a success.

'So, brother, do I gather that you're planning to buy an apartment now in Israel,' Reuben asked.

'Yes,' replied Shaul, 'We're going to have a look at some in the morning. Both ourselves and Aviv and Khaista reckon we'd better invest in some property now while the prices are still reasonable – they're already going up, due to the destruction of the war, plus all the thousands of new *olim* that have already arrived. We can rent the apartments out while we're still on duty in Basra.'

'I really don't understand why you'd want to settle down in a third-world country, when you could be back home in New York,' Reuben stated.

There were some startled looks between Rebekkah and her family.

'You mean because of all the new immigrants, I suppose,' Shaul answered. 'There will probably be a year or too of austerity to put up with while the government and the *New Israel Plan* get things really under control. But by then we should start to reap the benefits of a greatly increased population. These are not refugees who are coming, they are voluntary *olim* who really want to contribute to the new Israel – just like Aviv and Khaista, here, do.'

Aviv and Khaista both nodded in agreement.

'I think you're being a bit naive, brother,' said Reuben complacently. 'There's no guarantee that Israel will ever achieve that. You're going to be hard put to rebuild after all the war damage, never mind running a whole new set of territories with an immigrant population who have never set foot in the Middle East before. Most of them don't even speak English, never mind learning Hebrew.'

'I think maybe you are unaware of the nature of Israel, young man,' Yuval began, politely – though to the observant his frustration could be detected. 'Especially now. This country has been built on adversity and a pioneering spirit, which – to be honest – I thought we were beginning to lose. But with the recent war and our complete victory in it, and now all the new *olim* coming in – who have a spirit of expectation and the willingness to build a great new country – we are regaining that great pioneering enthusiasm.

'Back in 1948 we were building almost from scratch – and none of the *olim* then spoke Hebrew, either. That's no longer the case. Israel is now a world leader in technology, in agriculture, in solar power, water distribution, even in our military industries. Israel supplies tanks to India and water systems to China – and we will now be building on that secure foundation.

'Plus now we now control the oil and gas of the Middle East, in addition to the vast oil reserve we've discovered in the Golan – even Europe and the USA itself are in need of our resources. We're already beginning to turn that situation to our advantage. What Israel needs most at the moment is investment to rebuild the infrastructure in the new territories and we are getting that investment. You could not find a more secure place to invest.'

'Yes,' agreed Shaul, 'You could do much worse than invest in the new Israel, Reuben. I was going to suggest it myself.'

'Huh, we'll see.' replied Reuben, bluntly. 'I'd like to see some proof of that before committing myself to any investment.'

Yoel joined the conversation. 'You're welcome to come with me after the wedding and I'll show you just what Israel is achieving right now,' he offered. 'I manage an electronics company in Petah Tikvah, just east of Tel Aviv. We're developing some state of the art technology, there. If you have time, my brother Daniel is involved in R&D

for a company in Haifa and I'm sure he'd be only too happy to show you around there, too. We're not known as the 'start-up nation' for no reason, you know.'

'Well, it can't hurt, I suppose,' Reuben agreed reluctantly.

The conversation wandered from there to the progress in re-construction of damaged buildings and infrastructure in Israel; to the new railway system being built in former Lebanon, Syria, Jordan and Saudi Arabia and the twelve new airports now available in the new territories; to the success of the *New Israel Plan* in governing and developing the new territories and in settling the new *olim* and putting them to work. Shaul, Aviv and Rebekkah also shared with the others their recent experiences of the war and their work in Basra facilitating the new aliyah.

By this time the restaurant was almost deserted and they thanked the proprietor for a great meal and promised to come there again. Dev suggested he squeeze into the truck with Aviv, Khaista and Rebekkah's brother Yoel and wife, Batya – leaving room in the MPV for Reuben and Leah on the way back to the Leonardo Plaza. Shaul then took them and Rebekkah's family in the MPV over to their rooms in Ramat Rachel.

'Why don't you guys relax tomorrow morning – have a swim, or whatever,' said Shaul. 'Bekkah and I will be busy looking at apartments all morning, and you and Yuval have only to get measured for the suits at some stage – so why don't we pick up Dev and Brandon and join you here for lunch – say around one, one thirty?'

'Sounds good to me, bro,' agreed Reuben. 'We're both feeling pretty jet-lagged by now. It would be good to chill out for a bit.'

'Yes, Shaul,' said Leah, 'I'm looking forward to getting out in the sun and into the pool, too. This is a welcome break from New York for us. We'll see you at lunchtime, then.'

Leah gave Shaul a friendly hug and Reuben simply nodded to him.

Shaul returned to the hotel, where the others had already gone to bed.

Rebekkah was still awake when Shaul got to their room.

'We'll meet up with them at lunch, tomorrow.' said Shaul. 'Maybe Yoel and your Dad will have worked some magic on Reuben by then – I hope!'

'He has never been to Israel before,' said Rebekkah. 'Maybe if Yoel can show him some of our achievements he will change his mind a bit about this country.'

'Yeah, I think it would be great if he considered investing in the country. He couldn't lose, really – especially if he allows your brother to give him some advice.'

'My brother and your dad are quite different people, aren't they?' he observed, 'from opposite ends of the political spectrum.'

'Well, my dad is not such a dyed in the wool socialist as he used to be – since my brothers left the army and went into business – but he's still a long way from being the kind of capitalist that your brother is. Let's hope they can find some common ground, eh?'

'Ken,' said Shaul, with feeling.

28 – Weddings and interactions

Next morning while they ate breakfast Shaul and Rebekkah, Aviv and Khaista discussed their requirements with Niamh and Dev and scanned through the details of properties currently available. Shaul had inherited quite a lot of money from his father's estate, which he wanted to invest a good proportion of in a fairly up-market property, and he preferred to buy one outright for cash.

Aviv and Khaista, although now with a certain amount of money saved and transferred from Afghanistan – enough for a deposit on a reasonable apartment, they hoped – and though with two salaries coming in, would still need a mortgage. Niamh had already brought this up with the realtor. The trick would be to find two apartments in different price ranges in close proximity to one other.

The four couples set off in the MPV for the realtor Niamh had chosen as having the best selection of properties. Dev and Niamh were already involved in the process and Brandon was keen to learn more about living in Israel, so he and Alyssa tagged along.

They were to meet the realtor at her office, so Shaul drove straight there through the busy Jerusalem traffic. They confirmed their needs with the realtor, Rivka Levy, a young, ambitious – and pretty! – dark-haired woman of around thirty. She had Aviv and Khaista fill in a form applying for a mortgage. Then they discussed the currently available properties.

The first apartment was not far from Highway One, in the north east of the city, and near to the Light Rail. There were two apartments available in the area. The first was a two bed stone-faced apartment on the second floor of a six storey block, with mature trees and adequate parking just outside. It was clean and reasonably roomy, but with only stairs for access. The second was only a hundred metres from the first, but in a newly built twenty storey tower, with great views out over the city and towards the desert to the east.

The realtor was very keen to get the cash sale from Shaul and Rebekkah and so was prepared to go out of her way also to accommodate Aviv and Khaista as well. She would also be responsible for letting out the apartments until such time as both couples finished serving in Basra and would be in a position to occupy the premises. Both properties seemed suitable, but they moved on to see apartments in another area nearby.

After nearly three hours of viewing apartments, Shaul decided enough was enough. Most of those they had seen would have been acceptable to himself and Bekkah, though several were probably outside the present budget of Aviv and Khaista – and Shaul knew better than to offer any financial help to his comrade.

He summed up their position. 'Listen, Rivka, we really appreciate your help in showing us around today, but we're both getting married tomorrow and I think we need to bring things to a conclusion now. Rebekkah and I are willing to settle for one of three of the apartments you've shown us, but we particularly liked the first one we saw. It really depends on what Aviv and Khaista decide. Do you two have a preference at the moment?' he asked.

'Khaista and Aviv whispered together, then Aviv answered,'Actually, I think we also like the first apartment we looked at. Perhaps we could see them again, briefly, and then try to finalise a deal on both?'

'Beseder,' said Rivka, also tiring from a morning's viewing – even though it was her normal occupation, she normally dealt with only one couple at a time. Finding dissimilar apartments near to one another was a challenge. 'Let's take another look at the first two.'

When they had done so Aviv and Khaista assured Rivka that they would be happy with the apartment if the mortgage could be arranged. Aviv also mentioned that they had some furniture and other objects which they had brought all the way from Afghanistan. Most of this they could make available to rent out with the property. Any of Aviv and Khaista's more personal items could be locked up in a small store cupboard within the apartment.

Rivka, looking pleased as well as relieved, said she would endeavour to get everything arranged as soon as possible. 'I'll dedicate the rest of the afternoon to getting this set up. You're both getting married and having a reception at the Ramat Rachel Kibbutz Hotel tomorrow, isn't that correct?' she asked.

'Ken,' Shaul agreed.

'Well, then, if I can get all the paperwork sorted out I could bring it over there tomorrow afternoon for your signatures. I'll need a check from

Aviv for the deposit then, also. Normally, this would take a week or so to set up, but the IDF and NIP have both made it clear that they would like this expedited, so that will help us greatly with the mortgage company. What time would be convenient, do you think?'

Shaul suggested a time late in the afternoon, when their meal would mostly be finished.

'As for your furniture, Aviv, I understand it's stored at the kibbutz you mentioned, *ken?*' she said.

'Ken,' Aviv agreed.

'Beseder, if you can give me a number and a person to contact there I should be able to arrange with them to have your stuff brought up to the apartment. When you are returning your truck you could label any items you want locked away – mebbe put them in a separate box – and I'll make sure they're stored in the cupboard. Would that work?'

'Ken,' said Aviv, becoming more confident in his grasp of Hebrew, *'Toda raba.'*

Shaul wrote down the name and phone number of a good friend at the kibbutz and they shook hands with Rivka and thanked her again.

'Congratulations to both of you. Have a great wedding,' she said. 'And I'll see you later in the day.'

'L'hitraot!' they replied as they climbed back into the MPV and Shaul quickly turned on the air-conditioning.

'Well,' said Rebekkah, 'It looks like we just bought two apartments. I'm beginning to feel like I'm really getting married tomorrow.'

'Hope you're not getting cold feet, Ms Bar-Ilan?' said Shaul.

'No way, Mr. Levine,' she replied, grinning at Shaul.

'Tov ma'od,' said Shaul, smiling, and the others smiled too.

They drove to Ramat Rachel to join the others for lunch and to celebrate their successful morning's work.

They found Yuval and Ronit, Reuben and Leah, Yoel and Batya either in or sitting around the swimming pool. Yuval swam leisurely toward them, climbed out and dried himself briefly.

'By the look of all your faces I'd say you've had a profitable morning, then?' he said.

'Indeed,' replied Shaul, 'We've decided on two apartments within a stone's throw of each other – in the north east of the city. The realtor hopes to bring us the paperwork to sign after the wedding and reception tomorrow.

'That's great news, boy. Congratulations. And by the way let me introduce you to my younger son, Daniel,' he said, pointing to a young man seated nearby.

Shaul shook Daniel's hand.

'And this is his lovely wife, Gavriella – the angel of the family.'

Gavriella smiled shyly as Shaul took her hand in turn.

Shaul then introduced his friends and their other halves.

'We're none of us in any hurry to eat yet,' said Yuval, 'if you guys want to relax in or by the pool, here. We can eat in a little while. If you need swimming togs you can buy them in the hotel foyer.'

'Beseder,' said Rebekkah, turning to Khaista, 'I think I for one need to relax. Coming, Khaista?'

'Sure,' she replied, and Aviv, Dev, Shaul and the others joined them in the foyer. Soon there were eight more people enjoying the sun and the water.

As Shaul lay in the sun on a lounger provided by the hotel, he could hear his brother in conversation with Daniel and Yoel, as they explained their involvement in their respective companies.

'Sounds like some barriers are coming down,' he said quietly to Bekkah beside him.

'I think we'll just leave them to it,' said Rebekkah lazily. 'By the way, Ilana is joining us later in the afternoon. We're going to try out all our dresses and make sure everything is finalised for tomorrow.'

'Beseder,' said Shaul. 'I'll have to take your Dad and Reuben to make sure their suits fit and collect ours.'

'By the way, where are we going for our honeymoon?' she asked. 'You've been rather secretive about that. I take it we're NOT staying on in this hotel? And do you know where Aviv and Khaista plan to go?'

'That's several questions at once, Shaul grinned. 'I'll answer the last one – Yes, I do.'

'That's not good enough,' complained Rebekkah. 'At least tell me if we're going north, south, east or west?'

'Beseder,' said Shaul, 'I can let you know that much. Mainly south, I would say.'

'Hmmm, interesting. And what about Aviv and Khaista, then?' she asked.

'I don't think it's meant to be a secret, so I can tell you. They'll be spending a couple of days in Tel Aviv and then travelling up to Tiberias to see a bit of the Galil. Your dad has promised to show them around for one of the days they'll be there. He's promised to show Reuben, Dev and Brandon around before that. I've offered Dev and Brandon the MPV and I've hired another car for ourselves for the evening of the wedding, so we'll have it ready to leave next morning.'

'Beseder, you seem to have it all worked out. I'll leave it in your capable hands, husband to be,' she said, raising one eyebrow.

'*Tov ma'od,* wife to be!' he replied with a grin.

Late in the afternoon Shaul received a call from Rivka, the realtor, to say that both offers had been accepted by the respective owners and that she was continuing to work on the paperwork and would see them the next afternoon.

They stayed in Ramat Rachel for their evening meal – no-one felt like driving somewhere else – and most went to bed early. Next morning there was a flurry of activity after breakfast as the women got dressed, hair and make-up sorted, and the men dressed in suits and dress shirts.

Although the hotel had a synagogue, which they could have made use of, they had elected to have the ceremonies out in the open air. Two chuppah – canopies – had been erected in the garden and Rebekkah's brothers, plus some of her former comrades from the army and friends from the kibbutz were already seated, along with Reuben's wife, Leah, and several of Shaul's friends from his kibbutz.

Shaul's former IDF commander, *Seren* Jacob Gefen, now recovered from his shoulder wound in the recent war, had arrived with his wife. With the waiting Rabbi – a bearded young man from the Reform movement, called Alon Gilad, who sat patiently at the front, facing the others – it comprised a reasonable gathering, although there were conspicuously more people seated on the bride's side of the area. A quartet of double bass, cello, violin and viola was playing softly to one side.

At noon Shaul, led by Reuben and Dev walked slowly to the *chuppah* on the left and Reuben and Dev sat down at the front. Brandon led Aviv to the *chuppah* on the right and also sat down at the front. After a short wait the music changed to Mendolsohn's Bridal March and everyone stood as first Rebekkah, led by her father, Yuval, mother, Ronit, and her IDF friend, Ilana, was escorted to the chuppah, leaving her beside Shaul. They were followed by Niamh and Alyssa, who escorted Khaista to join Aviv.

Rabbi Gilad came forward and welcomed everyone, commencing the ceremony. Two cups of wine were blessed for each couple, rings were given and at the end the two bridegrooms each crushed a glass that bride and groom had first drunk from and there was a cheer and shouts of *mazeltov* from the company, as the quartet began to play fast klezmer tunes in celebration. The two couples made their way to the rear and into the hotel itself, where they were able to be alone for a few minutes in two rooms set aside for the purpose.

The guests made their way to the tables set for the occasion, the quartet joining them and continuing to play. After a short time the two newly married couples took their paces at the head table, the rabbi gave a blessing and the meal was served. The photographer stayed around until after the meal and arranged the guests into different groupings for more photographs.

As the proceedings were drawing to a close the realtor, Rivka, arrived and took Shaul and Aviv aside. She had a contract ready for Shaul to sign, but in Aviv and Khaista's case, she explained apologetically, there had been a delay with the mortgage company, who were still checking Aviv and Khaista's employment status.

She assured Aviv that this would just be a formality and that once the papers were ready to be signed he could come to her office and sign everything before they headed back to duty in Basra. Shaul and Aviv arranged to meet in Jerusalem the night before they were due back at the southern airbase, when Shaul could return his hire car – which had just been delivered – and the two couples could travel in Aviv's truck back to Shaul's kibbutz.

The next morning Shaul and Rebekkah, Aviv and Khaista joined the others for a farewell breakfast.

Chapter 28 – Weddings and interactions

Dev stood up and tapped a fork against a glass.

'Could I have your attention for a few minutes. I didn't want to say anything until now and detract from the weddings yesterday, but I just wanted to let you all know that Niamh has agreed to marry me, so we'll be joining the old married couples club in the very near future.

A chorus of 'Congratulations' was heard from around the table.

Shaul stood and lifted his glass of grapefruit juice, 'A toast to Mickey and Niamh,' he said. 'We wish you both all the best. *Mazeltov!'*

The others also raised glasses and again chorussed, *'Mazeltov!'*

'Where will you get married, Niamh,' Rebekkah asked.

'Oh, I think it will have to be in Ireland,' she answered. 'My family would never forgive me if we just went ahead and then sprung it on them. You'll all be welcome to come and join us, of course. We'll let you know when.'

Shaul and Rebekkah set out for Eilat/Aqaba shortly afterwards and Aviv and Khaista once more climbed into their pickup truck and set out towards Tel Aviv.

Dev and Niamh, Brandon and Alyssa, Reuben and Leah, Yuval and Ronit, Yoel and Batya, Daniel and Gavriella, and Ilana remained for a while, chatting and socialising. Reuben and Leah were also travelling to Tel Aviv, as Reuben had agreed to come and visit Yoel's electronics company in Petah Tikva. He was also now planning to travel up to Haifa to meet up with Daniel. Both couples had invited he and Leah to join them for a meal while they were there.

Brandon and Dev and their partners were planning to see a little bit more of Israel while they had the opportunity and had arranged to meet up with Yuval and Ronit in Tiberias the next day, to be shown some of the sites in Galilee. Later in the week Aviv and Khaista had also arranged to come and visit them.

Reuben was impressed by both Yoel's and Daniel's companies, and by the vibrant economy they were able to demonstrate to him. He was even persuaded to take a trip with Daniel into the new territories – he and Leah travelling by train with Daniel from Haifa to the city of Tyre in former Lebanon, on the newly re-built railroad.

He was not only impressed by the sleek and clean modern double-decker train, but also by the tour of new immigrant housing and shops and factories newly established by the *New Israel Plan*.

'So this is kinda like a modern day Marshall Plan – like Europe after the Second World War?' he asked Daniel.

'That's exactly right,' agreed Daniel. 'Our biggest resource is these new *olim* arriving in fresh from Afghanistan, Pakistan and the African countries. They have given up their old life and they are highly motivated to learn the language, find work of any kind and get themselves established as full citizens of Israel.'

'That's very commendable, Dan. But don't you think sooner or later Israel is going to be overwhelmed by the sheer numbers coming in?'

'Not really, we've already assessed the viability of homes, shops and factories, warehouses, etc. So every property that is usable is being assigned to a family, a business, or whatever. Any property too damaged to be re-used is currently being demolished – providing employment – and re-built – providing even more employment.

'By the time some of these new buildings are ready for occupation there will be viable existing businesses ready to expand and make use of them, freeing the old buildings for others. The gist of the plan is that tenants can become owner occupiers in due course – same with business premises. So, what do you think?'

'I think I'm going to recommend to some of my associates and friends that NIP is well worth investing in. I like your pioneering spirit here in Israel. We used to have that in the USA, too, but I think it has been disappearing for quite some time. Too many people on government welfare, who can't see any other option for their lives.

In too short a time Shaul and Rebekkah, Aviv and Khaista, were back in Jerusalem – Shaul and Rebekkah after several days in Eilat/Aqaba, with trips south into the Sinai and to Haql in Midian, where they had recently been involved in the war. Aviv and Khaista had spent several days in an apartment in Tel Aviv, then travelled up to Galilee, where they met up with Yuval, who, as promised, showed them around his part of the Galilee and a little of south Lebanon.

Aviv had met that afternoon with the realtor, Rivka, and finally signed the mortgage agreement, plus an agreement with the realty company to rent out the furnished apartment during their absence in Basra.

'I'm so glad we decided to organise these apartments, Shaul,' he said, as they shared a couple of ice-cold beers in the hotel bar. 'Now I feel much more a part of this country that I've been working for, but only just arrived in a week ago.'

'That's great, bro. I think we made a good decision there. I feel the same way – invested in what I now think of as *my* country.'

'Do you miss the USA at all, Shaul?' he asked.

'I can't really say that I do,'Shaul replied. 'I joined the military to see other parts of the world and to avoid being sucked into my father's business world. Then, when my parents were killed I began to wonder about Israel – especially after all the stuff Brandon told us back in Kabul.

'I guess my involvement with Israel has just grown from there. Beginning a relationship with Bekkah just cemented that for me. Now that we're married I feel joined to her family, too – even more a part of the landscape. And buying the apartment was another logical step. I needed to do something with that money, anyway. If there'd been any problem with your mortgage I'd have offered to buy your apartment for you both, in the meantime.'

'You are a very generous man, Shaul. *Toda raba,'* said Aviv.

'Not really,' said Shaul, 'I really don't care about money. I know I've been blessed by being part of a rich family – and I'm grateful for that – but continuing that lifestyle has never appealed to me. What about you?' he said, endeavouring to change the subject and remove the spotlight from himself. 'Do you miss Afghanistan?'

'I miss my family – my uncles and cousins – but I see myself as a pioneer. I hope they also will make aliyah in the future – if the door remains open. I write to them and tell them what I am doing, how I am getting on. I know my cousin, Elina, also writes to Khaista. She's always full of questions – especially now we can tell her more about Israel itself. I think maybe she is wanting to come here soon.'

'What *do* you think of Israel – now that you've seen just a little bit of it?' Shaul asked.

'Like I said, I see myself as a pioneer – so, now I have a much better idea of what Israel is like – although I'd love to spend much more time here. Seeing Jerusalem and Tel Aviv, and especially visiting with your father-in-law up in Ha Galil – that was special. I talked to lots of people in Tel Aviv – on the beach, in pubs and restaurants and hotels. They are a very interesting people and I feel I know a little bit more about them, now. I like their 'can do' attitude. They seem to love a challenge and no country has faced a bigger challenge, I think.

'Yuval and Ronit told us a lot about the old days – about pioneering in Ha Galil. They've never really had much money, but they own a real share in Israel – in the land and in the people. I want to feel like that, too. That is why I am so pleased that we were able to buy the apartment. It gives us a stake in the country, just like everyone else. I can say we belong in Jerusalem, we have a home there.'

'Aviv, what do you think you'll do when you are no longer working for the NIP in Basra? Have you any plans, ambitions?'

Maybe the NIP will offer me something else, perhaps in the northern territories? I know Khaista wants to use her computer skills, maybe even become a teacher. I'd like to continue to help my own people, the Pashtuns – along with the other *olim*. Perhaps one day – when I have fully mastered the language and know the land better – I would like to be involved in politics, helping to make good decisions for the future of this country.'

'Wow!' Shaul responded, 'that's a great vision to have.'

'What about you, brother? What do you think you will do after Basra?'

'I think I'll probably leave the IDF. It's a great organisation – and the only one that could cope with the problems of this aliyah. But back in Israel there is no real need, so I'll probably go back to civilian life – after many years now in the military.

'At least I've developed some leadership skills during this aliyah and certainly military experience is never a disadvantage in Israeli society. I don't know exactly what I'd like to do, though. I'll have to keep thinking about that. Maybe the NIP will offer me something, too.'

'Do you think your brother will ever bring his family to live in Israel?'

'I don't know – certainly not at the present time. But, if things are going to get much worse for Jews in the US, maybe he will consider it. I just hope he doesn't leave it too late – like all those millions of Jews who were unable to leave Germany and experienced the holocaust. I hope he got something out of his visits with Yoel and Daniel. I guess Bekkah will hear from her brothers in due course. Maybe he will seriously consider investing in this country.'

Brandon and Dev had travelled up to Galilee with Alyssa and Niamh, enjoying the sights and luxuries of Tiberias – a very lively tourist oriented town, with plenty to see and do and also many great restaurants. On their second day they met up with Yuval, who gave them a tour of the Golan heights, driving into the old town of Quneitra – blown up by the retreating Syrian Army in 1973, but now being rebuilt and with a new population. They drove up the hill of Merom Golan, to the lookout there, and gazed into former Syria from the binoculars placed on the height.

'The land of Bashan,' Yuval explained, 'Where some of the twelve tribes settled when Moses first brought them to the Promised Land. The ruins of Damascus are only sixty kilometres away. To the south is the land of Gilead, formerly northern Jordan. If we look over to the west you can see the mountains of Lebanon, where the tribe of Dan had their inheritance.'

'Can we go into Lebanon?' Brandon asked.

'Nothing simpler,' Yuval answered. 'Our kibbutz is right below what used to be the 'Good Fence.'

They drove north then west across the top of the Huleh Valley, passing the entrance to Kfar Giladi kibbutz, arriving at Metulla and then crossing straight over the old border into Lebanon and turning south again. They could see where the road had been repaired where the border had been.

'All these villages were deserted during the war,' said Yuval. 'Now they're full of new immigrants who are keen to be fully integrated into Israel. It's so refreshing to have friends living above us, instead of deadly enemies. Hezbollah, who used to control the whole of southern Lebanon, had more than 100,000 rockets aimed into Israel.

Many of them hit us and many of our people died, or were injured – including some from our kibbutz.

'But the IDF drones took out a lot of the launch sites and then the news about a nuclear attack on Damascus got around and suddenly there were fewer and fewer rockets being launched. I guess they believed Israel had fired the nuclear missile and that they would be next, although the missile was actually fired *from* Damascus and we only managed to divert it back again – same thing with Beirut and Gaza.

'If we hadn't they would have fired many more at us and maybe some would have hit and wiped out Haifa or Nahariyya or some other part of Israel. As it was we destroyed their nuclear capability in a few minutes and then they fled. When our ground troops went in they expected heavy resistance – they found none, only the last few civilians trying to flee from us – people whose cars had broken down, or had an accident. I was sent in with the Reserves and we just drove through Lebanon without any opposition.

'The biggest problem the IDF had was trying to catch up with the enemy. Northern Command eventually sent helicopters and ships with tanks and APCs, landing them in Lebanese and Syrian cities like Tripoli and Latakia, but they couldn't catch up with the enemy either. Our troops didn't stop until they reached the Turkish border. The Turks had lots of tanks and artillery lined up along the border, but they never fired a shot. Turkey weren't involved in the war at all – except to receive the millions of refugees, which they're still trying to cope with.

'Our company had mostly light APCs and trucks because we were never meant to be at the front line, but we found ourselves driving right across Syria and ended up at the Euphrates River – place called Deir Ezzor. Across the River we could see a lot of Kurdish Peshmerga fighters who were cheering us on. It was a welcoming party – like holiday outing, instead of a war! Some of them eventually came across the River to chat with us and they were very friendly.

'Israel now has a proper official friendship treaty with Kurdistan, though we always supported them quietly, anyway – supplied them with weapons we captured from Hamas, etc. Now Deir Ezzor is an Israeli city with a whole new population of Pashtuns, Menashe, Igbo – you name it.

'We could drive north or west from here for five hundred kilo-metres now and not see a single enemy. Same in every direction, really. The Turks don't want to mess with us, though they're not exactly allies any more, like they once were – but in every other direction we have just desert, or the Mediterranean, for company. And along the Euphrates, the Kurds, who are working closely with Israel to supply oil and gas to the rest of the world.

They had arrived in Kfar Kila, a former Lebanese village, and stopped there. New construction was going on in several locations and the village seemed to be thriving. Newly placed road signs were in English, Hebrew and Arabic – with some in Pashto, as well. Many of the population were black-skinned and obviously of African origin.

'Can we walk around,' asked Brandon.

'Sure, it's perfectly safe now, like I said earlier,' Yuval replied. 'Most of these guys probably speak English, anyway.'

Brandon and Dev climbed out of the MPV and Niamh, Alyssa and Yuval joined them. They walked through the centre of the village, where there were several cafes open. Brandon chose one that had a large tree giving some shade and they sat down at a table, ordering coffee once a young black waitress approached them.

'Where are you from,' Brandon asked her.

'From Nigeria,' she replied.

'What city in Nigeria are you from,' he asked again.

'Abuja,' she said. 'Have you ever heard of it?'

'Yes,' replied Brandon, 'I've been there. I've spoken in the synagogue and in a couple of churches there. I'm American, but my background is Igbo.'

'You are very welcome, then,' she said. 'Are there many Americans from Igbo background, then?'

'Yes,' he said. 'Several million of them.'

'Oh,' she replied, 'and are they also planning to come to Israel?'

'I think some would like to,' said Brandon, 'myself included, but it may not be possible.'

'Beseder,' she said. 'I will get your drinks, now. *Toda.'*

'Toda raba,' said Brandon in return.

'Really strange,' he muttered. 'A Nigerian Igbo, living and working in Lebanon and speaking some Hebrew!'

'You want to go over to the Euphrates – to Deir Ezzor and Raqqah. Raqqah is just over the border in Kurdistan, but that all used to be ISIS controlled territory at one time. Raqqah was their headquarters. Deir Ezzor is a real cosmopolitan city now.'

The girl returned with their drinks and they relaxed as they drank coffee, or grape juice. As they sat there a Nigerian man walked up smiling broadly. He greeted Yuval by name and shook his hands enthusiastically.

Yuval said, 'Yosef, this is Brandon, my Igbo-American friend.'

Yosef became excited, shaking Brandon's hand enthusiastically and welcoming him to Israel, *'Shalom, aleichem,'* he cried. 'you are very welcome.'

'Shalom, shalom,' Brandon replied, and Dev and the girls repeated the greeting.

'How do you know these guys?' Brandon asked, turning to Yuval.

'At the moment we supply them with fruit and vegetables and things like silage, hay and manure, help them get parts for tractors – stuff like that.

'Yes,' said Yosef, 'Yuval and his kibbutz are very helpful to us. They teach us many things.'

'Not for much longer, my friend. Soon you'll be supplying your own village with all the fruit and vegetables, milk and beef they can eat.'

He turned to Brandon, 'These guys are learning fast. They are very teachable and they listen carefully when we explain something to them – how we do things in Israel, and so forth.' When their crops are ready some of us will come over and help them to harvest, but next year they'll probably do it all themselves. It's creating quite a bond between their village and our kibbutz. We *are* neighbours after all.'

'Some of their traditions are different from ours, and some are the same, with maybe a different twist here and there. They invite us to join in their celebrations and we invite them to ours. And that's the main reason why that fence is gone for good – the trust we are developing between us. It's not just the Nigerians, the Pashtuns are just the same. We help them, too. They are all very keen to learn how to be good Jews.'

Chapter 28 – Weddings and interactions

'It's great to see the ingathering in reality – something that seems to be working. Is this what is happening in all the territories?' asked Dev.

'I believe so,' answered Yuval, 'though I haven't been down to the Gaza Strip – or the Sinai, or Midian – to find out for sure, but the same principles are being applied in all the new territories. I've taken a trip up north, though – skirting around the ruins of Damascus and up to Homs, Hama, Idlib and Aleppo – the roads are great, a lot of it freeway, but the cities were destroyed by the civil war and are now being reconstructed. Then we went over to Latakia and Tartus, and down the coast into Lebanon – Tripoli, Byblos and on down to Sidon and Tyre. Everywhere I've been there's new construction going on, people out on the streets – a lot of hard work and a lot of happy people, as well.

'Do you think there will come a crisis when the number of *olim* becomes too much to cope with?' asked Brandon.

'I don't think so,' said Yuval. 'Already they're talking about plans to build new cities out in the desert – and some kibbutzim, also, to farm the land out there. They're planning to bring water from the Euphrates to irrigate the desert – so anything's possible.'

Brandon was keen also to see the south of the country, so he, Dev and the girls drove back to the coast at Nahariyya, then south via Haifa and Tel Aviv to the Gaza Strip. They skirted the north of the Strip – where Beit Hanoun and a couple of kibbutzim – now being rebuilt – were cut off from the rest of the Strip by the still radioactive ruins of Gaza City.

Instead, they turned onto Highway 34, then south onto 232, bringing them quickly to Highway 25 running west from Be'ersheva. They turned right towards the Strip again and soon found themselves skirting the ruins of Gaza City on the south, where the re-erected former border fence now separated them from the hazardous area. *Danger, Radiation* warning signs were posted all along the length of the fence. Someone with some wit had added to one of the signs, 'HAMAS', between the two words, and then stroked it out with an X across the word.

'Meaning, 'no longer any danger from Hamas',' said Dev.

'That's true,' agreed Brandon.

They rejoined Highway 4, which took them south through the middle of the former Strip to Khan Yunis and Rafah. They passed several roads leading off to the right, to kibbutzim that had been evacuated by Ariel Sharon in 2005 but were now being rebuilt by some of the former kibbutz members and their families – a new generation rebuilding on the ruins of the past.

In Khan Yunis they saw only a few people who looked like Arabs – most seemed to be African or Pashtun, according to their dress. Most looked happy and industrious. They drove on into Rafah and came to the new city centre, which had originally been the area of the old border with Egypt – the Philadelphia Corridor.

All sign of the original huge razor wire topped border wall, with it's 1,000 metre security zone on the Egyptian side – had gone. In its place was a huge construction site, with some multi-storey buildings already partly constructed.

The area was buzzing with activity, trucks and delivery vans in evidence everywhere. Black Igbos were working alongside swarthy Pashtuns and Menashe – with evidence of a few Arab keffiyahs among them. Huge signs on the security fences explained what was being built, many with colourful artists impressions of the new structures.

North and south of the new city centre the construction became more residential – mostly high rise apartment buildings. To the north, heading towards the sea, Brandon and Dev passed a huge area of new construction on either side of the road, which – according to the signs outside – had been cleared of many acres of sand dunes and was now being made into a new residential area.

'Well, they didn't have to import any sand for all the concrete, at any rate,' said Dev.

'It's incredible,' said Niamh. 'This was the terrorist haven that kept on attacking Israel for years – and now look at it. It's a whole new world.'

'Yes, and some of the people building it and living here are original inhabitants of the Strip,' said Brandon. 'Now that they are free of Hamas and the PLO they seem to want to get on with their lives like anyone else. I guess seeing people like the Pashtuns – not so different from themselves – coming thousands of miles with their families, just to be a part of the new Israel – must have made an impact.'

They found themselves suddenly at the Mediterranean Sea and turned south on a narrow track along the edge of the beach, where the sea broke lazily among rocks at the water's edge. Less than a kilometre ahead they could see a breakwater jutting out into the sea, with a few leisure craft moored on the landward side. Here the beach became broad and sandy and they parked the MPV opposite it and changed into their swimming things.

After a time swimming they rested on sun loungers under the shelter of a couple of beach umbrellas – presided over by a young Igbo man, who collected a small fee from them. Brandon began a conversation with the young man, whose said his name was Bebo – asking him how he had arrived in Israel.

'We travelled right across Africa in a pickup truck – my whole family,' he explained. 'It took us nearly two weeks. Our truck broke down several times along the way, but the Israeli soldiers came along and helped us. They also gave us water, bread and fruit. We drove through many countries – Cameroon, CAR, South Sudan, Sudan and then Egypt,' he said. 'then, finally, we arrived here in Khan Yunis and registered with the *New Israel Plan.* They offered jobs to my dad and my brother. My mother also works in Khan Yunis, in a bakery.

'How long have you been here, then,' Brandon asked him.

'About two weeks, sir,' he replied. 'My father and older brother are working on the building site just down the road here. We live not far from here in a trailer camp – on the site of Gaza airport – but when the new apartments are complete we will be able to move into one of them.'

'What do you hope to do in the future, Bebo?' Alyssa asked him.

'I would like to finish my education and go to university here in Israel, he said.

'How do you find life here in Israel? Is it what you expected?' asked Brandon.

'We are very happy to be here in Israel,' he replied. 'We expected to have to work hard here, but we also have freedom. We are able to meet and worship in total freedom, here. In Nigeria we had to be careful of Boko Haram and the Fulani tribesmen, all of them Muslims who hated us.

'Now many, many Igbo are coming to Israel. Here, if we work hard we will prosper and live in peace. So we are happy here. Life will be even better when we have a proper home in our new apartment.'

'Thank you for talking to us,' said Brandon.

'You are from America?' Bebo asked.

'Yes, but my ancestors were Igbo, also. I have been to your country – to Abuja and Lagos. I have spoken in synagogues and churches there.'

'Ah, there are some Igbo living in America, then?' he asked.

'Yes, there are many – thousands were taken there as slaves in the 1800s. Many Black Americans are descended from the Igbo – several million, in fact,' said Brandon.

'And will these Igbo Americans come to Israel, soon?' Bebo asked.

'There are some who would like to. Maybe, if life becomes difficult in the USA many more will want to come. I don't know.'

'But surely this is your real home, just like us?' he asked, puzzled.

'Yes, you are right,' said Brandon quietly.

PART TWO – Babylon rising

The judgement to come
Just a few years on ...

29 – Time to flee Babylon?

When Dev and Niamh returned to Boston, and Brandon and Alyssa to Raleigh, they began to notice that America was now taking a much stronger stand against the newly revived State of Israel. The government tone was becoming harsher and government spokespersons were still in total denial of the USA's responsibility for the recent nuclear war – having allowed Iran to obtain nuclear weapons.

The previous Republican government had been strongly supportive of Israel, but they had been replaced by a very anti-Israel government who were now talking seriously about withdrawing all aid from their supposed ally. There was anger and great resentment that the super-power now had to negotiate with lowly Israel to obtain essential oil from the Middle East – even though the shipping costs were now greatly reduced because it was now possible to pipe oil directly to the Mediterranean ports.

Anti-Semitism – already becoming rife in America before the *Six Hour War* broke out – was now being actively encouraged by many statements even from government departments and agencies. Some congressmen were calling for restrictions on Jews wanting to make aliyah to Israel, or on Jewish businessmen considering investment in the *New Israel Plan*.

A law had just been introduced to greatly limit the movement of funds to Israel and some Jews were taking this as a sign that now was the time to make aliyah. Others were sure this would only be a temporary hiccup and that things would settle down and get back to normal in a reasonably short time.

Dev and Niamh discussed the new situation as they made plans for their forthcoming wedding in Ireland.

'It's just as Brandon told us it would be,' said Dev, 'that America would turn against Israel and that the USA would become a dangerous place for Jews and other believers. I think we need to have a back-up plan ourselves to make sure that, if it becomes necessary, we can get out of here once things become too difficult.'

'Well, I'm an Irish citizen and once we're married, you will have the right to reside in Ireland, too – in fact you qualify anyway because your grandfather came from Ireland.'

'Is that right?' asked Mickey.

'Definitely. I've been researching all this stuff for the website, so I ought to know,' she replied.

'Mebbe I should arrange to get together with Brandon sometime soon, and discuss all the possibilities. I remember him saying something about certain Jewish businessmen planning ahead for this scenario – buying land in Maine and building hidden bunkers to hide escaping Jews. We might even be able to arrange a sort of halfway house in Ireland, do you think?'

'It's certainly worth discussing. Brandon has a lot of contacts with both ordinary Jews and with the Igbo black Jews. We're already involved in getting Irish Americans back to Ireland, so it wouldn't be a big stretch to also help Jews – and, if it comes to it, maybe Christians, too – to escape via Ireland.'

'Yeah, if they get to the stage of actually forbidding Jews to go to Israel, we could possibly mask their real destination by sending them to Ireland, first. I think it would be good to have a proper discussion with Brandon pretty soon – before this government get around to making any actual laws about it.'

A couple of days later Niamh was on a plane flying back home to Kilkenny, to begin making preparations for her wedding to Micky in a few weeks time. Her parents were delighted to see the ring she proudly displayed to them and she and her mum began planning trips to various stores for wedding dress, shoes, bridesmaid's dresses, etc.

She was also planning to spend some time getting her and Dev's new business up and running. Once she had given in her notice to her boss she soon got involved in scouting out several properties in the greater Dublin area and eventually decided to buy two of them – near to one another in the same development – both of which she was able to purchase for a greatly reduced price.

The funds had been made available partly from her and Dev's own savings, boosted by a large investment from Dev's father, Brendan. With two properties now owned by their new company, she quickly organised for a local business to carry out minor repairs and redecorate the houses. They also agreed to give the gardens a make-over as well.

When the work was completed she picked a sunny afternoon, took a digital camera with her and shot a series of pictures inside and outside the two properties. Then she chose a selection of the best pictures and began to add them on two new pages she created on their company website.

Brandon and Alyssa had been discussing the same topic as Dev and Niamh, at their home in Raleigh, North Carolina.

'The government are really getting serious about restricting the Jews from investing in Israel, or making aliyah there,' said Brandon.

'It's unbelievable that our country should come to this – making the Jews feel unwelcome in the US,' said Alyssa. 'It's just like what we read about Nazi Germany in the thirties.'

'Yes, and I believe it will follow the same pattern – more and more restrictions, more and more limits on Jewish freedom, leading to actual violence and arrests of not only Jews, but eventually probably bible-believing Christians as well – anyone who insists on taking their bible seriously.'

'So, this could soon apply to us and our friends, too?' Alyssa asked.

'I truly believe it will. And the bible tells us to, *"Flee Babylon, and do not be a partaker of her judgements."'* said Brandon. 'When is the right time to flee? I believe the scripture in Matthew 10:23 answers that question, *"When you are persecuted in one place, flee to another."* In other words, when the persecution gets really serious it's time for us to leave this country.'

'Well, we'd better have a proper plan made before that time comes,' suggested Alyssa.

'Exactly,' agreed Brandon. 'We need to know where we're going and just how we're going to get there – long before we actually have to go.'

'Will we need to sell our house, then?' Alyssa asked.

'I think we will have to. If we leave it until a lot of other people are wanting to leave then we will get much less for it, or mebbe not be able to sell it at all.

'We also need to start teaching others about this. We have a responsibility as watchmen to make sure other believers are aware of what we believe is coming. And we need to organise an underground movement to aid people in getting out when the time comes.

'There are some who have foreseen this day coming and have already been making plans – buying land and building secret bunkers to hide people in. We need to link up with those people and know how to pass people on to them when the time comes.'

'And where do you think we should move to, Brandon.' she asked. 'Have you a particular country in mind?'

'Well, we're Igbo and therefore of Israelite background, so I think Israel would be the natural place for us, don't you think?

'I do,' agreed Alyssa. 'Ever since we went there I've been thinking what it would be like to go and live there. We would need to start teaching the children some Hebrew, don't you think?'

'Yes,' agreed Brandon, 'but maybe we shouldn't tell them where we are planning to go until we are safely out of the country.'

'Don't Dev and Niamh have a business where they help people leave the USA to live in Ireland?'

'They do,' said Brandon, 'but *we* sure don't look very Irish, do we?'

'I guess we don't,' Alyssa laughed.

'But their business might be useful to get ordinary Jewish people out via Ireland. It's probably a good idea to talk it over with them. There may be some Jews who also have an Irish connection – there's a lot more inter-marrying of Jews today than there was in the past.'

Reuben, Shaul's brother, had been talking to several of his Jewish business associates about his recent trip to Israel. Some of them were quite interested and wanted details of what he had seen and learned there. However, when they decided to take action in terms of investing money in the *New Israel Plan*, there suddenly appeared to be technical difficulties.

Reuben was puzzled and contacted Shaul to explain the problem.

'Shalom, brother,

I hope you are settling down to married life with Rebekkah – seems like a nice Jewish girl.

I enjoyed talking to her father and brothers and both of them took some time out from their own businesses to show me a lot of what is happening in today's Israel. As a result I had decided to invest some of Dad's money in the New Israel Plan and have encouraged some of my associates to also consider similar investment.

However, when we actually tried to transfer money into Israel we began to find technical difficulties occurring, which has so far made that impossible. My bank are at a loss to explain the situation.

I wondered if you had any idea of why this should be the case?

Perhaps I should contact Yoel, in Tel Aviv and see if he has any ideas. What do you think?

Your brother,

Reuben.

Shaul was mystified, though encouraged that his brother and friends had enough confidence in the new Israel to consider investing. He still had money – quite a lot of it, in fact – in his account in New York and decided to try transferring some of it to his account in Israel.

When he tried to do so he discovered that an error kept occurring.

Hmmm, he thought. *Let's take this a step further.*

He emailed Dev, in Boston, explaining the problem he was having and asked him if he would do him a great favour and transfer ten thousand dollars to his Irish bank account for him, then transfer it again to Shaul's Israeli account. He gave Dev the details of his account in Israel.

When Dev replied, giving him details of his business account in Boston, Shaul found that he was able to transfer the money to Dev's account without a problem and emailed Dev again to say that the money had now been deposited in his account.

About a day later he heard back from Dev, saying that he had been able to successfully transfer the money to their account in Ireland and that Niamh would then transfer it on to Shaul's Israeli account. When he checked his account in Israel the money had in fact arrived.

He checked his New York account and again tried to transfer a similar sum to his Israeli bank. Again there was an error and the transaction failed. He tried with a smaller amount – only $1,000 this time, but to no avail. There was again a mysterious error. Shaul decided he had better let Reuben know about the whole experience and emailed him again.

Brandon and Dev agreed to meet together in New York. They also hoped to have time to meet up with Shaul's brother, Reuben, to discuss the deteriorating situation for Jews with him. They had booked a double room in the Holiday Inn, on Manhattan's Lower East Side which was relatively inexpensive, compared with other options.

When Brandon arrived from the elevator and opened the door of their room he discovered Dev had already settled in.

'Hey, bro, ya made it then? D'ya have a good flight?' said Dev as he embraced his old comrade.

'Sure, it was uneventful, which is good enough for me,' Brandon replied.

'Thank goodness for central heating,' he added. 'It's mighty cold up here, compared to North Carolina. Seems like only yesterday we were travelling around in Israel.'

'Yes, indeed,' agreed Micky, 'that was a great trip. Niamh really enjoyed it. I hope Alyssa did too?'

'Oh she did. In fact, that's something I was going to bring up with you. We have been discussing this and we've decided to sell our house as soon as we can get a reasonable offer, then rent somewhere suitable in the meantime. You see, we're planning to make aliyah to Israel.'

'Wow!' Dev responded. 'I see now why you were so keen to talk to all those Igbo immigrants when we were over there.'

'Yes, I suppose the possibility was already in the back of my mind when we were there. But it's only become a concrete idea since we came back and Alyssa and I have been discussing the changes we're seeing in this country – especially towards Jews. It won't be long before those attitudes are extended to people like ourselves, those who love Israel.'

'Speaking of which,' said Dev, 'I had an email from Shaul – about his brother Reuben. After visiting with Rebekkah's brothers he'd come home keen to invest in the *New Israel Plan* and to encourage some of his colleagues to do so. But guess what? When he went to transfer money to Israel errors came up on the system. So, he got in touch with Shaul about it.

'Shaul also tried to transfer some of his own money from his New York bank to his account in Israel and found the same problem – an error kept coming up. So he emailed me and asked if I would transfer money for him via our new business account in Ireland. I gave him the details of my account in Boston and he transferred the money across – no problem.

'Same thing when I transferred it to Ireland and when Niamh, after I'd sent her the details of Shaul's account, transferred it on to Israel. So, you might have a problem right there – getting your money out of this country. It certainly looks like the government are blocking any money transfer from USA to the Jewish State.'

'I see,' said Brandon, thoughtfully. 'Even more reason to try to get together with Reuben while we're here.'

They discussed the recent political developments in their country.

'I've heard that Homeland Security are beginning to round up people belonging to pro-life organisations and putting them in camps,' said Brandon.

'Yes,' agreed Dev, 'Well, the IRS have been giving such groups – and other Christian and Jewish groups – a hard time for quite a while now – hitting them with surprise audits, delaying tax exemption status and so forth.'

'So Christian and Jewish groups could be next to be rounded up?' Brandon asked.

'It seems very likely,' said Dev. 'Since the Republicans lost the election this new government have quickly begun to undo every positive move they'd made. And the slogan *With Jews we lose!* has been getting more and more airtime recently and all sorts of crazy accusations about Jews are being seriously discussed on air and in our newspapers.'

'Yes,' agreed Brandon. 'It reminds me of that scripture in Jeremiah 51 – you know, where it says, *"Get balm for her pain; perhaps she can be healed. We would have healed Babylon, but she cannot be healed ..."* The previous president and government had done a lot to heal this land, but even so everything they tried to do was strongly opposed. This lot seem to be capitulating to the tide of opposition – especially where it concerns Israel.

'That scripture goes on to conclude, *"let us leave her and each go to our own land, for her judgment reaches to the skies, it rises as high as the heavens."* So, Alyssa and I decided to put our home on the market a few weeks ago – and I think we may have a buyer, now. But then we'll need to transfer money out of the US and then somehow get ourselves and the kids out of the country, also. We wondered if you and Niiamh could help us with that in any way?'

'Sure,' said Micky. 'we'd be happy to be of help. We've been facilitating Irish Americans travelling to Ireland for some time now.

We've learned the ins and outs of Irish law on immigration and so forth. The only problem is ...'

'... that we don't exactly look like the typical Irish,' Brandon completed the thought for him.

'Yeah, exactly, bro,' agreed Micky. 'But here's a suggestion. We offer you a job with our company in Ireland and you move there first – ostensibly to take up a job with us. Then – once your funds are safely out of the USA – you can travel on to Israel from there. We can even offer you a house for a while in Ireland, if necessary.'

Well, that would be really great, bro. Thank you,' said Brandon.

'It's no trouble at all,' said Dev. 'We'll make a start on that plan straight away, shall we?'

'Yes, indeed.' answered Brandon.

The next day the two comrades met with Shaul's brother, Reuben, at his company offices.

Over coffee in Reuben's conference room they shared the plan for Brandon and Alyssa's family to leave the USA for Israel, via Ireland.

Reuben queried if they were being a bit hasty and suggested that the present situation was simply due to a bit of hysteria after the recent nuclear war in the Middle East and that he expected that things would calm down in a short while and return to normal, once the new government found their feet.

Even though Brandon and Dev attempted to show him that the problems with money transfer were only the tip of the iceberg and that these things had been foretold long ago by the Hebrew prophets, Reuben became increasingly sceptical.

'You can't base business or life decisions on the words of some prophet written hundreds of years ago,' he answered. 'It just doesn't make any sense.'

They both attempted to show him just how accurate those predictions had been about the recent war, but Reuben just couldn't – or wouldn't – see it.'

'I don't see any signs of a mass exodus of Jews from the United States,' he said.

They told him about how many Jews were even now being helped to leave via the underground, but he scoffed at that, saying that none of his contacts had shown any signs of wanting to leave the country.

They eventually left him in frustration, Reuben still confident that his ideas were the more soundly based.

'He's just blinded, that's all,' said Brandon, sadly, 'like so many other Jews – and Christians, too.'

'Or mebbe he's just plain stubborn and totally arrogant,' suggested Dev, with feeling.

The situation in the United States did not improve. The Department of Justice began to target more and more Jewish and Christian institutions with lawsuits and arrested and incarcerated many for dubious and seemingly made-up 'crimes'. The accused were forced to spend a lot of their hard-earned resources on their defence – often made even more difficult by the prosecution by extreme demands for thousands of unnecessary documents in the 'discovery' process.

The IRS continued to lend their weight to the persecution of Jewish and Christian-owned business, churches and organisations – and the jail cells and special camps continued to fill up with those accused of hate crimes and other such accusations.

Many Jews – and Christians, too – decided that enough was enough and decided it was time to leave the USA, but then discovered that the way was not open to do so. Some found their way to the underground, who had prepared for this hour many years earlier and were able to help many thousands to make their way to Canada, Mexico and other destinations via carefully planned escape routes.

30 – Um Qasr

Wedding and honeymoon over, Shaul and Rebekkah, Aviv and Khaista, eventually arrived back at their base in Basra and were given an ovation by their colleagues the next morning.

There were cries of 'You kept that very quiet, sir,' and various other jokes at Shaul's expense.

Shaul just smiled and replied, 'You guys are all just jealous, admit it.'

Both couples moved into larger rooms in the hotel. They soon got back into the routine of the aliyah, but a new angle to their work was looming. Shaul brought it up a few days later at breakfast.

'We're soon going to have to recruit extra personnel and also change some of our duties around,' he began. NIP and Israel Rail – along with our new Kurdish State neighbours – have been working hard to get the main line of the old Iraqi rail system working again. The plan is that in the near future we will bring aliyah ships into the port of Um Qasr – just seventy kilometres down the road from us here in Basra.

'At the moment those ships bringing the Indian aliyah – the Menashe from eastern India and the Kashmiris from the north – have to travel all the way up the Red Sea to Eilat/Aqaba, before disembarking. The new route will shorten the sea journey considerably. The Indian *olim* will in future disembark at Um Qasr and travel on the newly repaired rail line north through former Iraq and Kurdistan to Aleppo, in northern Israel.

'We may also be able to send some of the Pashtun refugees on those trains, as well – especially any whose vehicles have broken down beyond repair.'

'We've collected up quite a few of those already,' said Tamari. 'I've now got a graveyard full of broken down vehicles out there.'

'Yeah, and at the moment we have to organise coaches and extra trucks to take the passengers and their household goods to Israel,' agreed Shaul.

'What we'll need to do is appoint someone as manager of a new depot at Um Qasr – it's about an hour away from here – and set up the base. He, or she, will be responsible for the incoming *olim;* registering them with NIP, transhipping their goods onto trains – already in containers on board the ship – and feeding them, doing medical checks, etc. then getting them aboard the train – next stop Aleppo.

Rebekkah had a question, 'That's going to be quite a long train journey – I don't expect these will exactly be high-speed trains? Will there be personnel aboard to feed and look after the *olim* on the journey?'

'Ken,' said Shaul, 'The trains *will* be fairly slow moving, as far as I can tell, due to the state of the track. But NIP will have qualified personnel aboard, so our responsibility will end once the train departs from Um Qasr.'

'Beseder,' said Rebekkah.

'We'll need to have the depot set up and ready to go before the rail line becomes operational, so it will take a few weeks, maybe?' said Shaul. 'The person in charge will be working for NIP, essentially – though seconded to them from the IDF. I reckon that both Rebekkah and Alon are suited for the task, so I want both of you to consider it and let me know if either of you are interested in taking it on.'

Rebekkah and Alon looked at one another and raised their eyebrows.

'Beseder,' they both echoed slowly.

31 – The Ark revealed

All of Israel's TV channels and radio stations had been instructed by the government and the chief rabbis to broadcast a special message at 7 pm that evening.

People of Israel, the chief rabbi began, *we have an extremely important announcement to make, which I can guarantee will shock and surprise many of you – whether you consider yourself secular or religious. This news will profoundly affect every Israelite throughout the world.*

'As you probably know we began work some time ago on the foundation for the new third temple in the City of David, here in Jerusalem. Before we began we did extensive excavations in the Haram area and in the course of that began to explore a tunnel, leading from the quarry beneath the Temple Mount north beyond the walls of the Old City.

'The Israel Antiquities Authority have been aware of this tunnel since its discovery by an American amateur archaeologist quite a few years ago. The tunnel was originally hidden behind a wall in the cave, extends for about a kilometre and had been completely filled with large rocks. We now believe it was built in the time of Jeremiah, during the Babylonian siege, to hide objects removed from the temple.

'The team in charge of the excavation built a small railway to help remove these rocks from the tunnel. They were nearing the end of the tunnel – which led to another large cave – when they felt compelled to call in the Sephardi Chief Rabbi and myself.

'When we learned what they had discovered, my friends, we halted all work on the tunnel straight away and arranged for only certain Cohanim – men specially trained for the future services in the new temple – to continue the excavation. They reported to us that they had found what they believed to be the ancient Ark of the Covenant.

'We informed the Sanhedrin of Israel and the evidence has now been fully investigated by us. Our conclusion, my fellow Israelites, is that this is indeed the Ark of the Covenant! The Ark has since been

held in the cave where it was originally found, carefully guarded by cohanim, until such time as the new temple should be completed, which we can now confirm.

The dedication of the new temple will be held one month from now and that day will be a public holy day throughout Israel. It will be treated like Yom Kippur. All work will cease on that day. The Ark of the Covenant will be carried by poles on the shoulders of the cohanim to the Temple itself, and placed in the Holy of Holies. Animal sacrifices will commence on that day to dedicate the new temple.

'But that is not the whole story, my friends. When the Cohen Gadol – the high priest – went into the cave to confirm the presence of the Ark, he discovered that it was contained within a stone box – a sort of sarcophagus, which had a broken lid. The box containing the Ark had been placed beneath a crack in the cave roof, and around that crack a black powder was found, which was also found upon the exposed mercy seat of the Ark.

'The Cohen Gadol took a sample of this black powder and the sample was taken to a specialist laboratory in Jerusalem to be analysed. My friends that black powder was discovered to be none other than human blood – and not just ordinary blood, but blood with a different constitution from any normal human blood.

'Firstly, when the powder was mixed with distilled water the blood came to life – a previously unheard of result. But when it was examined under a microscope the blood was found to contain – not the normal forty six chromosomes – but only twenty four. In other words, my friends, the blood contained the normal twenty three chromosomes from the mother, plus one additional chromosome, meaning the blood is that of a human male.

The location of the cave is directly beneath a site in Jerusalem that many will be familiar with – known as the Garden Tomb. In the 1990s the Israeli Antiquities authority gave permission for an American archaeologist to excavate an area adjacent to the site of the Garden Tomb. He dug down through many levels of debris, discovering what he claimed to be the site of the crucifixion of Yeshua HaNotzrim – Jesus of Nazareth.

'The site contained a level rock platform extending out from a vertical cliff face. In the cliff face were three rectangles cut out of the rock, such as the Romans would have used to define the crimes of the one being executed. The level platform contained a square socket, which was covered by a stone tile. The platform extended outwards, then sloped down to a lower level – with three similar sockets.

Chapter 31 – The Ark revealed

This site has been under examination for several weeks now and we must confirm that we believe this to be the site where Jesus of Nazareth was crucified. The socket covered with a stone tile also contained evidence of the same unusual blood as was found on the Mercy Seat. The crack – no doubt caused by an earthquake – had allowed this blood to flow from the crucifixion area to the Mercy Seat below.

'Our sincere conclusion, my friends – and we have gone into this most thoroughly – is that Yeshua HaNotzrim was indeed the Moshiach, the redeemer of Israel. For two thousand years we have denied Yeshua, but we are now faced with incontrovertible evidence that he was indeed – and is – the true Messiah of Israel. We must repent and mourn over this my friends.

At this point the chief rabbi looked straight into the camera lens, grabbed the lapels of his shirt and tore it right down the front.

'My fellow rabbis of the Sanhedrin – together with myself and the Sephardi Chief Rabbi, here beside me – are calling for a national month of fasting and repentance, to begin at sundown today. This broadcast is being recorded and it and further evidence concerning the authenticity of our claims, will also be presented on the website of the Temple Institute after this broadcast.'

'My brothers and sisters we have been so wrong about our Messiah and we now repent publicly for our mistakes. I would ask you to please watch this broadcast again and the video which we have provided relating the full story of this discovery. We would encourage you to fast and pray and seek HaShem about this discovery over the next four weeks and to join us as we re-instate the true worship of HaShem in His newly built temple.

'Moshiach has already come to his people, Israel, and he is soon coming again to judge the world and to restore Israel as his people. In the meantime He has destined us – the Jewish people – to be the light of the world.'

32 – To your own land

Brandon had arranged with his partner, Josh, to sell his half of the auto business to him. In turn, he invested this money in Dev's company in Boston. Their house, too, had eventually been sold – though for a good deal less than market value – and they were now about to move out. Brandon and Alyssa were happy to agree the sale, – even though they lost out on the deal – just to be free to make their way out of the USA at last.

Brandon found himself speaking more and more to a situation where prophecy was being fulfilled before his eyes in modern day America. At their most recent gathering with those who regularly joined with him and Alyssa in the hotel meetings he told them:

'In recent months the social climate in the USA has been deteriorating rapidly – both for Christians and Jews,' he told the gathering who regularly met with him. 'The recent election, as we know, brought to an end the Republican government and this new Democrat/New World Order administration has proceeded to rapidly undo almost all everything that had been achieved by the previous government.

'Border restrictions have now been greatly eased and a new flood of immigrants – many escaping the recent upheaval in the Middle East – are pouring in. Many of these people do not have the good of America – or of us Americans – at heart.

'Many areas of the country which have achieved Muslim control are now effectively under Sharia law and ordinary Americans are increasingly being harassed in the streets. Our women, especially, are now afraid to venture out in public unaccompanied. Rapes and racial attacks have become more and more common. As we know, laws have been passed greatly restricting those of Jewish or Christian faith, confiscating property and threatening incarceration to anyone bold enough to speak out in public against these abuses.

'Our government's spending is now way out of control – in order to fund these ambitious and expensive new programmes they are proposing. FEMA has been greatly expanded and their actions are more and more reminiscent of the Nazi 'brown shirts' of Germany in the thirties. Riots on the streets of our major cities are now a frequent occurrence. Churches and synagogues have already lost any tax-exempt status and are being being carefully monitored for any signs of activism – especially those who are still encouraging their members to take the teachings of the bible seriously.

'The FEMA camps – which have long been the source of great speculation by those in the alternative media – are being filled up as I speak – with all kinds of so-called 'dissidents': pro-lifers, preppers and militia groups, Jewish activists, outspoken evangelicals, and many others, have been rounded up and the raids are becoming more and more frequent.

Our churches and denominations are in confusion – whether from the fear of reprisal, or from an already strong tendency towards political correctness – and many have pulled back even further from true bible teaching. They are openly endorsing such things as evolution, abortion and same sex marriage and apologising for the – real or supposed – failings of 'white people' in the recent past.

'As we know some have even begun to claim that Mohammed is actually a true prophet of God, that Jesus never claimed to be the son of God and that he did not actually die on the cross. The apostle John, in his first letter, chapter 2, warned us that anyone who teaches such things – denying the Father and the Son – is a liar, NOT of God, but speaking from the spirit of Anti-Christ.

'In schools anti-biblical attitudes are being more and more openly taught to our children– yet the same teachers are often openly advocating respect for the doctrines of Islam. Our children are being targeted and encouraged to report on families who hold to bible teaching, creationism, etc. We've seen many disaffected kids who've had their own families arrested and carted off to the camps as a result of their often distorted – and sometimes totally fictional – reports.

'The words of the prophet, Micah, that Jesus once quoted in Matthew 10, are being fulfilled in modern-day America, *"Do not trust a neighbor; put no confidence in a friend. Even with the woman who lies in your embrace guard the words of your lips. For a son dishonors his father, a daughter rises up against her mother, a daughter-in-law against her mother-in-law – a man's enemies are the members of his own household.* Micah 7:5,6."

'My friends I believe we are now at the crossroads. Over and over in the scripture we are so clearly told – NOT to hang in there and pray for deliverance, like the Jews did in the nineteen thirties,

NOT to wait and see if things will get better – no! What we are told to do is to flee!

'We are living today in the midst of what the prophets referred to as the 'daughter of Babylon'. And how do they tell us to respond to this Babylon? They say flee from her! Jeremiah, in chapter 51:6 tells us to, *"Flee from Babylon! Run for your lives! Do not be destroyed because of her sins. It is time for YHWH's vengeance;"* he says, *"He will repay her what she deserves."*

'In verse 45 he says again, *"Come out of her, my people! Run for your lives! Run from the fierce anger of YHWH."* We are to run for our lives – our lives may well depend on our obedience to these scriptures!

'In the same chapter, in verse 50, he says, *"You who have escaped the sword, leave and do not linger! Remember YHWH in a distant land, and call to mind Jerusalem."* 'Leave, and don't linger', we are told! To escape the sword of judgement that is surely coming upon this nation!

'In chapter 50:8 Jeremiah again tells us, *"Flee out of Babylon; leave the land of the Babylonians, and be like the goats that lead the flock."* In verse 28 he says again, *"Listen to the fugitives and refugees from Babylon, declaring in Zion how YHWH our God has taken vengeance."*

'Fugitives and refugees! And what are these goats like, then? They are the ones who push to the front, who take the lead. God is telling us to take the lead in this, NOT to 'wait and see' and then find that we've left it far too late and that judgement has arrived – for that judgement *will* come.

'Isaiah says the same thing in chapter 48:20, *"Leave Babylon, flee from the Babylonians! Announce this with shouts of joy and proclaim it. Send it out to the ends of the earth; say, 'YHWH has redeemed his servant Jacob.'"*

'Zechariah 2:6, 7 tell us the same thing, *"Come! Come! Flee from the land of the north,"* declares YHWH, *"for I have scattered you to the four winds of heaven,"* declares YHWH. *"Come, Zion! Escape, you who live in Daughter Babylon!"* Where are we living right now? In the 'daughter of Babylon'.

'In 2 Corinthians 6:17 Paul tells us, *"Therefore, "Come out from them, and be separate, says the Lord. Touch no unclean thing; and I will receive you."* In Revelation 18:4 – again referring to Babylon – mega-Babylon – John tells us, *"Then I heard another voice from heaven say: Come out of her, my people, so that you will not share in her sins, so that you will not receive any of her plagues."*

'Let's read a little more from Jeremiah 50, from verse 4 on: *"In those days, at that time," declares YHWH, "the people of Israel and the people of Judah together will go in tears to seek YHWH their God. They will ask the way to Zion and turn their faces towards it. They will come and bind themselves to YHWH in an everlasting coven-ant that will not be forgotten. My people have been lost sheep; their shepherds have led them astray and caused them to roam on the mountains. They wandered over mountain and hill and forgot their own resting place. Whoever found them devoured them; their enemies said, 'We are not guilty, for they sinned against YHWH, their verdant pas-ture, YHWH, the hope of their ancestors.' Flee out of Babylon; leave the land of the Babylonians, and be like the goats that lead the flock."*

'God's people – both Jews and Christians – are like lost sheep. Our shepherds – both Jewish leaders and Christian pastors – have led us astray. Whoever finds us devours us. Flee! Leave!

'And in verse 33 he continues, *"This is what YHWH Almighty says: "The people of Israel are oppressed, and the people of Judah as well. All their captors hold them fast, refusing to let them go. Yet their Redeemer is strong; YHWH Almighty is his name. He will vigorously defend their cause so that he may bring <u>rest to their land, but unrest to those who live in Babylon</u>."*

'Can any instructions be less ambiguous? There is no uncertainty here! The people of God are told to get out of the 'daughter of Babylon' immediately, to avoid 'suffering and turmoil and cruel bondage' and so they will not 'share in her sins' or 'receive any of her plagues'. They 'are oppressed ... their captors hold them fast, refusing to let them go.'

'God will defend our cause and bring us to a place of rest – but that place of rest will NOT be in Babylon. Jeremiah tells us clearly that there will be <u>unrest</u> to those who live in Babylon. Unrest and much worse – judgement, plagues, a sword!

'So we are admonished to flee, run for our lives, leave and do not linger. We must be obedient to God's word – or suffer the con-sequences.

'OK, you say, but *when* are we supposed to do this? When is the right time to leave? This is a question I've been asking myself for several years – ever since I first realised what these chapters were actually talking about. And I believe the Lord has given me a clear answer to that question – a very simple answer. An answer from his word.

'Let's look now at Jesus words to us in Matthew chapter 10:21 on – just before Jesus' quote from Micah 7, that we looked at earlier: *"Brother will betray brother to death, and a father his child; children will rebel against their parents and have them put to death. You will be hated by everyone because of me, but the one who stands firm to the end will be saved."* That all sounds pretty relevant to our present situation, doesn't it? Just like Micah prophesied. And then Jesus tells us one more thing, he says, *"When you are persecuted in one place, flee to another."*

'That is so simple. So, are we being persecuted? I think the answer is now overwhelmingly, 'Yes!' OK, then it is now time for us to flee. We are indeed being persecuted more and more in this place – the United States of America, the 'daughter of Babylon' – so we must now obey all these directions from God and flee. Leave the USA. Get out. Run for our lives. Do not linger.

'Some of you will undoubtedly tell me we should pray about this. We should wait a little longer. I say, NO! To do so would be to already disobey the clear instructions of the Lord in his word. We have a definite choice, brothers and sisters. Either we obey what God has said we are now to do, or we linger – in some vain hope of deliverance in some other way. Be we are clearly told to leave and NOT to linger. We are to *'Run from the fierce anger of YHWH.'* There IS no other way!

'Here's what Jeremiah has to say – *"Babylon will suddenly fall and be broken. Wail over her! Get balm for her pain; perhaps she can be healed."We would have healed Babylon, <u>but she cannot be healed</u>; let us leave her and each go to our own land, for her judgment reaches to the skies, it rises as high as the heavens.""* Jeremiah is saying it's too late now, we tried to heal America, but we couldn't. We had a chance to put back the clock, to undo the damage. We saw the result. We were resisted all the way. Now it's too late, America's judgement reaches to the heavens.

'So choose now, obey, and flee, or linger and in our disobedience – because that is what it amounts to – come under the judgement of God, judgement which is not meant for us, but for the 'daughter of Babylon'.

'OK, we should now be clear on exactly what choice we have to make. There is just one more question. Where? Where do we flee to? Well, *my* first thought is Israel. In Jeremiah 50:33 God has promised us rest in the land of Israel, but unrest in Babylon. Is Israel the place to go, then? Well, maybe, but there is another answer. We've just read it. *"Let us leave her and each go to our own land"*.

'Almost every one of us has a land – outside of these United States – that we think of as 'our land'. For some it's Ireland, for some the UK, for some Germany, or China, or Mexico, or ... Unless you're a pure-blooded Native American, there is pretty definitely a land that you can lay claim to. That should at least be the starting place to look towards. You might eventually end up in Israel – I certainly hope to, myself! – but that may not be the best place to start. Start with the land of your ancestors and take it from there.

'But my honest and sincere and final word to you, my brothers and sisters, is this – heed the clear direction of God's word. Decide tonight that you are gonna be obedient and start making plans to leave. For some of us it is too late – some are already in police cells, or in FEMA camps. Some are no longer with us. But *we* – here tonight – still have a choice. *Dear Father in heaven, please help each one of us here tonight to make the right one! Amen!'*

33 – The dedication of the Temple

The period of mourning and fasting which the Chief rabbis had called for all Israel to observe had been taken very seriously by a large proportion of the population – both religious and secular. Since the rabbis' announcement on television of the evidence concerning Yeshua as the Jewish Moshiach, several million people – from Israel and around the world – had accessed the website and watched the videos documenting the evidence.

In fact the servers were initially overwhelmed and additional servers had to be brought online as thousands of people started to complain that they were unable to access the information.

Local TV channels were not permitted into the tunnel leading from beneath the Muslim Quarter, where the Ark had resided since Jeremiah's time, so they reported from outside the Old City walls and interviewed many of the Messianic leaders regarding their faith in Yeshua HaMoshiach.

Attendance at synagogues, churches and Messianic fellowships trebled and many of the same Messianic leaders were invited to speak in Orthodox synagogues. There was great confusion at first as many Jews tried to comprehend how their rabbis and leaders could have got it so wrong – and for a period of two thousand years.

Copies of bibles that included the Brit Chadasha (New Testament) were soon sold out and the Bible Societies has to rush print new editions, both in Hebrew and in English. Translations were also in demand in Russian, Amharic, Igbo, Pashto, Kashmiri and other languages used by the new immigrants.

Many of these new immigrants – having already been open towards Yeshua as Messiah because of their previous Christian or Moslem upbringing, were having supernatural encounters with the risen Messiah. Many Jews also were having dreams and visions confirming his resurrection and authenticity as Messiah.

It was an unprecedented time in Israel and many Messianic Jewish leaders from outside Israel were invited to come and speak in synagogues and churches – though, unfortunately, those from the United States were prevented from coming by various 'problems' and hindrances with passports and visas.

The day appointed for the dedication of the new Temple had arrived and the newly trained and prepared Levites and Cohanim (priests) were assembled outside the Old City, near Herod's Gate. All of them were dressed in white linen tunics.

Shofars were sounded and the chosen Cohanim entered the underground quarry beneath the Moslem Quarter, from which the newly excavated tunnel led to the hiding place of the Ark, and other artifacts, including the table of the shewbread. Outside the city walls the President and the Prime minister – together with most of the Knesset members and many rabbis, pastors and priests – waited for the procession containing the Ark to re-appear.

Eventually, the shofars were sounded again by the Levites appointed for this task and the six Cohanim, carrying the Ark of the Covenant on their shoulders, emerged from the underground quarry and proceeded along the outside of the city wall towards Damascus Gate – preceded by musicians and singers praising the Name of YHWH. The waiting crowds celebrated by cheering wildly, shouting and dancing. Outside the gate the Cohanim halted and another six priests took over the task and the procession moved through the gate and inside the Old City.

Soon they arrived at the Kotel and proceeded across the plaza – where Jews had worshipped for centuries – and out through the Dung Gate, south of which the splendid new temple building could be seen. Once they had ascended inside the temple court only specially trained Levites and Cohanim would be allowed at present – preparing to make the first animal sacrifices in a Jewish Temple for nearly two thousand years. The noise of cattle bellowing and sheep and goats bleating was considerable. The High Priest – the *Cohen Gadol* – waited inside the inner court to receive the Ark, wearing the ephod on his breast, and the Urim and Thummim stones on his shoulders.

Ordinary Israelites would be allowed into the inner court later, after the Ark had been placed inside the inner sanctuary, and Gentiles also would be allowed into the outer court at that time. No press or TV cameras would be permitted inside the Temple courts – although a couple of helicopters hovered above giving an aerial view of the proceedings. Every TV and radio station in Israel was covering this momentous event, together with those from all over the world – many filming from the southern end of the so-called Temple Mount, now usually just referred to as the Haram.

Chapter 33 – The dedication of the Temple

Eventually the Ark arrived before the outer gate and halted. Shofars were sounded by the Levites and the Ark ascended into the outer court – the Court of the Gentiles. Again the shofars sounded and the Ark was then carried forward into the inner court – the Court of the Jews.

Here the Ark paused and the Cohanim carrying it stood in place as the first bulls were slaughtered by their fellow priests, using ultra sharp knives specially honed for the purpose. As their blood began to spill the animals simply went to sleep feeling nothing, and their blood was collected in basins specially made for this purpose. Other Cohanim began to sacrifice the first of many hundreds of sheep.

The slaughtered animals were divided and placed on the bronze altar just outside the main building of the temple. As the smoke went up from the carcasses incense also was burned by other Levites. Soon the whole temple area began to smell of cooking meat and incense.

The *Cohen Gadol* took a branch of hyssop and dipped it into one of the basins of animal blood and sprinkled it on the courtyard. He then entered the Holy Place – the outer room of the Temple building itself, now illuminated by the Golden Menorah, which had already been transported from the Jewish Quarter into the temple – and again sprinkled the blood there. The Ark was now carried into the Holy Place. The President and the Prime Minister of Israel remained in the courtyard outside the Temple building.

The *Cohen Gadol* went ahead and pulled back the veil – the curtain dividing off the Holy of Holies. Before he entered the Holy of Holies – normal something only to be attempted once a year on Yom Kippur – the Day of Atonement – Levites approached and attached a rope made of silk to his ankle. They also did this to each of the Cohanim who were carrying the Ark. This was in case any of them were found unworthy to enter the presence of YHWH and were suddenly stuck dead by God.

The cords attached, the *Cohen Gadol* entered the Holy of Holies first, again sprinkling the blood. The Ark was then carried into the Holy of Holies and set in its place. The two poles used for carrying it were removed from their rings and the six Cohanim moved out of the Temple back to the Court of the Jews. The *Cohen Gadol* replaced the veil across the entrance to the Holy of Holies and also returned to the courtyard, just outside the doors of the new temple, where the silk rope was removed.

He stood beside the President and Prime Minister and declared the words from the New Testament Book of Hebrews, saying, *"The law is only a shadow of the good things that are coming – not the realities themselves. For this reason it can never, by the same sacrifices repeated endlessly year after year, make perfect those who draw near to worship. Otherwise, would they not have stopped being offered? For the worshippers would have been cleansed once for all, and would no longer have felt guilty for their sins. But those sacrifices are an annual reminder of sins. It is impossible for the blood of bulls and goats to take away sins."* (**Hebrews 10:1-4**)

'So, why are we carrying out these sacrifices,' said the Cohen Gadol. 'It is because it reminds us that our Messiah shed his precious blood for us on the tree, and we now know that that precious blood ran down from his body through the rock and fell upon the Mercy Seat of the Ark itself. By this once for all sacrifice, Yeshua our Moshiach has cleansed us from all of or sins.'

As he spoke a cloud had appeared overhead and now descended upon the courtyard of the temple. The *Cohen Gadol*, President, Prime Minister – and all the priests and Levites gathered in the Temple court – were overpowered by the presence of the living God and fell to the ground, worshipping in awe. The shekinah glory had returned to the Temple in Jerusalem.

TV and radio reporters standing outside the Temple Gates could see what was happening inside and began to report it, but found themselves unable to remain standing either and fell about – some of them laughing, and others groaning or weeping. Anyone watching this event on their TV screens could not help but be affected by it. Many watching were also overcome by the power of the Holy Spirit in their homes and knew without a doubt that something tremendously holy was taking place.

Shaul and his task force has set up large video screens in the main squares of Basra and the aliyah halted while the new *olim* gathered to watch the proceedings in Jerusalem in awe. Shaul and his officers were watching on a large screen set up in the main lobby of their hotel HQ. They also were impacted by what was happening on screen.

'Now I understand,' said Aviv. 'When the High Priest spoke about the blood of Yeshua the presence of YHWH descended upon him and all those around him. For some time I have suspected that Yeshua is truly the Messiah of Israel, but now I know it is true. Yeshua is Lord!'

Chapter 33 – The dedication of the Temple

The others – Shaul included – nodded in agreement with Aviv, but there was a great reluctance to further interrupt the scenes they were witnessing from Jerusalem. A sense of awe affected them all. Eventually, after the TV channel had finished broadcasting the Dedication, they stirred again and went back to their duties. The large screens were removed from the squares and the aliyah convoys began to move again.

'Shaul and Rebekkah retired to their new room and looked at one another.

'That was truly amazing,' Shaul began. 'It was an incredible experience.'

'Yes,' said Rebekkah quietly. 'I think I agree with Aviv. 'I've been contemplating these things this last few weeks – since the Chief Rabbi made that announcement on TV. But tonight I think I've come to the point that I can no longer deny that Yeshua is our Moshiach and Lord. That event rocked me to the core.

'Me also,' agreed Shaul. 'Do you think we should pray?'

'*Ken,*' said Rebekkah. 'I have no experience of praying – except the kind of 'God get me out of this' prayer in the middle of battle – but I'm sure I can learn.

They sat on the sofa in their suite and – for the first time in their relationship – spoke to their creator together.

After a few minutes they were quiet, aware of a real sense of peace in the room, when there came a quiet knock on their door. Shaul rose to answer it and found Aviv and Khaista in the hallway.

'We wondered if you would let us pray with you,' said Aviv. 'We've just been praying to Yeshua together and we felt we should join you guys. I hope you don't mind?'

'Actually, we were just praying ourselves,' Shaul admitted. 'It's the first time we've ever done it, so we don't really know what we're doing – but please join us, by all means.'

Aviv and Khaista sat down on chairs next to Shaul and Rebekkah.

'Lord Yeshua,' Aviv began, 'we want to agree with your priests and rabbis who carried your holy Ark into your Temple today. Now we know and believe that you – Yeshua – are the Messiah and Lord of all. We thank you that it was your blood that spilled from the cross, down through the ground, onto the Mercy Seat upon the Ark.

'It is only your blood – represented, but not replaced, by the sacrifices of animals that we saw taking place in Jerusalem today – that can transform us from self-centred beings into those who love You, adore You and want to serve You. We offer ourselves up to you, oh Lord.'

'Yes, YHWH God,' said Shaul, 'We agree tonight that Yeshua is truly your son and we offer ourselves to You to serve Him from here on in.'

'Yeshua,' Rebekkah began, then hesitated, cleared her throat and began again in a stronger voice, 'Yeshua, Your name is such a strange sound to our ears. May that no longer be the case. Forgive us for how we have rejected You for so long. We can't do that any more, so we come to You asking for acceptance and forgiveness. Thank You, Lord, for everything that You have done for Your people, Israel, and for all those who love You, the Messiah of Israel.'

'Lord Yeshua,' added Khaista, 'I want to thank you for becoming the sacrificial lamb for the sins of all your people, Israel – and those of the whole world. Please come and be a part of my life – and of all our lives – from this moment on. We love You, Yeshua.'

'Why,' asked Shaul, after a few minutes of a peaceful silence has passed, 'do we find it so strange to say the name, Yeshua. It's almost like it's become a swear word, or something – not to be used in polite company. I mean in the US army it was normal for the name, Jesus, to be used regularly as a swear word, but no-one felt able to say it in a normal way, with reverence – except our friend, Brandon, of course.'

'Yes,' agreed Aviv, 'Even as Muslims, who regard Yeshua – or Issa – as a Muslim prophet who is now in heaven and expected to return to earth one day – yet we hardly ever use his name. That is truly strange.'

'I guess we've all had an inbuilt fear, or embarrassment, or something of that kind – about that name, Yeshua', said Rebekkah. 'Suddenly, I feel like I want to practice saying it over and over – Yeshua.'

'I feel the same way, Bekkah,' agreed Khaista.

'You know,' said Shaul, 'I'm gonna see if I can get hold of Brandon right now – hopefully, he'll be home from work by this time.'

He turned on his laptop and connected to Skype, clicking on Brandon's contact details. In a few seconds the connection was made and Brandon's face appeared on the screen.

'Hey, you guys,' he said, 'it's real good to see you. I took the morning off to watch the dedication of the Temple on TV – wow, that was some experience!'

'We watched it too, and it was indeed,' agreed Shaul. 'In fact, the four of us have just been praying together – to Yeshua – for the first time ever. We thought we should let you know.'

'I'm so glad you did – hang on a minute.'

They could hear Brandon calling Alyssa to come and see who was online. She hurried in, wiping wet hands on a towel as she arrived.

'What is it?' she asked.

'Look who's on the screen,' he replied, 'All the way from Basra.'

'Hi, guys,' she said, once she realised who she was looking at. 'So great to see y'all.'

Brandon quickly explained why Shaul and the others had called them.

'Oh, that's so good to know,' she said with a grin spreading across her face. 'Brandon, myself and the kids have been praying for you guys every night – especially since we came home from your wedding. That is just unbelievable news. Brandon and I watched the reporting from Jerusalem this morning. That was just an amazing experience, wasn't it?'

'It sure was,' agreed Rebekkah. 'The first Temple service in almost two thousand years!'

'Yes, and to hear the Chief Priest relate it all to the blood of Yeshua,' she said. 'That was just so unbelievable. It's going to make such a difference to our relationship with the Jews in this country.'

'Yes,' Brandon interjected, 'I've already been asked to come and share in a couple of synagogues about Yeshua. What a turn around, eh?'

'Yes,' agreed Shaul, 'maybe we could do with you explaining some of that stuff to us, as well. We really know so little about Yeshua. We'll have to get hold of some New Testaments, I think.'

'Or you could just start online,' said Brandon. 'There's a great site called BibleGateway.com. It has several dozen different translations – including Hebrew. But what you said reminded me of something I wanted to tell you all.

'Alyssa and I have sold our house and are living in a rented home for now. We need to leave the United States as soon as we possibly can. I think Dev has similar plans, although he has the excuse of marrying an Irish girl, so he'll probably be allowed to go to Ireland. He and I met up in New York recently and discussed the way things have been going in this country lately.'

'So, where do you plan to go?' asked Shaul.

'Well, Alyssa and I both have a lot of Igbo in our background, so we naturally thought of joining all those Igbo who are already making aliyah. Trouble is we won't be allowed out of the country if they think we are going to Israel – so we are planning to move to Ireland initially, supposedly to work for Dev's company. Don't think we'll pass for Irish with our colouring, though!' he laughed.

'That's interesting,' said Shaul. 'I hope it all goes well. Let us know if we can do anything to help.'

'Sure,' said Brandon. 'By the way, when we were in New York we made a point of talking to your brother, Reuben, about our plans. We told him where we thought the country was heading and how important it was to get out in good time. He admitted that he had been unable to transfer money to invest in the *New Israel Plan*, but he just kinda laughed at us when we suggested he also should make plans to escape the USA and make aliyah to Israel. Maybe you could persuade him?'

'I don't think I'd have any better luck than you seem to have had,' said Shaul. 'My brother is pretty much deaf to anything I have to say.'

'That's a pity,' said Brandon. 'Listen, I'm gonna get things moving in the next week or so, and I'll be in touch when we know what's happening. We may have to make use of the underground to escape the country – and we may only get out with the clothes on our back, so to speak.'

'Well, we can always use a good mechanic out here in Basra,' said Shaul.

34 – Ireland: halfway house

Brandon and Alyssa had accepted an offer for their house which was well below the expected market value, but by now they both felt an intense urgency to leave the United States as soon as possible – which grew on them the more they prayed about it.

Dev had sent Brandon an official offer of a position in Ireland with their company and he had accepted this. They were allowed to leave the USA for Dublin, but it was only when the plane took off and they were far out over the Atlantic that Brandon and Alyssa eventually breathed a collective sigh of relief and began to believe that they had made it out.

The children were excited to be going to Ireland – as they thought – and were even more awed when they were eventually told that they would only be in Ireland for a short holiday and would then be flying on to Israel, where they would be living in the future.

'You mean we'll be living where Yeshua and his disciples lived and did all the miracles?' asked Hannah, enthralled.

'Yes,' said her father, 'and where Moses brought the children of Israel and where Joshua fought all those battles.'

'Can we go see where David fought Goliath and where Samson pulled the temple down on the Philistines?' asked young Caleb.

'Sure we can,' assured Alyssa. 'But Israel is a modern country with cars and freeways and trains and airports and malls, as well,' she explained.

'Are there lots of black people there, like us?' asked Hannah.

'Yes, darling,' said her mother, 'there are a lot of them living there now – mostly from countries in Africa, like Nigeria and Zimbabwe.'

'There are lots of beaches in Israel, too,' added Brandon.

'Oh great,' exclaimed Hannah. 'Can we live near the beach, then? Can we?'

'I don't know yet,' her dad answered, 'but we won't be too far away from one, that's for sure.'

This seemed to satisfy the kids for a while and Hannah and Caleb fell into a conversation about all the things they were going to do and places they wanted to see when they got to Israel.

The Aer Lingus plane landed at Dublin Airport and they found Niamh waiting for them at Arrivals with a welcoming smile.

'Slainte!' she said, 'Welcome to Ireland.'

Alyssa and Brandon congratulated her on her coming wedding, for which they planned to stay long enough to attend. Dev was still in Boston, but intended to be with them in a few days time.

'Come on. I've got the car outside. I'll take you to your temporary new home. The weather is typically Irish, today' she added. 'It's raining, just for a change! – what we call a 'soft' day.'

They followed her to the car and loaded their luggage into the rear, before settling in for the reasonably short drive – mostly by busy motorway, as they called freeways here – to the outskirts of north east Dublin and their new home for the next couple of weeks.

Shaul and Bekkah, Aviv and Khaista arrived from Israel a couple of days later – as did Micky and his parents and several other family members from Boston. The Israelis (and the potential new Israeli family) were welcomed to a great family reunion in Dev's uncle's house in Kilkenny.

The wedding – also in Kilkenny – was a great success. It took place in what Niamh had originally dubbed the 'born again' church, and the service was conducted by the same young pastor who had prayed with Micky and Niamh less than a year ago. The reception was held in the same Newpark Hotel in Kilkenny where Dev's cousin (and Niamh's friend) had held hers and that evening Dev and Niamh said goodbye to their friends and families and headed off for a short honeymoon in Spain's Canary Islands.

Brandon and Alyssa were able to have several conversations with Shaul and Rebekkah, Aviv and Khaista about their future life in Israel. Aviv offered for them to live in their apartment in Jerusalem, as did Shaul, once the present tenants finished their lease. Brandon and Alyssa thought they would prefer to live in a low-rise apartment, like Aviv and Khaista's, because of the children, but in the meantime they'd be happy to stay for a while in a small hotel.

Once they were settled and had seen a bit of their new country and picked up more of the language, they hoped to buy a home of their own in an area where there was work for Brandon and suitable schools for the children.

35 – The conspiracy of ten

Ten leaders were gathered in a luxury hotel in Paris, France. They occupied a boardroom and were seated in expensive comfortable chairs around a large polished rosewood conference table.

Between the ten they represented some of the most powerful nations on the planet, and thus a huge proportion of the earth's population. Although these were all individually men of great power and influence in their home nations, and also internationally, yet each of them deferred to another man who was present there with them.

This man's authority did not originally come about because he himself represented any major power. Though the populations of several nations did hold him in great esteem, he held no official political position at present and represented only himself and his religion, but that, seemingly, was enough to garner great respect – even awe – from these powerful men seated around him.

The meeting was chaired by the Russian, who welcomed the others briefly, then quickly got down to business:

'Gentlemen, we are here on very serious business – a business that affects not only the hundreds of millions of people we represent between us, but the whole world. We have proposed various solutions in the past – a new base world currency, trade agreements, etc., etc. – but I think we have now moved beyond such solutions.

'I have spoken with each of you individually in the past and I am confident we are all here now with one mind and we know what has to be done. We cannot allow this rogue state to continue its destructive course any longer. They have ridden on our backs for far too long. It is time now for us to shake them off.

'I refer, of course, to that nation which is in such great debt to each of us – a debt that we will never see repaid in our lifetimes – the debt owed by the United States of America. This nation is determined to carry on living in luxury at our expense, to continue to interfere in our internal affairs, to issue currency that it cannot stand over. Their military are stationed all over the world, protecting their unequal slice of the world's resources. It is time to put a stop to this. Are we all agreed?'

There were enthusiastic nods and murmurs from each man seated around the table. The Russian continued:

'But we must prepare ourselves for the results of our proposed action. Once this cancer is removed the world will be stunned and bewildered. We must be ready to provide the answer, before they even get around to asking, 'What now?' Otherwise our economies will go into free fall, our people will be confused and there would be great danger of uprisings and serious conflict.

'My friends there must be no uncertainty, there must be no political vacuum, no hesitation whatsoever on our part. We – the nations represented here – must be ready to take the lead, to provide the answer – the *only* possible answer for a viable future. When this cancer has been eliminated we must immediately announce to the world our solution. We must show solidarity, unity and confidence.

'We must present our friend here to the world as someone in whom each of us has the utmost confidence. And we must express that confidence by publicly handing over our authority – our economies, our military, our communications – into his control. Can I assume that we are all now agreed on this?'

This time the Russian looked directly at his Chinese counterpart, who nodded slowly and said, 'Yes, comrade, the Chinese people are agreed.'

He next turned his gaze on the Japanese representative, who also voiced his agreement. The Turkish representative was next, also agreeing enthusiastically. His gaze continued one by one around the table and each national representative confirmed his country's commitment to this drastic course of action.

'Good. It remains for us then to iron out and co-ordinate the details of our coming action. To that end I will now hand over the control of this meeting to our good friend, Adonikam – a man of exceptional gifts, authority and ability and to whom we look with the utmost respect and confidence. Mr Suleiman, please continue.'

The Russian sat back in his chair and visibly relaxed – his responsibility mostly over.

Adonikam Suleiman – for that was the name they all knew him by – was a man of exceptional gifts and charisma. When he chose to speak it was with such presence that the room would fall silent, every eye fixed on him. He stood slowly and allowed his gaze to travel calmly around the table, looking each person in the eye. He exuded confidence and authority. When he eventually spoke it was in a quiet, but deep and powerful voice.

'Gentlemen, we are about to embark on a very great adventure. We are about to change the world as we know it – for the better. We are about to usher in a time of great peace and prosperity – not only for the nations and people we represent here – but for the whole of the earth. I thank you for your confidence in me.

'As you know I already hold the confidence and esteem of the majority of the Islamic world. They have waited patiently for my coming and now the time of my rule is here. Unfortunately our people have been divided in the past – even in the recent past, to our detriment – but now that division is in the process of being healed. Those differences will become a thing of the past.

'The rest of the world do not yet know me and it will take a little time for me to demonstrate to them my authority and my abilities. I have someone working with me who will make that transition so much easier, and your support will also be a great help in boosting their confidence in me. I have great plans for this future world of ours. We will make great strides forward together.

'But first we must deal with the obstacle my Russian comrade has referred to – the cancer in our midst, the 'great Satan'. When that problem is dealt with everything else will fall into place.

'We have a plan which we have already discussed. The forces are in readiness and on the alert?'

'Yes', the Russian, Chinese and Japanese representatives said. The Chinese added, 'We have arranged a joint command and have placed the details at your disposal. I believe you already have the dossier with all the necessary codes?'

'Yes,' Adonikam replied with a slight smile. 'That is all very satisfactory.' The Russian nodded.

'And our sleepers, they are all in position and expecting my command in due course?

This time the Russian replied. 'They have all been given clear instructions on which cities to target and are now in position ready to receive your order.'

'Excellent', replied Adonikam. These brave warriors will soon meet Allah in person and their great sacrifice will benefit us all.'

'Your excellency?' the Turkish representative spoke now.

'Yes, comrade?' Adonikam replied.

'My comrades and I have assembled the support and liaison staff for you in the new headquarters building in that great city that we have previously discussed. 'I would be happy to escort you there now and introduce you and your assistants to the personnel involved. I can assure you they have all the latest and best communications equipment – both in terms of intelligence, command and control, and the media – for future broadcasting to the world at large. Everything has been tested and is working satisfactorily. You will be in command of an army previously unheard of in size and capability.'

Adonikam smiled, his eyes like black holes. 'Again, excellent, my comrade. We will travel there presently. Then my staff will finalise our plans while you gentlemen fly back to your respective countries in readiness for the action.'

Adonikam looked steadily around the men seated at the table. He smiled again, briefly, seemingly happy with what he saw and said, 'Well, gentlemen, to our glorious future. Let us go to work then.'

The leaders arose slowly from the table and took turns to shake hands with Adonikam and embrace him. They made their way out of the hotel to their waiting cars, while Suleiman and his Turkish colleague left ahead of them to travel to their new headquarters.

Three days later, in the early hours of the morning Eastern US time, a plane took off from a secret airbase far to the east of Siberia. It was armed with a nuclear missile and flew at high altitude over the Arctic, then over Alaska and the Pacific just west of the Canadian coast, veering east then across northern Washington State and towards the heartland of America.

Shortly after hundreds of nuclear missiles were launched in the same direction, and many hundreds of planes – bombers and fighters – took off from a number of airfields in China, Mongolia, Japan and eastern Siberia, their destination the same.

On receipt of a coded signal several dozen men and women left their hidden locations within major American cities and travelled by public transport to central locations in each of those cities. Others travelled by private car to strategic locations, including military bases all over the USA. Each individual carried a suitcase with them.

The fall of Babylon was at hand!

36 – The lights go out in Times Square

It was the most prestigious hotel in the city and the post-election victory party for the new mayor of New York had continued on extremely late into the evening. The president and his wife were there to congratulate his party's candidate on a successful outcome. The wine and spirits were flowing, the entertainment provided by some of the best known rock bands and comedians in the country, and the mood was one of mutual self-congratulation.

The president had been enjoying himself immensely and had just excused himself for the fourth time as he lurched unsteadily towards the washrooms. While there he took the opportunity to snort another line of coke – not his first of the evening, by any means – so he could keep up with the party celebrations for an hour or two longer. His wife, meanwhile, was enjoying the rapt attention of several male admirers.

The alarm call came in at 4 am, just as the flushed and ebullient president returned to the party – planning to continue his pursuit of a young and pretty staffer, whom he'd spent the best part of the last hour with. An aide rushed to his side, ignoring the young lady on whom the President's attention was focussed.

'Mr President, Mr President. We are under attack. The USA is under attack. An unidentified aircraft is approaching our airspace from the north over Canada and the Pentagon calculate that it is possibly of Russian …'

At that point the lights went out and the music died. Some of the women screamed and there was widespread consternation.

Someone rushed to pull back the curtains and by the pre-dawn light beginning to filter in the President struggled to get his confused brain around the unwelcome news, "Under attack? From where? Who …' He faltered, unsure what was required of him.

In his inside pocket he carried the launch codes which could instantly send nuclear missiles against any hostile target. Was this the occasion when he would be forced to employ them for the first time ever in US history?

The Afghan-American man wheeled his suitcase from the subway train up the escalator to Times Square in the early hours of the morning. Before leaving his classy apartment in the Brooklyn suburb of Prospect Heights he'd hugged his children and kissed his wife of twenty years– telling them he had to go see a friend urgently as an errand of mercy.

Actually, he'd walked to a storage facility a few blocks from his home and retrieved the suitcase, which had been delivered to him many years before by a Russian man he'd only met that one time. As they had made the exchange the only words spoken by the Russian were, 'Death to America!', and he had replied in sympathy, 'Death to the great Satan!'

He wheeled the suitcase to the subway and headed for Manhattan. He'd received the coded message earlier that day that his friend, Mustapha Shinwari, was very ill and was asking for him. Of course he didn't know anyone of that name but nodded to himself with satisfaction that the time for revenge had finally come.

He'd worked for the American military as a translator back in Afghanistan, then came to the USA and managed to get work, studying at the same time and ending up in the financial services business. He now worked as a senior consultant, with the private office, sharp suit and income to match. He did not fit anyone's idea of a terrorist.

After leaving the subway he found a seat in Times Square and sat near some tourists, watching the famous illuminated advertising display purporting to offer all the transient material things that Americans seemed to hold dear. He snorted to himself at their petty foolishness.

All his life he had blended in well, never drew attention to himself, become as American as they were. But not even his wife knew of the hatred he harboured deep in his psyche. These were the people who had carelessly and remorselessly annihilated his family – father, mother, brothers and sisters. One day they were going to pay for that atrocity and that day had finally come.

He waited patiently as the sky lightened. When the lights of Times Square suddenly went out, and the traffic around him drifted to a standstill, while people looked confusedly at their stationary vehicles he calmly reached over to the suitcase beside him, ready to press the tiny button set into the handle. 'Death to America!' he said to himself. Then he shouted for all around him to hear, 'Allahu akbar!' God is great! and pressed the button.

Another aide rushed into the darkened hotel banqueting room, 'Mr President, the Pentagon are reporting nuclear strikes against several of our cities – LA, San Francisco, Chicago ...'

The President felt numb. He stared around him at his now frightened and expectant fellow party-goers, his hands hanging limply by his sides. He could see his wife coming anxiously towards him, eyes now upon him, face full of concern. A sharp pain suddenly gnawed at his insides and he doubled over, groaning loudly.

He blinked up at the aide who'd brought the news. He opened his mouth to speak – but the words never came.

At that moment there was a blinding white flash of light and the President, his wife, the luxury hotel with its celebrity entertainers and important high-flying guests, the Afghan-American gentleman in Times Square – and most of central New York – were no more!

None of them saw the mushroom cloud that erupted above the city. None of them saw the planes flying in from the north to deliver even more destruction. None of them saw the military commanders grinding their teeth in confusion as no orders came, or the pilots cursing in frustration at their stationary multi-billion dollar F35 fighter jets, now rendered useless because their delicate electronics had been fried by the EMP blast.

As foretold by the Hebrew prophets, in one hour 'Babylon' had been destroyed! That great mega-city, which influenced the nations of the world – exporting pornography, abortion, aggression and exerting financial control, the city to which the nations of the world flocked – had fallen, never to be re-built. The influence of Wall Street upon the rest of the world had come to an end.

37 – Death of America

BBC News:

'We interrupt this programme to bring you an urgent news bulletin:

'America has been attacked!

'In the early hours of this morning what is believed to have been a nuclear missile exploded high over central USA. Since then all electronic communication in or out of the USA has been completely cut. The explosion is thought to have caused a huge Electro Magnetic Pulse (EMP).

'Shortly afterwards nuclear missiles followed by thousands of war planes attacked the United States of America. Warplanes are still flying across Canada – which has also been impacted by the EMP device – but there has been absolutely no response, or any sign of counter-attack, from the USA.

'All communications from the USA have been cut off since four am Eastern Time. We are relying on reports from ships off the coast of the United States, who are reporting huge fires and smoke all the way along the Atlantic coast as far as the eye can see. Reports are also coming in of similar devastation on the Pacific coast.

'I honestly can't believe what I'm reading. This seems like a fairy-tale, but I repeat, America has suffered a devastating nuclear missile attack! At this stage, we don't know what damage has been inflicted, but military experts say this has the hallmarks of an all out nuclear attack.

'The last news report received by Reuters was of the US President attending a major celebration in New York City – expected to continue into the early hours. No communication has been received from there since but, from the one satellite we still have access to, it would appear that most major American cities are now a smouldering ruin!

'US satellites are not responding. We have no internet, phone or radio communication whatsoever with the United States. What-ever has happened there is terrifying to contemplate.

'The world's only superpower appears to have been destroyed – annihilated – in a totally unprecedented attack! We don't know yet if anyone has survived, but there has been absolutely no sign of a counter-attack, or any kind of response, from the US.

'The British Prime Minister reports that he is dumb-founded with shock. "I've been trying the hotline to the president all morning", he said. "There is NO reply!"

'Meanwhile, stock markets in London, Brussels, and around the world, have suspended trading indefinitely!'

The attack was totally unexpected. A single high altitude plane flew miles above Alaska and continued south east, exploding a nuclear EMP device over the northern centre of the country during darkness. Power lines, electricity sub-stations and almost all electrical and electronic devices were destroyed as a result of the high voltage pulse induced. The entire country was plunged into darkness – including military bases. The internet ceased to function on the continental United States and in parts of Canada also. Motor vehicles, trains and aircraft ceased to function. The underground system in major cities ground to a halt.

The EMP was immediately followed by co-ordinated nuclear ex-plosions in almost every major city of the US. Suicide bombers exploded hundreds of devices in major population centres – these were many of the 'suitcase nuclear devices' which had gone missing after the defeat of communism in Russia. A further hail of Inter-Continental Ballistic Missiles rained down from the north in a follow-up attack, then waves of thousands of warplanes arrived across Alaska attacking anything left standing from the previous attacks.

The president of the USA, attending a late night celebration in New York City, was interrupted to be told the devastating truth. He hesitated, unsure how to respond, overcome by the suddenness and scale of the attack. News continued to come in of the total devasta-tion of his country without a retaliatory shot being fired. Without electronic communications the military were paralysed. He was doubled up in pain, unable to act, when the first nuclear device was triggered in New York City.

Before anyone could put together any nuclear cohesive plan of defence paratroops were falling from the sky in thousands and moving in to mop up any military survivors. Any citizens foolish enough to produce a weapon were also mown down without mercy.

Hospitals that remained undamaged – those in the suburbs, mostly – were inundated with casualties, until they ran out of even the basic medicines and equipment. Stores and supermarkets were raided by a population terrified and frenzied. People began to realise that they must vacate any cities, but even the countryside had been devastated, so great was the intensity of the attack. Nuclear blasts had stripped forests of foliage, rivers were polluted and many animals were also dead.

In the days after it became obvious that the only way to survive was to escape the country – either north into Canada, or south into Mexico. Rescue groups were heading across the borders from both countries, with emergency food rations, clean water and medical supplies. Countries around the world in turn offered to take in those with previous nationality – or parent's nationality – in their states.

Ships were diverted towards Canadian and Mexican ports, to await the arrival of the survivors. Those who managed to make it out were a sorry lot, carrying only the clothes that still clung to them. Blankets were wrapped around them as the rescuers found them. They were taken to vehicles and driven to refugee centres, where their details were recorded.

Any attempt at burying the dead was abandoned when it was realised just how impossible a task that would be. The exposed bodies began to decompose and there was an increasing danger of disease and epidemic. The rescuers had to work quickly to save as many as they could.

Israel was one of the first countries to respond. There were many in Israel who had read the words of the prophets and realised this disaster was coming. Preparations had been made and several hundred well-equipped rescue teams, with experienced personnel, were despatched to different areas of the former USA. Israeli ships and planes were also diverted rapidly, once the news of the fall of America became known, to go to nearby Canadian and Mexican ports to await the arrival of survivors.

In One Hour – Babylon will fall – *Raymond McCullough*

38 – Nightmare journey

Reuben, Leah and their two sons had been en route to their vacation home in Massachusetts when the EMP exploded. Their SUV drifted to a halt amidst a freeway of now motionless vehicles. Then the first mushroom cloud appeared, followed by several more in the near vicinity. One of the boys – the younger one, Levi – was tapping on his cellphone:

'It was only charged a short while ago,' he complained, 'and now it seems to be lifeless.'

He threw the phone to the floor in disgust.

'EMP,' his brother Samuel announced, mysteriously, then seeing the dangerous look on his mother's face, quickly went on to explain, 'Electro Magnetic Pulse – it'll have knocked out every electrical or electronic circuit in the whole country. We have no way of communicating with anyone, or calling for help ...' His voice faltered as the implication of what he had just said began to sink in.

Reuben turned to his family, 'Please forgive me he said. This is all my fault. I realise now I have been completely wrong all along. Shaul and his friends told me this was coming and I refused to believe it. I laughed at what I saw as their naive foolishness. I should have listened. I was so wrong, so wrong.' He placed his head against the steering wheel and began to weep.

Leah waited a few seconds, then spoke up in a strong voice, 'Yes, Reuben, you are correct. You got it very badly wrong – but it's much too late for remorse now. We *are* all still alive – thank HaShem! Providentially we were not back at home in the city to be destroyed along with it.

'Here we are – able to walk, and so walk out of this predicament we must. Above all we must stick close together. There may be others who may panic, or quite possibly resort to violence. We must do our best to avoid such people and just keep going.

'The homeland we knew as the USA has gone – never to rise again. But we still have a homeland – it's called Israel. All that matters now is that we keep going, keep moving, until we reach someone who can help us to get to Israel. Understand?'

Her two sons looked at her for a second, then muttered, 'Yes, mum.'

'Do you understand? she said again, in a slightly louder voice.

'Yes, mum,' the boys responded, more animatedly this time.

Reuben also managed a quiet, 'Yes, my dear. Yes, of course you are completely right. My brother is already in Israel. He will be concerned about us. The people of Israel will know about us. They will surely send help. Your mother is right. We are alive and unhurt. We must start walking towards the Canadian border. It may take us many days to get there, but we must stick together and help one another through this. And I think maybe – er maybe we should pray together before we start, eh?'

Leah said, 'Yes, indeed.' and the boys nodded in assent.

'Baruch ata adonai elohaynu, ha melech olam ..' Reuben began, but Samuel interrupted him.

'Oh God of Abraham, please be merciful to us. We need your help right now. We have no other help – except for one another ..' he faltered.

'Leah continued, 'Give us the strength and the will power to survive this disaster, oh Lord. Keep us safe from harm and give us the strength to keep going until we can get to a place of safety. Amen.'

Reuben added, '*Shmai Israel, Adonai Elohaynu, Adonai echad –* Hear oh Israel, the Lord our God, the Lord is one.'

'Amen,' the boys and Leah agreed.

They climbed out of the paralysed SUV, collecting their coats and the boys reaching to lift their bags from the rear.

'No,' commanded Leah. 'We'll need only the bare minimum with us. Any extra weight will only hinder us in the long run. If we make it out to safety with nothing but our lives – and the clothes we stand in – then we will have succeeded. We should change into shoes that are more suited for walking in. You boys are OK with those trainers, but I'll need to wear a pair of your spare shoes, Levi. They're the most likely to fit my feet.'

Levi quickly dug into his bag and produced his spare pair of shoes for his mother, who tried them on and seemed satisfied that they fitted her.

'Bring any water bottles, or cups. We may find a clean stream and we'll be glad of water and something to drink it from if we do. Oh and

Samuel, bring the torch and the map from the front glove compartment – we'll need to know what route is the best and the safest.'

They studied the map for several minutes and decided just when they ought to turn off the main highway east and begin to head north instead. They were apparently several miles west of New Haven, Connecticut, and chose a small road which headed north, crossing another highway.

'OK?' said Reuben, asserting leadership once again, 'Lets move, then. Remember, we'll have to skirt around the bigger cities – they're sure to have been targeted. Too much danger of radiation and of enemy activity. We need to keep to a route that avoids them, through smaller places that the enemy hasn't bothered with.'

The Levine family began walking in the same direction as most of the other stranded refugees. They headed east along the turnpike for several miles before a road sign directed them to the beginning of the route they had chosen as hopefully the safest – leading north towards Naugatuck, CT, initially. Some others joined them and they found themselves walking along with a small group of people – three other families – who had decided on the same route.

After walking for a couple of hours they stopped by common consent. Most of the women were wearing unsuitable shoes and were complaining of sore feet. Leah was very glad she had had the foresight to change into more suitable footwear. They rested briefly with the others, even discovering a small stream from which they were able to obtain clean water to drink. They shared their water with the others, but decided to move on when the others decided they needed longer to recover – Leah ensuring that they collected all their water bottles again.

When they were a few hundred yards away she explained to the rest of her family. 'I'm determined that this family will stick together and survive this,' she told them. 'And that means not being foolish. Sure, we should share our water, but we keep the means to obtain it with us. In fact, we should hide the bottles of water away. Things are not going to get easier as we travel. We have several hundred miles to cover before we reach the Canadian border – and we may not find help straight away even then.'

'How far do you think we ought to walk before we need to stop for the night,' Reuben asked.

'We are none of used to this – though you boys are used to sport and so forth in school. Let's try and cover thirty or forty miles before we call a halt. We'll need to find somewhere safe and hopefully hidden, where we we can protect ourselves and feel safe. We've done about ten miles so far, but we better get used to walking. This road has turned east, but we should hit another road soon which will take us north again.

'That road swings west after about ten miles and leads into Nauga-tuck, but I think we'd be better avoiding even somewhere that big – and Waterbury, which is even bigger – so I suggest we take this route here ..' She pointed to a smaller route to the east of Waterbury.

'This road crosses the 84 here. I think we want to get north of the 84 and then begin to look for somewhere we can bed down for the night – maybe an abandoned car, or similar. OK?'

Her family nodded in unison.

'Sounds fine to me,' said Reuben.

They continued walking north, stopping briefly for a few minutes, before Leah urged them on again. After another hour, or so, they crossed underneath Route 84 and turned east for about a mile before turning north again into another small road. Eventually, they came to a sign that showed Wallcutt only a mile ahead.

'Right, this is where we turn right into a small road going north. Maybe we can find some shelter nearby.'

'Thank goodness for that,' sighed Reuben. 'I thought you were going to keep walking forever.'

'Me too,' added Levi.

Samuel, although just as exhausted as his father and brother, decided it would seem more macho if he appeared willing to keep going, so wisely said nothing.

A short distance along this road they spotted an unpaved lane leading off to the right into some woodland. They decided to explore it for a short distance. Soon they could see the outline of a wooden shed, with a turning area beside it. The lane seemed overgrown and little used so they approached the shed and Reuben tried the door.

It was fastened with a hasp and staple, with a padlock affixed, but the wood was old and soft and Reuben managed to prise it off with an iron bar he found leaning against the side of the shed.

Inside the shed smelled slightly musty, but dry and – apart from some dust – reasonably clean. They decided it was not exactly the luxury accommodation they had originally intended to spend the night in but it would have to do. There were some plastic sacks of compost which they used as pillows and a folded tarpaulin which they spread over all four of them to give some warmth. It smelled mostly of grass, mixed with oil – so wasn't too unpleasant.

They huddled fairly close together enabling some warmth to build up and, eventually, they all fell asleep.

Reuben woke to find the daylight penetrating the murky, cobweb covered window and awakened the others.

'Guess we can forget about breakfast, eh?' murmured Samuel.

'Listen boys, we're alive and still fit and well. Let's have a drink from the water bottles and give thanks to Hashem for life and health and strength, eh?'

'OK,' agreed Levi, 'but just because we're heading for Canada we don't have to start talking like Canadians, do we – eh?'

The others laughed and Reuben said, 'That's the spirit, son. If we can hold onto our sense of humour, we can make it, I think.'

'I agree,' said Leah.

They prayed together briefly and left the shed, returning again to the paved road leading north.

There were several homes along the road they were walking – most set well back with woodland behind. At the edge of the grass lawn of one house they could see a greenhouse, which appeared to have various fruits growing. Reuben and Samuel crept quietly along the fence at that side and slipped into the greenhouse.

Along one side were several tomato plants, with quite a few ripened tomatoes. On the other side were some cucumber plants – again with ripe cucumbers – and, beyond them, a collection of strawberry plants with ripe strawberries.

'Looks like we may have breakfast after all,' said Reuben, quietly.

'Mmmm,' said Samuel, who was already eating a large tomato.

Reuben looked around for something to carry the bounty in, spying some plastic compost bags folded on the bench.

'We can use one of these bags,' he said to Samuel. 'If we turn it inside out the fruit will stay clean.'

They collected as many ripe tomatoes as they could, a few cucumbers and quite a lot of strawberries.

'OK, let's get out of here, now,' Reuben urged.

They made it back to the road without incident, rejoining Leah and Levi.

'Breakfast,' announced Reuben. 'We'll find somewhere quiet and eat some of it there. We'd better keep a lot of it for later. We can take turns carrying the bag.'

'Thank you, Lord,' cried Leah.

A short distance up the road they entered a small clump of trees and sat down on a log to distribute the bounty. Samuel produced a penknife and Leah used it to cut the cucumbers, giving a half one to each of her family, along with a couple of juicy tomatoes and a handful of strawberries.

'We'll have to be as careful as we can carrying the rest,' she said, 'otherwise it'll get all squashed together. OK?'

Her family nodded and grunted – still occupied with eating.

They finished breakfast, each had a small drink from one of the water bottles and began their trek north again. As they walked they heard jet planes scream overhead, heading south west.

Shortly after they found themselves walking alongside a lake. There were some shapes near the shore of the lake and Samuel trotted closer to investigate.

Suddenly he let out a shout, 'They're all dead,' he cried.

Reuben approached and could see five bodies – two adults and three children in their teens.

'Looks like the water must be polluted,' said Reuben, 'probably fallout from the nukes. We'd better be very careful what we drink from now on. All of the rivers and lakes could be dangerous.'

'Yes,' agreed Leah, 'and we need to be careful with the water and food that we have. If others see we have it they could well steal it from us. We have no way of defending ourselves and we're getting close to a built-up area.'

As she spoke Levi noticed some people ahead of them, moving north like themselves – several men amongst them. Leah suggested they took a parallel route and they turned into a narrow lane, which had once been the original road. As they neared the end of this they approached the junction carefully. The other group were just ahead of them to the right, but there was another narrow lane across the road, leading north, while the main road led east, then north, through the town.

They scooted quickly across the road and, as far as they could tell, were unnoticed by the other group.

'This lane cuts off the main town and joins the main road which runs west, turning north again and into the country,' said Leah, holding the map. 'Personally, I'd prefer to stay off the main road as long as possible. We'll meet less people that way.'

'Does it really matter, mum?' asked Samuel. 'Surely we are all in the same boat.'

'When people are under threat – stressed – they can behave in a totally different way from their normal behaviour. This is *not* a normal situation we are in. It's apocalyptic. We can't rely on people being normal, or 'nice'. It's best to avoid other people as much as we can.'

They followed the small residential lane north for about half a mile, turning west for another couple of hundred yards, where they found themselves approaching the main road west. There was no-one presently in sight.

'I think we can turn off to the left in about a hundred yards,' said, Leah. 'and follow a parallel route again.'

They soon found themselves in a winding road among trees and followed it west. After about fifteen minutes they heard the sound of hooves coming toward them.

'Quick,' said Leah, 'into the trees.'

They had barely hid themselves among the trees at the side of the road, when two figures on horseback trotted by. The horsemen must not have seen them, as they carried on without hesitation. Reuben and his family waited for a few minutes, then emerged onto the road again, which began to turn more to the south.

'We turn right here soon,' Leah explained.

Sure enough another road led off to the right. After a few hundred yards it joined another street, which they turned left into. It led them north west, curving more to the north after a little. It led to Route 6, which ran east-west and was currently deserted.

They made their way westwards along Route 6, but then crossed the highway and entered another small street leading roughly north again. They continued in this way for another mile and crossed the main road again into another smaller road, which they followed for a few miles, until it again rejoined the main road.

Now there was no alternative route but the main one, which they travelled for another four miles, until it met an east-west road. Opposite and continuing north was another small road. Another four miles brought them to the 202 Litchfield Turnpike. Visibility was limited in each direction, so they crossed hurriedly and found a small park surrounded by trees on their right. This seemed a good spot for a brief rest and some food.

'We're about fifteen miles from the Massachusetts border now,' Leah informed them. 'Then another forty miles until we cross into Vermont. We should be able to cover that today.'

'How far to Canada from there,' asked Levi.

'Maybe two hundred and fifty miles,' she answered.

'Phew, that's quite a distance,' Samuel responded.

'It is, indeed,' Reuben agreed.

Just then they heard the sounds of warplanes flying overhead again. They disappeared to the southeast, but then they heard the low rumble of explosions in the distance.

'They're still attacking us,' said Reuben.

'Who are they?' asked Levi, 'and why do they hate us so much?'

'We don't know,' Leah answered. 'But the planes always seem to come from the north, so maybe Russia have a hand in it. I seem to remember Shaul – or maybe it was his friend, Brandon – saying something about ten different nations who would join forces to attack America. I think Russia and China were mentioned, but I don't remember who the others were – perhaps North Korea?'

'Do you think they've attacked Canada, as well?' asked Leah.

'According to Shaul, or Brandon, this was a judgement against the United States, specifically – which they referred to as 'Babylon, the great' – so maybe Canada has been spared. I really hope so, for our sakes.'

'If Israel send help, Dad,' Samuel began, 'do you think Uncle Shaul will come?'

'I doubt it, Sammy,' replied Reuben, 'as far as I know he's still tied up with the aliyah in Basra. It's unlikely.'

'We haven't seen him for a long time,' added Levi.

'Yeah, last time we saw him he was going back to Israel – turned out to be the start of the war. He was in the thick of it, wasn't he, Dad?'

'Yes, son, apparently he led a company fighting in Saudi Arabia – that area is part of Israel now. It's where Moshe herded sheep in the desert, the ancient land of Midian.'

'He got promoted, too, didn't he, dad?'

'Yes, his commander was injured in Aqaba early on, so they made him up to Captain, then he got promoted again at the end of the war, so he's a Major now – leading a whole company in former Iraq.'

'OK, boys,' Leah interrupted, 'we need to get moving again. Can we hide any food and water we have as best as we can. We need it to survive. We may not find any safe water for some time.'

They organised themselves and began walking again.

'There's a road running north just along the Turnpike to the west, here. If we take it – and another small road running off it to the right, we'll cross Route 44 in about five miles, near Winsted. If we follow the old road to the east for a bit we can then head north again, by-passing Winsted.'

'OK,' the others assented.

After an hour they crossed the highway and turned right into the old road. After half a mile they were able to go north again. They had spotted some people further along Route 44, but were able to cross without having any interaction with them. About four miles along this road they detoured right into another small road and, after less than a mile crossed Route 20.

'We're sort of running parallel to Route 8,' Leah explained, 'but very soon we'll be forced to join it, as it's the only way further north.'

They travelled north for another mile, until they were forced to turn left to cross a small river, then right onto a road that crossed another river, then left again and were once more travelling north. They could see Highway 8 ahead – the Colebrooke River Road – which passed the Algonquin State Forest to the east, and then just to the west of Colebrooke River Lake, which prevented any detour eastwards.

After another three miles they crossed the state border into Massa-chusetts. There were people walking northwards ahead of them now and some others a good way behind. However, there was no good alternative to the route they were on. The road crossed Route 8 to the east and then ran parallel to it until, after just over a mile it reached Sandisford, where it crossed route 57.

Next to the bridge they could see a small grocery store on the right. As they looked they saw several men leaving the store carrying cases of beer and armfuls of food they had just stolen from the store. The men had obviously already been drinking as they looked unsteady and were holding one another up as they left.

One of them – a young man in his twenties in jeans and a torn T-shirt – spotted Reuben and his family approaching the junction and shouted to his comrades, 'What have we here, eh?' he muttered loudly, 'Some lonesome travellers?'

His accomplices turned around and also spotted Reuben and his family.

'Hey, pretty lady. You not gonna stop and chat to us?' he asked, leering drunkenly at Leah.

Levi, annoyed and also intimidated by the way the man spoke to his mother, informed them, 'That's my mum you're talking to, sir.'

Leah quickly tried to intervene, 'Be quiet, Levi,' she said, but the men heard her.

'Levi, eh?' said the first man with disgust. Don't tell me we got us some fuckin' Jews here, then?'

'Yids, eh?' the second man replied – a big hairy ginger man, with balding head and wearing dirty overalls.

'Bloody Jews. They're the cause of all this trouble in the first place, aren't they? Dirty fuckin' money-grubbing Jews! They've been suckin' us all dry for years.'

Reuben could see that this was only going to get worse and tried to usher his family past the four men.

'Not so fast there, Jew-boy,' said a third man – small, weaselly and mean looking. 'We don't take kindly to Yids around here, so we don't. Do we boys?'

The others grunted in assent.

Leah began to pray in Hebrew as others gathered at the scene. None of them looked as if they might intervene, though.

'Baruch HaShem ...' she prayed quietly, standing behind Reuben and holding her two sons close to her side.

'I reckon we're gonna teach you Jew-boys a lesson,' said Ginger.

'Reckon we are, indeed,' agreed Torn Shirt.

'I think I saw some rope in that there store,' said Weasel-face and turned back to fetch it.

The fourth man – a fat man in rubber boots, who looked as if he was perhaps mentally retarded – just grinned stupidly at them and downed another long slug of the stolen beer, belching loudly.

39 – Saved by 'Alice!'

Reuben stood protectively in front of his wife and sons as the men moved slowly and menacingly towards them. Weasel-face had now returned from the store with a coil of rope in his hand.

He took the lead now, stepping in front of his companions and swinging the loose end of the rope suggestively. 'We need a tall tree, here, don't we?' he asked his comrades.

'Hey, ain't we gonna have ourselves a little fun first,' whined Torn Shirt.

Rubber boots giggled in anticipation as all four looked lasciviously in the direction of Leah.

'Yeah, why not,' said Weasel Face. 'We got time for that. He looked around menacingly at the growing crowd of watchers, challenging anyone to contradict him. No-one did. They were fascinated by this interlude in their trek and had no intention of falling foul of Weasel Face and his trio of buddies.

Torn Shirt marched forward towards Leah, intending to grab her.

'Stop!' commanded Leah, stepping out from behind Reuben to face the four men.

'No way,' said Torn Shirt, continuing towards her, a leering grin on his face in anticipation of the fun to come.

'Stop, in the Name of Yeshua!' Leah shouted in a voice suddenly filled with authority.

The young man halted, looking confused. He turned to his buddies, who had also halted at the sound of Leah's command.

'Stop this now – in the Name of Yeshua! In the Name of Jesus,' Leah shouted once more.

Now all four men looked equally bewildered and hesitant, as if they has suddenly forgotten their previous evil intentions. They looked around them in confusion at the people watching. No-one moved.

Then a sudden sound exploded onto the scene. 'Out of my way, ye rotten varmints,' came the firm voice of an old-timer, who looked like he'd stepped off a page from a history book of the old west. He was well tanned, wore a battered, shapeless old hat, looked about ninety, if he was a day, and sported luxurious white whiskers around his gnarled, weatherbeaten old face.

The raucous sound came from an ancient narrow tractor, which had two small wheels at the front and two large ones behind. The tractor had no safety cab, but was running smoothly and the old-timer rode on the high seat brandishing an equally ancient shotgun, which he waved in the direction of the four evil-doers. The crowd watched with anticipation.

'There'll be no rapes and no lynching here today,' he cried. 'So ye'd all best be on yer way, hadn't ye? Nothing more to see here. Move out!'

The crowd looked sheepishly at one another, now embarrassed at their tacit participation in the ugly scene. One by one and in small groups they began to walk away from the junction.

'Quick!' said the old-timer to Reuben, 'Get your family into the drop box!

'On the back of the tractor,' he added, as Reuben hesitated.

Reuben, Leah and the two boys quickly climbed into the small rectangular compartment attached to the rear of the tractor and held firmly onto the sides as the old-timer operated a lever which raised the box higher.

He turned to the four men, now alone at the junction, 'You boys had better not be thinkin' a followin' me,' he shouted. 'Mebbe you'd just be best finishing your drinkin' right here an' then sleepin it off. First one I see again will get his ass filled with lead from 'Old Faithful' here. Understood?'

The men looked glum and fearful also. They nodded ungraciously as they began to slouch back towards the store they'd recently vacated.

The old-timer put the tractor into gear and pulled a lever to accelerate across the bridge northwards, away from the scene. They passed some of the recent spectators, who looked away from them as the tractor passed, embarrassed to catch their eye.

The old-timer looked over his shoulder and shouted to Reuben and Leah, 'Name's Jed,' he said, 'Pleased to meet y'all.'

'Thank you so much, Jed, for coming just in time to rescue us,' shouted Leah above the noise of the tractor. Reuben and the two boys chorussed their agreement.

'No problem, lady. I heard that Name you shouted there, an' I reckon th'Almighty mebbe sent me in answer to yer prayers. My old dad always taught me to do right by the Jews and God'll do right by you.'

He turned to concentrate on the road ahead and Reuben took the opportunity to ask Leah, 'Yeah, why exactly did you shout *that* to those guys? You took me by surprise, too?'

'Well, I don't really know. I've been thinking about stuff that Shaul and Brandon were talking about back in Israel. And then the rabbis in Jerusalem made their announcement about the Ark being found – y'know, with the blood on it and all? But I guess something just took me over. It surprised me just as much as it did you, I guess.

'But I found that the more I said that Name, the more authority I felt over the situation. Those men could easily have raped me and killed all of us – and not one of those people there watching would have stopped them – but I felt all the fear leave me when I spoke those words. I just knew that HaShem was in total control of the situation. And those men back there seemed to recognise that, as well.'

'Well, whatever led you to do it, it sure worked!' Reuben agreed.

'You were amazing, mum,' said Samuel.

'Yeah, totally, mum,' Levi agreed.

'No, I think it is HaShem Who is amazing – and Yeshua, His son, too. It was *his* Name that gave me that authority. Now I know that the rabbis were right – that Yeshua really is the Messiah and also the Son of God.'

'OK,' mused Reuben. 'I guess we'll have to think about that.'

'By the way, Jed,' Reuben shouted to the old-timer. 'How come your tractor is going, when no other vehicle is able to operate?'

'I keep a collection of old tractors and farm machinery,' Jed shouted back, 'take them on vintage runs – to agricultural shows, that sorta thing. I tried my normal working tractor and several of the others, before I got this one to go. This is an ancient Aliss – with two esses, one of the first tractors ever made – but I call her, 'Alice' – with a 'c', see?' He pointed to a badge on the tractor steering wheel, which said 'Aliss'. She already had the drop box hitched on,' he explained, 'so I brought her just as she was – glad I did, now!'

'OK. I think I get it,' shouted Reuben. 'You mean this tractor is so old that it wasn't affected by the EMP, or whatever it was that took out all the electrics across the country?'

'Amen! I guess so,' Jed shouted in reply.

'Well, we're sure glad you did, too,' said Reuben.

'By the way,' Jed continued, 'I got a friend who lives a way north of here. He may not be there any longer, but I know where he keeps his food and fuel and so forth, and he won't mind me making use of it. We can stay there for tonight. It's just into Vermont a little – about four hours or so from here at this rate. He might also have some kind of trailer with a little more room and comfort than this here drop box. We could find some straw and sacks and so forth, too.'

'Thank you, again,' shouted Reuben.

'No problem at all, 'Jed replied. 'I also got a few bottles of water here. I reckon you folks might just be a mite thirsty after that little adventure, eh?' He passed a bottle back to Reuben and Leah and they all drank enthusiastically.'

Leah got the boys to produce some of the food they had hidden and she offered some to Jed.

'Thank you kindly, ma'am,' he said.

'Would you really have opened fire on those people if they hadn't stopped?' she asked.

'Opened fire?' repeated Jed. 'Why no ma'am, this old gun hasn't been fired for years – it's not even loaded. I don't really believe in firearms, but I've had this old thing just decorating my wall for ages and something made me grab it before I left home. Guess we all know why, now, eh?'

'Indeed,' replied Leah. 'God really did send you, you know?'

'Yeah, I reckon He did, ma'am,' agreed Jed with a knowing grin. He winked at her, 'Reckon He did.'

They reached the farm belonging to Jed's friend well before dark overtook them. It appeared deserted. After retrieving the key and letting the others inside, Jed went back out to re-fuel his tractor and to search the barn for a more suitable vehicle to tow them in. The boys followed him outside.

He found a covered animal trailer and, after getting the boys to brush it out, fitted it out with sacks filled with soft hay for them to sit on next day. He also got them to help him add two drums of diesel fuel and secure them so they wouldn't move about on the journey. He removed the drop box from his old Aliss tractor and the boys helped him hitch the trailer to it. They were only too glad to help.

Leah, meanwhile, had made herself at home in Jed's friend's kitchen and cooked them up a wholesome meal from the food she found abandoned inside the house. Reuben had found plates and cutlery and laid the old farmhouse table.

'Use whatever you can find that's usable,' Jed had told her when they arrived. 'I don't reckon old Peter's ever gonna come back here – or any of us again for that matter.'

When Jed and the boys returned they all sat down to a nourishing and welcome meal. Leah would have offered to give thanks, but the old man took the lead and prayed over the food for all of them, 'Lord, we thank you for this day and all your blessing in it,' he said. 'We know you brought us all together for your good purpose today, Lord. Thank you for delivering us all from evil. And thank you for this good food, which you have provided. And help us all to reach safety together. In your name, Jesus – Yeshua, that is – amen.'

'Amen,' the others all added – including Reuben.

Leah asked Jed if he had lived alone and he told them of his wife, Jeannie, who had died ten years before. 'Reckon I'll be joining her in glory in not too many years,' he told them. I guess you know I'm not originally from around here – born in Texas, then moved back here when I met Jeannie, bought a farm and settled here. Farm's mostly sold off, now. My boys weren't interested in farming no more. Went off 'n' got themselves jobs in the city. Just me on my own, now.

'Reuben has a brother living in Israel,' Leah explained. 'We're hoping we can get to Israel and settle there.'

'Yes,' agreed Reuben. 'I realise now we should really have left the USA a few years back, but I refused to believe anything bad could happen to us here – even though my brother and his bible-believing friends had told us what was prophesied about the 'daughter of Babylon' and persecution and all that stuff. I realise now I was just being stubborn. And today we nearly paid the ultimate price for my stubbornness,.'

'Well, I reckon the good Lord has already forgiven you for that – just as long as you continue to learn from it,' said Jed.

'Yes, I will,' said a new and much humbler Reuben.

'Where will you go, Jed,' Leah asked the old-timer.

'Reckon I don't know,' replied Jed, 'I'll just be glad to reach civilisation again, I suppose. But I don't really know anyone up in Canada.'

'Well, why don't you just stick with us and come to Israel, then?' she asked.

'Israel?' he murmured. 'Israel? Well, I've read about it in the good book, of course, but I never thought to see the place at my age. Israel? Well, why not. I don't belong nowhere else, neither. And at least I'll know four people in Israel, eh?'

The others laughed and Leah said, 'Well, that's settled, then. You're coming to Israel with us – after all, we owe you our very lives! If anyone has a problem with it we will ask Reuben's brother, Shaul, to sort it out. Let it be our way of repaying you for all your help.'

'Thank you,' said Jed, his old eyes shining.

When they had finished the meal, Jed showed them the bathrooms, where they could shower, and bedrooms where they could sleep for the night. The house was reasonably modern and comfortable and they soon said 'Goodnight' and settled down to sleep quickly after all the excitement of earlier in the day.

40 – Brothers reunited

Next morning they woke early and had a hearty breakfast – stocking up with food from the kitchen and with water from Jed's friend Peter's unpolluted well – before setting off again on their trek north towards the Canadian border. The old tractor could only travel at about ten to fifteen miles per hour – and Leah and Jed had agreed that they should continue to stick to small back roads and avoid other people as much as possible.

Jed showed Reuben how to drive the tractor and they took turns driving during the day and on into the evening. While Reuben was driving Jed entertained Leah and the boys with anecdotes from his past. When the tractor ran low on fuel, Jed took it off the road into a lane or field and, with Reuben and the boys' help, they re-fuelled it from one of the drums stored in the trailer.

Travelling this way they covered the two hundred and fifty miles, or more, to the Canadian border in a day and a half. They had no more serious incidents and reached the small Canadian town of Frelighsburg, Quebec, before midday. The Canadians greeted them warmly, supplying them with food, showers and fresh fuel for their tractor.

They were informed that there were several Israeli teams in Canada, helping to rescue refugees from the USA. Many facilities in Frelighsburg had also been knocked out by the EMP and they were advised to keep going towards Montreal, where they could make contact with the Israelis directly.

The Canadians looked askance at their mode of transport, but Jed refused to be parted from Alice, so the Canadians finally produced a truck and loaded Alice onto it – leaving the trailer behind.

From Frelighsburg the truck took Canadian Route 35 and then Route 10 to Montreal. The driver delivered them to the Israeli HQ, where helpful Israelis unloaded Alice and stored her safely, directing them to a nearby hotel, after taking details of their former home in New York City and their contacts in Israel.

At the hotel they found several dozen other Jewish refugee families and individuals and soon began sharing stories of their recent experiences leaving the USA. After a filling evening meal Jed joined them in watching the news of the recent attack on the USA, via CBC, Canada. They watched in horror as reporters showed the still burning cities of the United States.

As the news began to repeat itself there was a loud knock on the hotel room door and Reuben was summoned by an Israeli agent, who told him that an IDF officer wished to speak with him downstairs. Wondering what this could be about, Reuben headed down to the hotel reception – to find himself grabbed enthusiastically by a sun-bronzed young man in the khaki green uniform of an IDF Major.

'Reuben, you made it! You're alive. I'm so glad to see you, brother!' said his brother Shaul.

'Shaul, brother, What are you doing in Canada?' said Reuben. 'I thought you'd still be in the deserts of Iraq somewhere? It's good to see you, though. Really good,' he said enthusiastically.

'I volunteered as soon as we heard the news of the attack on the US. I was given permission to attach myself to one of the special Israeli rescue teams, because I had family involved. And here you are – and in one piece, by the look of it? And are Leah and the boys OK, too?'

'Only by the grace of God we are all safe and unharmed,' said Reuben with feeling. 'Come on up to our room and meet them and we'll tell you the whole story.'

So Shaul joined his newly-rescued brother and his family in their temporary accommodation, was introduced to Jed and told the whole story of their ordeal and rescue. He was especially struck by Leah's re-telling of her command to her would-be attackers and the authority she experienced when she spoke to them in the name of Yeshua.

'There is a power in that name that is greater than any other,' she said. 'I just can't explain it, but I know it is real.'

'Yes, I think I know what you mean,' Shaul answered her.

'Yes,' agreed Reuben. 'I think we are all learning that there is something very special about that Name.'

Epilogue

A week later the Israelis – at Shaul's request – had made arrangements for 'Alice' to be shipped safely to Israel at a later date, but in the meantime he, Reuben, Leah, Jed and the two boys were on board an Israeli ship en route home to eretz Israel.

Due to the annihilation of their headquarters in New York City, the United Nations were forced to re-locate their base to Geneva, Switzerland, where a week later – at the first General Assembly since the fall of America – the United Kingdom proposed a two minute silence in honour of all those lost in the devastating attack. Most delegates stood reverently and faced the empty seats reserved for the former nation of the United States of America.

Muslim states and those ten nations involved in the attack, however, were conspicuous by their absence – though they were all present at a later UN session to propose the introduction of their choice of new world leader. Strangely enough he would turn out to be the very same man who had master-minded their attack!

The End

If you have enjoyed this series please consider writing a short review on *Amazon*. Thank you.

If the books have caught your imagination and you want to know what basis there is for them you may enjoy reading the short non-fiction follow-up to the series: *Neighbours from Hell* – available from *Amazon*, etc.

This 70-page book gives all the relevant prophecies, plus other helpful information, to help you understand the biblical basis of the story.

Glossary

Hebrew	**English**
Boker tov	Good morning
Ken	Yes
Leila tov	Good evening
L'hitraot	See you
Lo	No
Oleh, Olim	Immigrant, Immigrants (pl.)
Shalom	Peace (greeting)
Toda	Thank you
Toda raba	Thank you very much
Tov	Good
Tov ma'od	Very good
Ulpan	Hebrew language school

Arabic	**English**
La	No
Na'am	Yes
Salaam alekum	Peace to you (greeting)
Shukran	Thank you
Insh' allah!	If God wills

IDF Personnel

Rav Seren (Major) Shaul Levine – promoted *Seren* (Captain) at beginning of war, *Rav Seren* (Major) at end of war

Lieutenant *(Segen)* Alon Peled, tank commander at start of war, promoted *Seren* (Captain) a month after war

Sergeant Ari Gold, Peled's second in command; promoted after war

Second Lieutenant (*Segen Mishne*) Rebekkah Bar-Ilan, promoted full lieutenant (*Segen*) a month after the war

(Sergeant, *Samal* during war, promoted to *Segen Mishne* at end of war)

First Sergeant (*Rav Samal*) Musa Tamari, promoted second Lieutenant (*Segen Mishne*) a month after war

(Corporal in 2014, promoted *Samal* after Gaza conflict, *Rav Samal* at end of war)

Corporal (*Rav turai*) Avi Katz – *Rav turai* in war, promoted after war

Corporal (*Rav turai*) Samir Junbalat (promoted end of war)

Corporal (*Rav turai*) Doron Lev.

Seren Moshe Ben Ezra, commander Airfield Damage Recovery unit, Basra (and subsequent deployments)

New Israel Plan (NIP) personnel

Khan Ali (Aviv) Yusufzai

Khaista Yusufzai

IDF rank	**UK/US equivalent rank**
Rav seren	Major, Battalion executive officer
Seren	Captain, Company commander
Segen	Lieutenant
Segen mishne	Second lieutenant, Platoon leader
Rav Samal	Sergeant First Class
Samal	Sergeant
Rav turai	Corporal
Turai	Private

Bibliography

A Rabbi Looks at the Last Days
Jonathan Bernis

As America Has Done to Israel*
John P. McTernan

Blood Brothers
Elias Chacour

Britain and Zion
Frank Hardie and Irwin Herrman

Brother Shall Not Lift Sword Against Brother:*
The Roots and Solution to the Problem in the Holy Land
Tzvi Misinai

DNA and Tradition:
The Genetic Link to the Ancient Hebrews*
Rabbi Yaakov Kleiman

Fighting Hamas, BDS and Anti-Semitism
Barry Shaw

Guards Without Frontiers:
Israel's War Against Terrorism
Samuel M. Katz

Israel: Reclaiming the Narrative*
Barry Shaw

Israel's Lebanon War
Ze'ev Schiff and Ehud Ya'ari

Jews In Places You Never Thought Of *
Karen Primack

Like Dreamers*
Yossi Klein Halevi

O Jerusalem!
Larry Collins and Dominique Lapierre

Operation Babylon
Shlomo Hillel

The Lonely Soldier*
Adam Harmon

The Israel Solution:*
A One-State Plan for Peace in the Middle East
Caroline B. Glick

The Biblical Hebrew Origins of the Japanese People
Joseph Eidelberg

Phantom Nation:*
Inventing the 'Palestinians' as the Obstacle to Peace – Volume 1
Sha'i ben-Tekoa

Story of My Life
Moshe Dayan

The God of the Mountain*
Penny Cox Caldwell

The Igbos: Jews in Africa
Remy Ilona

We Belong to the Land
Elias Chacour

*Recommended

About the author:

Raymond McCullough, from Co. Down, near Belfast, Northern Ireland, has been a professional writer for over thirty years, originally writing a regular series – plus other articles, reviews and reports – for several UK technical magazines.

From 1990-96 he edited and published the Irish magazine, *'Bread'* – releasing his first book, *'Ireland – now the good news!'* from this in 1995; co-edited by his wife, well-known fiction author, Gerry McCullough. He has also had articles published in the *Irish Times*, Dublin, and the *Presbyterian Herald*, Belfast.

In 1993 he hosted a radio show, *'In tha Name a' Gawd!'* on *96.7 BCR*, in Belfast, which later developed into his current satellite radio show of music, news and faith-based interviews – broadcasting around the world on several satellite networks. From 1996, for seven years, he and Gerry led a cell-based Christian fellowship in the Belfast area and are currently involved in a church in Downpatrick, Co. Down.

Since then he's been involved in media of all kinds – from web design to podcasting, satellite and internet radio, plus documentary TV production – producing an album of Celtic & Hebrew worship music, *'Into Jerusalem,'* in 2005 and a Celtic pop-folk album, *'Different,'* in 2008.

Since 2008, Raymond has produced and hosted *'Celtic Roots Radio'* – an *iTunes* podcast and also a web-station – with several thousand downloads per month in over 100 countries. He published the craic from his *Celtic Roots Radio* shows as, *'A Wee Taste a' Craic,'* in 2011 and is currently editing a TV documentary, filmed mainly in Canada, entitled, *'Broken Treaties.'*

He has also produced and hosted the *'In tha Name a' Gawd!'* international series of personal testimonies and, more recently, *'Fresh Bread: Your Kingdom Come (WHM)'* – broadcasting each week on satellite radio in most countries of the world. His *'Kingdom Come Trust'* website has hundreds of enthusiastic emails from satellite radio listeners in US, Canada, Australia and the Caribbean.

In 2011, Raymond published *'The Whore and her Mother: 9/11, Babylon and the Return of the King.'* He researched the subjects in this book for about forty years, off and on, but the events of 9/11 brought a new focus to his research and a real sense of increasing urgency encouraged him to complete the book in just four months! He felt the subject was too interesting and dramatic to simply be confined to the fairly narrow, evangelical Christian world.

He followed this with, *'Oh What Rapture'*, in 2012 – another book on bible prophecy; and *'In Six Hours'* in 2015. *'What Kinda People?'* is planned as a follow-up to *'The Whore and her Mother'* – expanding the contents of the last two chapters on how we should respond to these prophecies soon to be fulfilled.

Raymond is also working on another non-fiction book, *'The Coming Six Hour War in the Middle East'*, dealing with the prophetic background to the first book in this fictional, *'Six Hours'* series.

More info at:

http://raymondmccullough.com

http://kingdomcome.org.uk

http://preciousoil.com

In Six Hours

... the world changed

Book #1 of the Six Hours thriller series

The debt will be called in and in one hour her destruction will come!

As bitter enemies race towards nuclear conflict, only a miracle can save Israel from the hostile Islamic forces surrounding her. The USA, Russia and the western world are playing with fire, as Iran rushes towards a nuclear climax. In just six hours the face of the Middle East – and the world – will change forever.

While fighting the Taliban with the ISAF forces in 2010, four young men from very different backgrounds meet in Afghanistan:

Shaul *'Solly'* Levine, an Orthodox Jew from New York;

Mickey *'Dev'* Devlin, an Irish Catholic from Boston;

Brandon *'Doubtin'* Thomas, a black Pentecostal from North Carolina;

Khan Ali *'Zai'* Yousefzai, a Muslim Pashtun from Afghanistan.

Through Brandon they discover they have more in common than they first thought and make a pact that one day they'll meet up again in Jerusalem, if the promised Six Hour War in the Middle East should actually come, taking separate ways to a common destiny.

Meanwhile they keep in touch with one another as much as possible and work towards making that meeting a possibility. Will these prophecies come to pass? Will Israel itself survive the coming nuclear holocaust?

"a page-turner and yet it cannot be read in one sitting. I learned so very much from this book" – **Barbara Silkstone**, Amazon, USA

"a roller coast ride with peaks of tension and troughs of inquisitive quests for 'The Truth'" – author **Roy Murry**, Amazon, USA

"You will learn more about the Middle East in the first few chapters of this book than you have ever known" – **Tom Elder**, Amazon, USA

"Raymond McCullough writes with conviction and clearly knows his subject well" – author **Melanie SJ Dent**, Amazon, UK

Neighbours from Hell:

Israel and the coming nuclear attempt to destroy her

Israel has not been blessed with good neighbours!

An end time war is prophesied in the Middle East: an attempt by the Arab nations surrounding Israel – with help from other Islamic nations – to eliminate the State of Israel once and for all.

But all will not go according to their plan and in approximately *six hours* the face of the Middle East – and the world – will change forever!

Will these prophecies be fulfilled?

Will this war involve nuclear weapons?

Can Israel survive the coming onslaught?

Who will survive and who will be destroyed?

Will Israel control the Middle East?

Could this war trigger the Ingathering of the Ten Tribes?

How will the rest of the world be impacted?

The Whore and her Mother:

9/11, Babylon and the Return of the King

Could the writings of the ancient Hebrew prophets be relevant to events taking place in the world today?
These Hebrew prophets – Isaiah, Jeremiah, Habbakuk and the apostle John, in The Revelation – wrote extensively about a latter day city and empire which would dominate, exploit and corrupt all the nations of the world. They referred to it as Babylon the Great, or Mega-Babylon, and they foretold that its fall – 'in one day' – would devastate the economies of the whole world. Have these prophecies been fulfilled already?

Is Mega-Babylon:

> **the Roman Catholic Church?**
>
> **A world super-church?**
>
> **Rebuilt ancient Babylon?**
>
> **Brussels, Jerusalem, or somewhere entirely different?**
>
> **Should this city/nation have a large Jewish population?**
>
> **Why all the talk about merchants, cargoes, commodities, trade?**

Can we rely on the words of these ancient prophets?
If so, what else did they foretell that is still to be fulfilled?
Do they refer to other major nations – USA, Russia, China, Europe?
What about militant Islam?

"AMAZED when I read this book ... in awe of your extensive knowledge on so many levels: Christian, Jewish, and Muslim culture; the Jewish diaspora ... Greek & Hebrew; ... thought-provoking and troublesome ... many will be offended, but you consistently build your case instead of being sensationalistic."

James Revoir, author of *Priceless Stones*

Oh What Rapture!

Is a *'Secret Rapture'* going to spare believers from the tribulation to come?

Raymond McCullough

Many are convinced that very soon an event known as 'The Rapture' will take place, where Bible believers all over the world will suddenly dis-appear, leaving society at a loss to explain the disappearance of so many. Many non-fiction books, fiction thrillers and movies have capitalised on this theme, earning a fat revenue for their authors/producers.

But is this really what the Bible teaches?

Is 'The Rapture' genuine, or a false hope?

Are those who trust in it being duped, so that they do not get ready for what is coming?

And are they being disobedient to the clear command of the Lord?

Written by the author of Amazon best-selling book, *The Whore and her Mother*, also on the topic of Bible prophecy, this volume focusses on the false teaching of a *'secret and separate Rapture'* – an event which is NOT supported by scripture!

This book investigates the scriptures used to back up the *'secret Rapture'* theory and clearly compares them to the other scriptures concerning the return of the Messiah, Jesus (Yeshua). The evident truth is revealed and the origins of the false *'secret rapture'* doctrine are exposed.

Believers around the world are taught to expect persecution, sometimes even death, for their faith. More have been killed in the past century than in previous centuries combined – in Syria, Iraq, China, Cambodia, Nigeria, Iran, Egypt, Indonesia, Vietnam, etc. Yet many believers in the west confidently expect to avoid any persecution and be *'beamed up'* out of any coming tribulation!

If you thought believers were soon going Fiction noto be lifted out of a worsening world situation, be prepared to meet the exciting challenge of scripture head on!

"Interesting and gave food for thought ... definitely worth a read"
Sheena, Amazon, UK

Other (non-fiction) books from

A Wee Taste a' Craic:

All the Irish craic from the popular
Celtic Roots Radio shows, 2-25

Raymond McCullough

*I absolutely loved this! I found it to be very informative
about Irish life culture, language and traditions.*
Elinor Carlisle (author, Reading, UK)

*a unique insight into the Northern Irish people
& their self deprecating sense of humour* – **Strawberry**, Amazon, UK

Ireland – now the good news!

The best of *'Bread'* Vols. 1 & 2 –

personal testimonies and church/fellowship
profiles from around Ireland

Edited by: Raymond & Gerry McCullough

*"…fresh Bread – deals with the real issues facing the church in Ireland
today"* – **Rev Ken Newell, Fitzroy Presbyterian Church, Belfast**

Fiction from *Gerry McCullough:*